Praise for *Secret Daughter*

"Gowda's flair for detail is evident in the way she describes the clothes, food, the streets and their smells of this land teeming with people and poverty. This story about motherhood, loss, family, and forgiveness is authentic in every way. . . . The prose is so achingly touching, it draws the reader in with every description and emotion of the characters."
—Associated Press

"Some of the best contemporary novels about families and what it means to be American are being written by Indian-Americans. . . . I've read and admired a lot of them lately, and *Secret Daughter*, Shilpi Somaya Gowda's debut, is my favorite. . . . Her novel is captivating and ultimately very wise . . . especially vivid and heart-rending. This novel travels far in the world, and deep into the human heart."
—*Minneapolis Star Tribune*

"A debut novel from [a] fresh, vibrant voice portraying a heroine straddling two cultures . . . offers readers cause for celebration. . . . A page-turning dual narrative."
—*Charlotte Observer* and *Raleigh News & Observer*

"*Secret Daughter* is an engaging read, with its quick shifts between characters and rapid movement through twenty years of familial narrative."
—*Boston Globe*

"Dualities abound in this engrossing first novel. . . . Gowda weaves her tale deftly. . . . The sounds, scents, and sights of India are vividly drawn, pulling the reader deep into a culture that most of us have only glimpsed, perhaps, in *Slumdog Millionaire*. Two worlds collide, then meld, in a story that intimately considers how we all are shaped, through fate or free will, nurture or nature, by the astounding power of family love."
—*Dallas Morning News*

"Gowda has masterfully portrayed two families . . . linked by a powerful, painful tie that complicates their lives. . . . A thought-provoking examination of the challenges of being a woman in America and in India—and in the psychological spaces in between."
—Chitra Divakaruni, author of
One Amazing Thing and *Sister of My Heart*

"It's moving and thought-provoking and informative and imaginative and beautifully executed. What a wonderful story!"
—Mary Jane Clark, *New York Times* bestselling author

"Set in California and the teeming city of Mumbai, *Secret Daughter* is a beautifully composed compelling story of love, loss, discovery, and the true meaning of family."
—Anjali Banerjee, author of *Invisible Lives*

"*Secret Daughter* is an unflinching yet compassionate story of mothers and daughters. In a tale that moves between Mumbai, India, and Northern California, Shilpi Somaya Gowda sensitively explores the balancing acts of international adoption and bicultural families. This book is a must for anyone touched by adoption or India or the delicate dynamic between adolescent girls and their mothers."
—Sujata Massey, author of *Shimura Trouble*

SECRET DAUGHTER

By Shilpi Somaya Gowda

SECRET DAUGHTER

SECRET DAUGHTER

Shilpi Somaya Gowda

WILLIAM MORROW

An Imprint of HarperCollinsPublishers

A hardcover edition of this book was published in 2010 by William Morrow, an imprint of HarperCollins Publishers.

HarperCollins books may be purchased for educational, business, or sales promotional use. For information please write: Special Markets Department, HarperCollins Publishers, 10 East 53rd Street, New York, NY 10022.

Designed and illustrated by Lisa Stokes

Library of Congress Cataloging-in-Publication Data has been applied for.

ISBN 978-0-06-192835-2 (pbk.)

13 14 15   OV/RRD   20 19 18 17 16 15 14 13

For my parents—
for giving much in their lives
so that anything might be possible in mine

HE CLUTCHES THE WORN SLIP OF PAPER IN HIS HAND, TRYING TO compare the letters written there to the red sign hanging on the door in front of him. Looking back and forth from the paper to the door several times, he is careful not to make a mistake. Once he feels certain, he presses the bell, and a shrill ring echoes inside. While he waits, he runs his palm over the brass plaque next to the door, feeling the ridges of the raised letters with his fingers. When the door opens suddenly, he pulls back his hand and gives another slip of paper to the young woman in the doorway. She reads the note, looks up at him, and steps back to let him enter.

With a slight tilt of her head, she indicates he should follow her down the hallway. He makes sure his shirt is tucked in underneath his slight paunch of a belly, and runs his fingers through his graying hair. The young woman walks into an office, hands the slip of paper to someone inside, and then points him to a chair. He enters, sits down, and clasps his fingers.

The man behind the desk peers at him through thin spectacles. "I understand you're looking for someone."

PART I

DAWN OF MOURNING

Dahanu, India—1984
KAVITA

SHE CAME TO THE ABANDONED HUT AT DUSK, WITHOUT A WORD
to anyone, when she felt the first unmistakable pulls deep within her.
It is vacant, except for the mat on which she now lies, knees drawn up
to her chest. As the next wave of pain shudders through her body,
Kavita digs her nails into clenched palms and bites down on the tree
branch between her teeth. Her breathing is heavy but even as she waits
for the tightness to ease in her swollen belly. She steadies her gaze on
the pale yellow shadow on the mud floor, cast by a flickering oil lamp,
her sole company in the dark hours of night. She has been trying to
muffle her cries until it is unbearable to do so anymore. Soon, she
knows, with the urge to push, her screams will beckon the village
midwife. She prays the baby is born before dawn, for her husband
rarely awakens before sunrise. It is the first of only two prayers Kavita
dares to have for this child, wary of asking too much from the gods.

The deep rumble of thunder in the distance echoes the threat of
rain that has been hovering all day. Moisture hangs in the air, settling
in small droplets of perspiration on her forehead. When the heavens

finally open and the downpour comes, it will be a relief. The monsoons have always held a particular smell for her: raw and earthy, as if the soil, crops, and rain have all mingled into the air. It is the scent of new life.

The next contraction comes abruptly and takes her breath away. Sweat has soaked dark patches through her thin cotton sari blouse, which strains at the row of tiny hook fasteners between her breasts. She grew larger this time, compared to the last. In private, her husband chided her for not covering up more, but with the other men, she heard him boast about her breasts, comparing them to ripe melons. She saw it as a blessing that her body looked different this time, as it led her husband and the others to assume this baby will be a boy.

A sudden fear grips her, the same suffocating fear she has felt throughout this pregnancy. *What will happen if they are all wrong?* Her second prayer, and the more desperate of the two, is that she not give birth to another girl. She cannot endure that again.

SHE WAS NOT PREPARED FOR WHAT HAPPENED LAST TIME. HER husband burst into the room just minutes after the midwife had cut the umbilical cord. Kavita detected on him the sickly sweet odor of fermented *chickoo-fruit* liquor. When Jasu glimpsed the writhing body of the baby girl in Kavita's arms, a shadow crossed his face. He turned away.

Kavita felt her budding joy give way to confusion. She tried to speak, to articulate something from the thoughts swirling in her head. *So much hair . . . a good omen.* But it was Jasu's voice she heard, terrible things she had never heard before from his lips, a string of obscenities that shocked her. When he spun around to face her, she saw his reddened eyes. He moved toward her with slow, deliberate steps, shaking his head. She felt an unfamiliar fear rising in her, tangling with shock and confusion.

The pain of labor had left her body weak. Her mind struggled to make sense. She did not see him pounce toward her until it was too late. But she was not quick enough to stop him from grabbing the baby out of her arms. The midwife held her back as she lunged forward, arms outstretched and screaming, even louder than when she had felt the baby's head tearing her flesh to make its way. He stormed out of the hut amid the cries of their daughter taking her first few breaths in this world. Kavita knew, in that terrible moment, they would also be her last.

The midwife pushed her gently back down. "Let him go, my child. Let him go now. It is done. You must rest now. You have been through an ordeal."

Kavita spent the next two days curled up on the woven straw mat on the floor of the hut. She did not dare ask what had happened to her baby. Whether she was drowned, suffocated, or simply left to starve, Kavita hoped only that death came quickly, mercifully. In the end, her tiny body would have been buried, her spirit not even granted the release of cremation. Like so many baby girls, her first-born would be returned to the earth long before her time.

During those two days, Kavita had no visitors except the midwife, who came twice a day to bring her food and fresh cloths to soak up the blood that flowed from her body. She wept until her eyes were raw, until she thought she did not have another tear to shed. But that turned out to be just the dawn of her mourning, which was punctuated by another sharp reminder when her breasts produced milk a few days later, and her hair fell out the next month. And after that night, every time she saw a young child, her heart stopped in her chest and she was reminded yet again.

When she emerged from her grief, no one acknowledged her loss. She received no words of support or comforting touches from the other villagers. In the home they shared with Jasu's family, she was given only scornful glances and uninvited counsel on how to conceive a boy next time. Kavita had long been accustomed to having little dominion over her own life. She was married off to Jasu at eighteen and settled into the daily toil of fetching water, washing clothes, and cooking meals. All day she did what her husband asked of her, and when they lay together at night, she succumbed to his demands as well.

But after the baby, she changed, if only in small ways. She put an extra red chili in her husband's food when she was angry with him and watched with quiet satisfaction as he wiped his forehead and nose all through dinner. When he came to her at night, sometimes she refused him, saying it was her womanly time of month. With each simple rebellion, she felt her confidence grow. So when she learned she was pregnant again, she resolved this time things would be different.

2

CLEAN

San Francisco, California—1984
SOMER

THE MEDICAL JOURNAL DROPS FROM SOMER'S HAND AND SHE clutches her abdomen. She rises from the couch and stumbles toward the bathroom, supporting herself down the long corridor of their Victorian flat. Despite the sharp pains forcing her to double over, she pulls aside her robe before sitting on the toilet. She sees the bright red blood dripping down the pale skin of her thigh. "No. Oh god, please no." Her plea is soft but urgent. No one is there to hear. She squeezes her legs together and holds her breath. *Sit perfectly still, maybe the bleeding will stop.*

It does not. She puts her face in her hands, and the tears come. She watches the red pool spread in the toilet bowl. Her shoulders begin to shake, and her sobs grow louder and longer until her whole body is overtaken by them. She manages to call Krishnan after the cramps have subsided somewhat. When he arrives home, she is curled into a ball on their unmade four-poster bed. Between her legs, she has stuffed a hand towel, once plush and the color of French vanilla, a gift for their wedding five years ago. They selected that particular hue together—not hospital white, not dull beige—an elegant shade of cream, now soaked with blood.

Kris sits on the edge of the bed and puts a hand on her shoulder. "Are you sure?" he asks softly.

She nods. "Just like last time. Cramps, bleeding . . ." She starts crying again. "More blood this time. I guess because I'm further along . . ."

Kris hands her a tissue. "Okay, honey. I'll call Dr. Hayworth and see if he can meet us at the hospital. Do you need anything?" He arranges a blanket on top of her, tucking it around her shoulders. She shakes her head and rolls onto her other side, away from Krishnan, who is behaving more like a doctor than the husband she desperately needs. She closes her eyes and touches her lower belly, as she does countless times a day, but this gesture, which usually brings her comfort, now feels like a punishment.

THE FIRST THING SOMER SEES WHEN SHE OPENS HER EYES IS THE IV stand next to her bed. She shuts them again quickly, hoping to recapture the dream about pushing a baby in a playground swing. *Was it a girl or a boy?*

"The procedure went well, Somer. Everything is clean now, and I didn't see anything that would lead me to think you can't try again in a few months." Dr. Hayworth, in his crisp white coat, looks down at her from the foot of the bed. "Try to get some rest and I'll be back to see you before discharge." He pats her leg lightly through the sheet before turning to leave.

"Thanks, Doctor," comes a voice from the other side of the room, and Somer becomes aware for the first time of Krishnan's presence. He walks to the bed and leans over her, laying a hand on her forehead. "How do you feel?"

"Clean," she says.

He furrows his brow and tilts his head sideways. "Clean?"

"He said *clean*. Dr. Hayworth said I was clean now. What was I before? When I was pregnant?" Her eyes focus on the fluorescent light humming above her bed. *A girl or a boy? What color eyes?*

"Oh, honey. He just means . . . You know what he means."

"Yes, I know what he means. He means it's all gone now: the baby, the placenta, everything. My uterus is nice and empty again. *Clean*."

A nurse enters the room, smiling. "Time for your pain meds."

Somer shakes her head. "I don't want it."

"Honey, you should take it," Krishnan says. "It'll help you feel better."

"I don't want to feel better." She turns away from the nurse. They don't understand it's not just the baby she lost. It's everything. The names she runs through as she lies in bed at night. The paint samples for the nursery she's collected in her desk drawer. The dreams of cradling her child in her arms, helping with homework, cheering on the sidelines of the soccer field. All of it, gone, disappeared into the thick fog outside. They don't understand that. Not the nurse, not Dr. Hayworth, not even Krishnan. They just see her as a patient to be doctored, a piece of human equipment to be repaired. Just another body to be cleaned up.

SOMER AWAKENS AND ADJUSTS THE CONTROL ON THE HOSPITAL bed to sit up. She becomes vaguely conscious of canned laughter emanating from a television set in the corner, some game show Krishnan left on before going to the cafeteria. She never thought she could feel this uncomfortable in a hospital, the place she spent five straight years of her life. She used to get a rush of excitement walking down the sterile corridors and hearing the buzz of the speaker overhead. The rituals of slipping on her white coat or picking up a patient's chart gave her a shot of confidence. It was something she and Krishnan used to share, that sense of purpose and mastery in being a doctor. Now, she knows, this is another thing that will pull them farther apart. She resents being the patient, hates that she can't fix this.

She wasn't supposed to be here yet, in this hospital she chose deliberately for its focus on obstetrics. Eight thousand deliveries a year. Twenty babies born here today. Today, while her dead baby was being scraped out of her. On the floor just below hers, every woman in the ward has a baby sleeping in her room. It seems so easy for everyone else: the mothers she sees in her practice every day, her friends, even the idiot on that game show, waving to her kids in the audience.

Maybe this is nature's way of telling her something. *Maybe I'm just not meant to be a mother.*

3

NEVER AGAIN

Dahanu, India—1984
KAVITA

ANOTHER PAIN COMES NOW, THIS TIME FROM EVEN DEEPER within her, its dull edges sharpened to jagged blades. Kavita can no longer catch her breath between the waves of pain coming one upon the other. Her thighs tremble, her back throbs, and now she cannot help but cry out in anguish. When this sound reaches her own ears, it no longer resembles a human voice. This body is no longer her body, it is driven by primal impulses that belong to the earth, the trees, the air. Outside, a sudden flash of lightning illuminates the dark sky, and an eruption of thunder shakes the ground beneath her. The branch in her mouth cracks from the pressure of her clenched jaw, and she tastes the bitter flavor of raw green wood inside. The last thing she feels is a wet warmth envelop her body.

When she opens her eyes again, Kavita feels the midwife arranging her legs and positioning herself between them. "*Beti,* you should have called earlier. I would have come. How long have you been here by yourself? As it is, the baby's head is showing already. It won't be too long now. The second time is much . . ." Her voice trails off.

"*Daiji,* listen to me. No matter what happens, you must not let my husband take this baby. Promise me . . . *promise me!*" Kavita shrieks.

"*Hahnji,* yes, whatever you say," the midwife says. "But now, child, it is time to push."

She is right. Kavita bears down only a few times before she hears a reassuring cry. The midwife works quickly to clean and wrap the baby. Kavita struggles to sit up, pushes the damp strands of hair out of her face, and takes the child in her arms. She strokes her baby's matted black hair and marvels at the tiny fingers grasping at the air. She pulls the small body close to hers, drinks in the scent, and then places its mouth to her breast. Once the infant begins to suck in a sleepy rhythm, Kavita slowly unwraps the cloth around its tiny body.

No one heard my prayers. Kavita closes her eyes and her body shudders with silent tears. She leans forward, seizes the midwife's hand, and whispers, "*Daiji,* don't tell anyone. Go quickly, fetch Rupa, and bring her here. *No one,* you hear?"

"*Hahnji.* Yes, my child. Blessings to you and your baby. You rest now, please. I will bring some food." The midwife steps outside into the night. She pauses for a moment, arching her back slightly, then picks up her steel urn of supplies and walks away.

As the early light of dawn seeps into the hut, Kavita awakens and feels the throbbing ache in her pelvis. She shifts her body, and her gaze falls upon the newborn sleeping peacefully beside her. Her stomach groans. She is suddenly ravenous. She reaches for the bowl of rice next to her and eats. Satisfied but still exhausted, she lies back down and listens to the sounds of the village stirring to life outside.

It is not long before the door creaks open and bright sunlight spills in. Jasu enters, his eyes gleaming. "Where is he?" He beckons play-fully with his hands. "Where is my little prince? Come, come . . . let me see him!" He walks toward her, arms outstretched.

Kavita stiffens. She clutches the baby to her chest and awkwardly tries to sit up. "She is here. Your little princess is right here." She sees blackness cloud his eyes. Her arms tremble as she wraps them tightly around the baby, shielding her small body.

"*Arre!* Another girl? What is the matter with you? Let me see!" he shouts.

"No. I will not. You are not taking her." She hears the shrillness of her voice, feels the tension flood into her limbs. "This is my baby, *our* baby, and I will not let you take her." She sees bewilderment in his eyes as they search her face for some understanding. She has never spoken to anyone, let alone her husband, with such defiance.

He takes a few steps toward her, then his face softens and he falls to his knees next to her. "Look, Kavita, you know we can't keep this baby. We need a boy to help us in the fields. As it is, we can hardly afford one child, how can we have two? My cousin's daughter is twenty-three and still not married, because he can't come up with the dowry. We are not a rich family, Kavita. You know we can't do this."

Her eyes fill again with tears, and she shakes her head until they spill out. Her breath becomes ragged. She squeezes her eyes closed for several breaths. When she opens them again, she looks squarely at her husband. "I won't let you take her this time. I won't." She straightens her back despite the terrible pain. "If you try, if you even *try*, you will have to kill me first." She draws her knees up in front of her. From the corner of her eye, she sees the door and envisions the five quick steps it will take to reach it. She wills herself not to move, not to shift her fierce and determined gaze away from Jasu.

"Kavita, come, you're not thinking straight. We can't do this." He throws his hands in the air. "She will become a burden to us, a drain on our family. Is that what you want?" He stands, towering over her again.

Her mouth is dry. She stumbles over the words she has not quite allowed to form except in the distant corners of her mind. "Give me one night. Just one night with my child. You can come fetch her tomorrow."

Jasu remains silent, looking down at his feet.

"*Please.*" The hammering sound in her skull grows louder. She wants to scream to be heard over it. "This is our baby. We created her together. I carried her inside me. Let me have one night before you take her." Suddenly, the baby awakens and cries out. Jasu looks up, startled out of his trance. Kavita puts the infant to her breast, restoring the silence between them.

"Jasu," she says, signaling her seriousness by her uncharacteristic use of his first name. "Hear me now. If you do not allow me even this, I swear to you, I will fix it so I can never have another baby. I will destroy my own body so I will never birth another child for you. Never. Do you understand? Then where will you be? Who will marry you now, at your age? Who else will give you your precious son?" She stares at him until he is forced to look away.

4

WITHOUT MUCH EFFORT

San Francisco, California—1984
SOMER

"HELLO, I'M DR. WHITMAN." SOMER ENTERS THE SMALL EXAM-
ination room to see a woman struggling to control a flailing infant.
"What seems to be the problem today?"

"He's been like this since yesterday—crying, irritable. I can't do
anything to console him, I think he has a fever." The woman has her
hair in a loose ponytail and wears a stained sweatshirt over jeans.

"Well, let's take a look." Somer glances at the chart. "Michael?
Do you want to see my nifty flashlight?" Somer shines the ear probe
light on and off until it captures the boy's interest and he grabs for it.
She smiles and opens her mouth wide. When the boy mimics her, she
inserts a tongue depressor. "Has he been eating and drinking normally?"

"Yes. Well, I think so. I'm not quite sure what normal is, since
we've just had him a few weeks. We adopted him at six months." The
mother's sudden and proud smile almost camouflages the shadows
under her eyes.

"Mmm hmm. How about this, buddy? Do you want to play with

this cool stick?" Somer hands the tongue depressor to the boy, swiftly picks up the abandoned ear probe, and looks into his ears. "And how's it going so far?"

"He bonded quickly, and now he always wants to be carried around. We're pretty stuck on each other, aren't we, buddy? Even though you were up three times last night," the mother says, poking a finger into his pudgy belly. "It's true what they say."

"What's that?" Somer feels the boy's lymph glands for swelling.

"You don't know until it happens to you. It's the strongest love you can imagine."

Somer feels a familiar pang in her chest. She looks up from the stethoscope on the boy's back and smiles at his mother. "He's lucky to have you." She pulls a prescription pad from her pocket. "Well, he has a pretty bad infection in his right ear, but the other one looks clear right now, and his chest and lungs are fine. These antibiotics should clear it right up, and he should be a lot more comfortable tonight." She touches the mother's arm as she hands her the prescription.

This is why Somer loves her work. She can walk into a room with a crying child and an anxious mother and know that when she leaves, they will both feel better. Her Peds rotation was the first time she calmed down a hysterical child, a diabetic girl with collapsed veins who needed blood work. Somer held the girl's hand and asked her to describe the butterflies she saw when she closed her eyes. She successfully drew blood on the very first poke and had the bandage on before the girl was finished with the wings. Her classmates, who did everything possible to avoid the "screamers," were impressed. Somer was hooked.

"Thank you, Doctor," the mother says, with visible relief. "I was so worried. It's hard not knowing what's wrong with him. I feel like he's a little bundle of mystery, and I'm just getting to know him a little every day."

"Don't worry," Somer says, her hand on the doorknob. "All parents feel that way, no matter how their children come to them. Bye, Michael."

Somer returns to her office and closes the door, though she's already running twenty minutes late. She lays down her instruments, then her head, on the desk. Turning to the side, she sees the plastic model of a human heart Krishnan gave her when they graduated from medical school.

"I'm giving you my heart," he said, in a way that didn't sound as corny as it would have from someone else. "Take good care of it."

IT WAS ALMOST A DECADE AGO, UNDER THE DULL YELLOW LIGHTS of Lane Library at Stanford's School of Medicine, that they first noticed each other. They were there night after night, and not just on the weeknights when the rest of the class studied, but on Friday nights, instead of going out for dinner, and on weekends, when the others went hiking. There were only a dozen of them, the Lane regulars: the most studious ones, the hardest workers. Looking back, Somer realizes, they were the ones who had something to prove. Everyone thought of Somer as the odd one out. With her hippie-dippy name and dirty blond hair, it was easy for her fellow students to dismiss her as a lightweight. It used to roil her, that kind of assumption. But she had learned, over the years, to deal with it. She had ignored her high school chemistry teacher's suggestion to let her male lab partner run the experiments. She had endured the teasing that came with being the only girl in advanced math classes. She was used to being under-estimated by others: she turned others' low expectations into fuel.

"Summer, like the season?" Krishnan said when she introduced herself. "Winter, spring . . . like that?"

"Not exactly." She smiled. "It's *S-o-m-e-r.*" She waited while he considered this. She liked being a little bit different. "It's a family name. And you're . . . Chris?"

"Yes. Well, Kris with a *K*. It's short for Krishnan, but you can call me Kris."

She was taken right away with his British-infused accent, which sounded worldly compared to her nondescript Californian tone. She loved hearing him answer questions in class, not only for his alluring accent, but also because his answers were unfailingly, beautifully correct. Some classmates thought he was arrogant, but Somer had always found intelligence to be a turn-on. It wasn't until later she noticed his dimples, at Gabi's house party in the spring. Somer sipped her rum-spiked tropical punch slowly. She knew how that type of drink could sneak up on you. Kris, on the other hand, appeared to have consumed several drinks already by the time he approached her.

"So, I hear Meyer also asked you to work in his lab over the summer?" His speech was slightly slurred as he leaned toward her, sitting cross-legged in the plastic white lawn chair.

Him too? Somer's heart skipped a little. An invitation from Professor Meyer was one of the most coveted prizes for a first-year. "Yes, you too?" she asked, trying to sound neutral. She could sense Krishnan's eyes lingering on the tiny bells trimming the neckline of her peasant blouse and was glad she had taken time to change.

He shook his head and took another big gulp of his pink drink. "No, I'm going back to India for the summer. Last chance I'll get before rotations. My mother will have my head if I don't." When he smiled then, his dimples appeared. She felt a tingling travel from the pit of her stomach up to her head and wondered if she'd had too much punch already. She fought the urge to reach out and smooth the tousled black hair falling into his eyes, which made him look like a little boy. As he would tell her later, he was smitten with the way her green eyes sparkled in the light of the tiki torches, and how she laughed at everything he said that night.

They began studying together every evening, drilling each other before exams, pushing each other to do better. Kris enjoyed sparring with her intellectually and didn't seem to mind when she occasionally outperformed him. It was a pleasant change from her last boyfriend who, after two years of struggling through premed classes and preparing for the MCATs with her, had dumped her once she got into Stanford and he didn't. It had taken Somer years to realize that she wasn't the one who should feel badly about this.

As much as she enjoyed sharing the intensity of school with Kris, it was his tender side she loved most: the way he spoke, when they lay in bed at night, about missing his brothers back home, or walking along the ocean wall with his father. "What's it like?" she would ask him repeatedly. India sounded intriguing. She envisioned tall swaying coconut trees, warm tropical breezes, and exotic fruits. She had never traveled outside the country except to Canada to visit her grandparents. She had always longed for a big family like the one he described: the two brothers with whom he did everything, the pile of cousins that formed an impromptu cricket team at family gatherings. As an only child, Somer had a special relationship with her parents, but she couldn't help feeling she had missed out on the camaraderie of siblings.

Those early years of medical school were blissfully simple, when they spent their days and nights in a tight circle of friends. They had a single purpose, and they were all students living the same modest lifestyle. They studied all the time, and their whole world was contained within the outer limits of the Stanford campus. Vietnam was over, Nixon was out, and free love was in. Somer spent hours showing Kris how to drive on the right side of the road. Later, he would tell her how much he appreciated that she didn't make him feel self-conscious about being different. But the way she thought about it, they were more alike than they were different: she was a woman in a man's world, just as he was a foreigner in America. Besides, they were both struggling med students before anything else.

By the time of their first board exams, Somer had fallen deeply in love. It was the first thing in her life that had happened without much effort on her part. Soon, they were so intertwined in each other's lives she could not imagine a future without Krishnan. When their final year of school arrived, they began discussing their choices for residency programs—pediatrics for her, neurosurgery for him. The University of California at San Francisco had good programs in both, but it was competitive.

"What are our chances?" Krishnan asked her.

"I don't know. Six spots for my program, maybe fifty applications? Ten percent for me. Definitely lower for you."

"What if we applied together?" he said. "As a couple. A married couple."

She looked at him. "I'd . . . say . . . our chances would be better." She shook her head a little. "Wait, so . . . is that what you want?"

He wore a hint of a smile and shrugged. "Yeah, don't you?"

"Yes." She smiled as well. "I know we've talked about it, but now?"

"Well, it makes sense, doesn't it? It's just a matter of timing, if we're both sure." He took both her hands in his and looked into her eyes. "And I am sure. I'm sorry I don't have anything to make it official. I know it's not the most romantic proposal." He smiled.

"That's okay," she said. "I don't need any of that."

"I know." He kissed her hands. "That's why I love you."

They made a quick trip to the courthouse, with plans for a proper wedding later. After graduating, they found a small flat near the UCSF hospital, eager to start the next chapter of their new life together.

A LOUD KNOCK COMES AT HER OFFICE DOOR. "DR. WHITMAN?"

"Yes." Somer replaces the model heart on her desk and stands up. "Be right there."

5

A LONG JOURNEY

Dahanu, India—1984
KAVITA

THE LIGHT OF MORNING HAS BARELY BROKEN WHEN KAVITA AND Rupa set out from the village. Kavita's wounds are fresh and her body is still recovering, but despite her sister's concerns, she is determined to make this journey. Yesterday, Rupa agreed to take her to the orphanage in the city. Rupa had four children in six years already, so last year, when the fifth was born, she found an orphanage in Bombay. Kavita knew, though no one in the village spoke of it. She begged Rupa to take her, despite the risks involved. Even if they survive the journey and the city, they will have to face the ire of their husbands when they return.

It is already quite warm and the dirt roads have absorbed most of the rain, with only a few telltale puddles left at their edges. These too will be gone by the end of the day, sipped up by the sun's waking rays. Traveling to the city could take several hours by foot, but they are fortunate to get picked up in the next village by a man in a bullock cart carrying his rice crop into town. They ride in the back, amid a dozen burlap sacks, using the loose corners of their saris to cover their eyes and mouths from the clouds of dust kicked up by the animal's hooves. The unpaved road is bumpy, and the blistering sun beats down on them as it rises higher in the sky.

"*Bena,* lie down for a little while. Take some rest," Rupa says, reaching out her arms for the baby. "I'll hold her. Come, give her to *masi.*" She offers a weak smile.

Kavita shakes her head and gazes at the fields. She knows her sister is trying to spare her the pain of what lies ahead. Rupa has told her how difficult it was to give up her own baby at the orphanage last year, and she had four children already. She has confided to Kavita that she still thinks about that baby when she lies in bed, her own child lost somewhere in the world. But Kavita won't give up the little time she has left. She will endure whatever she must in Bombay, but not before then.

EVEN WHEN THEY WERE GROWING UP, KAVITA BEHAVED MORE like an adult than other children. Instead of frolicking in the first downpours of the monsoons, Kavita ran to fetch the clothes hanging on the lines outside. When they found a stack of cut sugarcane at the edge of a field, Rupa grabbed as much as she could carry and chewed on the fibrous stalks all the way home. Kavita merely took one piece and used it to prepare afternoon tea for her parents. When it came time to find a matrimonial match, Kavita's family did its best to compensate for her plain looks. "Don't forget," Rupa reminded her sister as she carefully lined her eyes with dark *kajal,* "when you meet him, look up ever so slightly, not so much to meet his eyes, just enough so that he can see yours." Her sister hoped the prospective groom would be intrigued by Kavita's best feature, her striking hazel eyes.

But Kavita found it hard to smile, even demurely as instructed, when interested families came to visit. Afterward, the boy always found a reason to object to the match. Only after they scraped together a disproportionate dowry were her parents able to secure a husband for Kavita, fulfilling what they considered to be their most important duty. Though Jasu could be a difficult man, Kavita knew she should be grateful. Other husbands in the village were lazy, beat their wives, or squandered their earnings on liquor. And no one wanted to suffer the fate of the poor old women who lived alone, without the protection of a man.

WITH EVERY BUMP OF THE BULLOCK CART ON THE DUSTY ROAD, another jolt of pain shoots through her pelvis. Kavita has been bleeding since soon after they began walking this morning. She wipes up the blood trickling down her leg with the folds of her sari before Rupa notices. She knows that making it to the orphanage in the city is the only chance Usha has. *Usha,* dawn. The name came to her in the quiet hours of early morning after the midwife left them alone. It echoed in her mind as she gazed at her baby girl, trying to memorize every detail of her face. Amid the first rays of light that crept into the hut, as the cocks crowed the daybreak, Kavita silently named her daughter.

What power there is in naming another living being, she realizes, looking at the child. When she married Jasu, his family changed her name to Kavita, which suited them and the village astrologer better than Lalita, the only name her parents had chosen for her. Her middle and last names came from her father: it was expected these would change to her husband's. But she resented Jasu for taking her first name as well.

Usha is Kavita's choice alone, a secret name for her secret daughter. The thought brings a smile to her face. That one day she spent with her daughter was precious. Though she was exhausted, she would not sleep. She didn't want to miss a single moment. Kavita held her baby close, watched her small body rise and fall with breath, traced her delicate eyebrows and the folds of her tender skin. She nursed her when she cried, and in those few moments when Usha was awake, Kavita saw herself unmistakably in the distinctive gold-flecked eyes, more beautiful on her child than on herself. She could hardly believe this lovely creature was hers. She didn't allow herself to think beyond that day.

At least this baby girl will be allowed to live—a chance to grow up, go to school, maybe even marry and have children. Kavita knows, along with her daughter, she is forsaking any hope of helping her along the path of life. Usha will never know her parents, but she has a chance at life, and that will have to be enough. Kavita slides one of the two thin silver bangles she always wears from her own frail wrist and slips it onto Usha's ankle. "I'm sorry I cannot give you more, *beti*," she whispers into her downy head.

6

A FAIR ASSUMPTION

San Francisco, California—1984
SOMER

SOMER FROWNS AT HERSELF IN THE MIRROR. SHE TRIES SMOOTH-ing out her skirt, but it is still snug over her waist and hips, which haven't quite returned to normal even after a couple months, another cruel reminder of her loss. Her blond hair hangs limply to her shoulders; she cannot remember when she last washed it. As a last effort, she swaps her flat sandals for a pair of sling-back pumps, and applies a touch of lipstick. *No need to look as lousy as I feel.*

She arrives at the house, where two bunches of pale blue balloons tied to the porch railing announce IT'S A BOY! She takes a deep breath and rings the bell. Almost immediately, the door flings open, and a brunette in a floral dress beams at her. "Hi, I'm Rebecca, everyone calls me Becky. Come in. Here, I'll take that." She reaches for the pastel alphabet-covered box under Somer's arm. "Isn't this exciting for Gabriella?" Becky claps her hands together and bounces slightly on her toes. Somer looks around and sees a living room full of women like Becky, all holding plates decorated with blue booties.

"How do you know Gabi?" Somer asks, thinking she hasn't

heard her friend called by her full name since the first day of med school.

"Oh, we're neighbors. This is such a great place to live with kids, you know, much easier than the city. We were so glad when Gabriella and Brian moved here. More playmates for little Richard." She laughs, running a hand through her wavy brown hair. "And you?"

"Medical school," Somer replies. "We were classmates." She looks for an escape route, glancing at the buffet table, which features a punch bowl filled with a suspicious-looking blue concoction. She's relieved to see Gabi waddling over and tries not to stare too conspicuously at her enormous belly.

"Hi, Somer," Gabi says, leaning sideways to try to hug her. "Thanks for making the big trek out here to suburbia. I see you've met Becky."

"Gabriella, I was just telling your friend how much we love living in Marin," Becky says. "Are you married, Somer?"

"Yes, she took pity on one of our classmates . . . some lowly neurosurgeon," Gabi answers for her with a wink. Somer braces for the inevitable next question, but it comes too quickly.

"Do you have kids?"

Somer swallows deeply. It feels like someone has opened the freezer door in her face on a hot day. "No, not . . . yet," Somer says, her throat tightening.

"Oh, that's too bad," Becky says, scrunching up her face into a look of exaggerated pity. "It really is the greatest thing. Well, when you're ready to make the leap, come join us out here." Becky leaves to answer the door, and Somer has a momentary vision of grabbing a fistful of her bouncing brown hair.

"Somer, I'm so sorry—" Gabi puts a hand on Somer's elbow.

"It's fine," Somer says, crossing her arms. She feels the lump in her throat growing and her face getting flushed. "I'll be right back. I need to find the bathroom." She slips into the hallway, but rather than stopping at the bathroom, she keeps walking right through the front door, getting tangled in the blue balloons as she runs past them and down the driveway. She sits down on the street curb. She cannot face it all again. She can't go through the baby food tasting contest, or the "guess how big Gabi's tummy is" game. She can't watch everyone oohing and ahhing over each darling little outfit. She can't listen to the women discussing stretch marks and labor pains as rites of passage. Everyone acts as if being a woman and a mother are inextricably intertwined. A fair assumption, since she made it herself. Only now does she know it's an enormous lie.

THE FIRST TIME SHE HAD A MISCARRIAGE, IT WAS A RELIEF. THEY were only a couple years into their marriage then, still in their residencies, when a pink line on the home pregnancy test ignited their discussions. They had planned to wait until Somer finished her pediatrics residency, when one of them had a steady income and reasonable hours. So when the pregnancy ended a few weeks later, they told themselves it was for the best. But somehow that surprise pregnancy, taken away as unexpectedly as it was received, changed things. Somer found herself noticing pregnant women everywhere, their protruding bellies proudly announcing themselves.

After the miscarriage, she felt guilty for ever having been conflicted. Of course, as a physician, she knew a miscarriage couldn't be caused by ambivalence. But the obstetrics textbooks neglected to describe the enormous sense of grief that had replaced the tiny speck of baby growing inside her. They didn't explain how she could feel utterly lost without something she had known about for only a month. Something awakened in her with that first pregnancy, a deep yearning that must have been there all along. She was raised to believe her gender didn't have to handicap her aspirations. She spent her

career thinking she wasn't like other women. Now, for the first time
in her life, she felt exactly like other women.

Somer spent all her free time reading up on fertility in medical
journals—eliminating any potential causes of miscarriage, charting
her ovulation cycles, and changing her diet. She reported each new
finding to Kris but soon recognized the glazed look of disinterest in
his eyes. He was still in his neurosurgery residency and didn't share
her intensity about getting pregnant. Fortunately, Somer had enough
drive for both of them, so it didn't seem to matter that for the first
time since they'd met, they weren't forging down the same road.

Now, sitting alone on a suburban sidewalk instead of
drinking blue punch, Somer knows that day, three years ago, has
become the dividing line of her life. Before that miscarriage, she
remembers being happy—with her work, the house with a view of
the Golden Gate Bridge, the friends they saw on weekends. It seemed
enough. But since that day, she has felt as if something is missing,
something so immense and powerful that it overwhelms everything
else. With each passing year and every negative pregnancy test, that
void in their lives has grown until it has become an unwelcome member of their family, wedging itself between her and Krishnan.

Sometimes she wishes she could return to the naïve happiness of
their earlier life. But mostly, she aches to go forward, to a place her
body doesn't seem willing to take her.

7

WHEN THE BULLOCK CART DRIVER DROPS OFF KAVITA AND RUPA
in the city, the sun is high and they are parched and hungry. They are
engulfed by chaotic noises: honking lorries, yelling vendors. The
street is crowded with overflowing trucks, assorted livestock, intrepid
bicycles, rickshaws, and scooters. They stop to share a single coconut,
first drinking the water, and then waiting while the tender coconut
flesh is cut from the shell. On both sides, the road is lined by makeshift shacks with corrugated tin roofs; women squat in front, cooking
over small fires and scrubbing clothes in buckets of dirty water.

Rupa asks the *chaat-wallah* for directions to Shanti Orphanage,
but he simply shakes his head as he takes in the two women with
their conspicuous bare feet and rural garb. She asks a cabdriver leaning idly against his car, who spits *betelnut* juice onto the road and
looks Kavita up and down. They all try to ascertain whether the baby
is deformed, or Kavita is unwed or just too poor to keep the child.
Finally, a bearded old man roasting peanuts on the corner helps them.
He shovels the warm nuts into hand-rolled newspaper cones, and in

between his calls of "*sing-dhana, garam sing-dhana,*" he tells them where to go.

Rupa takes Kavita's hand tightly in hers and ushers them through crowded footpaths and across busy streets. Kavita struggles to keep up with her sister, stopping only once to nurse the baby. Rupa looks up at the darkening sky and at the people scurrying around them. She leans in and says, "*Challo, bena,* hold her like this." Rupa helps her position the nursing baby so she can keep walking. "We have to hurry. It won't be safe for us here after dark."

Kavita obliges, walking faster. A few hours from now, she knows, after Jasu has finished his evening meal and sat around the fire drinking and smoking *beedis* with the other men, he will come looking for her. She will tell him only that he need not worry about the baby, it has been taken care of. He may be angry, perhaps he will even beat her, but what punishment is that compared to what she will already have suffered? For nearly two hours, Kavita and Rupa walk without speaking. Finally they come to the two-story building with peeling blue paint. Standing outside the gate, Kavita's legs feel like lead and her feet drag with each step. She turns to her sister, shaking her head. "*Nai, nai, nai . . . ,*" she repeats.

"*Bena,* come, you must," Rupa says softly. "There is nothing else you can do. What can you do?" Rupa pulls her by the hand up to the door and rings the bell. Kavita stares at the red-lettered sign, carving into her memory the illegible markings that promise SHANTI, peace. An elderly hunchbacked woman in a faded orange print cotton sari opens the door, holding a short-handled broom.

Kavita watches Rupa speak to the old woman, but all she can hear is the ringing sound in her ears. *Who will take care of my baby? This woman? Will she love Usha?* Kavita's mouth feels dry and dusty. The old woman gestures for them to follow her inside and leads them down the hallway to the end. A tall woman in a blue silk sari stands in the doorway of the office.

"*Shukriya.* Thank you, Sarla-ji. See you next time." A man's voice comes from somewhere within the small office. The tall woman turns to leave. In her elegant sari and diamond earrings, she looks as out of place in the orphanage as a Bengal tiger. Upon seeing the sisters, she smiles and nods slightly, then continues past them.

Inside the office, a middle-aged man with a mop of black hair is squinting at a typewriter through horn-rimmed glasses. "Sahib," Rupa says, "we have a baby for your orphanage."

The man looks up toward the door. His eyes focus first on Rupa, then on Kavita standing behind her, and finally rest upon the baby in her arms. "Yes, yes, of course. Please have a seat. I am Arun Deshpande. You must have had a long journey," he says, noting their disheveled appearance. "Please, will you take some tea or water?" he asks, gesturing to the old woman to bring it.

"Thank you, yes," Rupa answers for both of them.

At this small show of kindness, Kavita begins to cry silently, the tears tracing two lines on her dust-streaked cheeks. She is thirsty— yes, of course she is thirsty. Her head is throbbing from heat and hunger. Her feet ache with cuts and blisters from walking through the city. She is exhausted from the journey, and from the childbirth, and from the hours of labor before that. She has slept little in the past few days. She is tired from all this, and even more from the looks she has seen on so many faces she has encountered today, looks of shame.

"Just a few questions," he says, picking up a clipboard and a pen. "Child's name?"

"Usha," Kavita says quietly. Rupa looks over at her, a startled sadness in her eyes.

Arun makes a note. "Date of birth?"

These are the last words Kavita hears clearly. She holds Usha close, the baby's head tucked under her chin, and begins to sway slightly. In the distance, she hears Rupa answer him. Kavita closes her eyes, and her crying becomes louder until Arun's questions and Rupa's answers fade to a background murmur and she almost forgets they are there. She almost forgets where she is. Kavita continues like this, weeping and rocking, oblivious to the persistent ache in her pelvis, and the bloodied, cracked soles of her feet, until she is interrupted by Rupa shaking her shoulder.

"*Bena,* it's time," Rupa says, gently reaching for the baby in Kavita's arms. And now, all Kavita can hear is screaming. As she feels Usha pried from her hands, she hears only the screaming inside her head, then the shrieks coming from her own mouth. She hears Usha wailing. She sees Rupa yelling at her, watches her mouth moving, making the same silent words over and over. She feels Rupa firmly pulling her up by the shoulders and pushing her down the hallway toward the front door. Kavita's arms are still outstretched, but they hold nothing. After the metal gate clangs shut behind them, Kavita can still hear Usha's piercing wail echoing inside.

8

OUT OF OPTIONS

San Francisco, California—1984
SOMER

"HONEY, DID YOU HEAR ME?" KRIS HOLDS BOTH OF HER HANDS
in his lap as they sit facing each other on the sofa in their living room.
Somer tries to recall what he just said.

"I said, we have other options," he says.

She looks around the room and notices he has lit some candles
and drawn the window shades. A bottle of red wine and two glasses
sit on the coffee table, next to a thick brown envelope. She hears the
sounds of rush hour traffic and the N-Judah streetcar squealing outside. *When did all this happen? Wasn't it just an hour ago we were sitting in
the doctor's office?*

Somer had finally insisted they go to a fertility specialist. She was
tired of waiting for nature to take its course, fed up with opening a
bottle of wine every month as her consolation prize for another negative pregnancy test. If they knew what their problem was, she reasoned, they would be able to do something about it. She suspected it
was her fault. Kris came from a big family, and each of his brothers
already had a couple of children. Somer was an only child, though
her parents never discussed the matter.

This afternoon in the doctor's office, they were given the diagnosis she had been dreading. It *was* her fault. *Premature ovarian failure.* Early menopause. It all made sense now. For the past year, she'd been having irregular cycles: missed periods followed by heavy ones. She thought it was her hormones fluctuating with the symptoms of early pregnancy, but all this time, it was her reproductive system slowly grinding to a halt. Within another year, the doctor said, her menopause would be complete. By the time she reaches the age of thirty-two, she will no longer have the ability to bear children, the one thing that defines her as a woman. *What will I be then?* She has spent her whole life competing with the boys, compensating for her femininity, tempting fate it would seem.

"Have you given any thought to what we discussed?" Kris asks. "Adopting? My mother says the orphanage can move quickly—maybe even less than nine months," he says with a lopsided smile. He's been intent on this orphanage in Bombay where his mother is a patron. The process is supposed to be quick if at least one prospective parent is Indian and can show proof of sufficient assets.

"That's not funny." She lays her head against the cushions. "You're giving up on us."

"No, honey, I'm not . . ."

"Then why do you keep bringing this up? We can keep trying. The doctor said—"

"—the chances are extremely low. "

"Low, not impossible." Somer pulls her hands back into her own lap.

"Honey, we've tried everything. Dr. Hayworth said you're not a good candidate for that new in-vitro technique, and even if you were, I don't want them experimenting on your body. Honey, look at what this is doing to you. This isn't good for us. Look, you want to have a family, don't you?"

She nods, digging her fingernails into her palms to hold off the tears.

"So, you can either keep killing yourself to get pregnant with very low probability of success, or we can start the adoption process, and this time next year, you could be holding a baby in your arms."

She nods again, biting her lower lip. "But would it *feel* like my baby?"

"Look, there are all kinds of families," he says. "Blood doesn't make you a family. Do you really want our kid to have my huge nose or be left-handed?" He smiles, as he usually does to get his way, but she doesn't feel like playing along this time.

"You'll be an amazing mother, Somer. You just have to let it happen." Kris moves closer, trying to peer into her eyes, as if he might find an answer there. "What do you think?"

What do I think? She doesn't know anymore. "I'll think about it, okay? It's a lot to take in all at once," she says, gesturing at the brown envelope. "Right now, I'd like to go for a run, clear my head a bit. Okay?" She stands up without waiting for a response.

SOMER JOGS DOWN THE STEPS OUTSIDE AND IN THE DIRECTION of the green expanse of Golden Gate Park. She doesn't feel like running, but she had to get out of there. Kris has been talking about adoption for months now, and she's been putting him off. She knows she has to consider it, but it's hard to abandon the idea of having her own child: carrying a baby, giving birth, nursing, seeing herself reflected in her own child. *How can I give all that up?* It's easier for Kris. He's not the one who has failed.

She reaches the water fountain, panting heavily, and realizes she has already run three miles. Normally, she does a two-mile loop on JFK Drive, but today, she feels like running all the way to the ocean.

She stops to get a drink from the fountain, which gurgles slowly to life and then blasts her in the face. The early evening park traffic continues past her: a Rollerblader with dreadlocks, a team of racing cyclists, moms with strollers, kids on bikes. It's been three years since she started running this route. Three years, she's been trying to have a baby. If her first pregnancy had survived, she would have a toddler by now. She would be like these mothers, helping her child ride a tricycle.

Premature ovarian failure. Her eyes begin to mist, but she wipes them quickly with the back of her sleeve and starts running again. She's only thirty-one, how did she run out of time for this? Four years for medical school, three more for residency. She did everything she thought she was supposed to. Being a doctor was the only thing she'd ever wanted in her life, until now. How could she know her body would betray her? The truth comes rushing at her as forcefully as the water from the fountain. Kris is right. The doctor's right. She got her answer, and she can't fix it.

When she gets home, Kris is gone. A note on the coffee table explains he was called to the hospital. She sits down on the cold hardwood floor, her legs in a V shape in front of her. She leans forward into a deep stretch, and just as the tip of her nose touches her knee, she begins to choke on the sob rising in her throat. The parquet design of the floor blurs with the tears filling her eyes. She lets out the deep, horrible wails waiting just below the surface. These tears are always accumulating, intensifying inside her. She pushes them down over and over, a hundred times a day—every time she hears a child's voice, or examines a patient's small body—until that moment comes. It always happens when she least expects it, a moment when she's doing nothing at all: rinsing her coffee mug, unlacing her shoes, combing her hair. And in that moment when she is unsuspecting, the tears finally rage uncontrollably, from someplace deep, deep inside her she barely recognizes.

AFTER SHE TAKES A SHOWER, SOMER SITS DOWN ON THE COUCH AND SEES that the bottle of wine is now open. She pours herself a glass, picks up the brown envelope sent by Kris's mother, and dumps out its contents. She reads, learning many of the children in Indian orphanages aren't truly orphaned but given up by parents who can't, or don't want to, raise them. The children are permitted to stay at the orphanage until the age of sixteen, when they are forced to leave in order to create space for new children. *Sixteen?*

She hears the echo of Kris's words. *You'll be an amazing mother. You just have to let it happen.* Somer fills her glass again and keeps reading.

9

SOLACE

Dahanu, India—1985
KAVITA

KAVITA ARISES BEFORE DAWN, JUST AS SHE HAS EVERY MORNING for the past several months, to bathe and perform her *puja* while everyone else still sleeps. These early hours of the day have been her only solace since returning from Bombay.

After she and Rupa came back from the orphanage, Kavita was somber and impenetrable. She barely spoke a word to Jasu and pulled away whenever he touched her. Before, as a newly married couple, the awkwardness between them was expected. But now, their mutual avoidance was based on seeing too much in the other. After surrendering two babies, Kavita was left only with resentment and distrust for her husband. She wanted him to feel the shame and regret she carried back from Bombay in Usha's place. And she knew her defiance in escaping his grasp, even temporarily, had shown Jasu the depth of her strength. In the months afterward, though he behaved awkwardly, he had allowed her the time and space she needed. It was the first genuine show of respect he had made toward her in their four years of marriage. Jasu's parents made no such concession, their

latent disappointment growing into relentless criticism of her for failing to bear a son.

Kavita walks outside and spreads her mat on the rough stone
steps, where she sits facing the rising sun in the east. She lights the
small *ghee*-soaked *diya* and thin stick of incense, and then closes her
eyes in prayer. The wisp of fragrant smoke slowly circles its way up
into the air and around her. She breathes deeply and thinks, as always,
of the baby girls she has lost. She rings the small silver bell and chants
softly. She sees their faces and their small bodies, she hears their cries
and feels their tiny fingers wrap around hers. And always, she hears
the sound of Usha's desperate cry echoing behind the closed doors of
the orphanage. She allows herself to get lost in the depths of her
grief. After she has chanted and sung and wept for some time, she
tries to envision the babies at peace, wherever they are. She pictures
Usha as a little girl, her hair wound in two braids, each tied with a
white ribbon. The image of the girl in her mind is perfectly clear:
smiling, running, and playing with children, eating her meals and
sleeping alongside the others in the orphanage.

Every morning, Kavita sits in the same place outside her home
with her eyes closed until the stormy feelings peak and then, very
gradually, subside. She waits until she can breathe evenly again. By
the time she opens her eyes, her face is wet and the incense has burned
down to a small pile of soft ash. The sun is a glowing orange ball on
the horizon, and the villagers are beginning to stir around her. She
always ends her *puja* by touching her lips to the one remaining silver
bangle on her wrist, reconciling herself to the only thing she has left
of her daughters. These daily rituals have brought her comfort and,
over time, some healing. She can carry herself through the rest of the
day with these peaceful images of Usha in her mind. Each day
becomes more bearable. As days turn to weeks, and weeks to months,
Kavita feels her bitterness toward Jasu soften. After several months,
she allows him to touch her and then, to reach for her at night.

When she becomes pregnant again, Kavita does not let herself think about this baby in the same way she has before. She does not dwell on her tender breasts or touch her growing belly. She doesn't even share the news with Jasu right away. When thoughts of the life growing inside her come to mind, she simply pushes them away, like the dust she sweeps from the floor each day. It is a practice she has mastered in the past many months after Bombay.

"It would be a good idea to go to the clinic this time, no?" Jasu says when she finally tells him. She detects a veiled urgency in his voice.

A new medical clinic in the neighboring village offers ultrasounds to expectant mothers, ostensibly to check the health of the baby. But it is well known that those who go there do so to learn the gender of their unborn child. The procedure will cost two hundred rupees, a month's earnings from their crops, as well as a full day to make the journey. They will have to use all the money they've been saving for new farming tools, but despite the hardship, Kavita agrees.

She knows if the test shows another girl growing in her womb, all of the possible outcomes are wrenching. Jasu can demand she have an abortion, right there at the clinic if they had the money. Or he could simply cast her out, forcing her to endure the shame of raising the child alone. She would be shunned, like the other *beecharis* in the village. But even this, becoming an outcast from her home and community, would not be as bad as the alternative. She cannot face the agony of giving birth, of holding her baby in her arms, only to have it taken away again.

Kavita knows in her soul she simply will not survive that.

10

A POWERFUL THING

San Francisco, California—1985
SOMER

SOMER SITS ON THE EDGE OF THE TUB, HER BARE FEET PRESSED against the cold aqua tile floor, her fingers clasped around the familiar plastic stick in her hand. Despite her tears, she can see the two parallel lines as clearly as she did eight months ago, when she learned she was pregnant. Today was to be her due date. It was to be a day of celebration for her and Krishnan, but instead she will mourn alone. The expressions of concern from other people trickled off a few weeks after her miscarriage. The only proof of the baby she lost is the home pregnancy test she now holds in her hand, and the persistent hollow she has not been able to fill.

The bellow of the distant foghorn brings her back, and from the other room, she hears Kris's radio alarm, the distinctive tones of National Public Radio's morning news. She stands and buries the plastic stick in the pocket of her worn terry cloth robe. She knows Kris is losing patience with her, growing frustrated with what he sees as her obsession. He is eager to move on. She reaches for her toothbrush as Kris pushes open the bathroom door.

"Good morning," he says. "What are you doing up so early?"

She turns on the shower and removes her robe. "My flight's at nine."

"Right. Tell your parents hello."

She steps into the shower and turns up the water until it's as hot as she can bear.

SOMER SEES THE GRAY VOLVO SEDAN AS SOON AS IT PULLS INTO the Arrivals Terminal of San Diego Airport. Her mother gets out of the car and comes around to the curb to meet her.

"Hi, honey. Oh, it's so good to see you."

Somer steps over her duffel bag and into her mother's open arms. Instantly Somer feels herself melt into the embrace. She buries her face in her mother's soft cardigan and the faint scent of Oil of Olay. She feels nine years old again as she begins to cry.

"Oh, honey," her mother says, stroking the back of Somer's head.

"I'LL PUT ON SOME TEA," HER MOTHER SAYS ONCE THEY'RE HOME. "And I made banana bread."

"Sounds good." Somer settles into a Windsor-back chair at the kitchen table.

"So, Kris is on call this weekend? Too bad, we'll miss him."

Her parents like Kris. She'd been unsure how they would react when she'd brought home her Indian boyfriend, but thankfully, they'd embraced him. Both her parents had grown up in Toronto during the postwar immigration boom of the 1940s, and had neighbors who spoke Russian, Italian, and Polish. They had always been open-minded, even before it became fashionable. As a physician, her father shared an immediate kinship with Kris and respected him for becoming a surgeon.

"Your father tried to cut back on his evening office hours, but then he went back to it one night a week, then a couple nights, and now he's right back where he started." Her mother shakes her head as she fills the kettle.

For as long as Somer can remember, her father has used a converted room on the first floor of their house to see patients. Some were patients he treated in his clinic during the day, for after-hours emergencies. But usually they were folks who otherwise wouldn't see a doctor at all: new immigrants without health insurance, teen mothers kicked out of their parents' homes, elderly people too scared to go to the hospital at night. Pretty soon, word got around that Dr. Whitman's home office was always open and he wouldn't charge those who couldn't pay. Somer's childhood was filled with memories of the doorbell ringing during dinner or a family Scrabble game.

"Look that one up, Somer," her dad would say as he went to answer the door after making a seven-letter word. "Use it in a sentence when I come back."

They often found freshly baked pies or fruit baskets left by grateful patients on the front porch, along with the morning newspaper. For her father, medicine was more than a profession; it was a calling. It was indistinguishable from the rest of his life, and Somer learned at his knee. When she was eight years old, he taught her to wear a stethoscope and listen to her own heartbeat. At ten, she could apply a blood pressure cuff. She never thought about becoming anything other than a physician. Her father was her hero. She hungered for the weekends, when she snuggled up to him in his brown leather wingback chair as he read.

"How about you, Mom? How are things at the library?" Somer notices the crow's-feet around her mother's eyes.

"Oh, busy as ever. We're reshelving the reference section to make room for some donated furniture. I'm organizing a series of workshops next fall on biographies of famous women: Eleanor Roosevelt, Katharine Graham."

"That's nice." Somer smiles, though she has never understood how her mother stays interested in such a mundane job.

Her mother brings two steaming mugs over to the table, accompanied by thick slices of banana bread. "So, what's going on, honey? You seem preoccupied."

Somer wraps her hands around the mug and takes a sip of her tea. "Well, we . . . I . . . can't have a baby, Mom."

"Oh, honey." Her mother puts a hand on Somer's arm. "It'll happen, just give it time. It's very common to have a miscarriage. Lots of—"

"No." Somer shakes her head. "I can't. We went to a specialist for tests. I'm going through early menopause. My ovaries aren't producing eggs anymore." Somer looks in her mother's eyes for the explanation she has not been able to find anywhere else, and sees them well with tears.

Her mother clears her throat. "So that's it. There's nothing more you can do?"

Somer shakes her head and looks down at her tea.

"I'm so sorry, honey." Her mothers clasps her hand. "How are you doing? How is Kris?"

"Kris is very . . . clinical about the whole thing, ever the doctor. He thinks I'm too emotional about it." She stops short of saying that she can't talk to him about this anymore, that she worries if she doesn't find a way to move on, she may lose Krishnan too.

"It can be hard for men to understand," her mother says, looking down into her mug. "It was hard for your father."

Somer looks up. "Is that why you didn't have more kids?"

Her mother takes a sip before answering. "I had one miscarriage before you, and then after you, I never got pregnant again. There weren't any tests back then, so we just accepted it. We felt so lucky to have you, but I did feel badly about not giving you a brother or sister." Her mother brushes away a tear.

Somer feels a rush of guilt for every time she wished for a sibling. "It's not your fault, Mom," she says. *Not your fault. Not my fault.* They sit in comfortable silence for a few moments before Somer looks up at her mother. "Mom, what do you think about adoption?"

Her mother smiles. "I think it's a wonderful idea. Are you considering it?"

"Maybe . . . there are all these kids over in India who need families, need homes." She looks down at her hands, twists her wedding band around her finger. "It's just hard to think that I'll never give birth, I'll never create a life." She chokes on tears rising.

"Honey," her mother says, "you'll be doing something just as important—*saving* a life."

Somer's face crumples like a tissue and she begins to cry. "I just want to be a mom."

"You will be a great one," her mother says, covering Somer's hand with her own. "And when you are, I promise you, it will be the most important thing you ever do."

On the flight home, Somer looks through the materials from the Indian adoption agency, focusing on the earnest faces of the children. It would be a powerful thing to change the course of one of those lives: to create opportunity where none exists, to make someone's life better. It reminds her of why she became a doctor. A quote from Gandhi graces the inside of the brochure, "You must be the change you want to see in the world."

Maybe there was a reason for all our pain. Perhaps this is what we're meant to do.

11

SPEND AND SAVE

Palghar, India—1985
KAVITA

THE MORNING OF THE PROCEDURE, KAVITA IS ANXIOUS, HER
stomach unsettled. She holds a protective hand over her swelling
abdomen as they approach the clinic. Outside the door is a placard—
SPEND 200 RUPEES NOW AND SAVE 20,000 RUPEES LATER—a transparent
reference to avoiding the wedding dowry associated with a daughter.
Other than this, the nondescript door through which they pass could
belong to a tailor or a shoe shop. Inside, pairs of women and men
stand together. Kavita notices she is the farthest along in her pregnancy, now in her fifth month.

Jasu approaches the desk clerk and exchanges words, then pulls a
bundle of bills and coins from his pocket and hands it over. The clerk
counts the cash, stashes it in a metal box, and with a sideways jerk of
his head, sends Jasu back to the waiting area. Kavita shifts over to
make space for him against the wall. While they wait, she keeps her
eyes focused on the rough concrete floor. The sound of muffled sobs
compels her to look up, and she sees a woman rushing toward the
front door from the back of the clinic. The woman's sari is draped

over her head, and a solemn man follows behind her. Kavita looks back down at the spot on the floor, and out of the corner of her eye, sees Jasu's toes squirming.

The clerk calls out their name and jerks his head toward the back of the clinic. When they pass through the single door, they find themselves in a room just large enough to hold a makeshift examination table and a cart with a machine. The technician hands several papers to Jasu that neither of them can read and instructs Kavita to lie down on the table. The gel he spreads on her belly is cold and uncomfortable. She feels a surprising pang of gratitude when Jasu stands beside her. As the technician moves the device around her firm belly, they both try to make sense of the grainy black-and-white images. Jasu squints at the screen, tilts his head, and glances anxiously over at the technician several times for a clue as to what lies in Kavita's womb. After several minutes, the technician says, "Congratulations, a healthy boy."

"Wah!" Jasu shouts, laughing. He slaps the technician on the shoulder and kisses Kavita on the forehead, a rare public gesture of affection. Kavita's only reaction is relief.

IN THE WEEKS AFTER THE PROCEDURE, WHEN THE REALIZATION slowly sets in that she will be able to keep this baby, Kavita finally allows herself to feel a connection to the child. This feeling gives way to a cautious anticipation, aided by the unbridled enthusiasm of her husband. Jasu's behavior changes after that day at the clinic. He begins giving up his extra *rotlis* at dinner so she will have more to eat, and he makes sure she rests when he notices her holding her lower back. At night, when they lie in bed, he rubs her swollen feet with coconut oil and sings softly to her growing belly. She knows much of the change in his behavior is because she is carrying a boy, but she wants to believe it is not the only reason. As Jasu tends to her in the last few months of her pregnancy, Kavita feels her remaining coldness for him melt away. She sees his capacity to be a caring husband, a good father. He too has changed since that first night in the birthing hut nearly two years ago. Kavita knows she cannot blame him entirely for what happened. He is no different or worse than the other men in the village, where sons are favored and always have been.

IT IS CLEAR THEIR SON WILL BE NO EXCEPTION. HIS ARRIVAL IS anticipated by all those in the family. Everything is different this time. Kavita is fed and pampered up until her first labor pains, and the midwife is called right away to provide her support. Jasu stays outside the door and rushes to her side as soon as he hears the baby's first cries. In the way of tradition, Jasu touches the boy's lips with a silver spoon dipped in honey even before the umbilical cord is severed. He leans down to kiss Kavita on the forehead. With his eyes glistening, Jasu cradles his new son in his arms.

Kavita wipes away her own tears. These rituals she shares with Jasu and their baby are beautiful and touching, but the joy cannot transcend her grief. For years, she has longed for this moment. Now that it has come, it is laced with sorrow from the past.

12

BEARINGS

San Francisco, California—1985
SOMER

IT IS ALL JUST THEORETICAL UNTIL THE DAY THE ENVELOPE arrives. When Somer sees it in the pile of mail, her heart jumps. She stashes a champagne bottle in the fridge and runs down the steps toward the hospital. They promised to do this together, but now, as she runs with the envelope in her hands, her fingers are itching to tear it open after so many months of waiting.

First, there were countless evenings spent at their kitchen table, poring over stacks of paperwork, completing forms, collecting educational transcripts, tax records, financial statements, and medical reports. Then came the scrutiny from the adoption agency—interviews, home visits, and psychological evaluations. Somer fought the urge to take offense when the caseworker investigated every corner of their flat, not only seeing where the baby's room would be, but also peeking in their medicine cabinets, even sniffing discreetly in the refrigerator.

They swallowed their pride and asked former professors, classmates, and colleagues who knew them as a couple to attest to their

suitability as adoptive parents. Even the local police department had
to give its approval. It was unfair, insulting to be subjected to so
many tests, to bare their souls when most couples could become parents without any judgment at all. But they did everything they were
told, submitted their application, and then they waited. They were
told only that it would probably be an older baby, perhaps not perfectly healthy, almost certainly a girl.

Somer arrives at the hospital, breathing heavily, and goes directly
to Kris's usual ward. "Have you seen him?" she asks a nurse at the
station but doesn't wait for an answer. She checks the doctors' lounge,
finds it empty, then ducks her head into the call room, briefly waking a sleeping intern, and finally returns to the nurses' station.

"I'll page him for you," the nurse says.

"Thanks." Somer sits in one of the hard plastic chairs nearby.
She taps her feet on the speckled floor, willing her eyes away from
the envelope. She hears Kris's voice, and sees him walking down the
hallway toward her. She can tell from his face—the steely look of his
eyes, the pulsing of his jaw muscles—that he's scolding the dejected
young resident walking alongside him. Even when he sees her, his
face remains serious until she stands and holds up the large envelope.
A hint of a smile appears on his face. He dismisses the resident and
strides toward her. "Is that it?"

She nods. He leads her by the elbow to the nearest stairwell.
They sit together on the top step, open the envelope, and pull out a
stack of papers with a Polaroid clipped on top. The baby in the photo
has curly black hair, and her almond-shaped eyes are a startling hazel
color. She wears only a plain dress, a thin silver anklet, and a curious
expression on her face.

"Oh my gosh," Somer whispers, one hand flying up to her
mouth. "She's beautiful."

Krishnan fumbles with the papers and reads, "Asha. That's her
name. Ten months old."

"What does it mean?" she asks.

"Asha? Hope." He looks up at her, smiling. "It means hope."

"Really?" She gives a little laugh, crying as well. "Well, she must be ours then." She grasps his hand, intertwining their fingers, and kisses him. "That's perfect, really perfect." She rests her head on his shoulder as they stare at the photo together.

For the first time in a very long time, Somer feels a lightness in her chest. *How can it be I'm already in love with this child, half a world away?* The next morning, they send a telegram to the orphanage, stating they are coming to get their daughter.

THEIR EUPHORIA CARRIES THEM THROUGH THE INTERMINABLE twenty-seven-hour flight to India. Somer is excited about so many things: visiting India for the first time, meeting Krishnan's whole family, seeing where he grew up and the places he's described for years. But most of all, when Somer closes her eyes, she imagines the moment she will hold her baby for the first time. She keeps Asha's photo in her pocket and looks at it often. That one photo vaporized her doubts and made everything come to life. She lay awake at night, picturing her daughter's sweet face. She consulted the growth charts at work and worried over Asha's weight. Now their house is ready, and they've been briefed by other parents through the agency, but they still aren't quite sure what to expect once they get to India. They've been warned about stranger anxiety, cultural shock, delayed development, malnourishment—the challenges of this adoption are too many to enumerate. Still, while other passengers roll their eyes at kids squealing on the plane, Krishnan and Somer squeeze hands and share an excited glance.

When they step off the plane in Bombay, the airport engulfs Somer with its pungent mix of ocean air, spices, and human sweat. She fights off her drowsiness while getting jostled by throngs of people in the unruly immigration line. Before they reach the baggage carousel, several men swarm around them, tugging at their clothes and talking rapidly. Somer starts to panic, then follows Krishnan through the human maze, watching as he calmly navigates among the people, the lines, and what appear to be a couple small bribes along the way.

When they get outside, the muggy weather settles on Somer's bare shoulders like an unwelcome shawl. The airport's roadways are buzzing with cars and beeping horns. She and Krishnan settle into the cracked vinyl backseat of a rickety taxi. She watches her husband hand-crank the window down, and does the same. Krishnan takes a deep breath and turns to her with a smile. "Bombay," he says, beaming. "In all her glory. What do you think?"

Somer just nods. Krishnan points out sights along the way—an elegant mosque in the distance, a famous racetrack. But all she can see are the dilapidated buildings and filthy streets that run like a nonstop movie reel outside her window. The first time they stop in traffic, a swarm of beggars in tattered clothing surrounds the car, extending their hands through her open window until Krishnan leans over to roll it up.

"Just ignore them. Don't look and they'll go away," he says, staring straight ahead.

Somer looks at the woman standing outside the car, holding an emaciated baby on her hip, silently gesturing with her fingers to her mouth. The woman is no more than twelve inches from her. Somer can feel the woman's hunger and desperation, even through the glass. She forces herself to turn away.

"You'll get used to it." He reaches for her hand. "Don't worry, we're almost there."

Somer is curious to see the house where Krishnan grew up. He has never given her much detail on his family beyond the basics: his father is a well-respected physician, his mother gives private tutoring lessons and does charity work. She's met them only once, six years ago, when they came for the wedding in San Francisco.

Although his parents stayed with them for an entire week, it was a hectic time, between work and wedding preparations. When Somer had a chance to talk to them, the conversation revolved around the weather (why it was so cold in the summer), the wedding plans (a casual ceremony for forty guests in Golden Gate Park), and which nearby restaurants served vegetarian food (the pizzeria and the bakery). Each morning, Kris's mother brewed tea on the stovetop and surveyed the scarce contents of their kitchen cupboards. His father studied the newspaper, as if he intended to read every single word printed there. Somer felt a guilty relief when she left for work every day. At one point, she asked Kris if there was anything wrong. It felt as if his parents were holding something back.

"They're not used to things here," he said. "They're just trying to get their bearings."

Now, looking out the window at the Bombay skyline, Somer wonders if she'll be able to do the same.

13

AMBITIONS

Bombay, India—1985
SARLA

SARLA THAKKAR LOOKS IN THE MIRROR AS SHE WINDS HER waist-length hair into its customary bun and pins it tightly in place. She lightly touches the gray strands at her temple. *Well why not? I am a grandmother, after all.* She lifts the freshly pressed yellow sari from the bed, and wraps it proficiently around her body until the embroidered pink border is aligned perfectly on her left shoulder. She leans in closer to the mirror to place a small yellow and gold *bindi* precisely in the center of her forehead. After applying her lipstick, she steps back for a look, then reminds herself to tell Devesh to clean the smudges off this glass. She has been keeping the servants busy all day. They know everything needs to be just so for the arrival of her eldest son from America. Though she laments to others that Krishnan has settled so far from home, foremost, she is proud. He always had big ambitions, ever since he was a child.

As a boy, Krishnan followed his father around on his hospital rounds, tugging eagerly at the corner of the elder man's white coat when he had a question. All three of her sons were smart, but Krishnan was particularly competitive. He raced home from school to declare he had earned the highest marks in science, or won the math competition. As he continued to be successful in school, Krishnan's ambitions expanded accordingly, and he dreamed of going abroad to study. When he gained admission to medical school in America, they had to muster the resources for him to go: their wealth in India didn't go as far in American dollars. Foreign students weren't eligible for loans, and they didn't want a job to distract Krishnan from his studies. Sarla can hardly believe a decade has passed since that day at the airport they saw him off.

SIXTEEN FAMILY MEMBERS TRAVELED TOGETHER, CARAVAN STYLE, IN four separate cars to the airport. The last driver's car was filled only with Krishnan's luggage, including one large suitcase full of sealed bags of tea leaves, ground spices, and other dry goods. Naturally, Sarla worried most about how her son would eat for the few years he was abroad. At the airport, they all passed the time together before Krishnan's flight. The children ran around in circles playing *kabbadi*, enjoying how their voices echoed in the high-ceilinged corridors. Sarla had brought a half-dozen stainless steel tiffin containers, so the adults could enjoy hot *chai* and snacks. No occasion, especially one as significant as this, was complete without a meal to mark the event. Sarla occupied herself with feeding everyone, organizing the group photos, keeping track of the time—anything to keep from getting sentimental. If she knew then that her son was leaving India for good, she would have permitted herself more emotion. It was her husband who shared the most touching farewell with their son. Normally stoic, he held Krishnan in his embrace for a long time. When he let go, his eyes were moist. The rest of the family looked away respectfully, and even the children settled down.

"Don't worry, Papa. I'll make you proud," Krishnan said, his voice cracking.

"I am proud already, son," his father said. "Today, I am very proud." Krishnan turned to wave to the cluster of relatives who had come to wish him well. It was not only his dreams that propelled him on his journey to America.

There was never any question he would return to India after medical school, to join his father's practice and get married. With his American degree and earning potential, Krishnan would have his pick of eligible young women. But when Sarla began looking for potential matches for him, he brushed her off, claiming he was too busy with school to think of marriage. Then suddenly, just before his graduation, he called to say he had found a woman of his own, an *American* woman, he planned to marry. And he was staying there, because of her, they understood implicitly.

Sarla and her husband were educated, progressive people: they weren't opposed to a love marriage on principle, but this seemed rash. They didn't want Krishnan to make a mistake—this girl came from a completely different culture, and they didn't even know each other's families. When they traveled to America for the marriage, their fears about Krishnan and his bride were confirmed. The wedding was quiet and small, the home they shared was soulless, their food bland. Sarla and her husband felt like guests in that home, rather than family. They wondered what had happened to their son.

Still, now he is married, and it is their duty is to support their son and his wife. When Krishnan inquired about adoption last year, Sarla saw an opportunity for reconnection. Maybe she wouldn't lose her son to America entirely. Each time she visited the orphanage, she got unofficial updates from the staff on new babies who had arrived. When she first saw the baby girl with the unusual eyes, she pointed her out to the director. Those eyes reminded her of Krishnan's wife's; she had a feeling the child might be a good match for them.

Sarla has always longed for a daughter, some female company in this house full of men. Of course, she would never trade one of her sons, but many times when they were young, she found herself wishing for a girl with whom to share not only her jewelry, but also her life lessons. Being a woman in India is an altogether different experience. You can't always see the power women hold, but it is there, in the firm grasp of the matriarchs who still rule most families. It has not been easy for Sarla to navigate the female path: she has become a master traveler, but one with no pupil. She thought she might develop this relationship with one of her daughters-in-law, but the others, like Somer, didn't quite fill the role. And when they had babies, they relied on their own mothers, leaving her once again in the company of men.

But now, Sarla muses as she glances at the clock, anticipating Krishnan's arrival, she will finally get her granddaughter.

14

MONSOON SEASON

Bombay, India—1985
SOMER

ON HER FIRST MORNING IN BOMBAY, SOMER WAKES WITH AN
upset stomach. She rolls over to a different position, but it doesn't
help. *Damn.* She tried to be careful at dinner last night with Krishnan's family, but clearly she couldn't handle the spicy food. That
wasn't the only thing that made her feel out of place. Everyone else
ate with their fingers while she sheepishly asked for a fork. She could
only understand part of the dinner conversation because Krishnan's
relatives kept lapsing into Gujarati. It was like skiing on snow and
suddenly coming upon a patch of grass. She was stranded, and Krishnan didn't bother to interpret for her.

Anyway, none of this matters, she tells herself. They're here for
one reason—to get Asha and take her home. *Stay focused. Don't worry
about the rest of it.* They have their interview at the government adoption office this afternoon, the final step in the approval process.
Somer feels a sudden curdling in her stomach and barely makes it to
the bathroom in time.

THEY ARRIVE TEN MINUTES EARLY AT THE ADOPTION OFFICE, then wait another forty minutes in the reception area. Somer looks at her watch and at the clock above the door.

"Relax, they know we're here," Krishnan says. "This is the way things work here."

Finally, they are ushered into an office that smells of stale tobacco and sweat.

"*Achha,* Mr. and Mrs. Thakkar, *namaste.*" The man wearing a yellowed short-sleeve dress shirt and a short necktie bows slightly to them. "Please, be comfortable." He gestures to two chairs across from the desk.

"Mr. Thakkar, you are from here, no?"

"Yes," Krishnan says. "I grew up in Churchgate, and did my BSc at Xaviers."

"Ahh, Churchgate. My aunt lives over there." The man asks him a question in another language. *Hindi?* Krishnan answers him in the same language, and they banter back and forth like that a few times without Somer understanding any of it. The civil servant consults his file, takes a long look at Somer, and turns back to Krishnan. "And your wife?" he says with a smirk. "You met her there, America? California girl, heh?"

She hears Krishnan answer, but the only English word she can catch is *doctor.*

The civil servant looks back at the file and says flatly, as if reading, "No children?" and then, looking directly up at Somer, "No babies?"

Her cheeks flush with familiar shame in this country where fertility is so celebrated, where every woman has a child on each hip. She shakes her head. After a couple more exchanges with Krishnan, the civil servant tells them to come back in the morning for an update on their case. Krishnan takes her arm and leads her out of the building.

"What was that about?" she says once they are outside.

"Nothing," he says. "Indian bureaucracy. Everything is like this here." He flags a taxi.

"What do you mean 'like this'? What happened back there? They kept us waiting an hour, that guy clearly hadn't even read our file, and then he barely even *talks* to me!"

"That's because you're—"

"I'm what?" she snaps at him.

"Look, things work differently here. I know how to handle this, just trust me. You can't come here with your American ideas—"

"I didn't come here with anything." She slams the taxicab door and feels the whole car reverberate.

When they return to the government office the next morning, they are told there is a delay in the approval process. Somer feels all her doubt surge back. She tries pushing it away, but it circles like the persistent mosquitoes that swarm the ripe mangoes at the corner fruit stand. They go back to the office every day, sometimes twice a day, to try to move things along. Each visit leaves Somer more frustrated. She sees the looks from the officers there—their skepticism as they size up her potential as a mother, the way their tone changes when they address Krishnan rather than her.

It is monsoon season. The rain pounds down in steady sheets until the alleys turn into rushing currents of water and debris. She has never before seen rain like this, another of many firsts since arriving in Bombay. It has been an assault on her senses: smells that suddenly overpower her, and heat she can taste, thick as dust on her tongue. Not only does she feel powerless in the face of Indian bureaucracy, but as further punishment, the torrential downpours also keep them trapped inside Krishnan's parents' flat.

An endless number of people circulate through the flat. There are Krishnan's grandparents, his parents, and his two brothers with their wives and children—fourteen people in all. Across the hall lives Krishnan's uncle, with a similarly expansive family. The front doors to the two flats are always unlocked and often wide open, so it feels like one labyrinthine living space, with people continuously milling about. Krishnan's relatives are polite, constantly offering her tea and small trinkets, but she notices they stop talking when she enters the room. No matter how much of an effort she makes, Somer still feels uncomfortable around them.

In addition to family, there are the servants: one who squats low and moves from room to room, sweeping the floors with a bundle of reeds; another who comes every day to wash clothes by hand and hang them on the balcony; the cook; the post boy; the paperboy; and the milk boy, among others. She grows accustomed to hearing the doorbell ring several times an hour and eventually learns to tune it out as the extraneous sound of a normal day's workings. The reality of this India clashes with the images she held in her mind, her hopes and expectations. As the days wear on, she longs for the simple comforts of home: a bowl of cereal, an ice-cold Coca-Cola, an evening alone with her husband.

As Somer observes this man she thought she knew, it becomes clear there is a side to him that is utterly foreign. This Krishnan wears white loose-flowing cotton tunics from morning to night, drinks milky tea instead of black coffee, and eats meals dexterously with his hands. He is not the least bit uncomfortable with the complete lack of privacy. She finds it curious, this person who seems to enjoy the din of a crowded household, so different from the quiet man she met at Stanford, living in a spartan bedroom with only a mattress on the floor and secondhand desk. Somer begins to wonder if she knows him at all.

15

VICTORY

Dahanu, India—1985
KAVITA

THE BABY GURGLES AS KAVITA KNEADS COCONUT OIL INTO HIS pudgy frog legs. He squirms and vigorously waves his arms in the air, as if to applaud his mother for this daily practice. She gently massages his delicate body, first stretching out one leg fully, then the other. She rubs circles on his belly, which is barely bigger than the whole of her palm. This is the one time each day she can delight in seeing every astonishing part of his body. She never tires of looking at him, inspecting every perfect detail: the soft curl of his eyelashes, the dimples in his elbows and knees. She bathes him in a wooden bucket, pouring small cupfuls of warm water over his body, taking care not to get any in his eyes. As she finishes dressing him, her mother comes to tell her dinner is ready. Kavita has been at her parents' home since the birth of her son, enjoying the luxury of focusing on her baby, free from any household responsibilities.

When she walks into the front room, she sees Jasu sitting there, his hair freshly oiled and combed. He stands, with a broad grin, to greet them. On the table between them, she sees, he has brought a fresh jasmine garland for her hair. Yesterday, it was a box of sweets. He has been coming here every day for nearly two weeks, and always with something for her. Now, walking toward him, she is struck by his smile, as wide as his arms, which reach out for his son. "Say hello to your papa," she says, handing him to Jasu. Unsure how to handle a newborn, he holds the baby tenderly, almost tentatively.

Jasu eats voraciously at dinner, scooping large bites into his mouth too quickly to taste the food. She suspects he is not having much at his other meals, but he hasn't pressured her about coming home. He told her he expects her to spend the customary first forty days with her mother. Not all husbands are so patient during this time. As she watches their son in his father's arms, she thinks of how fortunate this boy is, what a cherished life he will lead. Tomorrow, relatives are gathering for the baby's *namkaran,* his naming ceremony. Everyone has been overjoyed with the birth of their first son, bringing celebratory sweets, new clothes for the baby, fennel tea to bolster her milk supply. They have showered on her all the traditional gifts, as if this is her first baby, their first child. *What about the other times I've carried a baby in my womb, given birth, held my child in my arms?*

But no one acknowledges this, not even Jasu. Only Kavita has an aching cavity in her heart for what she's lost. She sees the pride in Jasu's eyes as he holds his son and forces herself to smile while saying a silent prayer for this child. She hopes she can give him the life he deserves. She prays she will be a good mother to her son, prays she has enough maternal love left in her heart for him, prays it didn't die along with her daughters.

THE NEXT MORNING, THE HOUSE HUMS WITH ACTIVITY. KAVITA'S mother has been up early frying *jalebis,* the sticky sweet delicacies essential at their celebrations. Family members arrive in a steady stream, each one seeking out Kavita and Jasu to offer their congratulations and gifts. When Jasu's parents arrive, they take Kavita aside and hand her a package wrapped in brown paper and tied with string.

"It is a new *kurta-pajama*," Jasu's mother says, "for the baby to wear at the *namkaran*." She smiles so widely her missing molars are visible. Kavita unwraps the package with care and pulls out a maroon silk outfit, embroidered with gold thread. A cream-colored vest covered in small round mirrors and a pair of impossibly small pointed ivory shoes complete the outfit. Kavita strokes the smooth fabric. It is genuine silk, and the embroidery is done by hand. The outfit is beautiful, impractical, an indulgence, and one that Jasu's parents cannot easily afford. She looks up to thank her mother-in-law and sees pride in the older woman's eyes. "We are so happy, *beti*," Jasu's mother says, grabbing Kavita to her large bosom in a spontaneous embrace. "May your son live a long life and bring you much happiness. Just as Jasu has for us."

"*Hahnji, sassu.* Thank you. I will go dress him in this now." Kavita can't remember ever seeing such a show of generosity or emotion from her mother-in-law. She feels her cheeks flush, a rising tightness in her chest as she turns away. She pushes her way through the guests, who are all drinking *chai* and admiring the baby. She has felt nothing but love for her son during these weeks she has been alone with him. But now, the adulation of others makes her cringe, the shameless celebration in his honor fills her mouth with a bitter taste, the bitterness of raw green wood.

When the *pandit* arrives for the ceremony, the two dozen relatives gather around him in the crowded drawing room. Jasu and Kavita take their places on the floor next to the *pandit,* with Jasu holding the baby in his lap. The *pandit* lights the ceremony fire and begins by offering prayers to Agni, the god of fire, to purify the proceedings. He begins chanting, invokes the spirits of the forefathers, and asks them to bless and protect this child. The priest's melodic voice is soothing. Kavita looks deep into the flames and is transported back to the stone steps of her morning *pujas*. The scent of incense mixed with *ghee* rises in the air, and she closes her eyes. Images flash through her mind—Daiji's face between her knees, the red-lettered sign on the door, the clanging iron gate of the orphanage.

"Precise time and date of the baby's birth?" she hears the priest asking from a distant place. Jasu answers him, and the *pandit* turns to his astrology chart to determine the boy's horoscope. Kavita feels her body tense even further. This reading will determine everything in their son's life—his health, prosperity, marriage, and today, his name. After some deliberation, the *pandit* looks up at Jasu's sister, seated next to him. "Choose a name beginning with *V*." All eyes in the room turn to her. She thinks for a moment, then a smile comes to her face and she leans down to the baby's ear to whisper the chosen name.

"Vijay," she says, beaming. Jasu turns to the crowd, and holds up his son for everyone to see. The *pandit* gives an approving nod, and everyone else cheers, repeating the name to one another. Somewhere in the noise of the crowd, Kavita hears a lone voice, an infant's piercing cry. She looks at her son, who is sleeping. Her eyes dart around the room, trying to find the origin of the cry, but she sees no other babies. Jasu places the baby in a cradle decorated with garlands of bright orange marigolds, white and red chrysanthemums, and begins to rock it from side to side. The other women in the room slowly come forward and surround them. Kavita is engulfed by their singing voices, but even this cannot drown out the high-pitched cry she still hears. For a moment, she is struck with the disturbing thought that everything in her son's life might be bittersweet for her.

She looks into Vijay's face to see whether his new name suits him. It means victory.

16

OFFENSE

Bombay, India—1985
SOMER

A QUIET KNOCK AT THE DOOR ROUSES SOMER FROM SLEEP. SHE hears Krishnan mumble something, then hears the door open and feet shuffle across the floor. Through half-opened eyes, she sees one of the household servants walking toward their bed with a tray. *What is he doing here before we've even woken up?* Suddenly aware of her thin nightgown, she covers herself with the bedsheet and waits for Krishnan to shoo the man away. Instead, he sits up in bed, propping a pillow behind him, and takes a cup of a tea from the tray.

"Do you want some?" he asks her.

"What? No." Somer turns over and shuts her eyes. She hears the clatter of a china cup and spoon, and the exchange of a few words before the shuffle of feet again, and finally, the door closes.

"Ah, bed tea," Krishnan says. "One of the great pleasures of Indian living. You should try it sometime."

Somer buries her face into the pillow. *Is there nothing that's off-limits here? Any corner of our lives that isn't subject to intrusions by your family or servants?* But she swallows back the words and says instead,

"What are we doing today?" Sunday is the one day of the week the government office is closed.

"Some friends of mine called me for a cricket match, if you don't mind. I'll play terribly, but it will be good to see them. Friends from high school, I haven't seen some of them in ten years. My mom can take you out shopping or something, if you'd like."

SOMER STANDS ON THE BALCONY LOOKING OUT TO THE DULL ocean, its gray waves lapping against the boardwalk. It is hot and muggy, but at least there is a respite from the rain. On the first day of clear weather in weeks, Krishnan has gone off by himself. Somer feels suffocated by the thought of staying inside again today, and even more put off by the prospect of spending it with his mother. She makes up her mind to go for a walk by herself, to get away from the stultifying pressure of this flat.

Stepping outside the building, walking past the tall gates and away from the watchful eyes of the doorman gives Somer a sense of freedom. Churchgate Station is up ahead at the end of the block, and on the opposite corner stands a sandwich shop advertising BURGERS on a placard out front. The thought of a burger after two straight weeks of Indian food is enticing. She walks up to the order window and says, "Two hamburgers please, with cheese." She'll eat one now and keep the other for later, something to break the monotony of curries and rice.

"No ham, madam. Mutton burger only."

"Mutton?" *As in, lamb?*

"Yes, very tasty, madam. You will like, guaranteed."

"Okay." She sighs. "Two mutton burgers please."

The burger is nothing like what she's used to, but Somer has to admit, it tastes pretty good. Feeling pleasantly full, she heads toward the ocean boardwalk, which has now become crowded with street vendors and pedestrian traffic. Men walk together in packs, laughing, chewing *paan* and spitting on the sidewalk. She sees a mustached man eyeing her, staring brazenly at her breasts, nudging his friends. Somer self-consciously folds her arms over her chest, and the men break into laughter. *Disgusting pigs.*

She walks, trying to breathe deeply and look at the water. But her eyes are repeatedly forced back to the crowds of people she must navigate. She expects the men to step aside and let her pass, to make some space for her in the crowd, but they don't. Each time, she must force her way through, squeezing her own body in between others. Pushing her way through a particularly reluctant group, Somer feels a body press up against her buttocks and a hand squeeze her breast. She darts around to see a couple young men snickering, one of them with stained teeth making kissing gestures at her.

Somer feels panic rise in her throat as she pushes through the crowd, looking for an opening to escape. Marine Drive is buzzing with six lanes of traffic that never seem to stop, so Somer weaves her way through, one lane at a time, with horns blaring and cars narrowly missing her. She walks rapidly down one of the side roads toward home. Once her fear subsides, indignation and anger percolate in its wake. *These men are pathetic. How can Kris be from here?*

She desperately wants to talk to him, but he is still out when she gets home. Thankfully, everyone else appears to be napping, so she stashes her leftovers in the fridge and retreats to their room. She fills two pails of water in the bathroom and washes every inch of herself before dressing in a clean nightgown and lying down on the bed until Kris gets home.

SOMER WAKES UP TO LOUD CLANGING NOISES FROM OUTSIDE THE bedroom door. She looks at her watch and realizes hours have passed. She hears Kris among the raised voices outside, steps into the hallway, and Kris's mother rushes past without acknowledging her. Somer walks into the living room, where she sees Kris arguing with one of the servants. The balcony outside is littered with various kitchen items—pots, pans, cooking utensils, dishes, cups—and another servant is furiously scrubbing each one of them. She walks toward the kitchen and sees a third servant dumping jars of flour, rice, and beans into the trash. Somer watches in disbelief as the servant empties out the entire platter of spices, at least two dozen small steel bowls.

"Kris?" Somer says. "What's going on?"

Kris spins around, his face creased in anger. Without a word, he takes her by the arm, walks her into their bedroom, and closes the door. "What were you thinking?"

"What do you mean?" She feels her heart rate quicken.

"What the hell were you thinking bringing meat into this house? You know my parents are strict vegetarians. You polluted the entire kitchen."

"I—I'm sorry. I didn't think—"

"My mother practically had a heart attack. She wanted to throw out every single dish and pot, but I convinced her they could be disinfected."

"Kris, I didn't know." She gets up from the bed. "I'll help clean it—"

"No." He grabs her arm. "Don't. You've done enough. Just leave it alone now."

"I'm sorry, I didn't know." She sits back down and begins to cry.

"What do you mean, you didn't know? Are you so wrapped up in your own head you don't notice where you are? I've told you they're vegetarians. Did we cook any meat when they came to visit us? Have you ever seen meat served in this house?" He shakes his head.

"I should go apologize to your mother," Somer says, standing up.

"Yes," Kris says, "you should."

Somer finds Kris's mother in one of the bedrooms, sitting with Kris's brother's wife on a bed draped with various multicolored silks. She gives the open door a polite knock. "Hello?" she says. "May I come in?"

"Yes, Somer," Kris's mother says, unmoving.

Somer perches on the edge of the bed. "These are beautiful," she says, running her hand over a pile of red silk.

"We are choosing saris for a wedding this weekend, one of Dr. Thakkar's colleagues."

"Oh. Well, I just wanted to come and apologize to you for the . . . for your kitchen. I didn't realize . . . I didn't mean any offense and I'm very sorry."

Kris's mother nods her head from side to side. "What's done is done. Let's put it aside."

"I guess I wasn't thinking. I was a little upset." Somer takes a deep breath. "I went out for a walk and had a disturbing experience. This man—or two men, I'm not sure—they touched me, on the boardwalk." Her mother-in-law, brow furrowed, peers at her. "They touched me," Somer continues, gesturing to her chest, "you know, inappropriately." She exhales and waits for them to understand.

Her sister-in-law speaks for the first time. "Krishnan let you go out by yourself?"

"Yes, well, no. He didn't let me, exactly. He was at his cricket game, so I went for a walk."

"No, of course he wouldn't do that. Krishnan knows better," his mother says. She turns to Somer. "It is not appropriate for women like you to walk on the streets alone. You should not have gone without one of us, for your own safety."

"Women like me?" Somer asks.

"Foreign women. Your bare legs and arms, your blond hair. It's asking for trouble." She shakes her head firmly with a disapproving look.

Somer thinks back to the midcalf-length skirt and T-shirt she wore this morning. *Not appropriate?* "I'll . . . remember that next time." She folds her arms and stands up. "Sorry to interrupt." She walks quickly down the hallway to their bedroom and pulls the door closed behind her. She tries to fight her growing resentment toward this country, the feeling that everything here is tainted: that the biased adoption process, the opaque cultural rules, and the oppressive weather, all are wrapped up with India as a whole. She expected to feel at home with Krishnan's family, not so utterly out of place. *Is this how I'll feel in my own family, like an outsider?* Asha and Krishnan will look alike, they will have their ancestry in common. Her daughter will always be from this country, which feels so foreign to her. She rummages through her suitcase for the pair of sweats she hasn't worn since the plane, and despite the sweltering heat, pulls them over her nightgown.

17

ALREADY ATTACHED

Bombay, India—1985
KRISHNAN

KRISHNAN LEAVES A DRIPPING TRAIL AS HE BOUNDS UP THE STAIRS TO his family's flat rather than waiting for the elevator. Somer hardly protested when he proposed going to the government office alone this morning, understanding this might be their best chance to finalize the adoption. Inside the flat, he finds her alone in their room, sitting on the bed, arms wrapped around her hunched knees, watching the downpour through the window. She doesn't notice him until he is standing before her, drenched from head to toe. When she looks up, her cheeks are wet. "Good news," he says. They share tears of relief, exhaustion, and joy and decide to go out for a celebratory dinner at the Taj Mahal Hotel.

Before their bottle of wine is half-finished, Somer is tipsy and begins to vocalize her complaints for the first time since arriving in India. She admits how frustrated she's been with the adoption process, how conspicuous she feels as a foreigner, how disconnected she feels from him and his family. Krishnan listens and nods, pouring himself more wine and then ordering one scotch, followed by another. He was worried how Somer would fare in India, and it has been even worse than he expected. He forces himself to listen, and though she doesn't blame him, he feels the weight of guilt nevertheless. He has known for a long time this reckoning would come.

BACK IN MEDICAL SCHOOL, EVEN AFTER HIS RELATIONSHIP WITH Somer became serious, he avoided telling his family about her. They would never think to ask him about a girlfriend: he was not expected to have any extracurricular interests, much less romantic ones. By waiting, he reasoned, he could prepare Somer to meet his family: teach her a few words of Gujarati, expose her to the food. But in reality, he didn't share very much with her about his life in India. She was, after all, thoroughly American, and he wasn't sure how she would react to reports of living in an extended family, or pigeons flying into the living room through windows that stayed open all summer. This love was new and intoxicating to him, and he didn't want to risk it. It would have required a concerted effort, and more courage than he felt at twenty-five, to bring the two spheres of his life together. As it turned out, it took very little effort to let them remain separate.

He hoped his parents would support him, but if he had to choose between their approval and marrying Somer, he planned to choose Somer. He was in love with her in a way he never could be with a woman chosen by his parents—she was his intellectual partner, and they had shared experiences. In India, such a relationship was unusual, if not impossible. So he chose a life in America, intending to embrace it completely. It was easier for him, and Somer, he thought, to assimilate to her way of life. But now it is clear to Krishnan that he'd done her a disservice. By the time she met his parents, it was clear that superficial gestures wouldn't make up for the reality that they were worlds apart.

THIS WOMAN BEFORE HIM BARELY RESEMBLES THE ASSURED young med student he first met. The miscarriages, the infertility, the adoption process, and now India—each has delivered a blow to her confidence. But he knows that woman is in there somewhere, and his job now is to reassure her.

"This process has been an emotional roller coaster," he says. "And India can be a hard place for Westerners. But soon this whole thing will be over, and we'll go home to begin our life together as a family." He smiles. "Won't that be worth it?"

Somer exhales and nods her head. "I can think of nothing better. I am so tired of never knowing what to expect in this country. I don't feel like myself anymore. I just want to get back to our home, our life. I want to put all of this behind us."

He hates to see her this wounded. And so, feeling disappointed with how his country and family have made her uncomfortable, and guilty that he hadn't adequately prepared or defended her, he says what he believes he must to heal his wife and his marriage. They will not need to come back to India anytime soon. They will pour their energy into building their family and their life in America. In time, he assumes, things will get better.

WHEN THE TAXI PULLS UP TO THE PLAIN CONCRETE BUILDING with peeling paint and a rusty metal gate, Somer grabs his arm. "It didn't look this bad in the pictures," she whispers.

"Come on." He puts his arm around her. They walk up to the front gate and hear the sounds of children playing in the courtyard inside.

They are met outside by Reema, the representative of their Indian adoption agency. "Welcome, *namaskar*," she says, greeting them with joined palms and a smile. "I know you have been waiting a long time for this day, so come, let us go in." Reema leads them inside the building. Krishnan glances over at Somer, who dons a bright smile, as if cameras might be waiting on the other side of the door. Inside, they are greeted by a throng of barefoot children in assorted sizes who cluster around Somer, clearly having never seen a white person before.

"Hullo, madam!"

"Come from America, madam?"

". . . speak English, madam?"

They reach out their hands to touch her fair-skinned arms, feel the jersey fabric of her shirt. They wear threadbare clothes and bright smiles. Reema ushers Somer and Krishnan through the children and into a small office where a stout, middle-aged woman stands, hands clasped in front of her sari, waiting for them.

"*Namaskar*," she says, bowing slightly, "I am the director's assistant. Mr. Deshpande could not be here for this very happy day, but he sends his best wishes. We have the final paperwork to sign, and then I will bring your baby."

Somer sits down in one of two chairs and takes the clipboard from her. Something at the top of the page catches her eye. "Usha?" she asks. "This says Usha. But isn't her name Asha?"

"No, madam," the assistant replies, "her given name is Usha. That is what *we* call her, but you can call her whatever you like, of course."

"I thought . . . we thought her name was Asha. That's what we've been calling her, all this time." She gives Krishnan a pleading look.

Reema shuffles through the papers in her manila file folder. "Yes, we also have Asha on everything. There must have been an error somewhere along the way, perhaps in reading someone's handwriting? But not to worry, there's no harm. You can call her Asha and she will know it as her name in no time."

"It doesn't matter, honey." Kris stands behind Somer and put his hands on her shoulders. "She won't know the difference. Don't worry about it."

Somer shakes her head. "Just once, I would like something here to turn out the way it's supposed to." She hands the clipboard back and takes a deep breath. "Never mind. We're ready." The assistant nods and leaves the office.

When the assistant returns to the office holding the baby, everyone in the room stands at once. Krishnan is closest and reaches out for her. The baby goes easily into his arms and immediately begins playing with his eyeglasses. "Hi, sweet girl. Hi there, Asha." He speaks slowly and softly as he cradles her head, and she moves on to pinching his earlobes. Somer walks over, and all three of them embrace. She reaches out her arms to hold Asha, but the baby turns and clings tightly to Kris's neck like a koala.

"See, nothing to worry," the assistant says. "She's already attached to you."

18

SILVER BELLS

Bombay, India—1985
SARLA

"WHAT A BEAUTIFUL BABY SHE IS. HELLO, ASHA *BETI*," SARLA reaches over to touch the child's cheek. "Very aware, very curious— just see how she's looking around. *Hahn,* baby?" She gives the child an exaggerated smile and nod. "So, how was it?"

"Long day." Krishnan pauses to drink his tea. "Lots of paper-work—orphanage, courthouse, government office. We'll sleep early tonight."

"Of course, it sounds very strenuous." Sarla wobbles her head from side to side in a weary compromise between nodding yes and shaking no. "Thank God we are here to help you. Dinner will be ready soon." She turns to Somer, who is holding Asha. "What do you need for Asha, *beti*? A cot, some towels? Come." They stand, and she places her arm lightly on the younger woman's back to lead her down the hallway. She can see her son's wife is unsure of herself. She's using both arms to hold the child, reluctant to let go even to take a sip of her tea. It isn't that unusual, of course: most new mothers don't know what they're doing, but then, they usually have more time to learn. Asha is already one year old and will be walking soon. Somer will have to earn her maternal confidence quickly.

When Sarla brought Krishnan home from the hospital, she was only twenty-two years old, still a young bride. She always said he was raised by a whole family of mothers. From the first day, there was always someone around to show her how to do everything— from cleaning out his tiny nose, to wrapping him up to sleep. Between her mother, her aunt, her sister, and the *ayah,* not to mention a host of well-meaning neighbors, she was never alone with Krishnan once in the first six months. At times, she found it stifling to have so many hands involved in caring for her child. But she knew she was fortunate, and even the frustration of interference was a luxury that many new mothers, like Somer, would never have. In America, she's heard, new mothers are sent home from the hospital after just a few days, with no support system at all.

"*Achha,* Somer, I'll just draw some warm water for Asha's bath . . . Here, please feel this. Is it a good temperature?" she calls out from the bathroom. "Okay, the basin is filled. Here's a towel and some talcum powder." She's about to leave when she notes the apprehension on Somer's face. "Would you mind if I stay while you give her a bath?" she says. "It's been so long since an old woman like me has been around a baby. I would quite enjoy it."

Somer's face relaxes. "Of course, please stay. I could use another pair of hands." Working together, thirty minutes later, they have Asha fully bathed, dried, creamed, and dressed.

"There's nothing I love more than the scent of a freshly bathed baby," Sarla says, then laughs. "Except perhaps the smell of a freshly opened coconut. That is my other favorite." Somer joins her in laughter as she combs through Asha's damp curls. There is a polite knock on the bedroom door and they hear Devesh's timid voice from the hallway outside.

"Madam, Doctor Sahib has arrived. Shall we serve dinner now?"

THEY ALL SIT TOGETHER AT THE LONG MAHOGANY CARVED TABLE while the cook and servants orbit around, leaning in to serve them from sterling silver dishes. Somer holds Asha in her lap as she feeds her a bottle of milk. Krishnan feasts on roasted cauliflower, stuffed eggplants, *saag paneer,* vegetable *pulao,* and light, crispy *puris.* "Ma, you shouldn't have gone to so much trouble," he manages to say in between bites.

"Nonsense! This is a special occasion."

After Krishnan finishes, he offers to hold Asha so Somer can eat. Her plate contains small quantities, no more than a tablespoon or two of each dish. She uses her fork to take delicate bites. "Mmm, this is delicious. It reminds me of India Palace in San Francisco. I wish I knew how to make spinach taste this good. I'll have to get your *saag* recipe."

Sarla smiles at her politeness and overlooks her mispronunciation. Somer is a nice girl, and in theory, she is part of their family, yet the gulf between her and the rest of them is unmistakable. Any twelve-year-old girl in India could make a respectable *saag paneer* without a recipe. She sighs to herself. Now that Somer is the mother of her only granddaughter, Sarla will have to make an extra effort to bridge the distance.

Asha, in Krishnan's lap, grins mischievously up at him and reaches for the silver *thali* and small bowls on the table in front of them. "Here you go, sweetie. You want some rice?" He scoops up some stray grains with his fingers and feeds them to her.

Sarla watches them discreetly. She cannot help but notice how comfortable he seems with Asha. This has been one of the unexpected joys of getting older, seeing each of her sons grow to be a father to his own children. As the eldest son of the extended clan, Krishnan has been around younger cousins all his life, so it is not surprising he would take to parenthood so naturally. Somer will be good at it too, Sarla hopes, once she is accustomed to the thought of being a mother.

"You both look tired," Sarla notes, after the servants clear the table and they move to the living room. "Before you retire for the night, your father and I have something for you." She walks over to an elegant wooden cabinet with inlaid ivory designs standing against one wall of the living room. The door hinge squeaks when she opens it. She reaches inside and turns back to them with two packages in hand. She gives the first, a small burgundy velvet box tied with a gold elastic ribbon, to Krishnan. "This is for Asha."

"Ma . . . you didn't have to do this," Krishnan says. He fumbles with the thin knot before opening the lid. "Ahhh . . . lovely." He shows the box to Somer. Inside are two delicately ornate silver ankle bracelets. Somer picks one up with a single index finger, and it makes a shy tinkling sound. She looks closer at the row of tiny bells that dangle from it.

"They're called *jhanjhaar, beti.* It is a custom here for little girls to wear them—some say, so you can always hear where they are." Sarla laughs. "As soon as you told us you were coming here to fetch Asha, we had our jeweler make them."

"They're beautiful." Somer moves Asha to Krishnan's lap, so she can unhook one of the strands and refasten it on Asha's ankle. "There . . . oh, look at that." She stretches out Asha's little legs, holding one foot in each hand: the shiny intricate anklet on her left foot contrasting with the simple silver bangle on her right. "Maybe I should take this one off?" she says, fingering the modest one. "I'd hate for them to get tangled."

"Whatever you like, dear. It is your choice." Sarla leans forward with the second package, holding it out to Somer with both hands. "And this one is for you, my dear."

Somer's face registers a look of surprise, soon replaced by the slow spread of a smile. "Oh, thank you."

"I hope you like it. I chose it myself," Sarla says. "I don't know your taste . . ." She pauses a moment while Somer lifts out of the box a lustrous silk shawl in the shade of bright peacock green. The border is richly embroidered in gold and aqua blue. "When a daughter-in-law becomes a mother, it is a tradition for us to give a special sari. I know you don't have much occasion for a sari, so I chose a shawl instead. This one reminded me of your lovely eyes." She catches an expression cross her son's face. Disappointment? *He told me not to expect the girl to wear Indian clothes, didn't he?*

"Thank you. It's beautiful." Somer clutches the folds of silk fabric to her chest.

Sarla sits back, pleased with herself and the way the evening has turned out. Sometimes, as she has well learned in life, one's actions must precede the emotions one hopes to feel.

19

MATERNAL INSTINCT

San Francisco, California—1985
SOMER

ON THE FLIGHT BACK FROM INDIA, SOMER AND KRIS TAKE TURNS
staying awake to watch Asha as she sleeps in the seat between them,
holding each other's hands across her small body. Somer feels a flood
of emotion every time she realizes Asha is truly their baby.

Back in San Francisco, Somer searches for that instinct her
mother-in-law told her to follow about what Asha needs. But she
never seems to get it right: Asha wants to stay awake and play at night
when Somer tries to put her to sleep, or she spits out the food Somer
offers her. Somer knows there are developmental reasons behind the
behavior, but it still feels like a personal rejection when Asha throws
her entire lunch on the floor. She's surprised at how hard it is to follow the advice she gives her patients' mothers not to get worked up
about these things.

On their third night home, Kris works an overnight shift at the
hospital, and Somer finds herself feeling anxious about her first night
alone with Asha. Sometime after midnight, Asha wakes up screaming. Somer warms a bottle of milk for her, but Asha cries again after

she drinks it. *OK, I'm a pediatrician, I can do this. Crying child: check temperature, check diaper, check for hair tourniquet around fingers or toes.* Panic rises. *Maybe she has a urinary tract infection? Or meningitis?* She examines Asha from head to toe. But there is no medical reason for her crying. In this situation, she is a mother, not a physician, and she feels helpless. Somer sings to Asha, rocks her and paces the floor. For two solid hours, Asha screams, and Somer can do nothing to settle her down. Finally and inexplicably, sometime around 3 A.M., Asha falls asleep on Somer's sweaty and tear-stained shoulder in the rocking chair. Shaken, Somer doesn't move from that position until morning, when Krishnan finds them there.

"I can't do it," she whispers when he gently wakes her. "I don't know how to do this. She was up all night screaming." Somer has always believed that not everyone is cut out for motherhood; she's seen how some of her patients take to it more than others. Nature already deemed she couldn't be a mother, and now she wonders if they made a mistake. The rational explanations she strains to hear in her head cannot drown out the doubt welling in her heart.

"What do you mean? You *are* doing it," Kris says. "Look at her."

She looks down at Asha, sleeping in her arms with her mouth slightly parted. Kris strokes Asha's hair and smiles at Somer. She tries to smile but is thinking ahead to the next night he's on call. It all seemed manageable in India, when Krishnan's family was there to help prepare Asha's food, bathe her, soothe her when she cried. But now, after spending so long trying to become a mother, she doesn't know *how* to be one. Somer worries she may never feel that instinct.

She expects it to get better when she goes back to work, but this only raises new issues. Once she returns to her pediatrics practice, Somer only sees Asha for an hour at each end of the day. She is relieved to finally feel competent at something again, but she feels conflicted when Asha becomes so attached to the young Irish nanny they hired, clinging to her in the evening after Somer gets home. At work, every patient Asha's age reminds Somer of her bright smile or her wobbly walk. The mothers and children she sees in her practice seem so comfortable together. Somer wonders if it's the biological connection that underpins their confidence, or is it the time they spend together, the time Somer spends at work? Would she know better what to do with Asha if they shared the same blood? Would Asha respond better to Somer if she didn't look so different from everyone she'd known in her short life?

Krishnan doesn't understand her anguish over this, and by now, Somer doesn't expect him to. She can't face the possibility of failing at this after everything she's been through. She still loves her work, but she is wary of overinvesting in her career, of placing too much emphasis on something she's learned will never be enough.

PART II

20

SHAKTI

Dahanu, India—1990
JASU AND KAVITA

JASU SEES HER, SITTING CROSS-LEGGED IN FRONT OF THE FIRE, and stops to watch from a distance. Kavita tosses the *rotli* onto the cast iron pan nestled in the fire. She wears a serious expression, absorbed with the daily task of preparing food for the entire joint family. Jasu likes it better when she smiles and takes it as a personal challenge to try to distract her from her work. He walks toward her and begins whistling, emulating the birds that sing in the early morning. "Here is my little *chakli*," he says with a playful smile. *Little bird.* He can usually count on this pet name to prompt a smile.

"Food will be ready soon. Hungry?" she asks.

"*Hahn*, starving," he says, patting his belly. "What are we eating?" He tilts the flat stainless steel lid of a covered vessel.

"*Khobi-bhaji, rotli, dal*," she replies in staccato fashion, reaching over to stir the cabbage.

"*Khobi* again?" he says. "Thank goodness my wife is such a good cook, she can make cabbage taste good day after day. *Bhagwan*, I miss *ringna, bhinda, tindora* . . ."

"*Hahn*. Me too. Maybe after harvest."

"*Chakli*," he says, lowering his voice so his parents in the next room cannot hear. "Harvest is not going to be good. We will be lucky to get by this year." Jasu tries to keep the anxiety he feels from showing on his face. Crop yields and market prices have been getting worse every year since they got married. He couldn't afford to keep his workers, so for the past two years, both Kavita and Vijay have been helping him in the fields.

"Vijay!" Kavita shouts through the open archway to where their five-year-old son is playing outside with his cousins. "Time for dinner soon. Come in and wash up."

"Kavi." Jasu feels the heaviness come over him. "I can't think of any other way. We must go." He rubs his forehead, as if to help the lines there disappear. "We will find better fortune in the city. I will get a good job. You won't have to work like this anymore, day and night."

"I don't mind working, Jasu. If it helps you, us . . . I don't mind."

"But I mind," he says. "In Bombay, we won't have to break our backs every day. Imagine, Kavi, you can do cooking or sewing—no more working in the fields, no more of . . . *this*!" He grabs her thin fingers, and runs his thumbs over the calloused tips and scraped knuckles, her weathered hands exposing his failings.

"There must be something we can do. We can try planting cotton like your cousin."

He looks down, shaking his head. *How can I make her understand?* Every cell in his body tells him they must leave this place now, the only home either of them has known. They must go away—from the crop fields that signal his failure as a man, from the family he can't seem to forgive, from this house they share with his parents, his childhood home in which he can't be contained any longer. Bombay beckons to him like a glittering jewel, promising a better life for them, and particularly for their son.

"Kavi, it's not like here, where everyone is scraping by all the time. Every day, I hear, truckloads of new people arrive, just like us. Hundreds of them, and there are homes and work and food for all of them!"

"But everyone we know is *here*. Bombay is not our home. What good will it do to have all the money in the world there, but no family?" Kavita begins to cry.

He moves closer to her. "We will have *our* family. You and me and Vijay. He can go to a good school, a *proper* school. He won't have to work like us or live like this . . ." Jasu gestures with his hands at the modest home they share with his family. "He can finish school and even get an office job. Can you see that? Our little Vijay working in an office one day?" He is trying hard now to make her smile. *Please, Kavi.* He holds her face in his palms and wipes away her tears with his rough thumbs. "*Good morning, would you like* chai, *Sahib Sir?*" Jasu mocks, gently prodding the corners of her mouth into a reluctant smile with his finger and thumb.

"How will he manage, being around strangers in that city?" she says. "Here, everyone cares for him. This whole village is his family. We had that. I want him to have that too."

"I want him to have *more* than that, Kavi. Our family will always be here, they will always love him."

"And what about us? No one there can help us if something happens." Her voice catches with emotion. "At least here, we have help when the harvest is poor or Vijay is sick."

"We won't be the first ones to go." Jasu folds her small hands in his. "My cousin's neighbor, and that sugarcane farmer—we'll find them. Kavi, I just want a better life for us . . ." He trails off with this thought and presses his forehead to their tightly clasped hands. Then it comes to him. In a single moment, he knows what to say to her, this woman who is a mother before anything else. He looks up abruptly. "Look at all your parents have done for you, how much they have sacrificed. Isn't this the right thing to do for our son? Doesn't Vijay deserve the best? It's our obligation as parents. It is our turn, *chakli*."

His words bring a flush of shame to her cheeks, and she begins to cry again.

"Just think of it—can you, *chakli*? Can you see a new life for us? Trust me, Kavi."

His eyes are hopeful and bright. Hers are shiny with tears.

WHEN KAVITA FIRST TELLS HER PARENTS SHE AND JASU ARE moving to Bombay, she can barely get the words out without crying. "*Ba, Bapu*." Kavita buries her face in her mother's lap. "How can I leave you? What will become of me in that place?" She remembers Bombay: the hot pavement under her feet, the way people looked at her with shame.

Her mother wipes at her own eyes, clears her throat, and then gathers Kavita in her arms. "*Beti*, you will be fine. Jasu is a good husband. He must have his reasons."

"A good husband? He's taking me away from you, from Rupa, all my relatives and friends, my home, my village."

"*Beti*, we will always be here for you. But your life is with him. You must trust in him. Your husband and son need you. *If the mother falls, the whole family falls*," her mother recites from a traditional poem. "You must be brave for them."

Kavita remembers the first farewell she shared with her mother— standing outside the temple after she was married, her body draped in layers of silk, flower garlands, and jewelry, her face heavy with bridal makeup that made her look more like a woman than the girl she still was. She wept that day as she went off to her new husband's home, feeling as if she were saying good-bye for the last time. Yet she went back home each time she was expecting, and again after Vijay was born, relying on her mother's care so she could learn to be a mother herself.

Now, her mother lifts Kavita's head up out of her lap and holds her face, hot with tears, in her cool hands. "I am glad it is you who is going," her mother whispers.

Kavita looks up at her with shock.

"I won't worry about you, Kavita. You have strength. Fortitude. *Shakti.* Bombay will bring you hardship. But you, *beti,* have the strength to endure it."

And through her mother's words and her hands, Kavita feels it— *shakti,* the sacred feminine force that flows from the Divine Mother to all those who have come after her.

It is a cool September evening when Kavita and Jasu gather together with their families and friends to say good-bye. The first sparkling stars are just beginning to show themselves in a deepening blue sky, like the glimpse of a diamond earring beneath a lock of dark hair. Kavita has worn one of her best saris for the occasion, a vibrant blue chiffon with the tiniest of sequins sewn onto the edges with silver thread. As the sky darkens, Kavita's cousins, with whom she has grown up as sisters, carry out large vessels of food. They spoon it onto several large banana leaves, laid out in a large circle on the ground. Each person—each family member, each childhood friend, each lifelong neighbor—takes a seat in front of a leaf. As always, the men gather around Jasu on one side, and the women flock together with Kavita on the other.

Jasu's booming laughter erupts from the men's side. Kavita turns in time to see Jasu throw back his head, and one of his brothers slap him on the back. A shy smile spreads across her face. He has been full of life these last few weeks as they have prepared for their move, and this has brought her happiness too. Her parents' blessing and their reassurance that her rightful place is alongside her husband have helped her see things differently. She has begun to envision a new life with more comfort, less work, and a home away from her stifling in-laws.

"What kind of work will Jasu *bhai* do, Kavita?" one of the women asks.

"First, he will work as a messenger or tiffin carrier, a *dhaba-wallah*," Kavita says. "There is plenty of that work, and they pay every day in cash. Then once we are settled, he'll do some less stren-uous work in a shop or office."

Rupa nods agreement. "And they already know so many people in Bombay. Just last night, Jasu *bhai* was telling us. It is exciting, *bena*," Rupa says, squeezing Kavita's arm.

Kavita forces away the ache that rises in her heart at the thought of being so far away from her sister. "*Hahn.* Jasu says we will have a big flat to ourselves, with a bathroom inside and a big kitchen. And Vijay will have his own room to study and sleep." She looks over to where Vijay and his cousins are chasing one another, each trying to grab the hem of the others' shirts. Whenever one falls accidentally, he sends up a new cloud of dust and prompts gales of laughter from the rest. "I worry about him most. He will miss his cousins," Kavita says. "God willing, we will make our riches in Bombay and come back here quickly, *futta-fut.*"

By the time the adults finish eating, Vijay and the other boys have returned, dirt ground into their clothes. Jasu comes over to Kavita, broaching the male-female divide that has separated them all night. "*Challo,* it is getting late, I think we better say good-bye." And with those words, Jasu breaks the spell that has permeated the eve-ning: the illusion that this is just another large gathering of their loved ones that happens for any reason, or none at all. Slowly, a clus-ter of people crowd around them to say their good-byes. One by one, they clutch one another, whispering wishes of safe journeys and promises to visit soon. Gradually, the well-wishers slip away until only Kavita's parents are left.

Kavita falls to her knees and touches her forehead to her mother's feet. Her mother pulls her up by the shoulders and holds her close, embracing her tightly. She says only one word to her, although she repeats it many times. *Shakti.*

21

AN UNEASY PEACE

Palo Alto, California—1990
SOMER

SOMER HEADS TOWARD THE RECEPTION DESK IN THE LOBBY OF Lucile Packard Children's Hospital to find her patient's room number.

"Somer Whitman?" A tall doctor approaches her, rolling a suitcase behind him. "Somer, how are you?" He extends his hand to greet her.

"Peter," she says, recognizing him from UCSF. He was an intern when she was a senior resident. "My gosh, I haven't seen you in, what, ten years?"

"Yeah, must be," he says, running a hand through his thick brown hair.

"I heard you went into infectious diseases. What are you up to now?" Somer remembers him being bright, going places. He reminded her of herself in that way.

"Well, I did my ID fellowship in Boston and tropical diseases at Harvard for a couple fun years. And I just got recruited as division head here, so it's good to be back."

"Wow, Peter, that's great," Somer says.

"Thanks. I'm heading to Istanbul for a couple days to give a talk. I'll be jet-lagged for the next week, but hey—the work's interesting, and it's better than dealing with coughs and colds, right? How about you, you were interested in cardiology weren't you?" He looks at her with genuine interest. She recalls how well they got along, how she encouraged him to pursue a subspecialty.

"Well," she says, bracing for his reaction, "I'm working over at the community medical clinic in Palo Alto, so lots of coughs and colds." There is simply no way to make it sound sexy. The cases are routine, there is little continuity of patient care, and the clinic never has enough resources. "But hey, I can pick up my six-year-old daughter from school every day." She smiles and shrugs her shoulders. *Is that a trace of disappointment in his eyes?*

"That's great. We have two boys, six and ten. Keeps you busy, doesn't it?"

"Sure does."

"Hey, I've got to head to the airport, Somer, but it was great seeing you. By the way, I never forgot that great diagnosis of neonatal lupus you made when I was a junior resident—I must have relayed that story a dozen times through the years, but I always credit Dr. Whitman."

Somer smiles. "Dr. Thakkar now, actually. But glad to hear it. Good seeing you, Peter."

As she rides the elevator, Somer watches the floor numbers light up in sequence. Where have the years gone, and what happened to that ambitious medical student she used to be? She recalls that desire to work up interesting clinical cases, do research, ascend in academia. Now, she barely keeps up with her medical journals. Her career choices have meant losing pace with her peers, and yet even in her unassuming clinic job, she can feel like an imposter.

Then she rushes to pick up Asha from school, where she is known only as "Asha's mom" by the other mothers, who seem to all spend a lot of time together. Somer has no time for the PTA and bake sales. She has no time for herself. Her profession no longer defines her, but neither does being a mother. Both are pieces of her, and yet they don't seem to add up to a whole. Somer didn't know that having it all, as she always believed she would, would mean feeling like she's falling short everywhere. She tries to reassure herself that life is about trade-offs and she should make her peace with this one, though more often than not, it is an uneasy peace.

SOMER SITS ON THE BENCH, SIPPING HER WARM SWEET COFFEE and watching Asha hang from the monkey bars in the playground. In the last year, Asha has become adventurous—climbing, hanging, and swinging from everything she can. All of her little-girl caution is gone, and she has the scabbed knees to prove it.

She loves bringing Asha to this park. They moved to this neighborhood a few years ago, when she was two. It was hard to leave San Francisco, the place where they learned to be a family together. After years of pain and estrangement, she and Krishnan enjoyed the novelty of their family time—going to Baker Beach on the weekend, where Asha would tiptoe just up to the water's edge and then run away screaming when the next wave came. Somer and Krishnan found a way to relate to each other again. Their conversations didn't center on medicine anymore: they rebuilt their tattered relationship, and did it around Asha.

They hadn't planned to join the exodus of their friends out of the city, but as Asha became more active, they began to lament their tiny backyard and the quality of the local schools. When Kris got a lucrative offer to join a practice in Menlo Park, a neighborhood with a good school district thirty minutes south of San Francisco, they started looking for houses nearby. Somer found a position at the community medical clinic.

"Asha, five more minutes," Somer calls out, noting the sun's position.

"She's lovely," says a woman sitting on the bench next to her. "I think I've seen you before. We come here almost every day." The woman gestures to a little blond boy digging in the sandbox. "He loves it, and I'm always happy to get out of the house."

"Yeah, Asha loves it here too. I'll have to pry her away soon." Somer laughs.

"You should come by here at noon on Fridays," the woman says. "I get together with some of the other nannies from the neighborhood every week for a picnic. The kids have fun together, and we get some grown-up company."

Nannies? After a polite moment, Somer stands and collects her belongings. "I'm not her nanny," she says, "I'm her mother."

"Oh, I'm so sorry. I just assumed . . . I mean, I thought because—"

"It's fine," Somer says, in a tone that indicates otherwise. "She looks more like her father, but she has my personality." She strides toward Asha. "Have a nice day."

On the way home, Asha rides her bicycle while Somer trails behind, reflecting on why the incident at the park bothered her so much. It's easy for people to assume she and Asha aren't related. She should be used to it by now. When the three of them are out together, people often look twice at Somer. Even she can see how natural Kris and Asha look together, when she rides on his shoulders or they sit side by side in a restaurant booth. At these times, Somer has to resist feeling she's the one who has been adopted into their family.

At an adoption seminar they attended years ago, they were told that adoption only solves childlessness, not infertility—a distinction Somer has come to understand. Asha's arrival into their lives brought many things—love, joy, fulfillment—but it didn't erase all the pain caused by the miscarriages, nor did it completely eliminate her desire for a biological child.

When they are together, just the two of them, Somer feels like Asha's mother and loves her as if she's her own child. She doesn't tell people Asha is adopted. Not only does it not seem pertinent, but she doesn't want to make Asha self-conscious about it. She doesn't see the dissimilarity evident to everyone else in Asha's dark hair, her tan skin. Now, when she sees Asha waiting at the corner, it is through the eyes of the nanny at the park. One of Asha's thin brown legs is perched atop a pedal, while the other barely touches the ground. Her thick black ponytail is peeking out from the back of her pale blue ladybug helmet. Somer looks at her daughter, who looks nothing like her daughter.

22

GOLD SPOT

Bombay, India—1990
KAVITA

KAVITA INHALES DEEPLY WHEN SHE FINALLY CLIMBS DOWN FROM
the open-air bus. For the past four hours she, Jasu, and Vijay have
shared cramped passage with dozens of sweat-drenched people, most
utterly disinterested in the scenery they passed along the way. Many
of them make this trip every week to sell their wares in the city.
Despite the fact they purchased three tickets, only Kavita could find
a seat on the bus. She held Vijay on her lap the whole way, numbness
slowly spreading through her thighs. Jasu was forced to stand for the
duration of the ride next to a man and his wire cage of chickens,
which swung repeatedly into Jasu's knee. Neither of them com-
plained, for some passengers hung out of the door and others clung
to the roof of the bus.

With three bags containing all their possessions, they now stand
outside the bus depot. Vijay leans against her leg, eyelids drooping.
Their plan is to make it to a settlement in the center of the city,
where they've been told they can stay for a night or two for very
little money. Right now, they need a good night's rest. Tomorrow,

they will see about finding a real home and jobs. Jasu leads them on foot, carrying a suitcase in each hand and stopping periodically to ask directions.

Kavita follows him, holding a bag in one hand and Vijay's hand in the other. As they move through the darkening landscape of Bombay, she is startled by how much it has changed since she was here six years ago. Defying all possibility, there seem to be even more people crowded into the same space, more vehicles on the roads, more noise and fumes filling the air.

Two thoughts keep entering her mind: how much she already misses the village, and the bitter memory of leaving Usha at that orphanage. These two ideas vie for prominence in her head, and Kavita fights a rising sense of resentment toward Jasu. *He forced me to give up my baby. And now he's forced me to come to this city, to leave everything I love.* For a moment, she loses sight of Jasu up ahead in the crowd and hurries to catch up with him. They only have each other in this strange new place. She hears her mother's soothing voice. *You must trust in him. You must be brave for them.*

By the time they arrive at Dharavi, the place about which they have been told, night has fallen. They are shocked to find not a building as they expected, but an enormous shantytown, occupying the space between a highway on one side and railroad tracks on the other. There is a long row of shacks, shoddily constructed from corrugated tin, cardboard, and mud: little one-room houses made of garbage. They walk slowly, to avoid the river of raw sewage that runs alongside the huts. Kavita clutches Vijay's hand tightly as she pulls him out of the way of the small children running around naked. A beggar with stumps for legs stretches one bony arm out toward her. Another man, obviously drunk, leers at her and runs his tongue over his lips. Kavita keeps her eyes on the ground, where the main dangers are discarded trash and scurrying rodents.

"You need place to stay? You need home?" A man dressed as a

woman in a garish yellow sari starts walking alongside Jasu. He has a pretty face, and when he smiles, two gold teeth are visible. Jasu exchanges a few words Kavita cannot hear, but soon they are following the man down the lane. He stops in front of a small mud shack draped in plastic sheeting with a rusting tin roof. When he tries to push open the crooked door, something inside blocks it from opening. In the dim light, they see it is a white-haired dog, so gaunt that each of its ribs can be easily counted. The sari-clad man briefly betrays his feminine persona to kick the dog out of the way, then gracefully holds out his arm to usher them in.

"Other family left just this morning," says the man. "You can stay here, if you please. Only a small donation is requested." He turns over his outstretched hand so that his palm is open, and smiles coyly at Jasu, who turns to Kavita.

"It's only one night," she says, to make the unavoidable choice easier for him. It is already dark outside. They have been walking a long time, and Vijay looks ready to fall asleep on his feet. Jasu puts down the suitcases, takes a couple of coins from his pocket, and drops them into the waiting hand without touching it, then shoos the man away. Jasu steps into the shack first, crouching down to pass through the doorway. Kavita and Vijay follow him. The small, windowless room is nearly bare, with nothing on the packed dirt floor but rotting food scraps. Kavita is suffocated by the stench of human waste, and fights her reflex to gag.

Kavita slips her arm into Jasu's. "Come, why don't you take Vijay to get some food, and I will fix it a little?" Jasu takes Vijay down to the nearby street stalls. Kavita steps outside to take a deep breath of the comparatively clean air, then covers her nose and mouth with the end of her sari. She props open the door to let in some light. Inside, she sets to work, gathering the food scraps and waste into a small plastic bag she finds balled up in the corner. When she takes the garbage outside and stops for another breath, she spies a broom leaning against the neighboring shack. She looks around, darts over to wrap the broom in the folds of her sari, and returns to the shack.

Working as quickly as she can, she squats down on her haunches and traverses the small room, banging the broom forcefully against the dirt floor. Her efforts create a dust cloud that makes her cough and her eyes water, but she continues anyway. If she can just remove this top layer of filth that carries the memory of other people's food and garbage and urine, if she can just sweep it outside, there will be fresh earth underneath, the kind she's used to. When her throat burns so much she can't continue, she sweeps the pile of dirt outside and returns the broom to its place. She waits outside for her lungs to clear, and the dust to settle inside. She steps into the hut again and inhales. Yes, the air seems cleaner, or could it just be she has become accustomed to the odor of this place? Finally, she takes out the bed-roll they have brought with them and lays it out, along with their three bags.

Jasu and Vijay bring back hot *pau-bhaji* and cold bottles of Gold Spot. Vijay is intrigued by his first taste of the orange soda, trilling it over his curled tongue, letting the bubbles tingle there, then slide down the back of his throat. So taken is he with this new experience that he is completely unfazed by their dismal surroundings. As they eat, they hear, from somewhere outside, the crackling sound of a radio that quickly turns to blaring music. An old Hindi film love song comes on, and Jasu begins singing along, making up the lyrics he doesn't know. He takes Kavita's hand, pulling her up to dance in the small, dank space. Kavita goes along, grudgingly at first, until she sees Vijay clapping and singing as well. Then a genuine smile comes to her face, and soon they are all laughing and dancing together. They spend their first night in hell closely bound in one another's arms until they all fall asleep.

THEY ARE AWOKEN EARLY THE NEXT MORNING BY THE LOUD honking of trucks outside their door. Kavita hears them first and cannot return to sleep. Jasu wakes up soon after she does. After a few minutes of lying together entangled, eyes open, they both rise quietly from the bedroll. Kavita steps outside to find the latrine. She sees a long queue of people gathering, but when she inquires, she learns they are waiting to get water from the public standpipe. There is no designated latrine area. With as much modesty as she can manage, she does her business by the railroad tracks and quickly returns to the shack.

"There is a long queue already for the water—over there," she says to Jasu, pointing. "But we don't have anything—a vessel or a pail—to collect it."

"You will need water today. It will be hot. Here, how about these?" Jasu says, retrieving the two empty Gold Spot bottles from the night before. "I will go. You stay here," he says, gesturing to the sleeping Vijay. When Jasu returns, nearly an hour later, he looks shaken.

"What is it, *jani*? Why did it take so long?" She uses the term of endearment infrequently outside of their nighttime intimacies, but the vulnerable look on his face compels her to.

"This place is crazy, Kavi. One woman thought another one tried to jump the queue, and started yelling at her to go to the back of the line. The first woman refused to go, and they started fighting with her—pushing and kicking her until she left. Women, fighting one another. For water." He shakes his head, still distraught over the memory. "Tomorrow, I will go earlier." He gives her the filled soda bottles, then sets out for the day, promising to be back by nightfall.

When Vijay wakes up, Kavita decides to take him out of the *basti* for the day, already feeling the hopelessness of the slum descending upon her. She takes their most important belongings and hides the rest beneath the bedroll. Kavita grips Vijay's hand while they walk through the streets of Bombay—broken pavement underfoot littered with garbage and animal droppings, people pressed in close to one another, with no choice but to move together like a flock of birds. Street hawkers call out, selling their wares.

"Hot *chai*! *Garam garam chai*! Hot tea!"

"See, madam. *Salwar khameez*! Only one hundred rupees. Many colors!"

"Latest films. Two films, only fifty rupees. Very good price. Your choice."

Kavita is reminded again of that day years ago when she walked these streets, being pulled by Rupa, just as she now leads Vijay. She finds herself searching for familiarity on every corner. *Have I crossed the street at this bus stop before? Doesn't that newsstand look familiar? Is this the same fruit market I recognize?* In the midst of this mad place where she has only been once before, this city bursting with over ten million people, Kavita tries to make some sense. Through the crowd of bodies and limbs, she glimpses a face that looks familiar, a little girl who looks just like the image of Usha she carries in her mind. Two glossy braids tied with ribbons, a round face, a sweet smile. The little girl holds the hand of a woman in a green sari. *Is it her? Could it be her?* She looks about the same age as Vijay. Kavita pushes through the crowd, following the couple, ignoring Vijay's protests that she's pulling him too quickly. The green sari fades from view, lost in a swirl of people and colors. Kavita stops in the middle of the footpath, breathing heavily, looking in every direction but finding no one left to follow.

"Mama?" She feels Vijay tugging on her hand and looks down at his questioning eyes.

"*Hahn, beta. Challo.* Let's go." She worries about losing Vijay in the throngs of people that push past them, and about the toothless beggars that follow them. Kavita keeps searching for the green sari and recalls Jasu's words about the baby girl. *She will become a burden to us, a drain on our family. Is that what you want?* Perhaps he was right then, even wise. It is hard to imagine having two children now, when it isn't clear they can properly care for one. They walk all day until Kavita is tired enough for sleep to come quickly tonight. After just one day, she feels stifled by this city, throbbing with its people and activity and noise. Her lungs, accustomed to the clean air of the village, struggle against this smog. Her feet long for the damp packed earth of the fields back home.

They walk back along the length of the settlement, passing hundreds of shacks like theirs. She navigates around a dirty goat pushing its nose through a large heap of smoking garbage on the corner. Every shack they pass has the same things out front: a cooking fire fueled with cow dung patties, a bucket of water to be rationed all day, and tattered clothing hung on lines. A few ingenious residents have devised ways of stringing up antennas for televisions or have transistor radios, around which more people gather. Kavita longs for something to soothe her: her mother's comforting hand, Rupa's bubbling laughter.

By the time Kavita and Vijay reach their shack, Jasu is inside already, sitting on the edge of the bedroll. He rubs the sole of one foot with his thumbs. When he hears them enter, he looks up and smiles. "What happened?" Kavita asks.

"I must have walked ten miles today in those old things." He nods at his worn *chappals* by the door. Kavita sits down next to him and takes his foot in her hands.

"I visited three messenger offices today." He closes his eyes and lies back on the bedroll. "They all said they had no work for me. They only want men who know the streets of Bombay—rickshaw drivers or taxi drivers. Tell me, if I was already a rickshaw or taxi driver, why would I need a messenger job?"

"*Hahn*, why?" Kavita speaks slowly, concurring but wondering what this means.

"Then, I went to see about a *dhaba-wallah* job," Jasu continues, "and as I suspected, it is very good money to carry those tiffins across town. One hundred rupees a day—can you believe? But there is a long list of men who want to become *dhaba-wallahs*. They told me to check back every week. They said it might take three, four months until they have a job."

Kavita, uncertain how to react to this news, watches Vijay draw circles with his finger into the packed dirt floor. *You must trust in him.*

"But good news—I met this fellow outside the *dhaba-wallah* central office. He knows the big boss and can help my name come to the top of the list. It should happen quickly with his help, two to three weeks. Only two hundred rupees I gave him."

Kavita looks up at her husband with alarm. The sum total they brought with them was one thousand rupees—their entire savings, plus gifts from their families.

"Don't worry, *chakli*!" He grins. "It's fine. This man showed me his papers, he is a good man. And also, he will help me get a bicycle to use for the job. He will let me use it straightaway, no money. At first, my earnings will pay for the bicycle, but after I own it, I will get to keep all my earnings." Jasu sits up and grabs her shoulders. "Don't look so worried. This is good, *chakli*, very good!" He wraps his broad palms around her head and kisses the top of it. "It's happening quickly, just as I thought. In no time, we'll have our own flat, with lots of space and a big kitchen for you. Heh?"

She finds it impossible not to smile when he is like this. Now it is her turn to exhale. "Okay, Mister *Dhaba-wallah,* let us have dinner then."

ONE MORNING TWO WEEKS LATER, KAVITA WATCHES FROM THE bedroll as Jasu carries a small basin of cold water to the corner of the room. Methodically, he washes himself and shaves. He has been going back to the *dhaba-wallah* office every day, but still they have not had a job for him. The man who took two hundred rupees from him has not been seen again either. Still, every day, Jasu rises early to stand in the water queue. He insists on doing this himself, though it's usually women from the *basti* standing in line. Today, he brings back reports of a typhoid outbreak on the north side of the settlement. Three children dead already, many more sick. "Keep Vijay away from the dirty water," he tells her. "These people do *susu* and *kaka* anywhere, like dogs they are. No shame." He dresses carefully and combs his hair. He hurries, as if someone expects him at a certain time. Each morning, he departs hopeful; every evening he returns to their temporary home dejected again.

Kavita steps outside to make *chai* in the dead embers of last night's fire. There is some leftover *khichdi* from dinner, which she divides into two portions, one each for Jasu and Vijay. As she prepares breakfast, other people emerge from neighboring homes to do the same. Women gather their crumpled saris between their knees to squat, and chatter together. They have lived here a long time, these neighbors. Kavita does not join in their conversation, though she does listen to the gossip they share over their cooking fires. It frightens her: tales of children gone missing, wives beaten the night before. Some of the men brew homemade liquor, then sell or trade it to the others. In their drunken state, these angry men turn on one another, their neighbors and families, to take out their rage.

It seems it is a whole city unto itself, this slum community. There are moneylenders and debtors, landlords and tenants, friends and enemies, criminals and victims. Unlike the village she has known, people here live like animals: packed into small spaces, fighting over every necessity of life. And worse yet, many people who have been here for years already have come to accept this place as their home. They do the dirtiest, most detestable jobs in the city—they are toilet cleaners, scrap scavengers, rag pickers. Not *dhaba-wallahs*, who live in proper homes like proper people. As soon as Jasu gets his job, they'll leave this place. Kavita knows they won't survive here.

LATER THAT NIGHT, WELL AFTER THEY HAVE ALL FALLEN ASLEEP, they are awoken by loud voices outside, men yelling. Jasu immediately jumps up toward the door. The empty Gold Spot bottles sit nearby, ready to collect water in the morning. He takes one in each hand. Kavita sits up and gathers Vijay, barely awake, in her arms. As their eyes adjust to the darkness, the voices get louder and draw closer. Jasu opens the door a crack and looks out. Quickly, he closes it and whispers to Kavita, "Police! They're banging down the doors, looking inside. They have sticks and flashlights." He stands with his back against the door. She moves her body in front of Vijay's, whose eyes are now wide and scared.

They hear pounding on doors. Bottles thrown against walls. Glass breaking. More angry voices. Then, a woman's scream, long and loud and laced with tears. After what seems like a long time, the angry sounds begin to fade away, giving way to sinister-sounding laughter that retreats slowly into the distance. Finally, it is quiet again. Jasu is still guarding the door. Kavita beckons for him to come to her. When she holds him, she feels the fear and perspiration the police have left in their wake.

"Mummy?" Vijay says. He is trembling. Kavita looks down to where his hands are clutching the front of his pants. They are wet. She changes his clothes, and covers the damp bedroll with an old newspaper. They all lie down in bed: Jasu with his arms around Kavita, and she with her arms around their son. In the dark, Vijay says simply, "I miss Nani." Kavita begins to cry without making sound or movement. Vijay's breathing eventually becomes heavy and regular, but neither she nor Jasu sleep any more that night.

The next morning, Jasu returns from the water queue with news about the police raid, apparently a common occurrence in the *basti*. One of the neighbors told him the police had been looking for someone, a man suspected of stealing from the factory where he worked. Even after waking dozens of other families, they didn't find the man at home.

But they did find his fifteen-year-old daughter. In front of her mother and young brothers, and while the neighbors listened in fear, they brutally raped her.

23

GIVE THANKS

Menlo Park, California—1991
KRISHNAN

"DID YOU MASH THE POTATOES YET? KRIS!"

Krishnan is so engrossed in the pages of *India Abroad,* he barely hears Somer.

"You need to mash the potatoes. The turkey will be ready in a half hour. And remember not to add any pepper this time. My dad doesn't like spicy food."

Krishnan exhales loudly. *Spicy food?* Only an American would consider mashed potatoes, quite possibly the blandest dish ever created, to be the least bit spicy. No, that would be the *battata pakora* his mother made—slices of soft boiled potato, dipped in spicy batter and studded with green chilies, then deep fried until they turned golden brown. She would barely lay one on the plate before his eager fingers snatched it up. It's been such a long time since he had a good *battata pakora.* He sighs as he begins mashing up the steaming potatoes in the large bowl. Somer obliges him by going out for Indian food occasionally, but she hasn't taken a true interest in Indian cuisine, and her own cooking skills are limited. He once showed her how to make *chana masala,* a simple dish made with a can of garbanzo beans and some packaged spices. Now, it is the one dish she makes over and over, with store-bought pita bread. The expensive bottle of saffron his parents sent from India sits unopened on their spice rack, after Somer admitted she didn't know how to use it.

He adds a couple tablespoons of butter into the bowl, pours in some milk, and stirs. The whole concoction is as smooth and white as hospital bedsheets, and about as appealing. How can one eat something with no color or flavor? These potatoes have become his designated task on Thanksgiving. One year, he took some latitude and added a handful of finely chopped cilantro leaves as a garnish. The next year, he stirred a teaspoon of his mother's *garam masala* with the butter. This year, he is restricted to salt and butter again.

"I still have to get the pie into the oven." Somer rushes to the oven, opens the door, and stabs the thermometer into the turkey for the umpteenth time.

Krishnan never understands why Americans, and his wife in particular, get so worked up over this one meal every year. His family celebrations at home regularly featured at least a dozen dishes, all of which involved more complex preparation than putting a turkey in the oven for a few hours. And none of it came out of a tin or a box. For Diwali every year, his mother and aunts would cook for days beforehand: light fluffy *dhoklas* dipped in rich coconut chutney, rich vegetable curry, delicately spiced *dal.* Every vegetable was individually selected from the *sabzi-wallah,* and each spice was toasted, ground, and mixed by hand. The tart, creamy yogurt was homemade, and the *parathas* were rolled and served hot from the flame. The women spent hours, gossiping and laughing while they peeled, sliced, simmered, and fried up a feast for twenty people or more. Never did he see the kind of frenetic worrying his wife now exhibits. He thinks back to his first introduction to the strange rituals of an American Thanksgiving.

IN HIS FIRST YEAR OF MEDICAL SCHOOL, HIS CLASSMATE JACOB invited him to Boston. Krishnan had only been in the United States a few months, and all that time in California, so when they arrived in Boston, the first thing that struck him was the crisp cool air and the brilliant colors of the leaves. It was the first autumn he had seen.

There were a dozen people there, and Krishnan was soon put to work with the other men, raking leaves from the ample yard of the regal Colonial house. This was disorienting enough—he wondered why there weren't servants to do this kind of labor—but Krishnan was even more confused by the game of touch football that ensued afterward. Inside, as they warmed their numb fingers around the fire, Krishnan could hear the tinkling laughter of Jacob's pretty sister from the kitchen. Her cousins were teasing her about the new boyfriend she had brought home for the first time. This concept was truly foreign to Krishnan. In India, parents and other relatives served as the first level of approval for prospective mates, not the last. Courtships between engaged couples were brief and usually chaperoned. Krishnan enjoyed the meal, though he couldn't help thinking a measure of hot sauce would make everything taste a good deal better. By the end of the weekend, Krishnan was enamored with everything he had seen: the beautiful house, the sprawling yard, the pretty blond girl. He wanted it all. He had fallen in love with the American dream.

When he first came to the United States for medical school, he was excited about the new possibilities his life suddenly held. Stanford's serene mission-style campus could not have felt more different from the bustling city he had left, but there was much about America he could appreciate: clean streets, huge malls, comfortable cars. He developed a taste for the food, particularly the french fries and pizza served at the campus cafeteria.

Krishnan went back to India for a visit after his second year to find things had changed. It was the summer of 1975, and Indira Gandhi had just declared a state of Emergency after being declared guilty of election fraud. Political protests were quelled rapidly, and government opponents were jailed by the thousands. It was difficult to believe anything in the propaganda-filled papers, but there was a distinct sense of fear and uncertainty about the future. When he accompanied his father on rounds, he found the hospital older than he remembered, particularly in contrast to Stanford. Some of his friends were getting married, but Krishnan managed to evade his mother's suggestion it would soon be time to start meeting girls. By the end of that summer, he found himself missing America, where life seemed good and the career opportunities superior. Going back to his homeland had tipped the scales for him, and when he returned to California for the last two years of medical school, he was quite certain he wanted to stay.

The past decade since med school has passed in one long blur of days and nights, working relentlessly toward becoming a surgeon. He made it through one of the toughest residency programs in the country. His colleagues now consult him on their most challenging cases, and he's often asked to guest lecture at Stanford. And he did get the pretty blond girl, now his wife. By every objective measure, he is a success. After fifteen years in this country, he has achieved that dream with which he was so taken.

THEY ALL SIT IN THE DINING ROOM, AT THE FORMAL TABLE, WITH a little too much space between them. Somer's father carves the turkey, and they pass around dishes filled with stuffing, cranberry sauce, gravy, mashed potatoes, and green beans. While Krishnan eats, he listens to Asha regale her grandparents with stories of her new teachers and the school uniform she loves. "The best part is there are no boys, because they can be so annoying." Everyone laughs, and Krishnan makes an effort to smile. They eat in this room only a few times a year, he realizes, looking around, and they never fill up the table. He blinks several times. The house is spacious and beautiful but feels sterile to him, just like their lives. He doesn't notice it as much when Asha fills it with her chatter and laughter, but even then, it never feels as full and rich as the family get-togethers he remembers from childhood. This is the life he envisioned, the life he hoped for, but somehow the American dream now seems hollow to him.

Just a few weeks ago, his family back home was all gathered for Diwali dinner at his parents' home, at least two dozen people in all. Krishnan was the only one missing, so they called him, passing the phone around so each could wish him a happy Diwali. He had been rushing out the door that day when the phone rang, but after hanging up, he sat motionless at the kitchen table with the phone in hand. It was evening in Bombay, and he could close his eyes and picture the millions of *diyas,* the tiny clay pots holding small flames lining the balconies, the street stalls, and the shop windows. Visitors came to exchange boxes of sweets and good wishes. Schools closed and children stayed up to enjoy fireworks. Ever since he was a child, it had been one of his favorite nights of the year, when the whole of Bombay took on a magical feel.

Krishnan has raised the idea of going back to India to visit and perhaps adopt another child, but Somer has resisted. She seems intent on preserving Asha in the little cocoon they have woven around her. It's not the way he sees family, as a precious thing that needs to be protected. For him, family is a wild sprawling thing, a strong thing that withstands years, miles, even mistakes. For as long as he can remember, there have been minor transgressions and major feuds erupting among his big clan, and it doesn't affect the endurance of their family's bond. Somer has good intentions, she tries to make an effort with Asha where she can: going through National Geographic, pointing out maps of India, reviewing facts on agriculture and animals. When his parents send a *chania-choli,* she dresses Asha in it and sends off photographs. But his daughter has no occasion to wear the festive outfits, so they accumulate in a row in her closet. Just like his weak efforts to teach Somer a few words of Gujarati, her gestures are, in the end, insignificant.

Perhaps all this wouldn't bother him as much if he felt he still had the woman he fell in love with—the intellectual partner, the equal companion. He misses talking to Somer about medicine. She used to be interested in his cases, but these days, she'd rather discuss the mundane details of Asha's schoolwork. Even when Somer talks about her work at the clinic, he finds it hard to feign interest in runny noses and muscle sprains after dealing with brain tumors and aneurysms all day. Though, technically, they're in the same profession, it's hard to have a conversation without one of them becoming disinterested or frustrated. At times, it seems the things that occupy and define his marriage today bear little resemblance to what once brought them together.

"Let's make a toast." Somer's cheery voice interrupts his thoughts. She holds her wineglass in the air, and the rest of them follow suit. "To family!" They all echo the sentiment as they stand halfway out of their chairs to reach awkwardly across the table and clink one another's glasses. Krishnan takes a deep sip of the chilled Chardonnay, feels the liquid trickle down his throat and the coolness permeate his body.

24

AFTERNOON REST

Bombay, India—1991
JASU AND KAVITA

JASU GROANS AT THE TINNY RING OF THE ALARM CLOCK. THE bedsprings creak as he lifts himself off the thin mattress, though it could just as easily be his joints making the noise. He touches Kavita's calf as he walks stiffly by the foot of the bed in the one room in which they all sleep. Once she stirs, he walks downstairs to use the common toilets for the *chawl* apartment. One fortunate side effect of waking so early is the latrine will not yet be overflowing.

When he returns, he sees that Kavita has already bathed and dressed. She is now cleaning her teeth, spitting over the side of the balcony railing. While he bathes, in the second small room they also use to cook and eat, he hears the tinkling of Kavita's prayer bell. Her soft singing will soon rouse Vijay. Even if they had more space here, Vijay wouldn't sleep by himself. Not only has he been accustomed to sharing his parents' bed for all his six years, but their ordeal in the slums also gave him repeated nightmares. Kavita enters the kitchen to make breakfast. Jasu walks briskly out to the common room to dress, running a thin black comb through his wet hair. He pauses in front of the *mandir* to press his palms together and bow his head. They pass each other like this several times each morning, sharing a silent, well-rehearsed dance.

"Food?" Kavita says.

"I'll take it with me," he says. The factory where he works in Vikhroli is forty minutes away, a short commute by Bombay standards, but he likes to be among the first to arrive in the morning. Luckily, the Central Railway train station is only a few blocks away, and he has now mastered the skill of running to catch a train pulling out of the station, able to jump aboard at the last possible moment. It is the most enjoyable part of his day: this sport of catching the train, the freedom of hanging off the outside while it rushes through the city, feeling a breeze through his clothes, already sticky with sweat. He's heard this is dangerous: apparently, a couple thousand passengers die riding like this each year. But considering several million people ride the commuter trains in Bombay, this does not seem unreasonable, nor particularly unsafe, to Jasu.

The bicycle factory where he works, on the other hand, feels decidedly unsafe. In his first month there, he saw two men lose fingers in the machines, and a third severely burned by a welding torch. By arriving early, he's more likely to get one of the less dangerous assignments, like painting frames or attaching bolts with a wrench. The factory is a large, dusty warehouse, filled haphazardly with machinery and tools. The dim lighting makes it difficult to see, and more than once, Jasu has tripped over electric cables that run all over the floor. The dust and fumes from the welding torches irritate his throat and eyes so much that stepping outside into Bombay's smoggy air at the end of the day feels like a relief. Nevertheless, Jasu feels fortunate to have this job, which he found a few days after the police raid on the settlement. The pay is not as much as he would have made as a *dhaba-wallah:* only eight rupees an hour. But if he works an extra hour in the morning and at night, he can earn over two thousand rupees a month, the equivalent of five months' income in the village.

Even so, it was not easy to find an apartment they could afford. The *chawl* on Shivaji Road is tiny; far smaller, in fact, than the house they left behind in their village. But Jasu's perspective has changed since arriving in Bombay, after the horrors they witnessed in the slums. What was meant to be a night or two there turned into weeks, and felt longer still. In all the things he'd heard about Bombay, in all the dreams in his mind, there was never a place like Dharavi. It was enough to make him want to pack up everything and flee back home.

But he knew there was nothing worth going back for, and he knew his family was counting on him. He had brought them here, and he would take care of them. The day after the police raid, Jasu bought a knife from the man in the yellow sari and began sleeping by the door with it in his hand. For several nights after that, Vijay woke up screaming and had to be coaxed back to sleep. Kavita, though she never said a word, clearly detested the place, and her hatred grew with each day they were forced to stay. Many days he came back to find her violently beating the ground of their shack with a broom while Vijay sat outside, looking frightened. The *chawl* on Shivaji Road met their basic needs and offered more security and privacy than the *basti*. There was even a good school nearby for Vijay. They used the rest of the savings they had brought, plus most of Jasu's earnings from the new job, in order to secure the lease. That first night their modest two-room apartment felt like a palace compared to where they had been.

The train slows as it approaches the station, and Jasu jumps onto the platform, glancing at his watch. Even after his walk, he will arrive at the factory before seven-thirty, as he has done every morning since starting this job. He will see the foreman who has, once or twice, even offered Jasu a lukewarm cup of tea that was left unwanted on the bosses' tray. Jasu goes to work like this, six days a week, from early morning to well after nightfall. He does what he is told and rarely takes a break, even when the other men go outside to smoke. When he comes home at night, he stinks of sweat and his body is sore. His days now are more grueling than the fieldwork back in the village. But Jasu doesn't mind. They are on their way to a better life.

KAVITA WASHES THE LAST STAINLESS STEEL DISHES. EVERY MORN-ing when she arrives at her employer's luxurious flat, the breakfast dishes are her first duty. She takes her orders from Bhaya, the head servant, who has worked here so long that Memsahib's instructions to her are partial sentences, understood only by the two of them like some secret language. Bhaya also has the preferred responsibilities of going to the market and overseeing the cooking, while Kavita washes dishes and does most of the cleaning. They go about their chores quietly, and when Bhaya speaks to Kavita, it is usually to ask her to add an item—durum wheat flour, *masoor dal,* cumin seeds—to the market list Kavita keeps in her head. Although she may not be able to read or write, Kavita has an excellent memory for words, and Bhaya has come to rely on her for this.

It is surprising how much of a mess two people can make, even with their children grown up and rich enough to live elsewhere. Sahib and his wife use several little cups and bowls for each meal, not like the single *thali* Kavita is used to. Bhaya is just as bad, using a different vessel to cook each dish. Sometimes, Memsahib will wear three different saris in one day, leaving the worn ones along with discarded petticoats and blouses strewn across the bed. Her jewelry, however, she takes great care to always replace in the locked metal cabinet. Each day, Kavita carefully irons and folds the saris and returns them to the cupboard. People drop by to visit often, and Sahib and

Memsahib have guests at almost every meal. Bhaya always makes enough food for at least six people, which means enough leftovers for both servants.

Kavita heard about this job from Bhaya's sister, who lives down the hall from them on Shivaji Road. It is not the kind of work Jasu wants her to do; he would prefer instead she take in sewing. But this job pays seven hundred rupees a month. And the flat is spacious and beautiful, with cool marble floors, sturdy wooden furniture, and a large kitchen. It is a nice place to spend her days, even as a servant. Most important, Bhaya allows her to leave in the afternoon to pick Vijay up from school and bring him back here while she finishes work.

Early afternoon, after the heavy midday meal, when it is hottest outside and the ceiling fan beckons, is the one time of day Bombay finally slows down. Cabdrivers turn down their meter flags and stretch out in their backseats. Servants in Memsahib's six-story building lie on bedrolls, lining the open hallways and the stairwell landings. Even the doorman sitting in the lobby nods off. Kavita sees him there with his head hanging forward, chin on chest and drool at the corner of his mouth, when she returns with Vijay. Kavita has never been one to rest during the day, so this arrangement works out well. Today, Bhaya has asked her to pick up some *paneer* on the way to Vijay's school. After stopping by the market, Kavita consults her watch. There is just enough time for a detour. If she walks quickly, she can make it. No lingering today.

Ten minutes later, out of breath, she reaches the familiar iron gates of the orphanage. She puts her face up to the metal bars and looks through them, to the red-lettered sign on the door. The sounds of laughter come from behind her and she spins around. A parade of children, two abreast and ascending in height, moves toward her. Quickly, she scans the faces of the little girls, searching for one that matches the memory etched in her mind. One girl smiles at her, but her complexion is too dark. Another one looks about the right size, but her eyes are dark brown. The children wear clean clothes, she notes as they pass her. They appear to be well fed, they look happy. Much too quickly, the last of the children walk through the iron gates and rush into the building. There is never enough time.

She must be in there somewhere. Of course, there are other possibilities, the ones that haunt her at night—Usha sold off as an indentured servant, or dead from starvation or disease. And this is precisely why Kavita keeps coming here, hoping to see a little girl with her eyes, so she can put an end to the thoughts that torment her.

Suddenly, she remembers the time. *Vijay.*

She walks quickly across the street. She'll only be a few minutes late. It is a nice day, perhaps she'll buy some fresh coconut water for them to share on their walk back. As she approaches the school, she can hear the raised voices of young boys who play in the yard after school. But today these voices sound angry rather than playful. Kavita begins to walk faster as dread builds in the pit of her stomach. When she arrives, she sees books strewn about the yard and a group of boys clustered near the brick wall of the school. She hurries to unlatch the metal gate and throws it open, now running as fast as possible in her sari. As she draws closer, she hears the boys' taunts.

"Village boy! *Gawar!*" they chant.

". . . Why don't you go back to your village and play with the other chickens!"

Kavita pushes her body between the boys and sees Vijay on the ground, leaning against the wall, his legs scraped with blood and his shirt ground with dirt. She rushes to him and cradles his head. "What is the matter with you boys? Have you no shame? Get out of here. Go, now! Before I beat you myself! Go!" she screams, waving one arm at them while holding her son's head with the other.

They scurry to retrieve their bags and run down the street, still laughing. She turns to her son to assess the damage. His lower lip is swollen, there are scuff marks on his cheek and tears coursing down his face. She sits down and pulls him onto her lap so she can hold his whole body in her arms. She rocks him and feels the wetness on his shorts and inner legs. "There, there, my sweet child, everything will be all right." Even while she speaks these words as calmly as she can manage, her eyes scan the school yard and the street beyond its gate for other dangers, which seem to come in new forms every day in this strange city.

November 1997

I wish you were here to help me.

I'm supposed to write a biography of myself for eighth-grade social studies, but I don't know where to begin. I don't know where I really came from. Whenever I ask my mom, she just gives me the same story—they picked me up from the orphanage in India when I was a baby and brought me to California.

She doesn't know anything about you, or why you gave me away. She doesn't know what you look like. We must look like each other, and I bet you would know what to do with my bushy eyebrows. My mom doesn't like to talk about this stuff at all. She says I'm just like everyone else now and it shouldn't matter.

My dad tried to help me find some photos for my project. He took out this old album with black-and-white photos and tissue paper between the pages. There were pictures of him in his cricket uniform and his uncle riding a white horse at his wedding.

He told me about the kite-flying festival that kids in India have in January, and the colored paint they throw for that holiday in the spring. It sounds like a lot of fun.

I've never even been to India.

25

OVERDUE

Mumbai, India—1998
KAVITA

KAVITA TASTES THE *DAL* AND ADDS MORE SALT TO COMPENSATE for the thinness of the lentil soup. She prepares two *thalis* of rice and *dal,* putting a small bit of mango pickle on Vijay's to add some flavor to this basic meal they have had so often lately. They eat alone, because Jasu is working late again. He's been adding extra hours nearly every day and taking on others' shifts. It took many months for him to find work again after the raid on the bicycle factory closed it down. They were forced to borrow from the moneylender in order to pay the *chawl* rent and Vijay's school fees until Jasu found a new job at a textile factory. Now, it seems every paisa they earn goes to the moneylender, yet half the amount is still outstanding. They have been late with Vijay's school fees, and now with the rent as well. They hoped the landlord, Manish, would be tolerant, since they've never given him a problem in the eight years they've lived here. But rents are rising all over Mumbai, and Manish is eager to get rid of old tenants so he can rent the place out for more.

"What did you learn today in school, Vijay?" Kavita looks forward to hearing about this all day.

"Same things, Mummy. Multiplication, exponents. The teacher says I have to properly learn those things to catch up with the others."

"*Achha*," she says slowly. She carries her empty *thali* to the sink and busies herself with cleaning the dishes so her son will not see her eyes water. It is her fault. Vijay has been working with her in the afternoons at Sahib's house for the past several weeks. When one of Sahib's regular messenger boys fell ill, Memsahib asked if Vijay could fetch her blouses from the tailor. She paid him fifty rupees and asked him to come back the following day. Since then, he has been delivering packages every afternoon, time he used to spend on schoolwork. She and Jasu decided it would do no harm if it helped them pay off the moneylender. She now realizes this was foolish. They have compromised their son's education, his only chance at a better life, all for a few hundred rupees. She scrubs furiously at the hardened rice grains on the bottom of the pot.

The front door opens. "Hello." Jasu stops to tousle Vijay's hair, then heads to the kitchen, where Kavita is heating his dinner. "Hello, *chakli*." He wraps his arms around her from behind and rests his chin atop her head. "Mmmm. *Dal-bhath*," he says, sniffing at the food. "Good thing my wife is such a good cook she can make *dal-bhath* so many different ways." He grins as he walks over to Vijay, patting his belly. "Heh, Vijay, aren't we lucky your mother is such a good cook?"

The momentary lightness is interrupted by loud banging at the door, followed by Manish's fierce voice. "Jasu? Heh, Jasu! I know you're in there. I can hear your fat, lazy footsteps over my head. Open up right now, or I'll break this door down."

"What is that scoundrel doing here at this hour?" Jasu strides toward the door and throws it open to reveal Manish, his hairy belly protruding between his worn undershirt and drawstring pants. There is a week's growth on his face, his eyes are bloodshot, and he smells of liquor. Kavita grips Jasu's forearm, hoping the pressure of her hand will restrain his reaction.

"Manish, it's late. What is so important it cannot wait until morning, heh?" Jasu's voice is firm, and he begins to close the door.

With surprising speed, Manish raises one flabby arm to block the door. "Listen, you lazy bastard. You are two weeks late with the rent, and I won't stand for it anymore," he shouts.

Jasu stands blocking the half-open doorway, shielding Kavita and Vijay behind him. "Manish *bhai,*" he says, his voice softening, "I will pay. Have I ever failed you in the eight years we've lived here? I've had some bad luck with my job lately and . . . it will just take a little time."

"Time? I don't have time, Jasu. You are stealing that money out of my pocket, you hear?" Manish waves his fist in the air. "You think you're the only ones who want this apartment? There is a line of people from here to the ocean waiting for this place, and all of them are ready to pay on time. I can't wait for you, Jasu!"

"Manish *bhai,* please. You can't throw us out. This is my family we're talking about." Jasu opens the door wider to reveal Kavita and Vijay. "You know us." His voice strains to sound respectable. "I promise I will get you the rent. Please, Manish *bhai.*" Jasu holds his palms together in appeasement. Kavita holds her breath.

Manish shakes his head and exhales loudly. "Friday, Jasu. You have until Friday, that's it. Then you're out." He turns and waddles briskly down the hallway, prompting cockroaches to scurry out of his path.

Jasu locks the door behind him. He lays his forehead against the closed door and sighs deeply before turning around to face them. "Greedy bastard. We've paid that man on time every month for eight years." Jasu strides back to the kitchen. "We put up with his filthy toilets and water shut-offs at all hours, and not once did we complain." He waves his fist at the door. "And now, he's ready to throw us out over nothing. Bastard." Jasu takes the *thali* from Kavita's shaky hands and strides back to the kitchen to sit down. "He's lucky I don't take care of him." He puts a bite of *dal-bhath* in his mouth and chews vigorously.

"Why don't you, Papa?" Vijay says, standing at the entrance to the kitchen.

"What?" Jasu says, without looking up from his food.

"Why don't you do something to keep Manish from getting mad and coming by here all the time? He came yesterday and Mummy was scared . . ."

Kavita sees the frustration and disappointment in her son's eyes, and knows Jasu will see it too. "Come, come, it's nothing. I wasn't scared. Papa has handled it, *achha*? Now come, finish your studies," she says, gesturing to his books and papers scattered on the floor.

"What, Vijay? What would you like me to do? That man is a scoundrel. He takes advantage of hardworking people. There's nothing else to be done," Jasu says, now shoveling large mounds of food into his mouth.

"I don't know, Papa, do something. Give him the money. Fight with him. Do *something*. Anything. Something besides begging."

Kavita draws in her breath quickly and moves instinctively toward her son. Suddenly, Jasu is on his feet again, and in a single stride he stands over Vijay, waving his fist. "Watch your mouth! You think you're better than your father, because you know how to read your fancy books at school? I break my back every day for you. You know nothing!" Looking down at his half-eaten dinner, he kicks the *thali*, making a clanging sound. "I'm sick and tired of *dal-bhath*." He turns to walk away. "Sick and tired."

Kavita follows him down the hallway. "Jasu, he's just a boy. He's doesn't know what he's saying." She watches him shove on his *chappals*. "Where are you going?"

"Out. Away from here." He slams the door shut behind him.

Kavita stands for a moment, staring at the closed door. She feels her fear percolate into resentment toward all of them—Manish, Jasu, and Vijay—for the anger they spray around like petrol, turning the landscape of her life into scorched earth. She breathes deeply before turning to face her son. *He's just a boy.*

"Vijay," she says, holding him firmly by the shoulders. "What is wrong with you? You must never speak to your father like that." Vijay bores into her, a steely expression in his youthful eyes. "Listen, Papa will take care of this." She touches his cheek with the back of her hand, noticing the facial hair beginning to sprout on his face. "You mustn't worry about these things, *beta*. You should focus on your studies." She leads him back by the arm to his books.

Vijay twists his body out of her grasp and violently kicks at his books on the floor. "Why? Why should I study? This is a waste of time. Don't you see? Where does this get us, Ma? You tell me to work hard. But it gets us nowhere."

She watches him turn and walk onto the balcony, the only place in the tiny *chawl* where he can retreat for some semblance of privacy. *Such big dreams, just like his father.* When did her little boy start carrying the worries of a man? Without bothering to undress, she climbs into the bed she shares with Jasu, buries her head in the thin, musty pillow, and cries, hardly making a noise. She lies awake in the dark for some time until she hears the creaking of the balcony screen, and then the deep, heavy breathing she would recognize anywhere as her son's.

Sometime in the early hours of morning, she hears the front door open, then close. When Jasu climbs into bed next to her, Kavita recognizes the smell of his breath. She remembers it from those dreadful first weeks in the Bombay slums, when the aroma of liquor permeated the night air. She remembers the sticky smell of fermented *chickoo-fruit* the night Jasu burst into the birthing hut. Each time, terrible things happened.

26

SIXTEEN YEARS

Menlo Park, California—2000
ASHA

ASHA ARRIVES EARLY AT THE *HARPER SCHOOL BUGLE* OFFICE, THE windowless room where she spends most of her lunch periods and spare time. She joins Clara, the editor, and Ms. Jansen, their faculty adviser, at the table and takes out her notebook and pencil. Asha can never bring herself to write in pen, either ballpoint or felt-tip. The permanency of it makes her uneasy, the way there's no going back once something has been written.

"Okay," Clara says. "Let's get an update on everyone's articles for the centennial issue next month that's going to all the alumni. Asha?"

Asha straightens up in her chair. "Well, in light of the school's anniversary, I thought it was important to take a look at our history. As we all know, Susan Harper endowed this school with her family fortune." She looks around the table at a circle of bored faces. Like her, they have heard about Susan Harper for years. "But that fortune came from her husband, Joseph Harper, and his company United Textiles, one of the largest textile manufacturers in the country.

"It turns out, about ten years ago when they had trouble with their unions, United Textiles began moving their factories overseas. Most of their plants are now in China, and most of their workers are child laborers . . ." She pauses for effect. "Kids as young as ten years old, working twelve hours a day in factories instead of going to a swanky school like this." Asha returns her pencil to her mouth and notes, with satisfaction, that no one looks disinterested any longer.

Clara manages to speak. "I don't think that's an appropriate topic, Asha, do you?"

"Yes, actually, I do. I think it's important we know our history as an institution and where the money comes from for all of this." She gestures around the room with her hands.

"It comes from our parents," another student mutters.

Unfazed, Asha continues, "We're always being taught to think about the world outside. Well, these kids in China are the world outside. We have an obligation to pursue the truth. Isn't that the whole point of journalism? Are you saying we should censor ourselves?"

Ms. Jansen exhales slowly and says, "Asha, let's discuss this when you come by my office—tomorrow, lunchtime." Her tone makes it clear this is not a suggestion.

"So, have you asked your parents about the party Saturday?" Rita bounces the soccer ball on her knee, aiming toward Asha.

Asha sighs. "No, my dad's been working late all week." She kicks the ball straight up in the air, watches for it, then catches it. "He's so uptight about these things. He says he doesn't see the *point* in my going to parties. What about having fun like a normal sixteen-year-old?"

"You know, Asha, my dad doesn't let me go out on weekends either." Manisha, the only other Indian girl in her class, intercepts the ball. She continues, now in a mock Indian accent, wagging her index finger. "Unless it is specifically for academic purposes." They laugh, and Manisha throws the ball back to Asha. "It's a cultural thing." She shrugs.

In the locker room, the girls change back into their uniforms with practiced discretion, and crowd around the mirror to check their faces. Asha tries to wrangle her thick black hair into a ponytail, but the elastic breaks, snapping against her fingers. "Ow—*crap*!" She shakes her head, retrieves a small pouch from her backpack, and walks over to the mirror to apply mascara.

"God, Asha, you *so* don't need eye makeup," one of the girls says, still peering directly at herself in the mirror as she speaks.

"I know, I would kill for eyes like that. They are so *exotic*. Did you get them from your mom or your dad?" another asks, brushing out her golden hair.

Asha tenses. "I don't know," she says quietly. "I think . . . they skipped a generation." She turns away from the mirror, her face burning, and returns to her locker. *I don't know who I got my exotic eyes from,* she wants to scream. Only Asha's closest friends know she is adopted; she lets everyone else make their own assumptions. It's easy enough to believe she could be the natural product of her Indian dad and American mom, and this has spared her many explanations. She doesn't want to share her whole personal history with the perfect mirror girls. She wonders if they would envy the black hair that sprouts every day on her legs, or her dark skin that tans after just ten minutes in the sun, even when slathered with sunscreen.

"Oh, Asha, you're so exotic." She hears someone behind her, in a low teasing voice. She turns around to see Manisha, rolling her eyes with a smile. "Come on, you want to get some frozen yogurt?" Manisha motions toward the locker room door.

"Sure," Asha says.

"I hate that 'exotic' thing we always get from people," Manisha says once they're outside. "I mean, come out to Fremont and you'll see it's not that exotic. Indians everywhere."

They sit together on a bench outside the small store, each holding a cup of frozen yogurt. Their conversation continues between bites of vanilla-chocolate swirl. "There's this ice cream shop near our house," Manisha says. "They serve *paan*-flavored ice cream. It is so good, it tastes exactly like the real thing. You have to try it sometime."

Asha just nods and keeps eating. She doesn't know what *paan* tastes like, her dad having given it to her only once when she was very young.

"Have you had ice *paan* in India? Last summer, I made my cousins take me to get one every night. Totally addictive. You have to try it next time you go."

Manisha talks without seeming to expect a response, for which Asha is thankful. She doesn't have to say that she's never been to India or fabricate an explanation. She remembers her father making a couple trips when she was in grade school. She recalls hearing her parents' discussions after they thought she was asleep, about whether or not Asha should accompany him. She does not remember any discussion over whether her mom should go. In the end, they decided it was not a good idea to take Asha out of school for so long. At the beginning of each trip, they drove her father to the airport with two enormous suitcases in the trunk, one filled with American trinkets and gifts. Every few days, there would be a crackly overseas phone call. When her father reappeared two weeks later, one of the suitcases was filled with tea and spices, sandalwood soaps, and colorful new outfits for Asha. There was also always a batik blouse or embroidered shawl for her mother, which she added to the others in the spare closet. Once the suitcases were stowed back in the basement, their lives returned to their normal routine.

Manisha stands up to start walking back. "Hey, are you going to

Raas-Garba next weekend?" she asks. "Don't think I've ever seen you there, but it's always so crowded"

"Um, no. I've never been," Asha says. "My parents aren't really into that stuff, I guess."

"Well, that makes them the only Indian parents in all of Northern California." Manisha smiles as she tosses her empty cup in the trash can. "You should come sometime, it's actually pretty fun. I mean, hey, it's the one time my dad actually *lets* me get dressed up and go dancing with friends on the weekend, you know?"

Asha nods again. But she didn't know. About any of it.

"WE NEED TO TALK ABOUT YOUR REPORT CARD." HER MOTHER'S tone is serious. Asha looks up from her dinner. Her dad is watching her, hands folded in front of his empty plate.

"I know, another A-plus in English, aren't you proud of me?" Asha says.

"Asha, a B in math and a C in chemistry?" her mother says. "What is going on? Your grades have been suffering ever since you started spending so much time on that school paper. Maybe it's time to cut back, so you can focus on your studies."

"Yes, I agree, Asha," her father joins in, nodding his head vigorously. "This is a critical year coming up. Your junior grades are the most important ones for college. You can't afford to have any Bs or Cs. You know how competitive the good schools are."

"What's the big deal?" Asha says. "I've had straight As all through high school; it's just one bad semester. Anyway, I won't have to take any more math or science after this year." Asha keeps her eyes focused on her plate.

"What do you mean by that?" her dad asks, his voice deepening to the pitch of disappointment Asha dreads. "You still have two years of high school, and *these* grades might hurt your applications anyway.

It's time to get serious, Asha, this is your future we're talking about!"
He pushes back from the table, chair legs screeching against the
kitchen floor to accentuate his point.

"Look, there's still time to turn your grades around this year,"
her mom says. "I can help you with chemistry, or we can get you a
tutor." Her mother grips the edge of the table with both hands, as if
she's expecting an earthquake to strike.

"I don't need a tutor, and I *definitely* don't want your help," Asha
says, choosing her words to sting her mother. "All I ever hear from
you is grades and studying. You don't care what's important to *me*. I
love working on the paper, and I'm good at it. I want to hang out
with my friends, I want to go to parties and be a normal teenager.
Why can't you understand that? Why don't you ever understand
me?" She's yelling now and feels a lump rising in her throat.

"Honey," her mom says, "we love you, and we only want what's
best for you."

"You always say that, but it's not true. You *don't* want what's best
for me." Asha stands up from the table and stumbles backward until
her back is pressed up against the kitchen wall. "You don't even
know me. You've always tried to fit me into some perfect image of
the kid you want. You just imported me into your little fantasy, but
you don't see *me*. You don't love *me*. You want me to be like you, but
I'm not." She shakes her head frantically as she speaks. "*That's* the
truth. Maybe if you were my real parents, you would understand me
and love me the way I am." She feels her body trembling, her hands
sweating. It's as if something alien has climbed into her body and
unleashed the venom spilling right out of her mouth. Despite the
hollow look on her father's face and the tears streaming down her
mother's, Asha cannot stop. "Why don't you ever tell me about my
real parents? You're scared they'll love me more than you do."

"Asha, we've already told you," her mom says in a cracking voice.

"We don't know anything about them. That's just the way things worked in India back then."

"And why don't you ever take me to India? Every other Indian kid I know goes all the time. What is it, Dad—are you ashamed of me? I'm not good enough for your family?" Asha stares at her father, looking down at his hands clenched so tightly the knuckles are drained of color.

"It's not fair." Asha can't hold back the tears now. "Everyone else knows where they come from, but I have no idea. I don't know why I have these eyes that everybody always notices. I don't know how to deal with this damn hair of mine," she yells, clenching it in her fist. "I don't know why I can remember every seven-letter Scrabble word, but none of the periodic table. I just want to feel that someone, somewhere, really understands me!" She's crying loudly now, wiping the mucus from her nose with the back of her hand.

"I wish I was never born," she lashes out. The look of pained shock on her mother's face brings Asha some satisfaction. "I wish you never adopted me. Then I wouldn't be such a huge disappointment to you." Asha is screaming now and feels a strange pleasure when her mother begins yelling as well.

"Well, Asha, at least I *tried*. At least I tried to be a parent to you. More than those . . . *people* in India who abandoned you. I *wanted* a child, and I've been here, Asha. Every single day." She bangs out each word with her finger on the table. "More than your father, more than anyone." Her mother's voice drops suddenly to a hoarse whisper. "At least I *wanted* you."

Asha slides down the wall and falls into a heap on the floor, head buried in her knees, sobbing. Right there, in the kitchen where she has celebrated birthdays and baked cookies, in the heart of the only home she can remember, she feels as alone and out of place as she ever has in her life. No one speaks for several minutes. Finally, Asha looks up, her face streaked with tears and her hazel eyes rimmed with red. "It's just not fair," she says quietly, between sharp sniffles. "I've spent sixteen years not knowing, sixteen years asking questions nobody can answer. I just don't feel like I really belong, in this family or *any- where*. It's like a piece of me is always missing. Don't you understand that?" She looks at her parents, searching their faces for something that will bring her comfort. Her mother is looking down at the table. Her father's eyes are closed, his forehead propped up by his hand. His entire face is still, except for the muscle pulsing in his jaw. Neither of them looks at her.

Asha collects herself from the floor, sniffling, and runs upstairs to her room. After slamming and locking her door, she throws her- self onto the bed, sobbing into the white eyelet duvet. When she finally looks up, it is dim in her room and the sky outside her win- dow is dark gray. She reaches into the bottom drawer of her night- stand, pulls out a small square box made of white marble, and lays it in front of her. Her fingers tremble over the geometric pattern carved into the heavy lid of the box her father bought for her at a flea market when she was eight. He said the design reminded him of India, of the carvings at the Taj Mahal.

She removes the lid and takes out several pieces of folded statio- nery. The paper is thin and worn at the creases, from having been unfolded and refolded so many times. Underneath all the papers, at the bottom of the box, she picks up the thin silver bangle. It is bent and tarnished. It is nearly too small to slide easily over the widest part of her hand, but she squeezes her wrist and manages to put it on. She curls up into a fetal position, clutching a large lace-trimmed pillow to her chest and closes her eyes. She lies there, in the deepening dark- ness of her room, listening to the raised voices of her parents down- stairs. The last thing she hears before falling asleep is the front door slam shut.

27

CRUEL COMPLICATIONS

Mumbai, India—2000
KAVITA

KAVITA OPENS THE FRONT DOOR TO THE *CHAWL*. "HELLO?" SHE calls out. Both Jasu and Vijay should be home by now, but the apartment is empty. She fears Jasu is out drinking again. Three weeks ago, he injured his right hand at the factory when another worker mistakenly turned on the fabric press as Jasu was adjusting the setting. The steel plates crushed his bones in three places before the machine was turned off. He was taken to the government hospital, where the doctor applied a brace to his hand and sent him back to the factory. But the foreman told Jasu he was slowing things down and sent him home until he could work properly. He asked Jasu to mark some papers with his thumbprint, then explained he wouldn't be paid until he returned to work.

The first few days, Jasu sat around at home, moping. Then he began wandering the streets, coming home darkened by the sun and covered in dust. Kavita tried to reassure him. At least they had almost paid off the moneylender, and between her income and Vijay's messenger pay, they could cover the other household expenses for a few weeks until his hand healed. This didn't bring Jasu much comfort; he only became more sullen. After the first week, Kavita began to detect that distinctive smell on him again. She has tried to ignore it. In truth, she doesn't have time to dwell on it. Each day, she rises early, goes to work, comes home to cook dinner, falls into bed exhausted, and does it all again the next day. If she has the energy, she tries to spend a little time with Vijay at night, though he too has become sullen these days.

She considers going out to look for Jasu but knows both he and Vijay will be hungry when they get home. It is better she get dinner ready first. An hour later, the rice and potato-onion *shaak* are ready. Kavita feels her stomach growl. She has not eaten in over eight hours. She picks gingerly at the food with her fingers. She cannot bring herself to sit down and eat properly without her husband or son. Vijay must be studying with a school friend, as he has been doing more often lately. But Jasu should be home by now. Her uneasiness escalates to worry, and then rapidly to fear. Making up her mind, Kavita covers the food and slides on her *chappals*. She tucks some cash and the key into the folds of her sari before leaving.

OUTSIDE, KAVITA WALKS QUICKLY. SHE KEEPS HER EYES FOcused straight ahead: the streets here are not safe for a woman alone after dark. *Where has he gone? How can he behave like such a lout?* Most of the time, she finds she can heed her mother's advice, to trust in her husband, to be brave for her family. Then occasionally, he will do something stupid like this, disappear in the night or come back smelling of liquor, and in a flash she will lose faith. She wonders if she has been wrong to trust him, if they were all bad decisions—giving up her daughters, leaving their village, trying to survive in this city that will never feel like home.

Her feet carry her down the path to the small park, fenced in from the shops and lights of the city streets. She walks past the rusted playground equipment that sits empty and toward a small cluster of men seated together under a large tree. As she approaches, she sees a large hookah pipe in their midst, and the trails of smoke drifting upward. It is almost completely dark now. She cannot make out the men's faces at this distance. They are laughing loudly, and for a moment, she worries what will happen to her at their hands if Jasu is not among them. When she draws closer, she is at first relieved, then disappointed, to see Jasu leaning against the tree, his eyelids drooping and his braced hand sitting lame in his lap. In his good hand, he holds a bottle.

"Jasu," she says. A couple of men glance at her, then turn back to their conversation. "Jasu!" she says again, loud enough to be heard over the crude joke about a woman and a donkey. She watches as her husband's reddened eyes drift over and slowly focus on her face. He tries to straighten up once he sees her.

"*Arre,* Jasu, your wife coming to fetch you like a schoolboy?" one man teases.

"Who wears your *dhoti, bhai?*" Another slaps him on the back, slumping him over again.

Jasu offers a weak smile to the taunting men, but Kavita sees the pain in his eyes. She sees the injured pride, the shame, the disappointment she knows he feels. In this moment, witnessing him in his messy, helpless state, Kavita feels her anger and fear washed away by sorrow. All this time, Jasu has had only one goal above all else, to provide for his family. And over the last twenty years, it seems as if God has been dreaming up one cruel complication after another to keep him from even this modest goal. The poor harvests back in Dahanu, the illusive *dhaba-wallah* job, the bicycle factory raid, the moneylender, and now his broken hand, dangling limply at his side as he tries to stand. Kavita rushes over to help him.

"Come, Jasu-ji," she says, using the respectful term of address for her husband. "You wanted me to tell you when dinner was ready. I've made all your favorites—*bhindi masala, khadi, laddoo*." Kavita steadies herself under the weight of Jasu's heavy frame. He looks in her eyes. They haven't eaten such a meal since they were married.

"Ahh, good thing my wife is such a wonderful cook," he says as they walk slowly away together. Jasu holds up his good hand to the men and says over his shoulder, "See how lucky I am? You poor bastards should all be so lucky."

BACK IN THE *CHAWL*, KAVITA HELPS JASU ONTO THE BED AND covers his forehead with a cold cloth. She feeds him cold rice and *shaak* with her fingers, which he eats clumsily before falling into a heavy sleep. Her stomach growls, and she remembers she still has not eaten dinner. It occurs to Kavita it is now after nine o'clock and Vijay is still not home. She feels the fear return, this time in the form of a bitter taste in her mouth.

Vijay finished his deliveries for Sahib five hours ago. The only reasonable explanation is that he is at a friend's house. They do not have a phone at home, nor do Vijay's friends. He probably got caught up with his studies and didn't notice the time. Yes, that must be it. He is a smart boy, responsible. Kavita breathes deeply a few times as she strokes Jasu's forehead with the damp cloth. Once he goes back to work, everything will be fine. She sits down on the floor next to the bare bulb that throws some light her way, and sews a button back on Jasu's shirt while she waits for Vijay. At least she can take some comfort in the fact that a fifteen-year-old boy is safer out there after dark than a woman is. When she finally hears the front door, she feels a wave of relief flood her for the second time this evening. Vijay enters the room.

"Vijay," she says in a loud whisper, standing up. "Where have you been? Have you no decency? We're sitting here worrying about you!"

Her teenaged son, who has the faint beginnings of a mustache on his upper lip, just shrugs his shoulders, hands in his pockets. He notices his father lying in bed. "Why is Papa asleep already?"

"You don't ask me questions, *achha*. You just answer my questions. Papa and I work hard every day to take care of you. You understand?" The anger in her voice is beginning to mix with fatigue. She feels, at once, utterly exhausted by all of this.

"I work too," Vijay mutters under his breath.

"Heh? What did you say?"

"I work too. I earn money." Vijay's muted voice gets louder as he points to his father. "Look at Papa! Drunk again. He's not working, he's sleeping."

Kavita's hand rises quickly and she slaps Vijay hard across the face. He pulls back, looking stunned, and touches his face with his hand. His mouth sets into a tight curl and he digs his hand deep inside his pocket. He pulls out a wad of cash and throws it down at her feet. "There! Okay? Now we have enough money. Papa can get drunk and sleep all day if he wants." He looks at her with defiance.

Kavita's heart stops. She looks at the money as if it is a cobra uncoiling itself from a basket. There must be at least three thousand rupees. He couldn't possibly earn this much from messenger work. She looks at her son with disbelief and fear. "*Beta,* where did you get this?"

"Don't worry about it, Ma," he answers, then turns away. "You don't need to worry about me anymore."

July 2001

My dad and I tried making two Indian dishes this weekend. The first one was a disaster—we set off the smoke detector when the oil and spices burned the bottom of the pan. But the second one, some kind of tomato curry with potatoes and peas, was actually pretty good.

I feel bad saying this, but I look forward to these weekends alone with my dad. Mom's been going down to San Diego every month or so since Grandma found the lump in her breast.

This morning, Dad called his family in India and I spoke to them again. It's still a little weird talking to people I've only seen in pictures, but it's getting better. He got those recipes from his mother, and we drove all the way down to the Indian grocery store in Sunnyvale for the ingredients.

Tomorrow, we're going to play tennis—Dad's been coaching me on my backhand. So, we're getting along pretty well now. The only thing that sets him off is when we talk about my future and I say I want to be a journalist and not a doctor. It actually caused a big fight between them when my mom helped me find an internship at a radio station for the summer. I thought that was pretty cool of her. She even seemed happy when I was appointed editor of the Bugle *next year.*

Finally, I'm not fighting with them as much anymore. And I can see the light—my senior year's going to fly by, and then I'll be off to college, where I can do whatever I want.

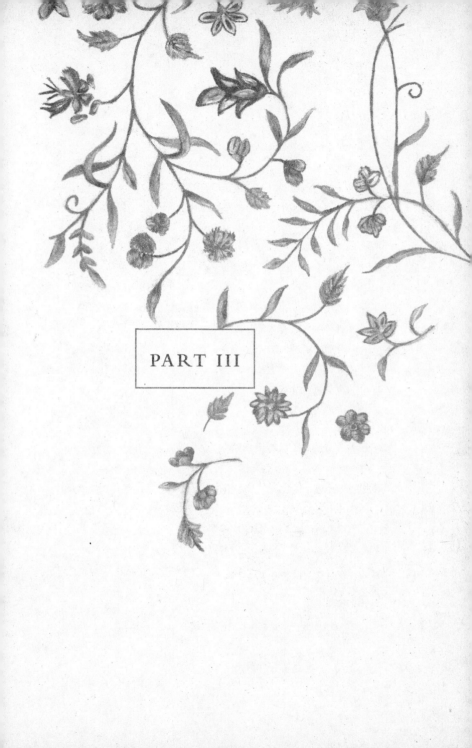

PART III

28

PARENTS' WEEKEND

Providence, Rhode Island—2003
ASHA

THE CAMPUS IS COVERED WITH CRISP LEAVES THAT RUSTLE underfoot as Asha walks across the main green with her parents. It is a cool day, but the bright autumn sun filtering through the tree branches and cups of apple cider keep them warm as she gives them a tour.

"The *Daily Herald* office is over there, a couple blocks down." Asha points through the ivy-covered buildings.

"I'd like to see it, since you spend so much time there," her mother says.

"Sure. More cider, Dad?" Asha asks, her cup poised under a steel urn on one of the tables on College Green, where hundreds of other students and parents are milling around. Asha feels a hand on the middle of her back. She turns and, seeing Jeremy, smiles broadly and turns back to her parents.

"Mom and Dad, this is Jer . . . Mr. Cooper. I've told you about him. He's the faculty adviser for the *Herald*."

"Jeremy Cooper," he repeats, extending a hand to her father.

"You should be very proud of your daughter, Mr. and Mrs. Thakkar. She really—"

"Doctor," her father interrupts.

"I'm sorry?"

"It's *Doctor*. Asha's mother and I are both physicians," he says. Asha sees her mother's eyes cast downward.

"Oh yes, of course." Jeremy chuckles. "Asha mentioned that. I always forget the 'Doctor' bit in my own name," he says, with a dismissive wave of his hand. Asha gives a small laugh. "As I was saying, you should be very proud of your daughter. Asha is one of the finest young journalists I have seen in my years at Brown." Asha smiles broadly.

"And how many years is that?" her father asks.

"Uh . . . well, five years now. Hard to believe. Did you see the piece she wrote this fall on campus military recruiters? Very insightful. Worthy of publication in any major newspaper. Really. Excellent." Jeremy smiles at Asha.

"Mr. Cooper, what do you do—" her father starts.

"Please, call me Jeremy." He puts his hands into the flap pockets of his brown tweed blazer, fraying at the edges of the lapels.

"Yes, what do you do," Krishnan says, "other than oversee the newspaper?"

"Well, I teach a couple classes in the English department, and I also try to do some freelance writing, when I have time." Jeremy rocks back on the heels of his worn brown loafers. "But I stay pretty busy on campus."

"Yes, I can imagine," her father says. "You must like it, the life of a professor? After all, there aren't too many other good career paths in your field."

"Dad . . . ," Asha pleads, her face in a grimace.

"No, no, your father's right," Jeremy says. "But I was never as talented as Asha. She could be our next great foreign correspondent, traveling to distant lands to bring us the news."

Asha sees her mother look stricken and is about to reassure her when her housemates bound up to them. "Asha! Oh, hey, Jeremy."

Jeremy excuses himself, saying something about a faculty reception where he is expected. Asha gives him a sympathetic look as he leaves, silently apologizing for her father.

"Hey, guys!" Asha turns to her parents. "Mom, Dad—you remember my housemates? Nisha, Celine, and this is Paula. I don't think you met her last time."

Nisha and Celine each wave and say hello. Paula perches her sunglasses on her head, revealing her thick-lashed brown eyes. She leans forward, her cowlneck sweater offering a glimpse of pale cleavage, and thrusts out her hand. "Very nice to meet you both. I've heard so much about you." Asha shares a look with Nisha and Celine. They used to tease Paula about being such a flirt, especially with her professors, until they realized she didn't know any other way to behave. Paula tilts her head to one side and smiles at her father. "Asha's been sharing some of your curry recipes with us. You must be a great cook."

"Oh, not really," her dad says. "We enjoy cooking together. I make a lot of mistakes, but Asha's patient with me." He puts his arm around her.

"You know," Paula says, "there's a *bhangra* party on campus later tonight. You should come. There's going to be a great deejay."

"Really, *bhangra*?" her dad says. Asha recognizes the confusion on her mother's face.

"Oh, we don't want to get in the way," her mom says, placing her hand on his elbow. "You girls have fun."

"Okay, so I'll see you guys at the hotel tomorrow morning for brunch?" Asha says.

"Sure, honey." Her mother leans over to kiss her. "See you then."

HER MOTHER SLIDES A WRAPPED BOX TIED WITH A LARGE YEL-low satin ribbon across the table toward her. Asha puts down her orange juice and looks back and forth between her mother's beaming face and her father's neutral expression. "What's this?

"An early birthday gift," her mother says. "Go ahead, open it."

Asha unwraps the box to reveal a new handheld video camera.

"I remembered how you liked using ours in Hawaii last summer." Her mother smiles and looks at her dad. "And you said you'd like to tape your interviews, so you don't miss anything."

Asha smiles. She recalls the conversation with Mom, when she meant audio-recording.

"You wouldn't believe how many different options there are," her mom continues. "But the man at the camera store said this has the most important features—a zoom lens and a computer connection. You can hook it right up to your Mac for editing."

"Thanks, Mom," Asha says. "This is great. I can't wait to use it." She holds the camera up to her eye and points it at her father. "C'mon, Dad—smile!"

29

REAL LIFE

Mumbai, India—2004
KAVITA

"Do you really think she would go off like that with his best friend?" Kavita says, linking her arm through Jasu's as they leave the cinema.

"Of course not, *chakli*. It's not meant to be real life. It's a film only." He wraps his arm around her shoulders and leads her across the busy street during a short break in the traffic.

"Then why do they make films like that? Something that will never happen?" she says once they make it safely to the other side.

"Time-pass, *chakli!*"

"Hmmm." The concept of simply passing time is almost as strange to Kavita as the idea that they can now afford to go to the movie theater on a whim.

"What would you like to do now, *chakli*? Something cold?" he asks as they approach an ice cream shop.

"Yes, I'll have a cold coffee, please," Kavita says. She's recently discovered this sweet, creamy indulgence and finds it hard to resist on a warm evening like tonight. She used to wonder about the people who lined up at these places, willing to spend their hard-earned rupees on such frivolity.

"*Ek* cold coffee, *ek pista* ice cream," Jasu says to the man wearing a paper Nehru cap behind the counter. A few minutes later, he hands the tall drink to his wife, and they continue strolling. The streets and footpaths are crowded. It is Saturday evening, the one night of the week when all of Mumbai seems to shake off its worries and go out on the town. The restaurants are full of families, and later, queues will form outside the popular nightclubs. This world too is a fairly recent discovery for Kavita and Jasu.

It started a few years ago, when Vijay took them out to a sit-down restaurant to celebrate his sixteenth birthday. It was the first time they had been to a restaurant with tables covered in crisp white cloths. Vijay had successfully finished his Tenth Standard and started a messenger business with his friend Pulin. Kavita and Jasu still wished he would pursue a different path. "*Beta,* you are such a smart boy. You've gone so much further in school than we did. Why do this messenger business like a common person?" Jasu said. "You can do better. Why not find a good office job?"

"Papa, this is a good job," Vijay said. "I am the boss. Nobody tells me what to do." Vijay ordered for all of them, since he was the only one who could read the menu. Kavita didn't recognize the dishes he chose, but all the food was wonderful, presented on gleaming silver trays and served to them by waiters. She felt like a queen, and she could tell from Jasu's boisterous talk, he was proud as well. At the end of the evening, Vijay pulled out a wad of cash to pay for the check. Kavita had seen it many times by then, but each time he unfolded the thick pile of bills and counted them out, a cold hand grabbed her heart.

"I LOVE PISTACHIO, I COULD EAT IT EVERY DAY." JASU FINISHES his pale green ice cream.

"You practically do eat it every day now," Kavita says, elbowing him in the ribs.

"Shall we take a rickshaw home?" Jasu holds her arm to guide her through the busy sidewalk. It is so much more pleasant to be able to take a rickshaw in the evening than ride the crowded train. Up ahead, a ring of people seems to be gathered around a street performer of some sort.

"What's going on there?" Kavita says. "Musician or snake charmer? Let's go see." The rhythmic clapping of the crowd draws them in. A couple of men are perched up on the low stone wall to get a better look. When Kavita and Jasu finally get close enough, both of them are shocked by what they see at the center of the circle of men. It is a woman, a girl really, not older than eighteen. She is down on her knees on the ground, crying, disoriented, groping about for something. A man in the circle is holding one end of her sari, which is almost completely unraveled from her body. Her sari blouse is torn down the middle, exposing her breasts.

Jasu pushes his way to the front of the crowd and crouches down next to the girl. He turns and rips the sari out of the man's hand and yells at him, "Dirty bastard! Have you no shame?" He tries to rewrap the garment around the girl, but finding this too cumbersome, he removes his own shirt and slips it onto her shoulders, shielding her bare skin from the hungry eyes devouring her.

"*Heh, bhaiyo,* step aside. Don't ruin our fun!" A man calls out from the circle.

The girl's hands finally find what they've been groping for—a pair of eyeglasses, now cracked and smudged with dirt. She puts them on her face, stands, and wraps herself tightly in Jasu's shirt. Kavita looks at the girl's face. Her forehead is too large, her eyes are set too far apart. She realizes, in an instant of horror, the girl is mentally retarded. She sees the same flicker of recognition on Jasu's face, which turns immediately to fury.

"Fun? This is your fun?" he yells at the men assembled around them, some of whom now peel away from the group. "*Arre,* this is shameful behavior. She is an innocent girl! How would you feel if someone treated your wife this way? Your sister? Your daughter? Heh?" Jasu, wearing only a sleeveless undershirt, gestures menacingly to the few men who remain there, unable to accept the untimely end to their entertainment.

Kavita quickly walks over to the girl and leads her away from the crowd. "You okay, *beti*?" she whispers as they stand against a tree trunk. The girl nods mutely in response. "Where do you live? You need paisa to get home?" The girl keeps nodding in the same rhythmic way, indicating neither comprehension nor agreement. Finally the crowd disperses, and Jasu joins Kavita and the girl. "I think we should escort her home," Kavita says, having finally learned her address. Jasu nods and steps down off the curb to hail a taxi.

"ARE YOU OKAY?" KAVITA ASKS JASU. THEY HAVE BEEN RIDING in silence since taking the girl to her building. Jasu spoke to the lift operator there, who said he would see she got safely upstairs to her parents' apartment.

"*Hahn,*" he says in monotone. "I was just thinking . . . that poor girl was so defenseless, and all those men just . . . If we hadn't walked by just then, what would have become of her?"

"You did a good thing. It was brave of you." Kavita puts her hand on his arm.

"It wasn't bravery so much, just chance we were there. Just chance . . ." He trails off again, then shakes his head. "No matter. It's done now. I hope it didn't ruin the evening."

"*Nai,*" she says, smiling at him. "Not at all." Kavita doesn't say what she is thinking, how nice it was to hold the girl's frail body in her arms until it stopped shaking, to wipe away her tears and stroke her long hair. To sing sweetly to her in the car, as her own mother used to sing to her. As she has imagined singing to her own secret daughter.

30

PART OF HER

Menlo Park, California—2004
SOMER

SOMER STANDS AT THE SINK AFTER DINNER, HER FOREARMS COV-
ered in slick yellow gloves, happy for the buzz of Asha's presence in
the house. It is her first night home for the summer after her sopho-
more year at Brown. Still, Somer is tentative, not sure how it will feel
to be a family again. Asha has made it clear since coming home that
she considers herself independent now—refusing any help with the
dirty laundry that came out of her suitcase and setting up her laptop
in a private corner of her room.

And Somer and Krishnan have finally managed to find a balance
predicated on plenty of space and avoiding conflict. They adhere to
the easy terrain and retreat when they feel the slightest crack underneath. There was a time they argued in the open. It started almost
suddenly, after Asha left. Without her presence in the house, there
was no common focus for their energy, no reminder to behave well
in front of her. They fought over the dozens of daily decisions that
suddenly fell to them alone. Somer was not prepared for the total
silence that took over the house without Asha. There was no music

emanating from her bedroom, no echoes of laughter as she chatted for hours on the phone. It was the small moments Somer missed—a good-bye at the front door, a quick poke of her head into Asha's bedroom at night—the moments that made their home and her day feel full. After so many years with Asha at the center of her life, Somer felt lost when she was gone. But Krishnan's life hadn't changed much: he was mostly consumed with work, spending mornings in the operating room and afternoons at his office.

Kris, now sitting at the table with Asha, flicks at a newspaper page with his middle finger and thumb. "I can't believe this nonsense. They're still fighting this thing in Florida—trying to keep this poor woman attached to a feeding tube. The woman's brain has been dead for over a decade and they won't let her go in peace." He removes his glasses, exhales loudly onto each of the lenses, then wipes them with a handkerchief.

"You think she's really brain-dead?" Asha says, taking the newspaper from him.

"Yes, I do. But that's irrelevant." He holds his glasses up to the light and, finally satisfied, replaces them on his face. "It's a decision between her family and her doctor."

"What if they can't agree?" Asha says. "Her parents want to keep her alive, and her husband doesn't."

"Well, her husband is her guardian," Kris says. "At some point, the family you create is more important than the one you're born into." He shakes his head. "Listen, I'm telling you both right now, if I'm ever in a persistent vegetative state, you have my permission to pull the plug."

"Isn't there a chance she could still be cured?" Asha says.

He shakes his head. "Not unless she grows a new brain. And now the politicians are trying to interfere with stem cell research too."

Somer observes from across the kitchen as Asha clearly enjoys engaging with Kris in vigorous debate. She calls out, "How about a puzzle tonight? I'll make popcorn."

"Cool." Asha clears the kitchen table. "I'll get the puzzle. Hall closet?"

"Yes." Somer retrieves the popcorn machine from the highest shelf. "I hope this still works," she says, energized by the familiarity of puzzle night, a regular event before Asha left.

Somer pours the kernels into the machine, producing a loud rattling sound.

Asha brings back a box portraying Venetian gondolas in assorted colors floating along the canals. "So what do you think of that proposition, Dad? To fund stem cell research?"

"I think three billion dollars for research in California would be brilliant. These stem cell studies are some of the most promising I've seen in neuroscience."

"You should write an editorial on that for the paper, Dad," Asha says, crossing the kitchen. "I bet the voters would love to hear from a neurosurgeon. I can help you."

He shakes his head, sorting through pieces. "No thank you, I'll stick with medicine."

The rapid-fire popping slows down and Somer shakes fluffy white popcorn into a large bowl. "Salt and butter?"

Asha tosses a piece of popcorn into her mouth. "Good, but it needs a little something." Asha takes the popcorn bowl from her. "You and Dad start." Somer sits down next to Krishnan, struck by how much easier it still is for him, how Asha seeks out common ground with him. Somer recalls fondly the times she played cards or Scrabble with her own father. Now, for the first time, she wonders how it made her mother feel when she blatantly favored him so.

Asha spins the spice bottle carousel. "I'm going to make a little concoction my housemates and I cook up." She joins them at the table and offers the bowl to Kris. "Try it."

Deep in concentration on several pieces of a blue gondola, he reaches into the bowl without looking up. "Mmm. Very good," he says.

Somer takes a piece and is shocked at its bright red color. "Oh," she says, putting it in her mouth, "what did you—?" She is interrupted by a cough as the pungent spices hit her throat. Somer reaches for the nearest glass of water but can't stop coughing long enough to take a drink. Her mouth burns and her eyes are tearing.

"Spicy, but good, isn't it? Red chili, garlic, salt, and sugar. And turmeric usually, but I don't think you have any." Asha takes a seat at the table with the bowl between her and Kris.

"So, I have some news." Somer looks up and Asha continues. "You've heard of the Watson Foundation? They grant fellowships for college students to go abroad for a year. I applied to do a project on children living in poverty. In India." Asha's eyes dart back and forth between them.

Somer tries to make sense of Asha's words, unsure what to say.

"I won." Asha's face explodes into a broad smile. "I won, so I'm going next year."

"You're . . . what?" Somer shakes her head.

"I can't believe I really won. The committee said they liked my idea of working with a major newspaper there to get a special report published, and—"

"And you're just bringing this up now?" Somer says.

"Well, I didn't want to say anything unless I won because it's really competitive."

"Where in India?" Krishnan asks, oblivious to Somer's shock.

"Mumbai." Asha smiles at him. "So I can stay with your family. My story's going to be on kids growing up in urban poverty. You know, in the slums, that kind of thing." Then she reaches for Somer's hand, still gripping a puzzle piece. "Mom, I'm not dropping out or anything, I'll be back to graduate. It's just a year."

"You've . . . done all this already? It's all planned?" Somer says.

"I thought you'd be proud." Asha pulls back her hand. "The Watson is a really prestigious award. I arranged everything myself, I'm not asking you for money. Aren't you happy for me?" she says, an edge of anger creeping into her voice.

Somer rubs her forehead. "Asha, you can't just drop this on us and expect us to celebrate. You can't make a decision like this without our input." She looks at Kris, expecting to see her anger reflected in his face. But she finds none of the shock she feels, none of the fear riddling her mind. *How can he be so calm about this?*

And, in that moment, it occurs to her. *He knew.*

THE PUZZLE LIES UNFINISHED ON THE KITCHEN TABLE DOWN-stairs while Somer strips off her clothes in the darkness of their closet. She runs the water in the bathroom faucet, listening for the sound of their bedroom door. She scrubs at her face in a way her dermatologist has warned against. When Kris enters the room a few moments later, she is fuming.

"So, you really have no problem with this?"

"Well." He stands at the bureau and removes his watch. "I think it might be a good idea."

"A good idea? To drop out of college and travel halfway around the world by herself? You think that's a good idea?"

"She's not dropping out. It's just a year. She'll come back and graduate, so what if it takes an extra semester or two? And she won't be alone, she'll have my family." Kris untucks his shirt and begins unbuttoning it. "Look, honey, I really think this could be good for her. It'll get her away from those liberal arts teachers, filling her head with the idea that journalism is a glamorous profession. My father can take her along to the hospital."

"That's your agenda? You still think you're going to make a doctor out of her?" Somer shakes her head.

"She can still change her mind. She'll see a whole different side of medicine over there."

"Why don't you just accept her for who she is?" Somer says.

"Why don't you?" he shoots back, in a tone quiet yet accusing.

There is a moment of silence while she stares at him. "What do you mean?"

"I mean, she wants to go to India. She's old enough to make that decision. She can spend time with my family, get to know her Indian culture."

Somer stands up and heads toward the bathroom. "I can't believe you. You are such a hypocrite. If she was talking about going any-where other than India, you would be just as upset as I am." She spins around to face him again. "Did you know about this?"

He rubs his eyes with his fingers and sighs heavily.

"Kris? Did you?" She feels her stomach knot.

"Yes!" He throws his hands into the air. "Yes, okay? She needed a signature on the form and she didn't want to get into it with you if she didn't win."

Somer tightens the belt of her robe and wraps her arms around herself, suddenly cold. She closes her eyes and takes in this news, the admission of guilt. She shakes her head. "I can't believe you did that. You went behind my back and—" She breaks off, unable to continue.

Kris sits down on the armchair in the corner and his voice soft-ens. "This is part of her, Somer. Just like it's part of me. There's no denying that." There is silence in the room for several moments before he speaks again. "What are you afraid of?"

She forces down the lump in her throat and ticks off the reasons. "I'm afraid of her leaving college and going halfway across the world by herself. I'm afraid of her being so far away we won't have any idea what's happening with her." Somer runs her hands over her face and then up over her head, continuing with a fresh string of concerns.

"I'm worried about her safety, being a girl over there, going into those slums . . ." She sits down on the bed again and clutches a pillow to her chest. Kris doesn't speak and doesn't move from his chair in the corner, where his head rests in one hand.

After several moments of silence, she clears her throat and speaks again. "Do you think she'll try to look for . . . them?" She cannot bear to use the word *parent*. It assigns too much importance to people who have no connection to Asha other than biology. They have become shadowy figures in Somer's mind over the years—nameless and faceless, distant but never far away. She knows there is no risk of them showing up one day, wanting a role in her daughter's life. Rather, it is Asha she has always worried about. She has waited in fear for the day her daughter reaches a point of dissatisfaction with her or Kris, and goes in search of more. Somer has tried to be faultless as a parent, but still she worries that in the end, all her love for her daughter will not compensate for the loss she suffered as a baby.

"Who? Oh." Kris rubs his eyes and looks at her. "She might, I suppose. She'd have a hard time finding them in a country like India, but she might try. She's probably curious. It doesn't really matter, does it? You can't still be worried—"

"I don't know. I realize we can't stop her from looking if that's what she wants, but . . ." She trails off, twisting a tissue around her index finger. "I just worry, that's all. We don't know what will happen. I don't want her to get hurt."

"You can't protect her forever, Somer. She's practically an adult."

"I know, but we've put all that behind us. She's in a good place now." Somer cannot give voice to her real fears. That she will lose Asha, even a little bit. That the bond she's worked so hard to build will be tainted by this ghost. This, after all, is the outcome she has tried to avoid all along—why she hasn't wanted to go back to India, why she's never encouraged Asha's questions about the adoption. It is at the core of almost every decision she has made since Asha came into their lives.

31

SAME AS ALWAYS

Mumbai, India—2004
KAVITA

THE TAXI DRIVER PULLS INTO THE DRIVE OF THEIR NEW BUILD-
ing. They've lived here for over a year now, but Kavita still finds it
strange to have someone waiting to open the car door for her, and
another standing outside the lift to ferry them up to the third floor.
Vijay insisted they move to a bigger flat a couple years ago once his
business began to prosper. "I'm nineteen now, Ma. I think it's time I
have my own room," he said.

They found it hard to argue with that, especially when Vijay said
they could continue to pay the same rent they did at Shivaji Road and
he would pay the difference. Kavita doesn't know what this new flat
actually costs, and she isn't sure Jasu does either. They have their own
bedroom now, as does Vijay, who comes and goes as his business
requires when calls come in on his pager and mobile phone at all
hours. Kavita appreciates the extra space, and the modern kitchen
with its always hot running water. But still, she misses the old place
on Shivaji Road, the neighbors to whom they had grown close, the
local shops where they knew her.

The best change to come out of their move is in Jasu. A weight seems to have lifted off him, and even his nightmares have abated. "I feel as if I can finally relax a little bit," he said. "Our family is stable, our son is grown. It is a good feeling, *chakli*." Kavita doesn't feel the same. It is unsettling to see her son as a grown man, living independently under their common roof, transacting business as an adult she barely recognizes. She still worries about Vijay spending so much time with his partner Pulin, the strange hours he keeps, the wads of cash, and various other things that enter her mind at dark times. As the elevator jolts into movement, she wonders if she will ever stop worrying about her son.

She wonders too about her daughter. Usha will be grown by now, perhaps even married. On the question of whether her daughter might now have children of her own, Kavita allows herself to speculate for just a few moments, only the duration of the elevator ride. Once the doors open, she will force her mind to change course. She has learned to make space in her daily life for such thoughts, which come without warning, without allowing them to take over completely. Kavita learned long ago she needed to find a way to live in the present while silently honoring the past, to live with the husband and child she has without resenting them for what is gone.

The elevator doors open and the operator steps out to allow Jasu and Kavita to exit. As they walk down the hallway, Kavita senses something is awry. "Do you hear that?" She turns to Jasu, gesturing with her chin to their apartment at the end of the hall.

Jasu keeps walking, swinging the key ring on his index finger. "What? Vijay probably has that television on. I don't know how he falls asleep with it so loud."

Kavita slows down, not reassured. By the time they reach the doorway of their apartment, they both know something is wrong. The door is ajar and the loud voices inside definitely are not coming from the television. Jasu holds his arm out behind him to keep Kavita back, and pushes open the door with his toe. He disappears inside, and she follows him quickly. It is the debris they see first: the familiar bits and pieces of their lives scattered about, as if Kali, the goddess of destruction herself, has paid a house call.

"*Bhagwan*," Jasu says under his breath as he steps over the broken glass of his dead father's portrait, which once graced the front hallway, intermingled with crushed marigold petals from the garland Kavita hung on it every morning. The loud voices come from the bedroom at the end of the hallway. *Vijay's room*. In the center of the common room, the table is overturned. The couch cushions have been slashed with a knife, their white synthetic stuffing belching out. In a trance, Kavita walks into the kitchen and sees the burlap sacks of basmati rice and lentils have suffered the same fate as the pillows, their contents spilling onto the concrete floor. All the cupboards are opened, and one of the doors hangs off its hinges.

"Kavi, listen to me," Jasu whispers hoarsely from the living room. "Go next door and wait there. Go, quickly!" He ushers her out of the apartment before she can think to ask whether she should call the police. She knocks on the neighbors' door, but there is no answer. She waits in the hallway for a few minutes, then returns to their apartment and walks down the hallway to the bedroom at the end, stopping outside. There are two men in tan uniforms standing inside, *lathis* in hand. *Who called the police? How did they get here so quickly?* A policeman is questioning Jasu. She steps to the side of the doorway so she is out of view.

"Mr. Merchant, I am going to ask you again, and this time you will tell me the truth. Where does Vijay keep his supply?" The officer jabs Jasu's shoulder with his *lathi*.

"Officer Sahib, I am telling you the truth. Vijay has a messenger business. He is a good boy, very honest. He would not do what you are accusing him of." Jasu looks up earnestly from the bed on which he sits. Only then does Kavita notice that coils are springing out of a huge diagonal slash across the mattress. *What are they look-ing for?*

"Okay, Mr. Merchant. If, as you claim, you don't know what type of business your son is into, then surely you can at least tell us where to find him. Heh? At this hour of night? If he's such a good boy, why isn't your son home?"

Kavita peeks around the doorway. She hasn't seen Jasu this fearful since the police raid on the slum. "Sahib, it is Saturday night, not even eleven o'clock. Our son is out with his friends like most young men."

"Friends, heh?" The officer snorts. "You might want to keep a closer eye on your son and his friends, Mr. Merchant." He pokes Jasu's shoulder again. "You tell him we're watching him." The offi-cer nods curtly at Kavita as he leaves.

LATER THAT NIGHT, KAVITA IS JOLTED AWAKE BY JASU'S SCREAMS. She turns to see him struggling to sit up, clawing at the sheets on top of him, yelling *"Nai, nai!* Give it to me!"

She touches his shoulder lightly at first—"Jasu?"—and then shakes him. "Jasu? What's wrong? Jasu?"

He stops thrashing and turns to her. His glassy eyes do not regis-ter anything, as if he doesn't know who she is. After a moment, he looks down at his open palms. "What did I say?"

"You said 'no' and 'give it to me.' Nothing, same as always."

He closes his eyes, breathes deeply, and nods his head. "*Achha.* Sorry to wake you. Let's go back to sleep." She nods, strokes his shoulder, and then settles back into bed. She doesn't bother asking him about the dream that haunts him. He always refuses to tell her.

32

CHANGE OF CURRENT

Menlo Park, California—2004
ASHA

ASHA SITS CROSS-LEGGED ATOP HER BED, SURROUNDED ON ALL sides by items to pack. In the corner of her room sits the largest suitcase she and her father could find at Macy's, thirty inches tall. In the hallway outside her room is another just like it. Her flight to India is in two days. Normally, she would wait until the last minute to pack, but she retreated up here a couple hours ago when her father was called into the hospital to treat an aneurysm.

She is accustomed to this, the abrupt comings and goings of her father when he's on call. It happened at her eighth birthday party at the bowling alley, the regional spelling bee in sixth grade, and on countless other occasions. When she was younger, she used to take it personally, burst out crying when her father suddenly left in the midst of dinner. She always thought she'd done something wrong. Her mom had to explain that her father's work involved helping people in emergencies, which could happen anytime. Eventually, it became part of their family pattern: Asha learned to always answer the call-waiting beep, and they took two cars when they went out on his call nights. Now, it no longer fazes her. The urgency of her father's work reminds her of her own, working under deadline at the *Daily Herald*—the pressure, the constant awareness of time ticking down, the need to stay singularly focused until the end. She loves that feeling, and the accompanying rush of adrenaline on which she thrives.

Still, over the past couple months, her father's presence in the house has been the only thing keeping the simmering tension with her mother at bay. When her dad's around, she doesn't have to face her mom's obvious disappointment with her decision, her constant fears and worries about this trip to India. Asha cannot bear it anymore. The more her mother tries to cling to her, control her, the more Asha wants to pull away. In her mother's presence, she always feels ready to burst, so when her father was called in for surgery earlier today, Asha escaped to pack.

She surveys the various piles scattered around her bedroom. On the floor is a large heap of clothes, some still dirty. On her desk are materials for her project: her laptop, notebooks, research files, video camera. On the corner of her bed is a bag of travel supplies she found sitting there one day last week when she came home. Even without a note, she knew it was from her mother: sunscreen, industrial-strength mosquito repellent, malaria pills prescribed for her, plus enough emergency medications to treat a small village. The anonymous bag of concern is one of the few acknowledgments her mother has made regarding her trip. Finally, there are the things she plans to take with her on the plane to keep her occupied on the long flight: a DVD player, her iPod, a crossword puzzle book, and two paperbacks. After some consideration, she adds a third book to this pile, a book of poetry by Mary Oliver, a parting gift from Jeremy. Inside the front cover, he wrote an inscription and included her favorite quote:

"Truth is the only safe ground to stand on"
—ELIZABETH CADY STANTON

To my brightest star—

Never hesitate in your pursuit of the truth.

The world needs you.—J.C.

There is a knock at her bedroom door, and her father pushes it open. "Can I come in?" Without waiting for an answer, he enters and sits down on the bed.

"Sure. I was just packing."

"I found these and thought they might be useful for your trip." Her father holds up two strange-looking plastic and metal contraptions. "They're electricity converters. You plug this side into the outlet in India, then your hair dryer or computer into the other side. It changes the current of the electricity."

"Thanks, Dad."

"And I thought these might be helpful." He holds out a stack of photographs. "Especially once you start meeting everyone. We have a pretty big family over there, you know." He moves around the bed to sit next to her, and they go through the photos together: grandparents, aunts, uncles, and several cousins about her age whom she knows only through sporadic phone calls and Diwali cards. She is most nervous about this, the prospect of living for almost a year with people she barely knows.

"I'll take them on the plane so I can learn everyone's names before I get there."

"So, did you get everything worked out with the *Times of India*?" he asks.

"Yeah, that name you gave me—Pankaj Uncle's friend—he was really helpful. Once the editor heard I was on a grant from America, he was very interested. They're giving me a desk and a senior reporter to go on location with me to the slums, but I'll get to do all the interviews. They might even run a special feature in the paper. Isn't that great?"

"Yes, and it's good you'll have someone with you. Your mother's been worried about that."

Asha shakes her head. "That, and everything else. Is she ever going to get over this? Or is she going to be mad forever?"

"She's just worried about you, honey," he says. "She's your mother. It's her job. I'm sure she'll come around."

"Are you going to come visit?" she asks.

He looks at her for a while, then nods. "We'll come. Of course we'll come, honey." He pats her on the knee before getting up to leave. "Good luck with the packing."

Photos in hand, Asha walks over to her old desk and sits in the chair. This desk feels small compared to the broad worktable she's used to at the *Herald* office. She opens the drawer to find an envelope for the photos, feels around the clutter, and sees a familiar shape in the back of the drawer. She reaches in and pulls out the carved white marble box. *My box of secrets.*

It has been years since she's seen this box, though she could still sketch it from memory. It too looks smaller than she remembers. She wipes off a layer of dust and leaves her hand there for a moment, on the cool surface. She realizes she's holding her breath, draws it in deeply, and opens the box. She unfolds the first letter inside, a small rectangular piece of faint pink stationery. Slowly, she reads the words written there in familiar childlike script:

Dear Mom,

Today my teacher asked our class to write a letter to someone in another country. My father told me you are in India, but he doesn't know your address. I am nine years old and in the fourth grade. I wanted to write you a letter to tell you I would like to meet you one day. Do you want to meet me?

Your daughter, Asha

The raw display of sentiment makes her cringe. She feels tears prick at the back of her eyes and the slow flood of emotions she has not experienced in a long time. She takes out the rest of the stack of letters, and unfolds the next one. When she finishes reading them all, her face is wet. Her eyes rest upon the only item left in the box, a thin silver bangle. She picks it up and turns it around and around between her fingers.

At that moment, she hears a knock and her bedroom door opens again. Asha spins around in her chair to see her mother standing in the doorway. She surveys the room, taking in the evidence of Asha's imminent departure. Her eyes come to rest on Asha's tear-streaked face and, finally, the bangle in her hands. Asha drops the bangle in her lap and hastily wipes her face.

"What? Could you at least knock, Mom?"

"I did knock." Her mother's eyes are pinned on the bangle. "What are you doing?"

"Packing. I'm leaving in two days, remember?" Her tone is defiant.

Her mother's eyes turn downward and she says nothing.

"Go ahead and say it, Mom. Just say it."

"Say what?"

"Why do you have to sulk around like it's the worst thing that's ever happened to you? It's not happening to *you*." Asha slams her hands down on the arms of her chair. "It's not like I'm pregnant, or going to rehab, or flunking out of school, Mom. I won an award, for God's sake. Can't you just be happy for me, just a little bit proud?" Asha looks down at her hands and her tone is steely. "Didn't you ever want to do something like this when you were my age?" She looks up at her mom, daring her to answer. "Forget it. You've never understood me. Why start now?"

"Asha . . ." Her mother walks toward her and reaches for her shoulder.

Asha yanks herself away. "It's true, Mom. And you know it's true. You've been trying to figure me out my whole life, but you still don't get me." Asha shakes her head, stands up, and turns back to her desk. Shoving the letters and bangle back into the marble box, she hears the door close behind her.

33

WELCOME HOME

Mumbai, India—2004
Asha

ASHA STIRS FROM A LIGHT SLEEP WHEN SHE HEARS THE PILOT'S voice. He announces that they are landing ten minutes earlier than scheduled, little consolation after twelve hours in the air. It is 2:07 A.M. Mumbai local time, according to the watch she adjusted soon after the stopover in Singapore. This last leg of her journey has felt unbearably long. It has been over twenty-six hours, a full day since she said good-bye to her parents at San Francisco International Airport, and the scene was even worse than she had expected. Her mother began crying as soon as they pulled into the airport. Her parents bickered, as they were doing a lot lately, about where to park and which line to stand in inside the terminal. Her father kept a protective arm on her back the whole time they walked through the airport. When it was time for Asha to go through security, her mother held her tightly, stroking her hair as she used to when Asha was a little girl.

When she turned to go, her dad pressed an envelope into her hand. "It's probably worthless by now," he said, smiling, "but you can make better use of it than I can." On the other side of the security gate, she opened the envelope and saw it contained dozens of Indian rupee notes in various denominations. She looked back through the maze of metal detectors, tables, and people and saw her mother, still standing in the same place they had embraced. Her mom smiled weakly and waved. Asha waved back and walked away. When she glanced back over her shoulder one last time, her mother was still there.

Asha gathers her things from the two-foot-wide space that has been her home for the past day. Her neck aches from sleeping awkwardly, and her legs feel stiff as she reaches for her backpack. Both her DVD player and iPod ran out of battery power on the way to Singapore. The paperbacks are largely untouched; she didn't have the attention span for them. She passed the time mindlessly, consuming the meals and movies served up to her with equal disinterest. The only thing she pulled out of her backpack, again and again, was the large envelope stuffed with her father's family photographs, and the contents of her white marble box. As the hours passed during the flight, and the miles put greater distance between Asha and her parents, she began to feel different. Nervous. Eager.

The two young boys sitting next to her stow their Game Boys, and their mother reappears from a visit to the lavatory, having exchanged her tracksuit for a sari and applied a fresh coat of lipstick. They introduced themselves as the Doshis, back for their annual summer visit after having moved from Bombay to Seattle six years ago "for Mr. Doshi's work." When the plane touches down with a slight bump, the passengers cheer and applaud. Asha shuffles off the plane with the others, getting used to the feeling of standing on her legs again.

Mumbai International Airport is complete mayhem. It seems ten other planes have all landed at this unlikely hour, and streams of passengers from all the flights are now converging upon the immigration checkpoints at once. Unsure of where to go, Asha follows the Doshis to a line at one end of the large open room. Once they've all secured their places in line, Mrs. Doshi turns to Asha. "It used to be much easier when we could stand in that queue," she says, indicating a much shorter line in front of a desk labeled INDIAN CITIZENS. "But last year we had to give up our Indian citizenship. Mr. Doshi's company sponsored him, and now we must wait in this queue. Always longer, this one." Mrs. Doshi says this matter-of-factly, as if it is the most notable impact of their decision to move to a new country.

Asha looks around at a sea of brown faces: some lighter, some darker than her own, but these variations are insignificant in light of the realization she has never been around so many Indians before. For the first time in her life, she is not in the minority. As she nears the front of the line, she reaches under her shirt to remove her passport from the travel belt her mother insisted she bring. The immigration officer is a young man, not much older than herself, but his trim mustache and uniform give him an air of authority that makes him seem older.

"Reason for visit," he says, without inflection. It is a question he asks so many times a day he no longer pretends to be curious.

"I'm a student on a fellowship." Asha waits for him to flip to the visa in her passport.

"Length of stay?"

"Nine months."

"What is this address you have provided? Where will you be staying?" he asks, looking up at her for the first time.

"With . . . family?" Asha says. It feels strange to say this. Though it is technically true, her palms sweat, as if she has just lied to the official.

"I see you were born here," he says, sounding slightly more interested.

Asha remembers that anomalous part of her American passport that lists BOMBAY, INDIA, as her place of birth. "Yes."

The officer bangs his stamp, leaving a deep purple rectangular bruise on her passport, and hands it back with a new smile beneath his mustache. "Welcome home, madam."

On the way to baggage claim, it is the aroma that greets her first. It smells salty like the ocean, spicy like an Indian restaurant, and dirty like the New York subway. Asha spots her bags among the other gigantic suitcases that fill the carousel. There are also enormous cardboard boxes wrapped completely in packing tape, Styrofoam coolers with the tightly bound lids, and one unusually large carton promising a small refrigerator inside. Mr. Doshi helps Asha lug her two suitcases off the belt, and motions to a scrawny turbaned man nearby. Just as she starts to wonder why Mr. Doshi summoned someone without a luggage cart to help her, the turbaned man squats to the ground and quickly hoists both bags on top of his head. Holding the stacked bags in place with one hand on either side, he raises his eyebrows slightly at Asha. She understands the subtle gesture to mean she should proceed; he will follow her somehow, through the thick crowd, balancing over a hundred pounds on his head.

As soon as she steps outside, Asha is met with a gust of hot wind. She realizes she has just left an air-conditioned building, though it didn't seem so inside. Metal barricades hold back throngs of people, at least six deep, who all crane their necks toward the sliding doors through which she has just passed. The crowd is comprised mainly of men who, with their trim mustaches and oiled hair, all look like the immigration officer, only without uniforms. And though they are all presumably waiting for someone in particular to come through that door, Asha feels several eyes lingering on her as she walks.

Every few paces, she turns back to check on the turbaned man behind her, half-expecting her suitcases to land with a thud on the ground after breaking his neck. But each time she looks, he is still there, his gaunt face expressionless and unmoving except for a slight chewing movement of his jaw. It occurs to Asha she will need to pay this man and wonders if the rupees her father gave her will be sufficient. Her dad told her that one of his brothers, her uncle, would pick her up at the airport. This seemed adequate information at the time, but now, as she scans the crowd of hundreds that line the airport walkway it seems impossible they will find each other. She nears the end of the walkway, and is about to retrieve her uncle's picture from her backpack when she hears someone yelling her name.

"Asha! A-sha!" A young man waves to her. He has wavy black hair and wears a white cotton shirt revealing his chest hair. She walks over to him. "Hi, Asha! Welcome. I am Nimish. Pankaj *bhai*'s son," he says with a grin. "Your cousin brother! Come." He leads her away from the crowd. "Papa is waiting with the car, over here only. Good, you found a coolie." Nimish beckons to the turbaned man to follow them.

"Nice to meet you, Nimish," Asha says, following him. "Thanks for coming to get me."

"Of course. Dadima wanted to come herself to fetch you, but we told her it wasn't a good idea, at this hour. The airport is always packed with overseas flights." Nimish leads Asha and the coolie through a maze of cars, each with its headlights on and a driver leaning out of the window. Asha remembers her father using the term *Dadima* when handing her the receiver on those weekly phone calls to India; she knows it means her grandmother.

"Here's Papa, come." Nimish ushers her toward an old-fashioned-looking gray sedan with the name AMBASSADOR in metallic script on the back. Asha is a little startled to see the man Nimish calls Papa. Pankaj Uncle looks quite a bit older and has significantly less hair than in the photograph Dad gave her. He is her father's younger brother, but looks a decade older than him.

"Hello, *dhikri*," he says, holding his arms out to embrace her.

"Welcome, I am happy to see you. *Bahot khush, heh?* How was your flight?" He holds her face in his hands and smiles broadly. And when he wraps his arm around her shoulders, it is such a familiar sensation that she leans into him. Out of the corner of her eye, Asha sees Nimish opening the trunk for the coolie. She wonders again about the envelope of rupees, but before she can say anything, Nimish has paid the turbaned man, who is already on his way back to the terminal. On the ride, her uncle peppers her with questions.

"How was your journey? Tell me, how is your papa keeping? Why did he not accompany you on this trip? He hasn't come to visit us in a long time."

"Papa," Nimish says, "enough questions. Give her a break. She just got here, she's tired."

Asha smiles at her cousin's defense. She yawns and leans her head against the car window. Outside, she sees the billboards that line the highway, advertising everything from fashion boutiques and Bollywood films, to mutual funds and mobile phone service. At some point, the scene outside the Ambassador shifts from high-rises to housing slums: dilapidated shacks, clothes hung on lines overhead, trash littered everywhere, stray animals wandering about. Asha has seen photos in her preparatory research, but those shots didn't give her an indication of how enormous the slums were. Mile after mile of the same depressing scenery, even shielded by darkness, begins to give Asha a heavy feeling in her stomach. She recalls her mother's anxious warnings about visiting such places and considers, for the first time, if she was right.

34

BROTHER AND SISTER

Mumbai, India—2004
ASHA

ON HER FIRST MORNING IN MUMBAI, ASHA WAKES EARLIER than she would prefer to the sounds of the household coming to life. She pulls on her yoga pants from the plane and shuffles out to the main room she passed through briefly the night before. An old woman dressed in a crisp green sari sits at the dining table, drinking from a teacup.

"Good morning," Asha says.

"Ah, Asha *beti*! Good morning." The old woman stands up to greet her. "Look at you," she says, taking both of Asha's hands in hers. "I hardly recognize you, you've grown so much. Do you know me, *beti*? Your father's mother. Your grandmother. Dadima."

Dadima is taller than she expected, with impeccable posture. Her face is soft and lined, and her gray hair is pulled into a large bun at the nape of her neck. She wears several thin gold bangles on each wrist, which jangle whenever she moves. Asha is a little unsure how to greet her, but before she can think about it, Dadima pulls her into her arms. Her embrace is warm and comforting and lasts for several moments.

"Come, sit, have some tea. What will you take for breakfast?" Dadima leads Asha by the arm over to the table.

Asha appreciates the bowl of fresh cut mango in front of her. It feels as if she hasn't eaten anything but airplane food in days. As she sips her hot sweet tea, they talk. She's surprised at how good Dadima's English is, though she does occasionally lapse into Gujarati.

"Dadaji, your grandfather, is at the hospital just now, but he will be back for lunch. Oh *beti,* the whole family is so excited to see you. I've called them all for lunch this Saturday. I wanted to give you a few days to get settled and adjusted to the time change and whatnot."

"That sounds good. They're not expecting me at the *Times* office until next Monday morning," Asha says. Just speaking these words gives her a thrill, the idea of working at a major international newspaper. After breakfast, Asha retrieves the envelope of photos given to her by her father, and asks Dadima to help name everyone again. Dadima looks through the pictures, laughing periodically at how outdated they are. "Oh, your cousin Jeevan has not been that thin in a long time, though she thinks she still looks just like this!"

Dadima shows Asha how to use the primitive shower in the bathroom, first turning on the hot water tank for ten minutes. Bathing takes more effort than Asha is accustomed to, with the weak water pressure and the ever-shifting temperature. By the time she's dressed, she is exhausted again and falls asleep on her bed, sleeping right through Dadaji's visit home for lunch. When she does finally meet her grandfather at dinner, she is taken aback to find him so serene. She expected someone more like her own father, ambitious and assertive. It is her grandmother who appears to have the bigger personality, telling stories, laughing and ordering the servants around with a snap of her fingers. Dadaji sits at the head of the table, eating quietly. When he smiles at one of his wife's stories, his eyes crinkle up at the corners and he nods his silver-crowned head.

Asha spends her first several days in Mumbai getting acclimated. The jet lag makes her feel as if she's walking around in a fog. Drowsiness overwhelms her in the middle of the day. The weather is stifling—hot and muggy, compelling her to stay indoors most of the time. When she does go outside to accompany Dadima somewhere, she is always shocked by the filth and poverty she sees on the streets, right outside the gates of their building. She holds her breath when they pass the putrid spots and averts her eyes from the beggar children who follow them.

Each time they return to the flat, she immediately heads for the air-conditioning unit in her room and stands in front of it until her body temperature returns to normal. Then there is the Indian food served thrice daily, which is spicier than she's accustomed to and forces her stomach through its own adjustments. She does not feel like herself, and every aspect of her surroundings—the bread that comes wrapped in small squares, the newspaper the color of pale pink nail polish—reminds her of how far she is from home. She considers calling home for some comfort, but pride holds her back.

FINALLY, SATURDAY COMES, THE DAY OF THE BIG FAMILY LUNCH. Asha wears a blue linen sundress and puts on a little blush and mascara. It's the first time she's worn makeup since leaving California. In the heat here, it feels like it may melt right off her face, but she does want to look nice. Dadima has been buzzing about the flat all morning, overseeing the servants as they prepare an enormous feast.

Once people start arriving, the stream never ceases. Relatives of all ages rush over to Asha wearing big smiles and pretty saris. They call her by name, embrace her, hold her face in their hands. They remark on how tall she is, her beautiful eyes. Some of them look vaguely familiar, but most do not. They introduce themselves to her in rapid, yet lengthy ways, such as: "Your father's uncle and my uncle were brothers. We used to play cricket out behind the old house." Asha tries to remember their names and match them up with the photos but soon realizes this is both improbable and unnecessary.

There are at least thirty people here, and despite the fact she is meeting them for the first time, everyone treats her as if they've known her for years.

When the initial rush of meeting everyone is past, people make their way through the buffet table. After getting her plate, Asha sees a group of younger women sitting together who introduced themselves to her earlier as her cousins of one sort or another. Priya, a twenty-something with auburn-highlighted hair and large gold hoop earrings, waves Asha over to join them. "Come, Asha, sit here with us," she says with a big smile, moving over to make space. "Leave the aunties and uncles to their gossip."

Asha sits down. "Thanks."

"You've met everybody, no?" Priya says. "That's Bindu, Meetu, Pushpa, and this is Jeevan. She is our eldest cousin sister, so we must treat her with respect." Priya winks at the group. Asha remembers Dadima's comment about Jeevan's waistline expansion and smiles.

"Don't worry, you don't have to remember everyone's names. That's the beauty of the Indian clan. You can just call everyone Auntie-Uncle, *Bhai-Ben*." Priya gives a hearty laugh.

"Okay, I understand Auntie and Uncle, but what do the others mean?" Asha says.

"*Bhai-Ben?*" Priya says. "Brother and sister. That's what we all are." Priya winks again.

Asha looks around at the dozens of people laughing, talking, eating, all gathered together for her. This family of her father's, who have known one another their whole lives, grown up together in this city, this very building. This warm, bubbling pool of people that promises to draw her in with its centripetal force, not seeming to care that she shares neither their history nor their blood. She smiles and takes her first bite of the food that has been prepared in her honor. It is delicious.

35

TIMES OF INDIA

Mumbai, India—2004
ASHA

ASHA PULLS THE DOOR OPEN BY ITS BRASS HANDLE AND FEELS A rush of cool air greet her. Inside, her heels click against marble as she walks toward the elevator. Ensconced in the middle of the wall is a large plaque with the inscription: THE TIMES OF INDIA, ESTAB-LISHED *1839*.

"Lift, madam?" The elevator operator wears a two-piece gray polyester suit.

"Yes, sixth floor, please." Asha is no longer surprised when some-one addresses her in English. Her cousins have explained that Indians can peg her immediately as a foreigner, with her Western-style cloth-ing and shoulder-length hair. Even the fact that she makes eye con-tact with people is a giveaway. Despite this, she enjoys the novelty of walking down the streets among a crowd of people who look like her. Asha shares the elevator with two other passengers and the oper-ator. They stand with only a few inches between them, and this space is permeated by the stale odor of sweat. This elevator, like most she's found here, isn't air-conditioned, with only a weakly circulating fan overhead to stir up the pungent air.

At the reception desk on the sixth floor, Asha asks for Mr. Neil Kothari, her main contact at the newspaper. She sits down in the reception area and picks up this morning's *Times* when Mr. Kothari appears. He is a tall gangly man about her father's age, with his necktie loosened and hair disheveled. She declines his offer of a cup of tea and follows him to his office. They walk through the *Times's* office, a large open room with rows of desks lined with computers. The place is noisy with ringing phones, clattering printers, and myriad voices. She can feel the energy pulsing here, the biggest newsroom she's ever seen, all filled with brown faces.

"I think I'm the last one with a typewriter still in my office," says Mr. Kothari. "Of course, I don't actually write much anymore, but I still like to have it." Around the perimeter of the open room are several offices enclosed by glass walls. Mr. Kothari leads her into one, with a nameplate that says ASSOCIATE EDITOR on the wooden door. "Please have a seat," he says, gesturing to the chairs. "Are you sure you won't take some *chai* . . . tea?"

"No, thank you." Asha crosses her legs and takes out her notebook.

"*Nai,*" he says, to someone over her shoulder. Asha turns to see that a short, dark-skinned man has appeared silently in the doorway. His toenails, thick and yellow, are splayed grotesquely across his thin worn sandals. He nods imperceptibly at Mr. Kothari and leaves as quietly as he came, never once glancing in Asha's direction. "Very well, so you are here, all the way from America. Welcome to Mumbai! How are you finding it?" Mr. Kothari asks her.

"Good, thank you. I'm very excited to be here, to be collaborating with such a great newspaper on my project," says Asha.

"And we too are excited to have such an accomplished young woman here. I'll introduce you to Meena Devi, one of our best field reporters. Fearless, she is, sometimes to a fault. She will be an excellent mentor for you." Mr. Kothari hits a button on his phone, and a young woman appears promptly at his door. "Please get Meena here right away." A few minutes later, another person appears in the door-way, but instead of waiting outside like the others, this woman breezes in and sits down.

"*Achha,* what is so important, Neil, that I had to come just this very minute? I'm working under deadline, you know?" She is a small woman, not much taller than five feet, but her presence electrifies the mild atmosphere of Mr. Kothari's office.

"Meena, this is Asha Thakkar, the young lady from America who's here—"

"Yes, of course!" Meena lurches out of her chair to pump Asha's hand.

"You remember," Mr. Kothari continues, "she's doing a project on children growing up in the slums. We have set up a desk for her near your office. Your job is to take good care of her. Show her the real Mumbai. But make sure she's safe," he adds quickly.

"Come on, Asha." Meena stands. "I have to finish this story and then we'll go for lunch. To see the real Mumbai," she says, glancing over her shoulder at Mr. Kothari as they leave.

Asha spends the next couple of hours reading through a stack of clipping files that have been gathered on her desk, along with a few basic office supplies and an outdated computer. As she flips through a folder containing the previous in-depth feature reports the *Times* has run, Meena intermittently taps away at the keyboard in her office nearby. Asha reads a story on the rise of the information services industry, and another on the operational efficiencies of the city-wide tiffin-carrier system. She is just beginning to believe Mumbai is the next great modern industrial capital of the world when she comes across a feature story on bride-burning.

She reads in disbelief about young brides who are doused with gasoline and burned alive when their dowries are deemed insuffi-cient. She turns to another story, about a member of the Untouchable caste who intentionally crippled his own children to foster sympathy and increase their begging earnings. The next feature is on the fantastic success of Lakshmi Mittal, the global steel-industry titan. The one after that is on the latest political scandal, detailing corruption and bribery charges against several government ministers. The last story in this folder is on the 2002 Gujarat riots between Hindus and Muslims, in which thousands of people were killed. After reading about neighbors who torched each other's houses and stabbed each other in the streets, Asha closes the folder, and then her eyes. She wonders whether a sample of stories from the *New York Times* would inspire the same intensity of both shame and pride in her.

"Almost done over here. Hungry?" Meena calls out from her office.

"THIS PLACE HAS THE BEST *PAU-BHAJI* IN ALL OF MUMBAI," MEENA says over the roar of the train. "If I'm anywhere within ten minutes of this spot, I have to go there, whether it's mealtime or not." Asha doesn't know what *pau-bhaji* is, or whether she will like it, but Meena doesn't seem concerned about this. Once they leave the noisy train, they can carry on a regular conversation again. "So, what did you think of the clippings you read?" Meena says.

"Good. I mean, the quality of writing and reporting is excellent, of course," Asha says.

Meena laughs. "I meant the subject matter. What do you think of our fine country? It's a five-star pile of contradictions, isn't it? I selected those clippings for you because they show the extremes of India, the good and the bad. Some people like to demonize India for her weaknesses, others only glorify her strengths. The truth, as always, lies somewhere in between."

Asha finds it hard to keep up with Meena as she maneuvers the sidewalk, darting through its assorted population: men who spit care-

lessly on the ground, scrawny dogs without owners, children begging for change. And as hazardous as it is on the sidewalk, the roads
seem infinitely worse: cars weave in and out of lanes and pay little
attention to traffic signals, double-decker buses careen dangerously
close to oblivious cows and goats. "There are one billion people living in India," Meena says, "and nearly ninety percent of them live
outside major cities, that means small towns and rural villages. Mumbai—even the real Mumbai, as Neil calls it—is only a tiny fraction of
the country. But it is a powerful fraction. This place draws people
like a magnet. It has the best and worst of everything India has to
offer. Ah, here we are." Meena walks up to a street stall. "*Doh pau-
bhaji, sahib. Ek* extra mild." She turns and smiles at Asha.

"This? This is where we're having lunch?" Asha looks at the
street vendor and then at Meena in disbelief. "I . . . I don't think I
should do this. I'm not supposed to eat street food . . ."

"Relax, Asha, you'll be fine. Anything the heat doesn't kill, the
spices will. Come on, you're in India now—you have to experience
the real thing. Wait until you taste it!" Meena hands Asha a rectangular paper tray filled with a reddish brown stew topped with
chopped raw onions and a lemon wedge and two glossy white buns
on the side. They stand at the edge of the walkway as a line forms in
front of the stall. Asha follows Meena's method of tearing off a piece
of the bun and dipping it in the stew. She takes her tentative first bite.
It is tasty. And very, very spicy. She looks around frantically for something to drink and recalls her mother's warnings about the dangers of
unsanitized water.

"How is it? I told him to make yours mild." Meena smiles.
"Tourist version."

"It's . . . a little spicy. What's in it?"

"Leftover vegetables mashed together with vegetables. It was
devised as a quick meal for millworkers. Now it's one of the most
common street foods in Mumbai, and no two places make it the

same. And no place in Mumbai"—Meena licks her fingers—"makes it like this place." After they eat, Meena says, "Come on, let's walk a little. I want to show you something." Asha follows, unsure after their lunch if she should really trust Meena. After only a block or two, they find themselves at the edge of an enormous settlement.

"Well, here we are. This is Dharavi," Meena says, dramatically extending her arm. "The largest slum in Mumbai, the largest in India and perhaps all of Asia. A dubious distinction, but there you have it."

Asha looks around, slowly. Homes—if you can call them that— half the size of her bedroom, crammed up against one another. People spilling forth from each of the doorways—an old toothless man, a weary-looking woman with stringy hair, small children barely clothed. And in all the spaces in between, filth—rotting food, human waste, piles of trash taller than her. The stench is overwhelming. She covers her nose, trying to be discreet. And then Asha sees something she can scarcely believe: right there on the sidewalk is a makeshift Hindu temple. A statue of a goddess in a pink sari draped with a small floral garland leans against a scrawny tree trunk. The goddess has a peaceful smile on her painted face, and there are flower petals and rice grains strewn at her feet. It looks so out of place, this little alcove of divinity amid all the squalor, yet no one else seems to think so. A five-star pile of contradictions, indeed.

"Over a million people live here," Meena says, "in just two square kilometers. Men, women, children, livestock. Factories producing everything from textiles to pencils to jewelry. A lot of what's 'Made in India,' according to those tags you see, is made right here in Dharavi."

"Where are the factories?" Asha looks again at the small huts and outdoor fires, trying to envision a factory floor full of machinery.

"Homes on this level, factories upstairs. Most everything is done by hand, or with primitive tools," Meena says. "Remember what I said about the extremes of India? Well, here you find it all: the good and the bad, living side by side. On the one hand," she says as they walk alongside the settlement, "poverty, filth, crime—some of the worst aspects of human behavior. On the other hand, you'll see the most amazing resourcefulness here. People make things out of literally nothing. You and I will earn more in one year than they will in their entire lives, and yet they find ways to survive. They've formed a whole society here: gang lords, moneylenders certainly, but also healers, teachers, holy men. So you see, Asha, there are two Indias. There is the world you'll see at your father's home, with spacious flats, servants, and outrageous weddings. And then, there is this India. It is a good place to begin your study."

36

IN GOD'S HANDS

Mumbai, India—2004
KAVITA

"IS VIJAY COMING TO THE TEMPLE?" JASU CALLS FROM THE BAL-
cony where he's shining his shoes.

Kavita waits a moment before answering. The small balls of
dough sizzle as she drops them carefully into the cast-iron pot. When
the crackling oil settles back down to a safe level, she turns her head
to the doorway and says, "I don't know. He didn't say."

"So, we don't need to wait for him." Jasu's comment could just as
easily refer to the past three months as to today's outing. After the
incident with the police, they tried talking to Vijay. He insisted the
police were only after him because he refused to pay bribes from his
messenger business. Since then, he has withdrawn, spending most of
his time out with Pulin and others.

Kavita pulls the last of the fried dough balls out of the pot and
slips them onto the paper-lined tray with the others. She wipes her
hands on the dishcloth tucked into her sari. "I can put these in syrup
after we come back. I'll go change." She decided to make *gulab jamun*
for Diwali, even though it's a great deal of trouble for just the three

of them. Both she and Jasu were feeling particularly sentimental about Diwali this year—they would have liked to go back to Dahanu for a visit, but Jasu couldn't get leave from the factory. She thought this little touch of home might help them, and she can also take some to Bhaya's luncheon this afternoon. She hurries to the bedroom to change her sari. They'll try to make it to the temple before the crowds descend. It is the busiest day of the year at Mahalaxmi Temple, and unlike Sahib and Memsahib, who gave her and Bhaya a rare day off, they do not have a driver to drop them near the entrance.

"KAVITA *BEN,* YOU SHOULD NOT HAVE GONE TO SO MUCH TROU-ble!" Bhaya says when she opens the door and sees her holding the large bowl of *gulab jamun.* "But, of course, we will be happy to enjoy the fruits of your hard work. Come in, please." Bhaya smiles and ushers them into the apartment. Kavita is surprised at how small the space feels, these two rooms that are almost identical to their old *chawl* apartment. It is filled with their old neighbors and Bhaya's family. Everyone greets them warmly.

"Jasu *bhai,* you've put on a little in the tummy, heh? What is your wife feeding you over there in fancy Sion?" Bhaya's husband chuckles.

"What a lovely sari," one of the neighbors says to Kavita, admiring its deep burgundy sheen.

"Thank you." Kavita looks away, uncomfortable with the attention. Fortunately, they are soon all sitting with full plates of food on their laps. They talk of the weather (poor), the quality of the tomatoes this year (good), the price of bread (high). They speak of their children and grandchildren, their achievements in school and their adventures on the cricket fields. Inevitably, the discussion turns to the latest Hindi films.

"Have you seen *Dhoom,* Jasu *bhai*? You must see it."

"Excellent film," another neighbor says, nodding.

"*Hahn,* we saw it last week," Bhaya's husband says. "It is excellent. First-rate. Not that standard Bollywood nonsense. It's about this gang of criminals who ride motorcycles, see? Not the scooters you see everywhere, but real fast motorcycles. They ride all over Mumbai, robbing places and creating mischief, see? Only the police can't catch them because they drive away so quickly. Every time!" He slaps both his hands on his thighs and rocks backward.

"Abhishek Bachchan is so smart and handsome, *nai?*" Bhaya says to her sister.

"*Hahn,* but I prefer John Abraham, so naughty!" They break into girlish laughter that belies their combined century of life.

"Speaking of gangs," Bhaya's husband says, "have you heard Chandi Bajan's criminals have come together again? *Hahn!* He has a whole crew working for him in Mumbai, see? Selling drugs. Very big drug trade. Heroin, they say." He raises an eyebrow and nods wisely, one of the few in the room who can read the newspaper.

Kavita takes a bite of the vegetable *biryani* and glances at Jasu to see his reaction, but sees a blank expression on his face. She decides to venture into the discussion.

"Where are they operating? The gang? What part of Mumbai?" She tries to sound only casually interested.

"Everywhere. Right here even, in our own neighborhood. You know that boy Vijay and Chetan used to play with at school? Patel . . . uh, Pulin Patel? They live over there on M.G. Road, two blocks over? I hear he's mixed up with that gang. The police have been watching him." Bhaya's husband shakes his head and puts a large bite of rice in his mouth.

Kavita has a raw feeling in her chest, as if a horrible truth is scratching at her from the inside to get out. She tries to focus on eating, but the food has no taste. The conversation turns to the latest government scandal, then meanders back again to films. Eventually, the women congregate near the kitchen and laud Bhaya's food, while the men stay behind in the main room.

"Kavita, when will you look for a wife for Vijay? He's almost twenty, no?" Bhaya says.

"*Hahn,* I know." Kavita is relieved to turn to the more mundane issues concerning her son. "I think it is time too, but he doesn't seem too interested—'too young, too young, Mummy' he says." She shakes her head and smiles for what feels like the first time since arriving.

"Don't wait too long, *ben.* It's getting harder now, with so many boys and not enough girls." Bhaya lowers her voice to a conspiratorial whisper. "Some families are even having to pay money to bring brides from abroad, Bangladesh and such."

Kavita's fleeting smile melts away as the raw feeling in her chest returns. So many boys. *Not enough girls.* The raw feeling escapes her body and surrounds her. She smells the earthy monsoon air, though it is November. She feels the deep rumble of thunder, though the sky outside is clear. She closes her eyes, knowing that next she will hear the high-pitched cry echoing inside her ears. When she opens her eyes again, Bhaya and her sister are laughing, teasing their husbands for poking around in the kitchen for sweets.

The rest of the afternoon passes in a blur. Kavita doesn't even taste the rich sweetness of the *gulab jamun* someone serves her, the dessert she spent all morning preparing. She feels as if she is standing outside on the balcony, watching her friends through the window. She is desperate to leave and run back to their home. Yet deep inside the same raw place, she knows there is nowhere she can run that will make the feeling better. Not even Jasu can do anything to make it go away. When the group begins to break up, Jasu and Kavita say good-bye to their friends. They walk in near silence for a few blocks. "Jasu? Do you think it's true what the police were saying? Do you think Vijay is wrapped up in that Chandi Bajan gang?" Kavita says.

He takes too long to respond, and when he does, it is an unsatisfactory answer. "We've done our best, Kavi. Now it's in God's hands."

At home, Kavita goes through the motions of lighting the *diyas* and placing them along the windowsills. As a child, she loved Diwali simply for the sweets and firecrackers. Only later, as an adult, did she come to understand the true meaning of the occasion, the commemoration of the battle of Lord Rama, a celebration of the triumph of good over evil. She steps out onto the balcony and sees the thousands of tiny lights that shine in the windows of people's homes across Mumbai. She thinks about what Jasu said about God's hands and wonders if they are holding Vijay tonight. *What else should I have done for him? How could I have kept him from this fate?*

In the distance she sees the first bright snap of light just before the crack of the fireworks. She watches for a while, so deep in her thoughts they are barely interrupted by the startling booms and bangs that splatter across the night sky. She doesn't register the sound of the front door opening and closing until she hears water running in the kitchen. She turns to see Vijay hunched over the sink. "Vijay?" She walks toward him, then stops and gasps when she sees the blood dripping down his shoulder. She rushes to him. "*Arre!* What happened, *beta?*"

"It's okay, Ma. It's not a deep cut," he says.

She insists he remove his shirt and sit at the table while she fills a bowl with warm water and gets some bandages. "*Beta,* what have they done to you? I knew it was just a matter of time before something like this happened. They're no good, these boys you go with—Pulin and the others. They're dangerous, Vijay. Just look what they've done to you!" She presses a cloth firmly against his shoulder until the bleeding abates, then begins cleaning it with water. "Please, *beta*, I'm begging you. Don't get mixed up with them."

"Ma, they're not the ones who hurt me," Vijay says with a defiant shake of his head. "They helped me. My brothers look out for me, defend me." Kavita flinches at the mention of Vijay's siblings, real or imagined. She bites on her lower lip to fight the tears that want to come. The phone rings. *Someone calling to wish us Happy Diwali?* "We take care of each other, Ma. Who else can you trust, heh? The police? Nobody helps anybody but themselves, Ma."

The phone stops ringing, and the fireworks outside continue cracking. Jasu comes into the living room. "Kavita . . . ," he says quietly.

Jasu never uses her full name. She looks up.

He does not appear fazed by the sight of his son, shirtless and bloody. He looks directly at her. "It's your mother."

37

TRUE INDIAN BEAUTY

Mumbai, India—2004
ASHA

"ASHA, *BETI*," HER GRANDMOTHER SAYS ACROSS THE TABLE OVER breakfast. "We are attending a big wedding this weekend. The Rajaj girl is getting married. You've heard of the Rajaj family? They make nearly every auto-rickshaw and motor scooter in all of India. Anyway, it will be a lovely time, and I've asked Priya to come this afternoon to take you to Kala Niketan to choose something to wear. A nice *salwar khameez* or perhaps a *lengha*?"

"Oh, that's okay," Asha says, "I don't want to impose, since I don't know them. You guys go ahead. I don't mind staying home."

"What impose? Nonsense!" Dadima says. "The family is invited and you are family, no? If we have twelve people or if we have thirteen people makes no difference. There will be thousands of guests there. Besides, I want you to see this. A true Mumbai wedding. Very fancy. So be sure to choose something special, *achha*? Something . . . colorful," she says, glancing at Asha's tan cargo pants and gray T-shirt. "Priya will come fetch you after lunch."

"Okay, Dadima." After only a few weeks, Asha has learned when not to argue with her grandmother. She is a formidable woman, exuding strength in everything she does, yet she shows pure tenderness toward Asha. It helps her see her father in a new light, as the boy who was raised and shaped by this woman. She can even see echoes of her dad in Dadima's smile. She really hopes her parents come to visit, though her father didn't mention anything during their last phone call. Her mother spoke up only at the end, to ask if Asha was taking her weekly malaria pill.

"HELLO, ASHA? WHERE ARE YOU?" PRIYA CALLS OUT, WALKING down the main hallway of the flat. She stops at the door of Asha's room, dressed in a sleeveless chiffon *salwar khameez* the color of mango sherbet and holding sunglasses in one hand. Her black hair hangs thick and straight to her shoulders, its henna tint glowing reddish in the sunlight. "Ah, there you are! Ready?" Priya flashes a confident smile and links her arm through Asha's. "We'll find you something *gorgeous* for the wedding. Strict instructions from Dadima."

Thirty minutes later, stepping into the sari shop, Asha is thankful to have Priya by her side. When her cousin sent the driver off with directions to return in two hours, Asha was baffled, but now she can see why this will take some time. The entire perimeter of the store is lined from floor to ceiling with shelves holding thousands of saris in every hue and fabric imaginable, a rainbow wonderland. The shop caters exclusively to women's fashion but employs only men. One of them engages Priya immediately, clearly having deduced who's in charge of this expedition. He points to bright bolts of fabric stacked on the shelves, talking without pause like an auctioneer, until Priya holds up her hand to silence him. Then, with a few curtly administered directions, she proceeds to navigate their way through the overwhelming selection.

"*Kanjeevaram bathau! Nai, chiffon nai. Tissue silk layavo!* Pistachio green, pastel colors?" As Priya issues her rapid commands, the man behind the counter unfolds the piles of silky fabric in front of them, pointing out the elaborate borders sewn with gold or silver thread in detailed patterns of paisley and peacocks. Asha sees each sari for a few seconds before it is buried beneath the next one. She catches only the odd word, watching in astonishment the quick-fire volley between her cousin, the man behind the counter, and his two clerks, who dart back and forth to distant parts of the store to retrieve armfuls of new saris.

No one asks Asha for her opinion, nor could she proffer one. Another clerk presents them with stainless steel tumblers of steamy fragrant *chai*. Asha, accepting her incidental role, busies herself with alternately sipping and blowing on her tea to keep a skin from forming on its surface. Periodically, she glances around the store, where every few feet an elegant mannequin with a black updo and feline eyes stands with perfect posture and a gracefully extended arm holding her sari. This is the quintessential garment for women across India, according to Asha's research, a six-yard rectangle of fabric wrapped and tucked around the body without a single button, hook, or zipper. It can be draped in a number of different ways, depending on the region, and one size is used to fit women tall and short, fat and thin. It all sounded very democratic when Asha read about it, but the smiling mannequins now seem intimidating.

Finally, Priya turns to her and says, "Okay, Asha, I've made a few selections. Tell me if you like any of these." When Asha glances down at the glass countertop, she sees most of the saris have been pushed to a big pile on the side and two are displayed in front of her. "This one is tissue silk," Priya says, showing her a papery thin pale green bundle with delicate gold beading. "Tissue is the latest thing. Very modern. You *cannot* be plump and wear tissue silk, it is too fluffy. You have to be thin like a rail," she says, holding up a pinkie finger. "This color would look lovely on you." She holds it up to Asha's chest.

"It is beautiful." Asha wonders if she is rail-thin enough to carry off the tissue sari.

"And this one is more traditional, very elegant," Priya says, sliding her hand over a deep-gold-colored lustrous sari with a dark red and gold border. "It has a bit of a shine to it. Good for night-time. The silk is a little slippery, but we could pin it in place. You could wear it with a gold and ruby choker. Dadima has the *perfect* one."

Asha pictures the six yards of slippery gold silk sliding off her into a puddle at her feet. "I don't know, Priya. They're beautiful, but . . . I've never actually worn a sari before," Asha admits quietly. "I'm not sure I can do it." She gestures helplessly to the nearest mannequin. "Is there something a little less complicated I can wear?"

Priya looks at her for a moment, head tilted to one side, an indiscernible expression on her face. Asha feels a rush of warmth to her face, ashamed she can't do this.

Suddenly Priya stands up, waves her sunglasses, and says to the men behind the counter, "*Achha, challo,* let's go upstairs. Show us some *lenghas* please. Wedding *lenghas*. Only your best ones. *Jaldi.*" Priya heads for the staircase, and Asha follows her upstairs. A *lengha,* Asha learns, is a two-piece gown comprised of an ankle-length drawstring skirt and matching top. There doesn't seem to be the same risk of it falling off, though the long skirt looks like it might trip her up. Priya selects one in a deep rose satin topped with a layer of sheer organza, the sleeveless tunic studded with shimmery silver beading. Asha agrees to try it on.

Standing alone in front of a narrow mirror behind a flimsy curtain, Asha is taken aback by the extravagance of the outfit. The *lengha* looks like something you might see at the Oscars or at a beauty pageant. She feels awkward, as if she has been caught wearing a Halloween costume on the wrong day. It feels uncomfortable on her body.

It hangs heavily upon her, the drawstring of the skirt cutting into her belly. It is itchy at her neckline, the metallic thread and beads irritating her skin.

"It's perfect!" Priya says, poking her head behind the curtain. "Look at you, a true Indian beauty! What do you think?"

"Fine," Asha says, relieved to get back into her cargo pants. "Let's go."

"WE'RE HEADED TO THAM'S RIGHT NOW. COME, MEET US. WE'LL go for dinner afterward," Priya says into her mobile phone as they leave the sari shop. "That was Bindu," she explains to Asha as they slide into the backseat of the car. She directs the driver and replaces her sunglasses.

"Who's Tham?" Asha holds on her lap a string-tied red box containing her new *lengha*.

"Not who, *bena*, what? Tham's is only the best beauty salon this side of Mumbai. I'm taking you for waxing, Asha."

"Waxing?"

"*Hahn, bena,* waxing. Your arms?" she says, raising an eyebrow above the rim of her sunglasses. "Your *lengha* is sleeveless, *yaar,* you can't show all this." Priya points to the hair covering Asha's arms.

"So, you *wax* your arms? Can you do that?" Asha asks, incredulous her cousin might have a solution for this embarrassing problem she has suffered from her whole life.

Priya throws her head back and laughs. "Are you kidding? I get everything waxed—arms, legs, face. I go every three weeks to Tham's, and I'm telling you, they practically wax me from head to toe. You've never done it?" Now it is Priya's turn for disbelief. "I can't believe it. Everyone here does it, *bena,* as common as coconuts at a *puja,*" she says.

"Doesn't it hurt?" Asha asks.

Priya shrugs her shoulders. "Not really. A little, I suppose, but you get used to it," she says, as if this is wholly beside the point.

One hour later, Asha is not sure she can be as dismissive of the pain involved in waxing. She is, however, very pleased with her resulting smooth arms, now fragrant with rose petal lotion. Tham's is filled with Indian women, most of them young like Asha and her cousins, but older ones as well. Just as Priya described, many of the women appear to be spending the day here, getting one treatment after another—waxing, threading, bleaching, plucking. Everyone here is completely comfortable discussing the bodily issues that have secretly haunted Asha since puberty. Bushy eyebrows, hairy arms, and splotchy skin are simply common annoyances to be treated here at Tham's. It doesn't take too much prodding from Bindu and Priya to convince Asha to give eyebrow threading a try. Since it appears no needles, razors, or hot wax are involved in this procedure, Asha concludes the pain must be negligible.

She is only partially correct. She is told to slide down in a salon chair until the back of her head rests on the top of the chair. The stylist, with a nameplate that says KITTY pinned to her white smock, instructs Asha to close one eye and hold the skin above and below it taut with her fingers. Kitty holds a long piece of thread looped between her fingers and her mouth, and begins bobbing her head uncomfortably close to Asha's. The vibrating thread burns against Asha's brow bone and causes a tickling sensation in her nose. Kitty stops a few times when the thread breaks, and a few more times for Asha to sneeze. Thankfully, the whole thing is over within ten minutes. Asha sits back upright in the chair, her eyes watering as Kitty hands her a mirror with which to inspect her freshly sculpted eyebrows. Kitty turns to Priya and says something in Hindi, which her cousin seems to acknowledge with a sideways bobbing of her head.

"What did she say?" Asha asks.

"She said you had a lot of hair. Don't wait so long next time and it won't hurt as much."

THEY SIT TOGETHER—ASHA, PRIYA, AND BINDU—IN A SMALL vinyl-covered booth at China Garden, famous for its Indian-style Chinese food. Bindu passes a plate of sweet and sour chicken to Asha as she and Priya discuss the upcoming wedding. Asha has learned all of her cousins, and even some of their parents, consume "nonveg" food when they dine out, though they still maintain the unspoken illusion of being complete vegetarians at Dadima's home.

"I heard the *jamai* procession has six white horses, one for each of the male cousins, and the groom himself is coming in a white Rolls-Royce," Bindu whispers across the table. Asha takes a bite of the chicken, which tastes far more spicy than either sweet or sour to her.

Priya nods her head while biting into a spring roll. "*Arre,* some-one told me they're spending close to a *crore*. They're planning to feed ten thousand people!" Priya explains to Asha. "A *crore* is one hundred *lakh,*" and then she whispers, "ten million rupees."

"The bride is wearing eight carats of diamonds in her necklace alone, not to mention the earrings and nosepiece. She is changing between three different sets—diamond, emerald, and ruby. And thirty bangles of twenty-two-karat gold on each arm. They'll need one security guard just for her jewelry." Bindu grins and pours more green tea for all of them.

"You came at a good time, Asha," Priya says. "This is going to be the wedding of the year. Lots of eligible bachelors there." Priya winks at her over the fried rice, and all three of them dissolve into the giggles of a bunch of old girlfriends. Asha laughs so hard that green tea comes out of her nose, and tears from the corners of her eyes.

BEFORE GOING TO SLEEP, ASHA CHRONICLES THE DAY'S EVENTS in her journal. She is surprised by her own discovery that, although the food may be spicy, the clothes uncomfortable, and the beauty treatments painful, this place is starting to feel like home, and these people like family.

38

SLIPPING AWAY

Menlo Park, California—2004
SOMER

SOMER INWARDLY COMMENDS HERSELF FOR COOKING THE chicken perfectly, as she knows the praise will not come from Kris. Since Asha left for India last month, all the conflicts they had spent years repressing erupted freely, living with abandon under their roof, a thousand disturbing houseguests. Somer has struggled to understand why Asha made the choice she did. She's tried to let go of her anger toward Krishnan, but his complicity lingers in her mind.

Kris takes several bites without comment, and then speaks with his mouth full. "We need to decide about India. Asha's going to keep asking until we give her a date." Looking up, she notices the Tabasco bottle next to his plate. He has a habit of dousing everything she cooks with some kind of hot sauce, one of the varied assortment he keeps in the fridge. It's as if he means to obliterate any delicate flavor she tries to impart to her cooking—a touch of rubbed sage on the chicken, lemon-scented rice—all of it lost under his red blanket of heat. She pokes her fork at the wandering green beans on her plate. "I can't just pick up and go to India on a moment's notice, I only have a week off over the holidays—"

"Just get someone to cover, Somer. They'll get by without you."
She bristles at the remark, though she should be used to it, his being
dismissive of her work, as if anything less than the brain-saving sur-
geries he performs is unworthy medical practice. Kris removes his
glasses and begins rubbing them with his handkerchief. "I don't see
what the big deal is. It's the perfect time to go. Asha's there, her first
trip, my whole family's there. I haven't been in nearly a decade. You
haven't been in . . . God knows how long. Why wouldn't we go now,
Somer? I thought you were worried about her, I thought you'd want
to keep an eye on her."

Of course Somer wants to see her daughter, but she is not sure
Asha feels the same. She thinks of the fight they had just before Asha
left, and the awkwardness at the airport. Her daughter has been pushing her away ever since she made her decision to go to India. The
idea of seeing her there, in that country that brings to mind only difficult memories, is hard to abide. She already feels like an outsider in
her own family, this family to whom she has given her whole life.
She doesn't have the strength to go to India now and feel out of place
in a country full of strangers.

"I haven't seen my family in eight years," Kris says, his voice getting louder. "Eight years, Somer. My parents are getting older, my
nephews are growing up. I should have gone earlier, but now will have
to do." Kris pours himself more Cabernet and sits back in his chair.

"Don't make it sound like it's my fault," she says. "You've always
come and gone as you've pleased. I haven't stopped you from going.
That's your own damn fault." He snorts and takes a deep swig of
wine. "It's harder for me, Kris. You know that," she says. "I don't
have a connection like you do, it's different. You don't know what it
feels like."

"What do you mean, you don't have a connection?" Krishnan
says. "Your husband is Indian, and your daughter is Indian, in case
you've forgotten."

"You know what I mean," she says, pressing her eyes closed and rubbing her forehead.

"No, I don't. Why don't you explain it to me? The way I see it, there are only a couple of explanations. Either you have a problem with Asha getting to know my family, which is also her family, I remind you. Or you have a problem with her becoming a little bit Indian. In either case, Somer, the problem is actually yours, not hers. We've done a damn good job raising her. But now she's an adult, and you can't control everything she does. You're always the one saying we should accept her as she is, we should support her interests. For God's sake, at her age, I moved halfway across the world and my parents didn't fall apart."

"It's not quite the same," Somer says, tears forming at the corners of her eyes.

"Oh yeah? How's that?" His wry smile does little to veil the cruelty in his eyes.

Because they were your only parents. They didn't have to worry about losing you. "It just is," she says, the only words she can speak out loud.

"It's different because I came to this fantastic country, full of milk and honey that no one would ever want to leave? Is that it?"

She shakes her head and the tears spill out of her eyes. She can't find the words to make him understand, to penetrate the impassive look in his eyes.

When he finally speaks again, his voice is calm. "I'm leaving December twenty-eighth, if you want to come." Every word out of his mouth cuts as precisely as a scalpel. She looks up at him in disbelief while he continues. "Yes, I bought tickets. It gets very booked up at this time of year, I didn't want to take chances."

She feels the hollowness expand to fill her stomach. "When . . . did you do that?"

"Why does it matter?" he snaps, and then takes a drink. "September. After Asha left."

"So, that's it? It's all decided then." It is now clear. She has no voice in this decision, just as she had no choice in Asha's.

"That's it." He stands up and carries his plate to the sink, where his silverware clangs against the basin. "Come if you want. Or don't. Maybe it's better that way."

THE NEXT DAY FEELS SURREAL. SOMER SEES HER PATIENTS, CONsults their charts, writes prescriptions. She goes through the same motions as every other day, but something has shifted. It feels as if someone has picked up her world and tilted it off its axis. Everything familiar to her is slipping away. Kris and Asha not only don't need her, but they also can't seem to tolerate her in their lives any longer, betraying her to make their plans.

At lunch, she walks the few blocks to Whole Foods and picks up her usual boxed salad and lemonade. On her way out of the store, she pauses in front of the community bulletin board. She scans the postings for dog walkers and garage sales until she sees one advertising a Palo Alto sublet. She tears off one of the dangling phone numbers and slips it into her purse. She calls and arranges it all quickly before she can change her mind.

That evening, she tells Krishnan she will not go with him. That it may be a good idea to each have their own space, just for a while, a few months. They agree Asha doesn't need to know. Somer is prepared to say more, but she is surprised at how unsurprised he seems.

"I hope you can find a way to be happy, Somer," is all he says. After he goes upstairs, Somer stays on the couch in the family room and weeps. The next morning, she begins to pack.

39

A PROMISE

Mumbai, India—2004
ASHA

DADIMA INSISTS ASHA ATTEND THE BRIDE'S *MEHNDI* CEREMONY with her cousins, though she herself is not going. "I am an old lady, these things are not for me. You girls go and enjoy."

Priya brings Asha a pale blue chiffon *salwar khameez,* thankfully less ostentatious than the outfit they purchased for the wedding. On their way to the party, Priya explains the *mehndi* is only for women, close family and friends who gather before the wedding to decorate the bride's hands and feet with henna. The Thakkars are invited because Dadima's mother was good friends with Mrs. Rajaj's mother from their days in Santa Cruz, though both women are long since deceased.

When they arrive at the palatial Rajaj home, Asha discovers that the allegedly intimate nature of the *mehndi* means this evening's guests will number only in the hundreds, rather than the thousands who will attend the wedding. Inside the vast marble foyer, there are musicians playing lively Indian music, a harmonium player and a *tabla* drummer. In the distance, Asha sees a dining table set with a magnificent buffet of silver dishes and begins to drift in that direction. Priya catches her by the arm and whispers, "First, we must say hello," nodding slightly with her chin in the direction of the grand living room. The bride is seated on a thronelike chair atop a raised platform. One woman sits at her feet, another works on her hands. Each of them holds a small plastic cone filled with olive green paste. As she draws closer, Asha sees the women are creating designs on the bride's skin that are indescribably intricate—a flowering branch climbing up the back of her hand and over to her palm, which is covered in swirls and spirals. Even more impressive, both *mehndi* artists appear to be drawing freehand, without looking at anything. In fact, they carry on a conversation with each other and the guests all the while.

"Come on now, make sure it's nice and dark." One of the bride's friends teases the hand artist. "We want the *mehndi* to last a good long time!"

"And make sure you make the initials as small as possible. We want him to really look hard." Another friend laughs, kissing the bride on her head.

Priya guides Asha toward a cluster of older women as she explains, "It's a tradition on the wedding night, the groom has to find his initials hidden in the design before the bride will let him . . . you know." Priya smiles and winks. "Come, here she is."

"Manjula Auntie!" Priya presses her palms together and bows slightly to one of the older women, swaddled in a burgundy silk sari, her artificially jet-black hair tied neatly into a bun. "Dadima sends her regards she couldn't come tonight. This is my cousin from America," she says, quickly turning to present Asha. "She's just arrived. She's come on a special scholarship. From America. Very prestigious."

"Hello, *namaste.*" Asha tries to emulate her cousin's easy way. "Nice to meet you."

"Welcome, *betis*. So nice to have you," Manjula Auntie says, taking Asha's hands in her own plump ones. "Are you enjoying your time here? I do hope you will come tomorrow—we have a charter boat sailing around the harbor. I always say, that's always the best way to see the lights of Mumbai at night, far away from the pollution!" She laughs heartily at her own joke, causing ripples through the belly rolls of fat exposed by her sari. "Please, help yourself to food. There is so much of it," she says before excusing herself to greet another guest.

"Okay, that's done," Priya says and they head off to the buffet table. On the way over, Asha sees two more *mehndi* artists creating less elaborate, but still beautiful, designs on the hands and feet of other guests. Asha piles her china plate with *samosas, kachori,* and *pakora,* but is sparing with the assorted chutneys, having learned these tend to be too spicy for her. She reflects on Manjula Auntie's comment about the harbor cruise and Mumbai's pollution. She's noticed the thick blanket of smog that covers the city most days and finds herself coughing quite often outside, but it also seems most of the fumes are emitted from the auto rickshaws and scooters that bear the Rajaj name. Manjula Auntie, old family friend, also happens to be quite the hypocrite. While they stroll around the vast house, Asha discreetly checks out the large marble statues of Indian gods and heavily embroidered tapestries that line the wall. Priya introduces her to several other women, but Asha misses much of the quick Gujarati banter among them.

Asha eats and watches the *mehndi* artists demonstrate their handiwork. When one of the artists is free, Priya nudges her forward. "Something simple," Asha says, "like that, maybe." She points to a sun design worn by another girl. In under five minutes, both of Asha's palms are adorned with radiant spheres. The *mehndi* artist applies a layer of lemon juice and then oil to the design after it dries, and tells her to leave it on for as long as possible for a dark stain. In the morning, she is fascinated by the beautiful red designs left behind

after she scrapes off the dried mudlike material, and can't stop looking at her own hands all day.

THE WEDDING TAKES PLACE TWO NIGHTS LATER. AS SOON AS
Asha walks through the gates of the Cricket Club of India, she stops
cold at the sight before her. The entire grounds, perhaps the size of
two football fields, are covered in luxurious furnishings that have
been transported here for the occasion: ornate chaise lounges, carved
tables, silk pillows, tented ceilings draped delicately overhead. It looks
like an enormous outdoor palace. There are thousands of guests milling about, and an almost equivalent number of servers holding silver
trays of food and drinks. Asha's concerns about looking too flashy
in her new *lengha* are supplanted by the realization that she is rather
underdressed compared to other women, draped in lustrous saris and
dripping with jewelry.

"Come on, *yaar,*" Priya says, grabbing her by the elbow. "Close
your mouth, you look like you've never been to an Indian wedding
before!" Asha follows her cousins around mutely for a while, staring
in wonderment at the transformation of the cricket field. She wonders whether her parents' wedding was like this, and then remembers
the framed photo that hangs in their bedroom, of her mother in a
simple sundress and her father in a suit at Golden Gate Park.

". . . And this is Asha, my American cousin. She's not only beautiful, but brilliant too," Priya says, nudging her in the ribs. Asha
shifts her attention to see an extended hand in front of her, and follows it all the way to its owner. Her eyes widen at the sight of him.

"Nice to meet you. I'm Sanjay," he says with a British lilt in his
voice.

"Yeah, me too. I'm Asha."

"Yes, I know, Priya just told me. That's a lovely name, do you
know its meaning?"

Yes, of course I do. I've only been told by my parents a thousand times. But she shakes her head mutely, hoping he will keep talking in his intoxicating voice.

"Hope. Your parents must have had big dreams for you." He smiles, and Asha feels her legs wobble.

"Yeah." *Shit.* Why can't she say anything else? She notices his eyes are the color of soft caramel. From the corner of her eye, she sees Priya and Bindu are already steps away.

"Just get some food . . . come right back," Priya says with a wink.

"So, from America? Do you come here often to visit your family?" Sanjay says.

"Well, actually, this is my first trip," Asha says, finally recovering her ability to speak. "How about you? Are you from . . . England?"

"No, no. I'm a native Mumbaiite, born and raised just a few blocks from here. But I've been in England the past six years for university and graduate school."

"Graduate school—for what?" She catches herself sounding like a reporter, but his easy smile reassures her.

"London School of Economics. I'm getting my master's and then I hope to work someplace like the World Bank. That is, if my father doesn't rope me into the family business first. How about you?"

"I'm in college, a place called Brown University in the United States. I'm here on a fellowship to do a project."

"And what's your project?"

"I'm doing a story on children living in poverty—in the slums, like Dharavi." His eyes widen. "What, are you going to tell me to be careful, like everyone else?" she says.

"No." He takes a sip of his drink. "I'm sure an intelligent woman like you understands the dangers." His smile radiates heat that makes her feel like she's melting. "So what have you learned so far?" Their conversation flows easily from there. At some point, they wander over to the buffet table, which features at least fifty varieties of food. He carries her plate over to one of the velvet sofas where they sit down. He eats with his hands and encourages her to do the same. They talk about the upcoming elections in the United States, the conversion to the euro, and the World Cup. He laughs easily at her jokes, and makes sure her glass is always filled. The evening passes quickly, and she begins looking around for her cousins.

"So, tell me. You said this was your first trip to India. Why haven't you come before?" Sanjay asks, his arm resting loosely on the back of the couch behind her.

His relaxed confidence has been contagious all evening, quelling the reporter in her. It feels as if he knows her already, and nothing she says can surprise him. Even so, she's not ready to talk about this. She swallows and pushes a strand of hair behind her ear. "That is a long story, too long to get into tonight. I'll tell you another time."

"Promise?" he says.

Her stomach flips over. "Promise." She extends her hand, and instead of shaking it, he raises it to his lips and kisses it lightly, then covers it with his other hand. When she takes her hand back, she sees he's left a card there, bearing his name and phone number.

Bindu and Priya appear next to her, as if on cue. "There you are. We've been looking for you. Absolutely impossible to find someone in this place. Madness." Priya wears a sly smile.

They say their farewells, and as Asha turns to leave, Sanjay touches her arm. "Remember." He smiles. "A promise is a promise."

On the way home, while her cousins tease her about Sanjay, Asha reflects on his question, which she can't answer because she doesn't know herself.

40

SEPARATE

Palo Alto, California—2004
SOMER

ON A FRIDAY AFTERNOON IN NOVEMBER, SOMER IS INVITED BY
Liza, another doctor at the clinic, to join a few colleagues for a drink
after work. In no hurry to return to her apartment, a sublet from a
graduate student in Madrid for the year, she agrees. The sparsely furnished one-bedroom apartment on a quiet tree-lined street a few
blocks from campus is unremarkable, featuring the beige carpets and
neutral walls characteristic of such rentals. Somer expected the place
to give her a sense of freedom, unencumbered by the constant presence of Krishnan and his things. But each day when she returns to it,
it simply feels empty.

They go to a wine bar in Palo Alto, one of the hip new places
that have been built here since Somer was in medical school twenty-
five years ago. Liza orders a glass of Shiraz and Somer, overwhelmed
by the selection, asks for the same. Somer doesn't know Liza well,
other than that she's single and an avid yoga practitioner, often showing up at work with a purple mat rolled under her arm. The clinic
doctors gather once a month for their staff meeting, but otherwise

rush past each other in the hallways. At fifty-two, Somer is one of the older doctors in the group and the most tenured, having been there for over fifteen years. The relentless pace of the clinic, combined with the unpredictable clientele and dismal pay, leads to high turn-over among the younger ambitious doctors.

Somer takes a sip of her wine and notices her colleagues seem able to shift from work to relaxation mode easily, shedding their white coats and swirling their wineglasses. Liza, whose hair is nor-mally pulled back in a low ponytail, now wears it loose around her face. From the wiry gray strands in her dark curls and the lines etched around her eyes, she looks to be in her late forties, a few years younger than Somer. The conversation circulates through the predictable topics of eccentric patients, ornery nurses, and the recent election debacle. After the first glass of wine, most of the group excuse them-selves to get home to waiting families.

"Well, I'm in no hurry." Liza slides down the now-empty wooden bench toward Somer. "I left food out for my cat this morning. How about you?"

"Nope, I have nowhere to be either," Somer answers, draining the last of the wine from her glass. She cannot bring herself to admit she and Kris are separated. It has only been a few weeks, and she is not yet used to the idea of living alone: she still makes too much cof-fee for one person in the morning and keeps the TV on all evening to compensate for the silence of the apartment. All her friends from medical school and the neighborhood are really their friends as a couple, and Somer hasn't told them either.

"Great, another glass then," Liza says to the waiter.

Somer watches, mesmerized, as the rich claret-colored liquid fills her glass again. Her head begins to feel pleasantly light.

"Hey," Liza says, lowering her voice. "I was sorry to hear about the director position. I was sure you'd get the job. You've been there longer than anyone, and the staff loves you."

"Yes, well, they found someone with more administrative experience, someone who's actually been doing it full force for twenty years, not half-assed like I have." Somer knows she shouldn't say this, but she was disappointed about the promotion, and it feels good to finally talk to someone about it.

"Do you know anything about the guy they hired?"

Somer shakes her head. "Just that he's coming from Berkeley." She had been flattered when her retiring boss suggested she throw her hat in the ring. For a while, she allowed herself to be intrigued with the idea of focusing on her work again, investing herself in something new.

"So, what are your plans for the holidays, Somer?"

"I'm going down to San Diego to see my parents." She wonders if it is possible this glass of wine tastes better than the first.

"That'll be nice. Does your family go there every year?"

"My . . . no, actually." Somer feels so warm all over, the rest of it comes tumbling out. "I'm going alone. My husband is going to India to visit his family. And our daughter, who's there right now." Somer takes another deep sip of her wine and continues. "I didn't want to go, but my husband was really stubborn about it, so . . ." She shakes her head. "It'll be good to have some time away from him. You're lucky you're not married, it's not all it's cracked up to be." Somer's laugh sounds a little loud for the small wood-paneled room, even to her.

"Well, I was married, actually," Liza says, "for six years. I got divorced ten years ago. No kids, thankfully. At least that made the breakup easier. And how about the kids part of it? Is that all it's cracked up to be?"

"Hmm." Somer considers this. "Normally I would say yes, but that seems like a very complicated question right now."

"That's fair. I always feel compelled to ask, since that's the reason—well, the main reason—my husband and I split up."

"He didn't want kids?" Somer says.

"No, he did, actually. Very much so. I didn't," Liza says. "I never had that driving desire to be a mother, and I started seeing what it did to my friends. It changed their marriages, their careers. It changed . . . them. They weren't the same people anymore, they were like empty shells of their former selves." Liza runs her index finger around the rim of the glass. "Maybe I'm selfish, but I really like who I am, and I didn't want to lose all that. I like staying in shape. My career's impor-tant to me. I didn't want to give up traveling for ten years. I just looked ahead to a life with children and didn't think I'd be happy with the trade-offs." Liza shrugs her shoulders. "I guess it's not for everyone."

"Do you still think it was the right choice?" Somer asks before she can stop herself.

"Sometimes I wonder," Liza says. "But most of the time, I'm really happy with my life. I love my job, my weekends are my own, I get to travel . . . By the way, I'm planning a trip to Italy next spring with a few friends, and my sister just canceled because she's having knee surgery. If you're interested in coming along, it'll be a great trip—bicycling in Tuscany, delicious food, great wine. Just the girls." Liza smiles as she lifts the glass to her lips.

"Hmmm. That's tempting. Especially the part about leaving my husband behind." Somer drains the rest of her wine, the warmth now spreading all over her body.

"You know, I'm meeting my Italy friends for dinner tonight at that new Singaporean restaurant. Why don't you join us, if you don't have plans?"

LATER, OVER PLATES OF CRISPY CALAMARI AND SATAY SKEWERS, Somer meets Liza's friends, both single women in their forties. "I'm Sundari," one of them says. She wears her sun-bleached hair in two braids, one resting on each shoulder. "It's my spiritual name," she explains. "It means beautiful in Sanskrit. And Hindi. And my cat is named Buddha. I've got all my bases covered." Sundari smiles as she picks up a menu. "I always forget how hard it is for me to order here. Aren't there any vegans in Singapore?"

"You know," Liza says, "Somer's husband is from India."

"Really?" Sundari puts her menu down. "That is so cool. I love India. I went to New Delhi a few years ago for a friend's wedding. Arranged marriage, the whole thing. They dressed me up in a sari and did the henna on my hands. I loved it. Did you do that? Then I traveled to Agra and saw the Taj Mahal. Such an amazing country. I would love to go back and see more of it. I hear the south is really beautiful. Have you been there? Where is your husband from?"

Somer waits to see if Sundari expects an answer this time, then simply says, "Mumbai."

"You're so lucky. I would love to get married in a sari. For a white girl from Kansas like me, it's all very exciting." Sundari giggles.

A woman in a blue pantsuit arrives at the table looking harried and pulls out a chair. "Can I get a cosmo?" she says to a waiter, not theirs, passing by. "Sorry I'm late, girls. I had a showing at five o'clock, then Justin insisted I read him three books. I only got out of there because I told the sitter he could watch cartoons. Resorting to bribery with my six-year-old, aren't I a great mother?"

"Yes, Gail, you are," Sundari says, holding up her martini glass for a toast. "Especially considering you have to be mother *and* father most of the time."

"Gail, this is my friend Somer," Liza says. "She works at the clinic with me. I'm trying to convince her to join us in Italy next spring."

Gail clinks glasses with Somer across the table. "Great, the more the merrier. I'm still trying to get Tom to take Justin for that week.

My ex," she says for Somer's benefit. "He's such a pain about switching weeks with me, he always has to check with his girlfriend first. I never imagined when I got divorced that my schedule would be at the mercy of the other woman."

"'Tis better to have loved and lost . . . ," Sundari says, with a dreamy look.

"Sundari's our hopeless romantic." Liza shakes her head, smiling.

"Still looking for Mr. Right, if you know any candidates," Sundari says. "Hey, maybe it's time for me to have an arranged marriage."

"Trust me, honey," Gail says after taking a gulp of her drink, "there are no Mr. Rights left, not at our age. The question is, how much wrongness can you tolerate?" She throws her head back and lets out a big laugh, causing the waiter who has just arrived to take a step back.

SOMER AWAKENS THE NEXT MORNING TO A HEAVY ACHE IN HER head and a dry mouth. She rolls over slowly and opens one eye to see her alarm clock showing 10:21 A.M. The aspirin is in the bathroom medicine chest, an unbearable distance away. She moves her head slowly back to the pillow and looks up at the white ceiling, the paint cracking at the corners where it meets the wall. She thinks back to the night before—two glasses of wine at the bar, a few more drinks at the restaurant—more than she's had to drink in a long time. She had a good time with Liza and her friends: they were fun and helped take her mind off things for a while. Still, Somer wouldn't want to trade places with any of them. Liza, who is perfectly happy being child free, as she calls it. Gail, struggling to make a living, raise a child, and manage an ex-husband. And Sundari, still looking for love in her fifth decade but settling for a relationship with a cat named Buddha.

Somer rolls over to escape the sunlight streaming across her pillow. *Too old for a hangover.* Fifty-two. Separated from her husband. Living in a student apartment. Working at the same place so long she's become a fixture but still isn't qualified to be in charge. *Not how I pictured my life.* It seems as if everything she's cared about over the past twenty-five years has disintegrated, oblivious to the time and energy she has invested. She can call herself a physician but can't take the same pride in this she used to. She is not really a wife at the moment, not much of a mother. Somewhere along the way, Somer realizes, she has lost herself.

She can't quite put her finger on when her marriage fell apart. When she thinks of Krishnan now, he hardly seems to be the same man she remembers from Stanford. This Krishnan is impatient and dismissive, like some stereotype of the egotistical neurosurgeon they used to joke about in medical school. He no longer has the tenderness and the innocence he had when he first came here from India. He doesn't need Somer the way he did when she taught him to drive and operate a microwave oven. He hasn't lost himself in her eyes over dinner or held her hand proudly as they walk down the street in a long time.

She tries to remember the last time they were truly happy. Asha's high school graduation? Hawaii, their last real family vacation? At some point after Asha went to college, the distance between her and Krishnan grew. By the time their daughter left for India, they were too far apart. It was as if they stood on opposite sides of a lake, neither of them having the ability to cross the distance between. The angry words they hurled fell like stones to the bottom of the water, leaving ripples of sadness on the surface.

Somer sits up slowly and waits for the pounding in her head to subside before getting out of bed. In the bathroom, she splashes cold water on her face and supports herself on the sink while she retrieves the aspirin from behind the mirror. After closing it again, she catches her reflection, the image of a middle-aged woman. *Fifty-two.* In a few weeks, Krishnan will leave to join Asha in India, and Somer will be left here alone. And although it is her husband who will be boarding the plane to fly away, just as their daughter did months ago, Somer cannot help wondering if she's the one who drove them to do so. If she, in fact, left them first.

41

TWO INDIAS

Mumbai, India—2004
ASHA

"PARAG SPEAKS SIX OF THE TWENTY-ONE MAJOR LANGUAGES IN India, as well as English. You'll need him, Asha." Meena has been insistent they bring a translator into Dharavi today to conduct interviews. "This way you can focus on your questions and getting everything you need. Don't worry, he won't get in your way."

Asha draws in a deep breath and exhales. "Okay." She is nervous, though she's not sure why. She has done her homework. She's researched the *Times* archives and interviewed several city-planning and government officials. Most of them concur about how this enormous urban slum came to be. Dharavi used to be the site of a mangrove swamp until the creek dried up and fishing clans moved away. By then, people were migrating from surrounding villages and towns to Mumbai in search of greater economic opportunity. The city's infrastructure was ill equipped to deal with the huge influx of people, and so Dharavi sprang up, this vast slum vibrating with the hum of misery and human resourcefulness. Asha knows the history, she has collected the statistics and facts. She has the framework of her story in place, but now she needs to add the human element. The personal stories she collects through her interviews will mean the difference between a compelling feature and just another news report.

"You want to record it, right?" Meena asks.

"Yes. Let's take this." Asha takes her handheld video camera. "If you don't mind holding it. That way, I can extract some still images afterward if I want."

"I'll take these too," Meena says, grabbing a bag of *Times*-branded trinkets—notepads, pens, canvas bags. "In case anyone needs a little enticing."

AS IT TURNS OUT, THREE OUTSIDERS ARE ALL THAT'S NECESSARY to attract a crowd, and Asha quickly has to decide whom to speak with first. She is drawn immediately to a little girl with penetrating eyes, and points her out. Meena turns on the camera and Parag approaches her. The girl looks to be about two years old, wears a plain beige cotton dress and a string around her neck. She is barefoot, and her hair is only a quarter-inch long all over her head. She holds the hand of an older girl in braids, whose dull gold nose ring sits in contrast to her dark skin.

"This is Bina, and her younger sister Yashoda." Parag begins translating to Asha, who smiles at the girls and crouches down to their level. "Bina is twelve years old, and Yashoda is three."

"How long have they been here, where did they come from?" Asha holds out her hand to the little girl. Parag translates, and Bina answers back promptly in a bold high-pitched voice.

"She says they arrived here just before the last monsoon season, so that would be about eight or nine months ago. They traveled for two nights to get here from their village," Parag says.

Yashoda is now playing with the rings on Asha's finger, twisting them around and around. "Ask her about their family. What do her parents do?" Asha says.

"Their mother is a house servant, their father works at a clothing factory. They have three brothers—the oldest works with his father, and the younger two are at school."

Asha looks up from her notebook. "Why isn't she at school too? Bina?" Parag stares at Asha in silence. "Ask her. Ask her why she isn't in school." Asha sees Parag hesitate another moment, then glance at Meena before finally turning to Bina. When he asks the question, Bina glances at Asha, and then down at her feet. She answers briefly and Parag translates, "She needs to take care of her sister, to prepare food and wash clothes." Asha is hardly satisfied with this answer but senses from the look shared by Parag and Bina she won't get much more.

"Ask her why her sister's hair is so short," Asha strokes the little girl's head.

"It's probably—" Parag begins.

"I want you to ask her. I want to hear *her* answer."

He turns to Bina, speaks, listens, and then turns back to Asha. "She says it was a problem with bugs," Parag says quietly. Bina is looking down at her feet again, kicking the dirt. Asha swallows hard. Yashoda is still watching Asha with sweet eyes and swinging one of her hands.

"Here," Asha says, crouching down and trying to remove one of the rings from her fingers that are now swollen with heat. Finally, she manages to get one loose from her pinky, a thin silver band with a small purple stone, which she holds out to Yashoda. The little girl looks first to her sister, then back to Asha. She snatches it with delight and throws her arms around Asha's neck.

"Thank you for talking to us," Asha says to Bina, standing up. Parag translates this, and Bina nods at her with a shy smile. Asha finally lets go of Yashoda's small hand.

Asha gestures to Parag and Meena, and they walk on down the settlement. A weary-looking woman, standing in front of a hut and yelling loudly, draws their attention.

"What's she saying?" Asha says.

"She's calling someone—telling her to hurry up," Parag says.

Just then, the woman turns and notices the camera, and walks over to greet them. She and Parag have a polite interchange, and he turns to Asha. "She's taking her child to school. The girl is always running late."

"Oh, cool. Can she talk to us for a minute? How old is her daughter?"

"She has four kids, only two still live here with her . . . one's left for school already this morning, he's thirteen. The one inside, her daughter, is ten."

"Her ten-year-old daughter goes to school? That's great."

"Yes, she says school is very important," Parag translates. "She takes her daughter both ways every day. Otherwise, she wouldn't be able to go."

"What does her husband do?" Asha says.

The woman answers in a single word, which Parag then translates. "He's dead."

Asha jots this in her notebook, uncertain what question could be appropriate after this. In that moment, she sees Meena shift attention behind her, and Asha turns to look. At first glance, Asha thinks she sees a child crawling out of the hut, but in the next horrible second, she realizes the girl is crippled. Both her legs are stumps, and she is propelling herself along the ground on her arms, swinging her torso between them. Asha draws her breath in sharply, and turns her head away from the grotesque sight. When she looks up, Meena is staring at her, nodding for her to continue. Asha turns back to her interview subject just in time to see the woman crouch down and her legless daughter somehow climb onto her back. Parag speaks before Asha can ask another question. "She must leave now, or she'll be late. School is two kilometers away." Parag thanks the woman by putting his palms together, and Asha repeats his gesture. They watch as the woman with the child on her back disappears into the crowd.

Asha feels her head spinning. *Is it the heat?* She tries to breathe deeply, but her nostrils fill with the oppressive stench of sewage and human waste. She shakes her head and turns to Meena. "I'll be back in a minute." She dashes across the street to a newsstand, thankful to get away for a moment. She didn't expect to be so affected by what she saw here today, she thought she was prepared. But all the photos she saw had edges, the film clips were framed by the screen. Here, in Dharavi, the misery goes on and on, pouring out in every direction as far as she can see. The cumulative effect of the putrid smells, oppressive living conditions, and despair in these children's lives has conjured up a deep sense of pity inside her. Asha buys a Limca, the lemon-lime soda for which she has developed a taste. After wiping the mouth of the bottle, she drinks half the soda in a single gulp. A double-decker bus passes before her eyes, and she sees Meena and Parag standing across the street, looking impatient. She needs to pull it together. After draining the bottle, she dashes back to join the others.

"Okay, just had to cool off a bit. I'm ready. Let's go," she says, trying to sound confident. They walk together until Asha stops in front of a shack where a woman stands in a dull green sari. She holds a baby on her hip, and two other young children cling to her legs. Her left arm, between the edge of her sari blouse and her elbow, is covered in charcoal bruises. The woman is intermittently stirring something on the fire and feeding rice to her baby with her fingers. "Will she talk to us?" Asha asks Parag. She watches as they speak, and the woman makes a gesture with her hands and mouth.

"She wants to know, will you give her something . . . some money for food?" Parag says. Asha pulls a fifty-rupee note from her pocket and holds it out. The woman tucks it into the folds of her sari. She flashes a crooked smile, displaying two missing teeth.

Asha takes a deep breath. "Ask her when she came here, and where she came from." Parag and the woman carry on a lengthy conversation, during which she gestures with her one free arm to the shack behind her, and then someplace in the distance.

"She has been here, in this house, since she got married two years ago. She used to live over there"—Parag points to someplace deep within the slum—"with her parents."

"Here, in Dharavi? How long did she live here with her parents?" Asha didn't think this was a place people lived for generations. The government officials made it sound like a temporary stopping ground.

"Since she was a child, as long as she can remember," Parag relays. "She says this house is better than her parents'. Here, it's just her husband and kids. There, it was eight or ten people." Parag communicates this information as if he's reporting on the weather, as if there's nothing shocking about its content. Asha considers if he might be doing it intentionally, to irritate her.

"Does she like . . . is she happy living here?" Asha asks. She knows it's an absurd question for a woman who's spent her whole life in the slums, but she can't think of a better one.

"She says it's fine. She would like to live in a proper home one day, but now there is not enough money."

Asha thinks of the fifty-rupee note now tucked into the woman's sari, and the dozen more still in her own pocket, a grand total of ten American dollars. "What does her husband do?"

"He worked as a rickshaw driver," Parag says, then pauses to hear the rest of the woman's answer and continues. "He used to share driving shifts with another man, but he lost his job two months ago because he was getting drunk and showing up late."

"What do they do for money, then?"

When Parag translates the question, the woman looks down at the pot on the fire. She puts the baby down on the ground, who promptly runs off with the other children. Her tone is muted when she answers. "She goes to the brothel in the evening," Parag says. "There's one just down the road. She can make a hundred rupees a night, for a few hours' work, then she comes home. She says she won't take her children, she leaves them with a neighbor. She doesn't want them to see that place, to see what goes on. She doesn't want them to know."

Asha swallows hard as she takes this in. "Is that enough? A hundred rupees? I mean—"

"She says it's enough to feed her family. If her husband gets a job, she won't have to go there anymore."

Asha feels dizzy again, unsure what to ask now and not convinced she can handle any more. She looks at Meena, who nods her on. She scans the list of questions in her notebook and blinks hard, trying to focus. "How old is she?" she says, stalling. He turns to the woman, whose children are back and pulling on her sari. The woman leans down to pick up the baby.

"Twenty," comes the answer. Asha shudders involuntarily as she looks at this woman who lives in squalor, prostituting herself to survive. She has spent her entire life in this place. She has three young children, a drunkard husband, and little hope of a different future.

She and Asha are the same age.

THEY SIT IN SILENCE ON THE DRIVE BACK TO THE OFFICE. ASHA'S mind is reeling with images of the faces she's just seen, the inconceivable stories she has heard. She can feel Meena's eyes on her.

"How do you feel about that?" Meena says. The question is gentler than Asha expected.

Can she say she's horrified people live like that in this country? That some little girls never even get the chance to go to school because they're doing housework at the age of three? That everyone else seems to think a child missing both legs is not uncommon? "I think it was a good start," Asha says. "What did you think?"

"I think you did well, all told. We found some good stories, very typical of life in Dharavi. Anything you missed, that you'd like to get next time?" Meena says.

"We didn't talk to any boys. Or men. I didn't really see any." Asha looks out the window at the full sidewalks. "Why is it that whenever I walk outside, the streets seem to be full of men, but at Dharavi today, all we saw were women?"

"Asha," Meena says, "just as there are two Indias for the rich and the poor, there are two Indias for men and women. A woman's domain is of the home—she takes care of the family, manages the servants. A man's domain is of the world—working, eating at restaurants. That is why, when you walk on the streets as a woman here, you can feel like a minority. It's the men who are out and about. And sometimes they like to taunt those of us who dare to venture out."

Asha thinks of the catcalls and leering men she sometimes encounters on the streets that make her want to use the self-defense moves she learned in her dorm workshop.

"Also, it's not just perception, it is also a fact. We are a minority in this country. You know the birth rates are all bungled up in India, don't you? We have something like nine hundred fifty girls born for every one thousand boys." Meena stares straight ahead. "Mother India does not love all her children equally, it seems."

42

ONLY ONE REGRET

Mumbai, India—2004
JASU

JASU WAKES IN THE MORNING, EXHAUSTED BEFORE HIS DAY HAS even begun. Last night again, he awoke in a panic, bolting straight upright in bed, his arms reaching out to grab the elusive shovel that always disappears when he opens his eyes. He woke up panting, his heart racing, with his face and chest drenched in sweat. Kavita put a cold cloth on his forehead and tried to soothe him back to sleep. Nothing she does or he tries to tell himself is ever enough. He will have to make a visit to the temple today before going to the factory.

He runs and hops on the train just as it's beginning to move. This morning, he feels his age and for a moment fears he might slip off the bottom step of the train. It is hard to believe he has been riding this train nearly every day since coming to Mumbai fourteen years ago. He shrinks from the memory of how little he knew then about the ways of this city and the hardships he would face. Sometimes he sees himself in the faces of the newly arrived: the men dressed in village garments who show up at the textile factory every day asking for a job. As the foreman, he is now the one who must turn away so many of them, knowing his decision means their families may not eat that night. When he looks into the eyes of these men, Jasu recognizes the pressures they face and the fears they suffer. They have all come here, as he did, with the expectation this city would bring riches and abundance, but they have found something else entirely.

Last week, one young man came to the back door wearing a ragged shirt and nothing on his feet. Standing behind him were his four children and pregnant wife. They had no place to stay, he told Jasu. He nearly broke down when Jasu told him there were no jobs at the factory. "Please, Sahib, please," he begged, speaking to Jasu in a quiet voice so his family would not hear his desperation. "I will do anything you need, anything. Sweep floors? Clean toilets?" He held his palms together in front of his face, as if in prayer. Jasu would have given him a job if he could, but even as foreman, he had little leeway in these matters. He gave the man a fifty-rupee note and told him to come back in a month. He feels badly when he sees these men, but even more so, he feels fortunate to have avoided their fate. Nearly fifteen years after leaving his home and coming to this strange city, he has a good job, a steady income, a decent home. It hasn't been without hard work, but in the end, he knows much of it has been due to fortune.

There were so many times along the way things might have gone wrong. The injury he sustained years ago could have been much worse. He might have lost a hand or foot like so many others and been forced to beg on the street with the other cripples. That one time he couldn't work, he almost lost himself to drink. He would have frittered away his family's money and his own life were it not for Kavita. Over the years, it has become increasingly clear to him that most of their fortune is really due to her—her strength, her love, her confidence in him. If they'd had more children, he might have ended up like that man in the ragged shirt, desperate to do anything for a few rupees. Of course, if they'd had more children, perhaps he would not have invested all his hopes in Vijay, now destined to lead the life of a criminal. He thinks of all the choices they've made since Vijay's birth, most of them for their son's benefit, and cannot think of a single one he would have made differently. He did everything he thought he should as a father, and still Vijay turned out to be a disappointment. He always thought he knew what was best for his family, but age and experience have humbled him.

Jasu gets off the train at Vikhroli Station and walks in the direction of the small temple a couple of blocks away. He is often drawn here after the nightmares; lately, he has been coming every few days. It is a modest temple—from the outside, it looks like any other building in the neighborhood. He leaves his slippers outside the door and walks past the white marble fountain at the entrance. When he kneels down on the floor and closes his eyes, his mind returns to the one decision he does regret: that horrible night Kavita gave birth to their first baby. It was only a few moments, a split-second decision, but twenty years later, he is still haunted by it. He remembers holding the squirming child in his hands and hearing Kavita's shrieks as he walked away. He handed the baby to his cousin who, it was understood, would dispose of her as quickly as possible. Jasu sat on his haunches outside the hut, smoking a *beedi,* waiting.

When he saw his cousin return from the woods with a shovel in his hand, he knew it was over. Their eyes met for just a moment and shared a horrible understanding. Jasu never learned where the baby was buried. He knew his cousin didn't tell him because he thought Jasu didn't care. The truth was Jasu didn't ask because he couldn't bear to know. He did what was expected of him, what his other cousins had done and his brothers would do. He had barely thought about it as a choice at all until he saw his cousin walking back with that shovel, and then it hit him.

He would not admit to himself for many years that what he had done was wrong, but it was a very long time before he could look into Kavita's wounded eyes again. Only God spared him from committing the same sin again with the second child. When the midwife told him the baby died in her sleep, too weak to survive the first night, he was relieved. Even that mercy didn't lessen the depth of Kavita's mourning. Still, he didn't have the strength to defend her against his family's continued criticism. *Two daughters means she has committed a sin in her past life,* his parents said. They wanted him to throw her out, get a new wife. They forced him to get the ultrasound with the third pregnancy and gave him the money for an abortion on the spot if it was necessary. He knew then, one day they would move out of his parents' house, even if it meant leaving Dahanu, no matter the risks involved. He never wanted to choose between loyalty to his parents and protecting his wife, but they left him no option. Though they came around after the birth of Vijay, Jasu never saw them in the same way again. Even now, when they go back to the village to visit, he cannot look at his cousin without seeing the vision of him walking with that shovel in hand.

He and Kavita have never spoken of that night, not once. He was both too proud and too ashamed. But Jasu knows in the eyes of his wife, and likely those of God as well, he was a monster for what he did. He has spent much of his life trying to make up for that one night, to show Kavita he can be a good man, to prove to God he is worthy of his family. He knows he can't undo the sin he's committed. But he has tried desperately to make it part of his past, and to build a new future: a new city, new home, new work. These things have given him some measure of pride, but they haven't erased the guilt that has weighed on his heart. The nightmares stopped for a while, for a few years when everything was finally going well. Then came that terrible night they came home to find the police ransacking their home.

The nightmares started again and have gotten worse since Vijay's troubles, with Jasu's realization that what was once his main source of pride will instead end up as his life's disappointment.

43

MARINE DRIVE

Mumbai, India—2004
ASHA

ASHA HEARS THE GUTTURAL PURRING OF THE PIGEONS OUTSIDE her window and turns to see the morning light glowing behind the dark cotton curtains. She rolls over and arches her back into a long stretch with a corresponding groan. Despite the loud hum of the air conditioner, she can hear Dadima scattering birdseed on the balcony, as she does every morning. Dadima says the pigeons, in addition to being holy creatures, are her most loyal visitors, keeping her company every single morning of the fifty-some years she's lived in this flat, ever since she married Dadaji and came to live here with his parents.

Dadima described her late mother-in-law as a gentle soul, a religious woman who visited the temple around the corner every morning. Her humility and tender nature made her a great deal easier to get along with than most *sassus,* and Dadima credits this fortune for smoothing over the early years of her marriage. After her in-laws passed away, Dadima inherited the mantle of matriarch of the Thakkar clan. Asha learned this bit of family history from her grandmother on the fourth day they took an early morning walk together.

It is the promise of these conversations that now motivates Asha to drag herself out of bed at such an early hour.

THE FIRST DAY, NEARLY TWO WEEKS AGO, ASHA HAPPENED TO be awake early, thanks to fireworks that had disturbed her sleep the night before. In the morning, when she walked bleary-eyed into the living room, she was surprised to see Dadima sitting at the table drinking tea. "Good morning, *beti*. Care to join me on my walk today? There's a lovely breeze this morning." And so, with nothing better to do at that hour, Asha laced up her running shoes, donned her baseball cap, and walked with her grandmother along Marine Drive, the boardwalk that lines the harbor of Mumbai. It wasn't a vigorous walk, since Dadima shuffled along in her light sari and *chappals,* so it took them almost an hour to get all the way to Nariman Point and back.

On the first day, Dadima pointed out a small white storefront with a green awning. "See there, that ice cream shop? That is where Dadaji used to take your father and his brothers on Sundays. It was their ritual, the one day Dadaji didn't go to the hospital." *Shuffle, shuffle.* Dadima's worn *chappals* slapped at the soles of her feet as they walked. Every few strides, she would use her hand to shield her eyes from the sunlight that bounced off the water's shimmering surface. "And here, there used to be a nursery school where the boys went. It was run by a lovely nun, Sister Carmine." As they walked, they averted their eyes from the people defecating along the seawall and the half-naked children who held out their hands in hopes of a spare coin.

The second day, Asha convinced Dadima to try on her extra pair of running shoes, and by some miracle, they had the same shoe size. Once she got used to the feeling of her feet being completely enclosed, Dadima said, she appreciated the comfort of the shoes and agreed to adopt them as her own. She refused, however, to wear the baseball cap Asha offered her, preferring instead to drape her sari modestly over her head, though it offered minimal sun protection. The shoes, Dadima pointed out, could at least be hidden beneath her long sari. If people saw her in that hat, they would think she had surely lost her mind. At her age, Dadima explained, people were always looking for signs of this, and she needn't give them any more evidence. On that day's walk and the next, Dadima asked Asha questions about her life in America. Asha talked at length about college, her classes, the newspaper, and her friends. She wasn't sure how much Dadima understood, given their differences in language, culture, and generation, and the fact that she nodded along but didn't ask any questions. But later, when her grandmother made reference to some small detail she had mentioned, Asha realized she had taken it all in.

On the fourth day, somewhere between the morning street vendors who hawk their roasted corn and those hacking the tops off fresh coconuts with machetes, Dadima shared the story about her mother-in-law. She described how the old woman brought her, as a new bride, into the kitchen to show her how to prepare roasted eggplant curry the way her son liked it. "It was too much for me," Dadima said. "I had just said good-bye to my family, and here she was trying to tell me how to make *bengan bhartha*. As if I didn't know! I had been making it with my mother for years. She made the best *bengan bhartha* in the neighborhood."

"So, what happened then?" Asha said.

"I left the kitchen and sat in our room. For hours. I could be a very stubborn girl back then." She chuckles. "Anyway, she came to me after some time. She told me to come into the kitchen and show her how I made *bengan bhartha*. She said this was my kitchen now and I was free to cook however I wanted. That's the kind of woman she was. So full of generosity toward others. No ego at all." It surprised Asha to hear her speak with such fondness and respect for her mother-in-law after hearing so many people complain about this relationship.

"This is the temple she went to every day," Dadima said as they walked past a nondescript white façade a few blocks from the flat. "Come, I'll show you." Asha had never been in a temple before, so she followed Dadima's lead, removing her sneakers outside the entrance. Inside was a plain room with a few statues of various Hindu gods. In front of one statue with the head of an elephant, Dadima stood for a few moments, her eyes closed and palms pressed together. "Ganesh," Dadima whispered to her, "remover of obstacles." Then she stepped forward, moved her open right palm over a steel plate that held a small flame, took a small handful of peanuts and crystallized sugar, and offered the same to Asha.

Outside, Dadima explained further. "In my family, we did our daily worship at home, and only went to the temple for the big occasions. Mahalaxmi Temple—you must see it while you're here—lovely temple, very big, people from all over Mumbai go there. In any case, after I married and moved here, I started coming to this little *mandir* with my *sassu*. There's one of these in every little neighborhood. People stop by here for a few moments in the morning or on their way home. I find it brings a little bit of peace to my day."

"Dadima? I hope this isn't too ignorant of me," Asha ventured on the fifth day. "How did you learn to speak English? Most of the other people your age in the building don't seem to know more than a few words."

Dadima chuckled softly. "That is my father's legacy. He was a real Anglophile. When everybody else was busy blaming the British for India's problems, my father insisted I take English lessons. He was a progressive man, my father. He wanted me to finish my college studies before he would let any boys look at me for marriage. He was ahead of his time, my *bapu*," she said, with a wistful smile. "He really understood the value of a woman. He always treated my mother like gold."

And so it went. Dadima doled out her stories in small doses, reaching further back into her memory as the days went on. Asha learned to navigate the delicate balance of being a good listener: asking just enough questions to keep Dadima going without disturbing the flow of her memories. After one week of their morning walks, Dadima began to speak about her family's migration during Partition, the division of the country into India and Pakistan that accompanied its independence from the British empire in 1947. Dadima's family had lived in Karachi, capital of the northern Indian state of Sindh. Her father owned a thriving grain export business and traveled often to the Middle East and East Africa. They had a beautiful home, two cars, and several hundred acres of land, on which Dadima and her sister and brothers played freely. All of it, they had to leave behind when they were forced to move.

Karachi was named the capital of Pakistan, the new Muslim state. The British drew their new lines on the map of South Asia without regard to those people who lived on the wrong side of them. And so people were forced to shutter their homes, close their businesses, and uproot their families to make the journey to the right side of the line. Dadima's family, like many Hindus in Karachi, moved to Bombay. Her father stayed behind to wrap up their affairs and salvage what he could of their assets, while Dadima traveled with her mother and siblings by sea to Bombay. They were lucky to afford ship fare, as she told it, since those who traveled by bus and train suffered the most bloodshed in skirmishes with travelers of a different faith going in the other direction.

"My brother was only fourteen then, five years younger than me," Dadima explained, "but he was the oldest boy in the family, so he stepped in for my father. He looked after us on the journey. When the ship drew close to the harbor, they put us in a small dinghy to go to shore. There we were, my mother and the four children, floating toward the lights of this city where we knew not a single person. Suddenly, my brother stood up and started yelling and waving back to the ship. He had counted our trunks—we had brought ten with us—so he had counted them, and there were only nine on the dinghy. My brother wanted to go back to the ship and get the last one. He would have to go by himself.

"That's all we had left in the whole world, those trunks." Dadima shook her head at the memory. "My mother was so frightened. She didn't want him to go. It was dark, and it was a huge ship. There was no certainty he would find the trunk, or even make it back to us. But he went. He was only fourteen, but he knew our father had trusted him to be the man of the family. My mother cried and prayed the whole time he was gone. I started wondering what would happen if he didn't come back. We had already left my *bapu* in Karachi, and—"

"What happened?" Asha asked.

"Oh, he made it back, a little shaken, but he found the final trunk. And we made it safely to the harbor, of course," she says, gesturing to the water.

"And your father?"

"Bapu joined us here after a few weeks. We all came together again after Partition. We were luckier than many," she said softly. "But my father was never the same man after we left Karachi. I think his heart ached to leave behind the city he loved and the business he had worked so hard to build. He was never quite the same." They walked in silence the rest of the way.

THIS MORNING, AS SHE LACES UP HER SHOES, ASHA HOPES TO hear some of her own history. Her parents rarely spoke about her birth or adoption in India, and when they did, it was the same few details over and over. She was given away at birth to the orphanage, a place called Shanti. She stayed there until she was one year old, at which time her parents came to India, adopted her, and took her to

California. This is all Asha has ever known about where she came from. She's not sure if Dadima will tell her anything more, but she's summoning the courage to ask today.

"Good morning, *beti*," Dadima greets her as she walks out to the living room. "I am ready to keep up with you today," she says, smiling. "That bothersome knee pain is completely gone."

Asha notices her grandmother looks younger when she smiles. Sometimes she forgets she is with an old lady, but then Dadima mentions something like her family getting the first icebox in the building, and Asha realizes again how much this woman has lived through. "Good, I'm ready too. Is this for me?" Asha asks, removing the saucer from atop the cup of hot *chai*. She never liked Indian tea before, finding it too heavy and sweet. But something about Dadima's *chai*, with a hint of cardamom and fresh mint leaves, makes it the perfect way to greet the day.

IT IS A BEAUTIFUL MORNING. THE AIR IS UNCHARACTERISTICALLY crisp, with a slight breeze blowing across the ocean's surface and onto the boardwalk.

"You are seeing India for the first time at twenty, *beti*," Dadima says. "What do you think of her?" Without waiting for an answer she continues. "You know, your father was not much older than you when he left for America. Oh, he was so young then. He didn't know the hardships he would face."

"I know. He always talks about how hard he studied in medical school. He thinks I don't study enough," Asha says.

"Studying was not hard for him. He was always smart. Top of his class in school, captain of the cricket team, best marks all the time. No, that part I never worried about. I knew he would do well at school. It was the rest of it. He didn't know anyone there. He was homesick. He couldn't find any good Indian cooking. People couldn't understand his accent at first. His professors asked him two, three times to repeat his answers. He would get embarrassed. He started listening to audiocassettes to learn how to speak like an American."

"Really?" Asha tries to picture her father listening to tapes, repeating words to himself.

"*Hahn,* yes. It was very difficult for him. At first he told us all these things when he called, but over time he said less and less. I don't think he wanted to worry us."

"Did you? Were you worried?"

"*Hahn,* but of course! That is a mother's burden to carry her whole life. I will worry about my children and grandchildren every single day until my deathbed, I am sure of it. It's part of being a mother. That is my *karma.*"

Asha ponders this and is silent for a while.

"Is something wrong, *beti*?" Dadima says.

"I was just thinking about my mother. My, you know, my biological mother. I was wondering if she ever thinks about me, if she worries about me."

Dadima takes her hand and holds it firmly while they continue to walk. "*Beti,*" she says, "I assure you. There is not a day in her life your mother does not think about you."

Tears fill Asha's eyes. "Dadima? Do you remember when I was a baby?"

"Do I remember? What, do you think I'm already some crazy old lady who's lost her mind? Of course I remember. You had one little birthmark on your ankle, and another on the bridge of your nose—yes, that one, it's still there." Dadima brushes it lightly with a finger. "You know, in our tradition, if you have a birthmark on your forehead, it means you are destined for greatness."

Asha laughs at this. "Really? In America, it means you're destined for concealer cream."

"And you loved to eat rice pudding with saffron. We had some the first day you arrived here, and we had to make a new batch every two days after that, just for you!" she says. "Your father had to adjust. He was used to all that food being prepared especially for him, but once you arrived, you became the focus." Dadima smiles. "Oh yes, and you would flip onto your tummy the moment we put you to sleep, curl up into a little ball, and stay there until morning."

"Dadima?" Asha says softly, feeling her heart beat faster.

"*Hahn, beti?*"

"I . . . I've been thinking about trying to find my birth parents." Asha sees the old woman stiffen almost imperceptibly and a flicker of something cross her face. "I love Mom and Dad more than anything, and I don't want to hurt them, but . . . I've felt this way for a long time, as long as I can remember. I just want to know who they are. I want to know more about myself. I feel like there's a little box of secrets about my life, and nobody else can open it for me." Asha exhales and looks out at the sea.

After another one of her long silences, Dadima says, "I understand, *beti*." An ocean wave crashes against the seawall as she speaks. "Have you spoken to your parents about this?"

Asha shakes her head. "It's a touchy subject with my mom. She doesn't really understand, and . . . I wanted to see if it was even possible first. There are a billion people in India—what if they don't want me to find them? They gave me away. They didn't want children then, so why would they want to meet me now? Maybe it's better if I don't look."

Dadima stops, turns to her, and places her wrinkled hands on either side of Asha's face. "If you feel it is important, you should do it. Those eyes you have are special, just as you are. You are meant to see things others cannot. That is your gift. That, *beti,* is your *karma*."

44

CHOWPATTY BEACH

Mumbai, India—2004
ASHA

"WHERE ARE WE GOING?" ASHA TRIES TO SOUND NONCHALANT as she asks the question that has been burning in her mind since Sanjay called three days ago. Looking at him now in the backseat of the taxi, she decides she did not overestimate his attractiveness the night of the wedding. His hair is still damp, and she can detect the faint scent of soap on him.

"Surprise," he says with a smile, his eyes hidden behind sunglasses. After a few minutes, he says something to the taxi driver and they pull over.

"Okay," she says, after he helps her out of the cab. "I'm surprised, where are we?"

"Chowpatty Beach. This is my favorite time to come here, just as the sun is setting. Right now, you see beaches and playground, but in a half hour, it will be lights and carnival games. I know it's a little cheesy, but I consider it one of the highlights of Mumbai. You can't leave the city without seeing Chowpatty." They walk together toward the water's edge, their sandals sinking into the sand as they go.

"So, how is your project coming?" Sanjay says.

"Okay, I guess. I did my first interviews last week."

"And?" He sits down on a bench and slides to one side.

Asha sits down next to him and looks toward the water. "It was kind of hard."

"Why?"

The wind whips her hair around and she pulls it to one side. "I don't know, I just found it so . . . depressing." She hasn't spoken to anyone about this, not even Meena. "Seeing those people, the conditions they live in, hearing their stories . . . it made me feel horrible. Guilty."

"For what?"

"For having a different kind of life. A better life. Those kids are just born into that, you know? They didn't ask for that. It's hard to find the hope."

Sanjay nods. "Yes. But there's still a story for you to tell, isn't there?"

"I don't know. I don't think my questions were very good. I lost my composure after the first couple of interviews. Everywhere I looked, all I could see was tragedy. The people at the *Times* must think I'm an amateur. Journalists are supposed to hold it together. And I didn't."

"Maybe. But that's not all you are, is it? A journalist?"

"No, but—"

"So," he interrupts, "maybe you need to look at it differently." He takes off his sunglasses and looks into her eyes. She feels a flutter in her stomach as he touches her cheek. He leans in toward her and she closes her eyes before she feels his lips brush lightly against her ear. "Beautiful," he whispers. When she opens her eyes, Sanjay is gazing out over the water and the orange-red glow of the sun is dipping below the horizon.

Beautiful? The sunset? Her eyes? Her? The way he said it makes her believe it might be true. Her mind is filled with a million questions, but his comes out first.

"Hungry?"

She nods, unable to speak.

They walk to one of the snack food stalls on the beachfront that have come to life with the darkening sky, and Sanjay gets them two dishes of *bhel-puri*. As they eat, standing, they watch the transformation of Chowpatty. The Ferris wheel is lit and begins to turn. A snake charmer attracts a crowd with his flute music, and another man beckons a costumed monkey to dance. Sanjay holds his arm around her back as they walk through the various attractions. When they reach the Ferris wheel, he looks at her and says, "Well?"

"Sure, why not?" They climb into the rickety bucket seat. The wheel begins to move, and she sees the scattered lights and sights of Mumbai spread out below her.

When they reach the top, Sanjay says, "So, how do you like Mumbai? What do you think of your first visit here? You must find it very different, being born and raised in the United States."

"Actually, I was born here," Asha says. She knows this information is unnecessary to their conversation, and yet she wants to share it.

"Really?" he says. "Mumbai?"

"Well, I don't really know. My parents adopted me from an orphanage here in Mumbai. I don't know where I was born. I don't know who my . . . birth parents are." She waits for his reaction.

"Are you curious?"

"Yes. No. I don't know." She turns away from his penetrating eyes and watches the children riding decorated ponies on the ground below. "I was curious when I was younger, and then I tried to put it out of my mind. I thought it was a childish dream I would grow out of. But being here in India has brought it all back up again. I have so many questions. What does my mother look like? Who is my father? Why did they give me up? Do they think about me?" Asha stops, realizing she probably sounds a little crazed. "Anyway . . ." She shakes her head and focuses on a white pony decorated with bright pink floral garlands.

Sanjay puts his hand on top of hers. "I don't think it's childish. I think it's a very natural instinct, to want to know where we come from."

She stays silent, feeling like she's already said too much. When the wheel stops moving, she feels at once disappointed and relieved their discussion has come to a natural conclusion.

"Do you want to get some dinner?" Sanjay says. "There's a great pizza place nearby."

"Pizza?" Asha laughs. "What, you think the American girl only eats pizza?"

"Well, no, I just . . ." Sanjay appears flustered for the first time.

"Where would you go to eat, with your friends?" she says. "Take me there."

"Okay, then." He flags down a taxi on Marine Drive. "Somewhere authentic."

45

ONE MORE LIE

Mumbai, India—2004
KRISHNAN

KRISHNAN REPOSITIONS HIS BAG ON HIS SHOULDER AND TURNS sideways to squeeze through the sliding glass doors that serve as the last barrier between him and his city of birth. After stepping outside, he closes his eyes and takes a deep breath of the Mumbai air. Just as he remembers. Behind the metal barricades, he sees Asha, the only young woman in Western attire, surrounded by men.

"Dad!" Asha waves at him with all the enthusiasm she used to show as a little girl waiting for him at the front door.

"Hi, sweetheart!" He drops his bag to hug her.

"Hello, Uncle," the young man standing next to her says.

"Dad, you remember Nimish? Pankaj Uncle's son."

"*Hahn,* yes, of course. Good to see you again," Krishnan says, though his nephew looks only vaguely familiar to him, in the way that almost anybody in this crowd could. He's thankful Asha is here to introduce him.

"How was your flight?" She links her arm through his as they walk to the car.

"Fine. Long," Krishnan replies. In the eight years since his last trip to India, the seats have gotten smaller and the airplanes fuller, but the anticipation of seeing Asha buoyed him through the long flight.

THE NEXT MORNING OVER BREAKFAST, ASHA SAYS, "LET'S GO out for lunch today, Dad. I want to take you to this place I really like."

Krishnan smiles at her over his steaming cup of *chai,* which never tastes as good as it does at his mother's home. "What's this? You've been here a few months and already you're an expert on my home-town?"

"Well, maybe not an expert, but it's changed a lot since you've been here. I can show you a thing or two." She smiles back.

She's right about the changes. On the ride from the airport, he was overwhelmed with the development that has taken place all over the city. Entire blocks of buildings have appeared where there used to be nothing, and American brands are everywhere: Coca-Cola bottles, McDonald's restaurants, Merrill Lynch billboards. The posi-tive signs of modernization are unmistakable, as are the negative effects. When he looked out from the balcony this morning, the familiar sight of the seashore he expected was all but obscured by the haze of pollution.

"Okay, I'm in your hands." Krishnan chuckles.

"Wise man," his mother says, entering the room. "Your daughter is as strong-minded as you are, perhaps even more so." She stands behind Asha with her hands on the girl's shoulders.

The sight of this, his mother together with his daughter, makes Krishnan's voice catch in his throat. "Yes, trust me, I know. Why do you think she hasn't applied to medical school yet?"

"Oh, *beta,* you must give up that notion. She has a career already.

You should see the wonderful work she's doing at the newspaper," his mother says.

"I'll take you there after lunch, Dad."

THE RESTAURANT ASHA HAS CHOSEN SERVES CLASSIC SOUTH Indian street food: gigantic paper-thin *masala dosas* that arrive at the table crispy and hot, moist *idlis* served with spicy *sambar* for dipping. This place is the equivalent of a neighborhood greasy diner. As they sit in the vinyl-covered booth, Krishnan notices they are the only nonlocals in the place. He is surprised and pleased his daughter feels comfortable here.

"This stuff is good, but it's so hot," says Asha, pointing to the dish of *sambar*. "You need yogurt for it." She requests some in broken Hindi from the waiter rushing by.

"So, have you had a chance to go to the hospital with your grandfather?" He notices himself slipping into the familiar language rhythms of Mumbai, a fusion of Hindi, Gujarati, and English.

"Not yet. He's usually gone by the time I get back with Dadima. Did I tell you we've been taking these morning walks together? It's been great. She's an amazing woman, Dad. It's too bad I didn't get to know her until now."

Krishnan feels the accusation in her last statement, though he doubts she meant it this way. "Yes, she is a remarkable woman, isn't she? She hasn't mellowed too much with age." Over lunch, they talk about the family members Asha's met, the grandiose wedding she attended, the people she works with at the *Times of India,* the places she's visited in Mumbai.

"Mmm. This *sambar* is good. How did you find this place, Asha?"

"This guy . . . a friend, Sanjay, brought me here. He dared me to eat someplace that doesn't cater to foreigners. He thought I wouldn't be able to keep up, but I did, with my secret weapon." She smiles, pointing to her dish of yogurt.

He raises an eyebrow. "Sanjay, huh? And how did you meet him?"

Asha finishes. "At that wedding I told you about. Someone in his family is friends with someone in ours, I don't know exactly."

"What does Sanjay do?"

"He's getting his master's at the London School of Economics." She smiles and makes a face at him. "Sorry, Dad, I didn't manage to find an eligible Indian doctor."

"Hey, two out of three is not bad." Krishnan smiles, despite himself.

"So, how's Mom?" Asha says. "She went to San Diego for the holidays?"

"Yes, she really needed to. She was worried about Grandma's last mammogram and she wanted to talk to her doctors. She hasn't been able to get down there during the week because the clinic's been busy . . ." Krishnan worries he's doing too much explaining. He and Somer agreed not to tell Asha about their separation yet, not until it's time for her to come home. In his heart, Krishnan hopes they will be reconciled by then. Being apart from Somer has been harder than he expected. The past couple of months, he has spent most of his time working, volunteering to cover his partners' call schedules and staying late at the office to finish paperwork. Home feels unbearably lonely without Somer.

Now, out of some deep-seated sense of loyalty to both of them, Krishnan presses out one more lie. "She really wanted to come, Asha."

"Actually, I'm kind of glad it's just you, Dad. I wanted to talk to you about something." Asha sounds tentative for the first time since he arrived. She wipes her hands and mouth with a small paper napkin and takes a deep breath. Krishnan puts down his food, sensing something important is about to happen. "Here's the thing, Dad. You know I love you and Mom so much. You've been great parents. I know how much you've done for me . . ." She trails off, now visibly nervous, twisting the paper napkin in her hands.

"Asha, honey, what is it?" Krishnan says.

She looks up at him and blurts it out. "I want to find my birth parents." After a moment, she continues, seeming desperate now to get the rest of the words out. "I want to know who they are, and see if I can meet them. I know it's a long shot, Dad. I have no idea where to start or how to look for them, so I really need your help."

He looks at his daughter, her beautiful eyes wide and searching. "Okay," he says.

"Okay . . . what?" Asha says.

"Okay, I understand . . . how you feel. I'll help you however I can." He has anticipated this discussion a number of times. He too is thankful Somer's not here right now.

"Do you think Mom will understand?" Asha says.

"It may be hard for her, honey," Krishnan says. "But she loves you. We both do, and that will never change." He reaches across the Formica table and puts his hand on his daughter's. "You can't forsake your past, Asha. It's a part of you. Trust me." She nods, and he squeezes her hand as they both acknowledge the implications of this decision.

Krishnan came to India knowing he would have to protect Asha from her mother's choices. Now he will return knowing he has to protect Somer from her daughter's as well.

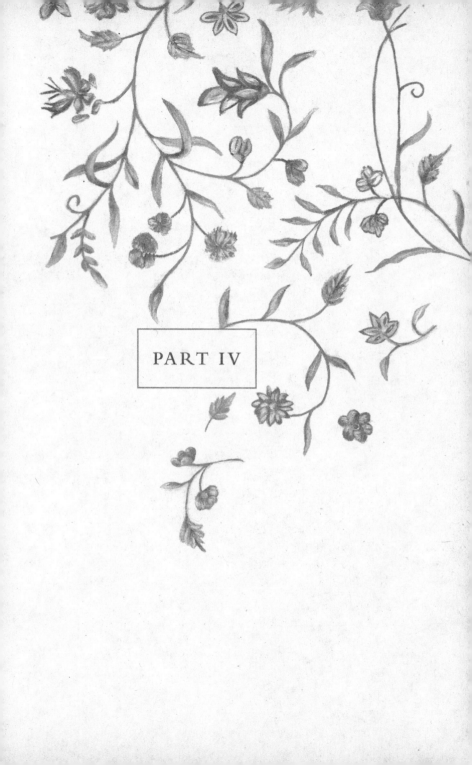

PART IV

46

A FATHER NEVER FORGETS

Mumbai, India—2005
KAVITA

KAVITA STANDS PATIENTLY IN LINE AT THE TELEGRAPH OFFICE, awaiting her turn. When she reaches the counter, the clerk smiles at her. "Hello, Mrs. Merchant. Money wire to Dahanu today?" She has been coming here every week for the past three months but still doesn't know this man's name—the one who instructs her to fill out the paperwork, the one to whom she hands the envelope of cash. He knows her name, of course, from the receipt he gives her each week, which she carefully files away with the others in her cupboard at home. Once she hears her sister has received the money, she puts a small mark on that receipt.

The seven hundred rupees she sends each week pay for the nurse and medicines for her mother since her stroke last fall. Kavita hopes to go for a visit soon, but she can take leave only once a year in the late summer, so as not to overlap with the other servants. Exceptions are only made in the case of a close family member's death. Jasu has told her to simply ask Sahib and Memsahib for the time off, but she won't. They have been fair and treated her well, and she feels the need to keep her job. It's not for the paltry money itself; it is the security of knowing she has some earnings, separate from Jasu's unreliable income and Vijay's illicit fortune.

"I SENT THE MONEY THIS AFTERNOON, *BENA*," KAVITA SAYS INTO the phone.

"Thank you, Kavi. I will call you when it arrives," Rupa says.

No one back home ever asks Kavita where the money comes from, an amount none of them could ever afford to part with. In truth, Kavita and Jasu wouldn't be able to afford it either, were it not for Vijay. She knows her family assumes, as they have ever since she left, that they have become prosperous in Mumbai as Jasu boasted they would. In the early years, out of loyalty to Jasu she refrained from telling them about their financial struggles. Now that they are finally comfortable, it is her shame about Vijay that is the basis of her silence.

"Rupa, how is Ba keeping?"

There is a deep sigh on the other end of the phone. "All right. The doctor came to see her just yesterday and said she's doing as well as possible. He does not expect a full recovery, *bena*. She will not be able to speak properly again, or see out of her right eye. But she is comfortable, and the nursemaid takes very good care of her, thanks to you, *bena*."

Every time Rupa thanks her for sending money, Kavita feels a snake crawling in her belly, not only because of where the money comes from, but also because it is all she has to give. She knows she should be in Dahanu herself. It is shameful that, instead of caring for her own mother, she spends her days washing Sahib's dishes and folding Memsahib's saris. This awareness makes her daily tasks even more burdensome. "And how is Bapu?" Kavita keeps her voice strong, not wanting her frailty and fear to travel through the wire to her sister's ears.

"Not well. He doesn't recognize his grandchildren at all, and some days, he doesn't even know me. It is good you are not here to see it, *bena,* it is not easy to watch him drift away."

This news is no different from what Rupa tells her each time they talk. Their father's condition has been deteriorating slowly for the past several years. But he is like the ancient *chickoo-fruit* tree behind their childhood home; though its branches get thinner each year and the leaves fewer, its proud trunk stands tall. Still, her next words catch in her throat.

"Does he remember me? Do you think he will know me when I come?"

There is a long pause before Rupa answers. "I'm sure he will, Kavi. Can a father ever forget his daughter?"

KAVITA PRESSES INTO THE SKIN OF THE SMALL MANGO WITH HER fingers to test it for firmness of flesh, then holds it to her nose. "I'll take a half kilo of these, please." Memsahib woke up this morning demanding fresh mango pickle, so after lunch, Bhaya sent Kavita out to find the best green mangoes she could. She tried three different markets, and now she's at least a half hour from Memsahib's flat, but no matter—everyone will still be resting when she gets back. Kavita walks briskly until she arrives at the iron gates, then stops and sets the cloth bag of mangoes down at her feet. She looks through the rusting bars of the gate, even stands on her tiptoes to get a better look. She knows it's pointless, of course. Even if Usha survived, she would be a grown woman by now, even older than Vijay. She certainly wouldn't be here in this orphanage anymore. *So what am I seeking here, why am I still drawn to this place?*

Is it to conjure up the pain of that day when she gave her daughter away, to punish herself for handing over her own flesh and blood? What kind of life could that girl have? No family, raised by strangers, no home to go to once she left this place. *Was it better? Better for me to have given her just life and nothing else a mother should give her child?* Or does she still come here simply because it's become a habit, like a scar etched onto her body, one that she can't help but think about, scratch at, pick at, all the while hoping it will miraculously heal one day?

47

ONCE BEFORE

Mumbai, India—2005
Asha

Asha feels her heart rate quicken as the train rumbles into Churchgate Station. The approaching train stirs about the dusty air and releases the persistent stench of urine from the steaming ground. The odor is overwhelming, but she can think only about where this train will take her. She moves forward on the platform, a wad of rupees safely tucked in her money belt. Her backpack, unused since the flight over here, now contains her notebook, city maps, and first-class train tickets—the only safe way for an unaccompanied young woman to travel in India, Dadima insisted.

Before he left, her father gave her the only details he could remember, the name of the adoption agency and the representative who helped them. When Asha called the agency, they directed her to the orphanage. Dadima gave her the address of the orphanage and the name of its director, Arun Deshpande. She wrote it in Asha's spiral-bound notebook, in English, Hindi, and Marathi, just in case. Dadima offered to come with her, but Asha wanted to do this alone. She settles into her seat on the train, pulls the silver bangle out of her pocket, and holds it for the duration of the ride. When she gets off the train, she makes her way to the front of the rickshaw line, where she shows the driver her notebook with the address of the orphanage. He nods, spits *betelnut* juice on the pavement, and pedals off on impossibly thin, sinewy legs.

The orphanage looks different from what Asha expects, a sprawling two-story building with outdoor areas where children play. She pauses at the plaque inscribed in English outside:

SHANTI HOME FOR CHILDREN
EST. 1980
KIND THANKS TO THAKKAR FAMILY
FOR GENEROSITY IN PROVIDING OUR NEW HOME

Thakkar? As she's learned since arriving here, there are thousands of Thakkars in Mumbai. It's a nice change to not have to spell it for everyone. She rings the bell at the front gate, and an old woman with a puckered mouth shuffles out. "I'm here to speak with Arun Deshpande." Asha speaks slowly, assuming the old woman doesn't understand English. Upon hearing the name, she opens the door and points to a small office at the end of the hallway. Asha puts her palms together to thank the old woman and steps tentatively into the building. She was so confident on the way over here, but now her legs feel weak, and her heart is racing. The door to the office is open, but she knocks nevertheless. A man with pepper-and-salt hair and bifocals perched on his nose speaks loudly on the phone in a language that doesn't sound familiar. He motions for her to come in and sit down. She clears a pile of papers from the one chair in the office. She sees a nameplate on the desk that says ARUN DESHPANDE, and her palms begin to sweat. She takes out her notebook and pencil while she waits.

He puts down the phone and gives her a harried smile. "Hello, I am Arun Deshpande, director of Shanti. Come in, please," he says, though she is already seated.

"Thank you. My name is Asha Thakkar. I am visiting here from the United States. I . . . was actually adopted from here, out of this orphanage. About twenty years ago." She puts the end of the pencil in her mouth as she waits for his reaction.

Deshpande pushes himself back from the desk. "Thakkar? As in Sarla Thakkar? She is your relation?"

"Sarla . . . uh, yes, she's my grandmother. My father's mother. Why do you ask?"

"We are very grateful to your grandmother. She made the donation for this building, must be, almost twenty years ago. She wanted to make sure we had enough classrooms upstairs for all the children. Every day, they continue their studies here after school. Music, language, art."

"Oh, I . . . didn't know that." Asha chews the end of her pencil.

"I haven't seen her in many years. Please give her my very best regards."

"Yes, I will." Asha takes a deep breath. "Mr. Deshpande, the reason I'm here is I'm hoping you can help me. I'm . . . trying to find my birth parents, the ones who brought me here, to the orphanage." When he doesn't respond, she continues, "I also wanted to say I am thankful for all that you did for me here. I have a good life in America, I love my parents"—she pauses, searching for the words to convince him—"and I don't want to create any trouble. It's just that I really want . . . I have always really wanted to find my birth parents."

Mr. Deshpande takes off his glasses and begins rubbing them with the tail of his shirt. "My dear, we have hundreds of children coming through here every year. Just last month we had over a dozen new babies left on our doorstep. The fortunate ones are adopted; the others stay here until they finish their schooling, sixteen at most. We can't keep records on every child. For most, we don't even know their true ages, and back then, well . . ." He sighs heavily and tilts his head to look at her. "I suppose I could check. Very well. Thakkar. Asha, you said?" He turns to the relic of a computer on his desk. After a few minutes of fumbling with the keyboard and squinting at the screen, he turns back to her. "I'm sorry, I can't find that name. There's no record of you. Like I said, our record keeping . . ." He shrugs and puts his glasses back on.

She feels a hollowness in her stomach and looks down at her notebook, where the page is blank. *No record of me.* She digs her nails into her palms to stave off the tears waiting anxiously behind her eyes.

"You know, we've had other children come here, like you, and it's been challenging to find the mother, even when they have a name. Sometimes these women don't want to be found. Many times they were unwed, and no one even knows they had a baby or brought the child here. It could be very . . . difficult for these mothers if people found out now."

Asha nods, gripping her pencil and trying to maintain her composure. *What is my next question? What do I write on this blank page?*

Suddenly, Arun Deshpande leans forward and peers at Asha's face. "Your eyes, they're so unusual. I have seen that color only once before on an Indian woman." A look of comprehension spreads across his face. "When did you say you were adopted?"

"Nineteen eight-five. August. Really? What—"

"And do you know how old you were?" He knocks over a stack of papers on his way to the steel filing cabinet behind her chair.

"Around a year, I think." She stands to join him, peering over his shoulder.

He shuffles through the files, which look even more disorganized than his desk. "I remember her . . . She was from Palghar or Dahanu, one of those northern villages. I think she walked all the way here. I remember those eyes." He shakes his head, then pauses and looks up at her. "Look, this will take some time. I have to go through all of 1984—these files, and then some more in the back. Shall I call you if I find something?"

She feels feverish at the thought that the information is here, somewhere in this disheveled office. She can't just leave now. "Can I help you look?"

"No, no." He gives a small laugh. "I'm not even sure what I'm looking for, but if it's here, I'll find it. I promise you. For Sarla-ji. Promise. One hundred percent." He nods his head from side to side in that confusing way people do here. This is the way things work in India, she's learned. You have to have faith. She tears out a sheet from her notebook to write down her number and lodges her pencil behind her ear. "Do you have a pen?"

SEVERAL DAYS LATER, SHE MAKES THE JOURNEY BACK TO SHANTI. She can hardly keep from breaking into a sprint to Mr. Deshpande's office after entering the front gate. She is jittery as she waits for him. When he enters, she stands up. "I came as soon as I could. What did you find?"

He sits down at his desk and hands her a manila folder. "I remember her. Your mother. I never forgot those eyes." Inside the file folder, there is a single sheet of paper, a partially completed form. "I'm sorry there's not much information," he says. "Back then, we thought it was best if things were anonymous. Now we do a better job collecting information, for health reasons and whatnot. Oh, but I did discover why I couldn't find you at first. You see right there . . ." He leans over and points to a spot on the form. "Your given name was Usha when you arrived here. I guess our records aren't so bad after all." He sits back in his chair, smiling.

Usha. Her name was Usha. Her given name. Given by her mother. *Usha Merchant.*

"That was my first month as the new director, when you came

here. We were full to capacity, and I wasn't supposed to accept any more children. But your mother came here with her sister, who convinced me to take you. She said you had a cousin here already, it wouldn't be right to separate you."

"A cousin?" Asha has spent her entire life without any cousins, and since coming to India, there seems to be another one everywhere she turns.

"Yes, your aunt's daughter. She said she was a year older than you, but that would've been before I was here, and there are definitely no records from back then."

"Mr. Deshpande, I want to find her . . . my mother, my parents. Do you know how I can?" Asha asks, trying to swallow back the lump in her throat.

He shakes his head. "I'm sorry. I'm surprised I found that file at all."

Mr. Deshpande helps her hail down an auto-rickshaw, and gives the driver instructions to take her to the train station. She clutches the manila folder tightly in one hand and, with the other, shakes Mr. Deshpande's. "Thank you so much. I appreciate your help."

"Good luck to you, my child. Please be careful."

BACK IN HER CHAIR AT THE *TIMES* OFFICE, SHE STARES AT THE single page inside the manila folder, although she has already memorized the few bits of information it holds.

NAME: USHA
DOB: 18 08 1984
SEX: F
MOTHER: KAVITA MERCHANT
FATHER: JASU MERCHANT
AGE AT ARRIVAL: 3 DAYS

Only a few details, and yet they have already brought discoveries. Her mother was not unwed. Her parents were married, and she knows their names. Her own name for her first year of life was Usha Merchant. Asha practices writing it out, first in block letters, then as a signature, and finally just the initials she uses to sign off on her edits. She looks at the reflection of herself in her darkened monitor.

Usha Merchant. Does she look like an Usha? "Usha Merchant," she says, extending her hand in introduction to the stapler on her desk. Asha rests her head on the back of the chair and stares at the ceiling. She calls out to Meena in her neighboring office. "I don't even know where to start. How am I going to find her?"

"Well, you're in the right place. The *Times* has access to the best database in India." Meena leans over Asha to type on her keyboard. "We have good information on all major cities."

"What if she's not in a city? What if she's in a village somewhere? The orphanage director said she came here, walked I think, from a village."

Meena stops and looks at her. "Really?"

"Yeah, why?"

"That's remarkable. For a woman to do that, especially back when transportation was less reliable. She must have been quite dedicated to get you here." Meena pulls up a chair. "Okay, I'll show you how to use this. It's only cities, but you might as well start here. Start with Mumbai. Good thing their name isn't Patel or something like that. It will be easiest to find her through a male relative, property holdings and such. Okay, here we go, tenant listings for Merchant . . . oh well, still quite a few."

There are no Kavitas, but there are dozens of listings for Jasu Merchant or J. Merchant in Mumbai alone, and they haven't even tried other cities yet. Asha begins with a long list of names and spends several hours trying to piece together scraps of information.

By the end of the day, she has narrowed it down to three valid addresses, none of which may yield anything. Still, she feels hopeful as she heads toward the elevator with her notebook clasped to her chest.

"Wish me luck," she says over her shoulder to Meena. "Who knows what I'll find."

48

REVOLUTION

Palo Alto, California—2005
SOMER

"PICTURE YOURSELF AS A STRONG TREE, A MAJESTIC TREE, AND breathe deeply into your lower belly." Genevieve, the yoga instructor, has a soothing voice that trails her as she weaves in between the dozen people spread out in the studio. Somer stands absolutely straight, holding her arms high up above her head, palms touching. The sole of one foot is lodged firmly against the opposite thigh, and her eyes are focused intently on a small white speck on the brick wall in front of her. *Vrikshasana,* tree pose, has been giving her difficulty since she began taking this yoga class with Liza a couple months ago. Invariably, Somer wobbled on one foot and fell out of the pose while others in the class stood serenely. After class one day, Genevieve told Somer the key to the pose was to calm her mind and concentrate on the moment. What a difference this made, this one small change in focus, this slight shift in her perspective. Instead of fighting and struggling to stay balanced, she found a point to gaze at, and suddenly, all her energy was aligned and the pose was simple. Today, Somer stands perfectly still in *vrikshasana*, along with the others, until Genevieve's calm voice beckons them on to the next pose.

Somer has been coming to this yoga studio, ambitiously named Revolution, two or three times a week. When she woke up sore after the first few classes, she realized how long it had been since she had done anything really physical, since she had run until her lungs burned or swum until her muscles were happily tired, as she had during each of her short pregnancies. Twenty-some years ago, after her body stopped working, Somer ceased to think of it as an important part of her. When her back gave her trouble or her allergies acted up, she felt resentment toward her aging body for failing her again and again. Each new yoga pose she tried was a challenge, not only in the stretching and the twisting, but also because she had to get to know her body again, which muscles were tight, which joints inflexible. She had to be gentle with herself—understanding at first her body's limits, and then how to push beyond them. In doing so, Somer learned to reclaim the body she felt had betrayed her so many years earlier.

The turning point came one day when Genevieve urged the class to pay attention to their breath. "Are you holding your breath?" she asked them. "Notice if you are holding your breath after inhaling, and if so, what are you afraid of letting go of? Or are you holding it after exhaling, and what are you afraid of letting in?" Somer realized she was doing both, and so, as Krishnan had accused her of many times, she was being governed by fear.

After three months of living by herself, she has found some ways to combat the loneliness. On Thursdays, she goes to her Italian class with Giorgio, who sounds much sexier than he is, a grizzled old Sicilian man whose white chest hair peeks out above his shirt. She's been learning the language slowly, in preparation for her trip to Tuscany. During the week, when her days are busy at the clinic, and the streets of downtown Palo Alto are buzzing with students, she finds the pace of her new life tolerable.

The weekends are more difficult. The open hours stretch on and on, and she finds herself without someone to talk to for long periods of the day. She usually makes dinner or hiking plans with Liza, who has perfected the lifestyle of an older single woman. Still, it is the weekends when she misses Kris most. She longs for the lazy mornings they spent lying in bed, reading the paper. As the day turns to evening, she wishes she could walk arm in arm with him down to their neighborhood Thai restaurant and share a bowl of rich coconut curry. She misses his heavy arm across her body as she lies alone in bed. When she sees students around town, she tries to remember the carefree feeling she had with Kris back then. She lingers over the memories of their early days with Asha, when she was just a small bud unfolding in front of them, and everything she said or did made them laugh: going to the zoo and spending all their time in front of the monkeys, Asha beckoning both her parents to make monkey sounds and gestures before they could finally leave. The vacation they took to San Diego when Asha was six and she buried Krishnan up to his neck in sand when he fell asleep on the beach.

The time alone has made Somer appreciate how much of her life was built around Kris and Asha. For all she gave them through the years and the regret she sometimes felt over her career sacrifices, without them, her life was devoid of its meaning and fullness. Even now, what she most looks forward to each week is Sunday morning, when she goes over to the house so she and Kris can call Asha at their scheduled time. He and Asha do most of the talking, but this doesn't bother Somer as much as it used to. Often, just the sound of Asha's voice from miles away can bring tears to her eyes. It is a false premise, she knows, she and Kris are presenting, that of a happily married couple. But for those thirty minutes when she shares the phone line with them, and a cup of coffee afterward in the kitchen with Kris, it doesn't feel false at all.

Now, much too quickly it seems, it is time for *shavasana,* the rest-

ing pose that takes up the last ten minutes of class. At first, this was
the part Somer used to dread, lying there with nothing but the anxious thoughts swirling around in her head: thoughts of Asha leaving,
her daughter's anger toward her, fighting with Krishnan, the promotion she'd lost, the uncertainty of her future. *Shavasana,* corpse pose,
meant to relax the mind and body, was her enemy—the one time she
was forced to confront her darkest thoughts. And once the thoughts
came, there was no confining them. They infiltrated her time alone,
when loneliness ached in her heart, when quietude engulfed her
apartment. It was a Sunday morning, as she lay in bed counting the
hours until her phone call with Asha, when it occurred to Somer that
all her efforts to protect her daughter had backfired. It was fear that
kept Somer from letting her go, but by holding too tight she'd produced the opposite effect. She had driven Asha away. Just as in tree
pose, her constant struggles had knocked her off balance.

One morning before work, standing in the shower until it ran
cold, Somer realized first that she had used all the hot water, and then
that there was no one left to save it for. It was then that Somer
admitted to herself that she had, at some point, stopped giving to her
marriage. She had always expected Kris to be the one to assimilate to
her culture, as he had in the beginning. Even after they adopted an
Indian baby, even when he missed home, even when he asked her to
go with him. Somer felt she had given so much to their family already.
But her mother always said the key to a successful marriage was for
each spouse to give as much as they thought they possibly could. And
then, to give a little more. Somewhere in that extra giving, in the
space created by generosity without score keeping, was the difference
between marriages that thrived and those that didn't. Every time
Sundari asked one of her many questions about India and its culture,
questions Somer couldn't answer and had never asked herself, it made
her think there could have been another way. She could have

embraced what she had tried to push away. A slight shift in perspective, one small change in focus, might have made the difference.

Now, as she allows her limbs to relax into *shavasana,* her fingers to curl up, Somer thinks of Asha and Krishnan, together on the other side of the world. For the first time, she is separated by an ocean from the two people who have formed the fabric of her life. When they each announced their departure for India, she thought they were rash decisions, designed to punish her. But now, Somer can see, those decisions had been coming for years. It was she who had acted out of anger and fear, she who had walked out on her family without considering the repercussions of this choice. Just as she had married a man from another culture without understanding what it meant to him. Just as she had adopted a child from India without thinking through the implications. Always so eager to achieve the next milestone on her path, she has neglected to question that path or to look ahead.

49

THE ONLY SAFE GROUND

Mumbai, India—2005
ASHA

THE FIRST TWO LISTINGS PROVE TO BE FRUITLESS, BELONGING TO other J. Merchants. It was a struggle for Asha to communicate enough to learn even that. On her way to the third address on her list, she wishes Parag were there to translate for her. She begins to feel as if this was a foolish idea, to think she could find her parents in this city of twelve million people, if they're even in Mumbai at all. What if they're in one of those villages Deshpande mentioned? Could she go out there? How would she communicate? When the driver stops in front of a dilapidated tenement, Asha is reluctant to get out. But he confirms with more incomprehensible language and vigorous hand gestures that this is the place she is looking for. There is no listing of residents downstairs, so Asha begins climbing the stairwell, which reeks of human waste. She covers her nose and mouth with her hand. Cockroaches crawl busily in the corners, and on the first landing, she carefully sidesteps a man sleeping on his bedroll. She averts her eyes but cannot avoid the sinking feeling in her stomach. Her mind hovers between the equally distasteful thoughts that her parents might live in this place, and if they don't, she doesn't know how else to find them.

On the second floor, most of the apartment doors are open. Small children run freely through the hallways and chase one another in and out of doorways. Through one of these doorways, Asha sees a young woman squatting and sweeping the floor. "Excuse me, do you know where I can find the Merchants? Kavita Merchant?" Asha says. The woman shakes her head from side to side, scoops up a crawling baby, and motions for Asha to follow her. They walk across the floor and directly into another apartment without knocking, where another young woman beats a rug on the balcony. The apartment is oppressively small—a single room from the looks of it—and barely furnished. The paint on the walls is peeling, and one bare bulb hangs from the ceiling. The smell of simmering onions and spices wafts out from the tiny kitchen. The two women speak, watching Asha curiously. They aren't much older than she is. If it wasn't for the difference in language, their conspiratorial talking could pass for Asha and her friends back home. Yet here these women are, living with husbands and children instead of roommates, their days occupied by household chores rather than textbooks. Asha feels claustrophobic at the thought of living in a space this small.

"Kavita *ben*? You want Kavita *ben*?" the second woman asks in halting English.

"Yes, Kavita Merchant," Asha says.

"Kavita *ben* no live here anymore. Move to Vincent Road. You know Vincent Road?"

ASHA RUNS DOWN THE TWO FLIGHTS OF STAIRS AND OUT OF THE building. *Someone knows where my mother is.* At last, she knows she's on the right track. The first taxi driver she approaches does not know where Vincent Road is. The second one does but is unenthusiastic about driving there at this time of day. Asha pulls some cash out of her pocket, but this does not seem to convince him. *Damnit.* So close. She's going to get to Vincent Road if she has to hijack this man's taxi and drive there herself. She empties her money belt and waves all its contents in front of him. Finally, he gives a slight nod and opens the rear door from the inside. Her mind races during the entire half-hour drive in the backseat of her fourth taxi of the day. The various revelations of the last twenty-four hours swirl through her mind. Her name was Usha. She has her mother's eyes. She has a cousin. She has parents living on Vincent Road, right here in Mumbai. Her heart is pumping so hard, it feels it's going to burst through her chest.

Vincent Road turns out to be a short street, only two blocks long with three tallish buildings that look like apartments. She pays the driver everything she promised him and only briefly considers that this leaves her without any money to get home. The first building lists no Merchants as residents. She enters the second building and sees a uniformed man sitting at a table in the lobby. "Can you tell me if a Kavita Merchant lives here?"

The uniformed man shakes his head. "Regular doorman on break. Come back later."

Asha sees a binder on the table in front of him. "Can you check, please? Kavita Merchant?"

The uniform, who looks as if he'd rather be on break himself, flips open the binder and runs his finger down the list of names. "Merchant . . . *Hahn.* Vijay Merchant. Six-oh-two."

Vijay? "How about Kavita? Kavita Merchant? Or Jasu Merchant?" she says, looking around to see if the regular doorman is anywhere in sight.

"*Nai,* only Merchant here is Vijay. Vijay Merchant."

She feels her pounding heart plummet all the way into her feet. *How can this be?* There's only one more building on Vincent Road. She turns to leave.

"Ah, here he is," the uniform says to another similarly dressed man, who must be the regular doorman. "This girl wants Kavita Merchant. No Kavita here on list. I told her only one Merchant here. Vijay Merchant."

"Heh? Stupid idiot. Do you know nothing?" the doorman says, then babbles something she can't understand, except for the names *Kavita* and *Vijay*. The doorman turns to her and explains, "Please, this man is confused. Kavita Merchant lives here, yes. Only the flat is in Vijay's name. That is the reason for confusion."

"Vijay?"

"*Hahn.* Vijay. Her son."

What? "No, that can't be her. She . . . she doesn't have children. I don't think this woman has children. Kavita Merchant?" she says again, consulting her notebook for clarity. "*M-e-r-c-h-a-n-t.* Her husband's name is Jasu Merchant."

"*Hahnji,* madam," the doorman says, looking directly at her and speaking with complete confidence. "Kavita and Jasu Merchant. And their son Vijay. Flat six-oh-two."

Their son. The word reverberates in her head as she tries to make sense of it. "Son?"

"*Hahn,* you know him!" The doorman mistakes her repetition for recognition. "Must be about your age. Nineteen, twenty years old."

My age? "Are you . . . sure?" The words and numbers bang around in Asha's head like billiard balls. Suddenly, the facts arrange themselves in an unmistakable order. It finally makes sense, and then again none at all. Her real parents had a child, another child. One they'd chosen to keep. Her mouth tastes of sour acid. They kept him. Their son. *They kept him instead of me.*

From somewhere in the distance, she can hear the doorman's voice but catches few of his words. "Kavita . . . gone away for some time . . . back to her village . . . return in few weeks."

The ground buckles under her feet. She stumbles and somehow finds the step beneath her to sit down. It wasn't that her mother wasn't married. It wasn't that they didn't want a child. It wasn't that they couldn't afford one. *It was just me. It was me they didn't want.*

She is vaguely aware the two uniforms are watching her now, but she can't stop the tears from rolling down her cheeks. "I'm sorry . . . it's been a long day. I'm not used to the heat," she tries to explain. "I'll be fine. Don't worry." Even as the words come out of her mouth, she realizes how absurd she must sound to these two strangers. They won't worry like Dadima, probably waiting at home for her with a cup of *chai.* Or her father, who called her before she went to the orphanage to wish her luck. Or even her mother, who mashed her bitter malaria pills into fruit smoothies so she could stomach them before she left for India.

She buries her head in her hands and cries helplessly in front of these two men, who don't know her any more than Kavita and Jasu would if they walked into this lobby right now. With this thought, Asha feels her stomach tighten. She panics at the thought of further humiliation. *I have to get out of here.* Sniffling loudly, she stands and scrambles to gather her bag. The pressure builds in her lungs, and all she can think of is the need to get outside. "I have to go." She turns for the door.

"What's your name?" one of them yells after her as she runs out of the building. "I'll tell her you came."

The air outside is thick with smog, but it is still a welcome change from that building and its revelations. She needs to get far, far away from there. A taxi driver pulls up to her. "Need ride, madam?" He grins at her with his mouthful of crooked, stained teeth.

She climbs into the backseat and says, "Churchgate, *jaldi!*" She has picked up Priya's habit of automatically telling drivers to go quickly, but never has she meant it this much.

He pedals off and says, "Where you go, madam?"

At that moment, she remembers giving the last taxi driver the rest of her cash. She has no money left. She desperately searches in her backpack, unzipping all the pockets and fumbling around. She feels something unfamiliar in the bottom and pulls it out. A bag of chocolates. Ghirardelli mint chocolate squares. Her favorite. *Mom.* She must have slipped them into her backpack at the airport, just as she used to put a single chocolate square in her lunch bag. Asha lets out a cry, and the driver turns around. She waves him off and keeps looking through her bag. There's no telling what he'll do if she can't pay him. Behind her notebook, she finds a worn envelope, the one her father gave her at the airport. A small laugh erupts through her tears. Her father's afterthought will help her get home. She opens it and counts out the rupees. She taps the driver on the shoulder and shows him the money. "How far will this get me?"

He spits on the road before answering. "Worli."

The driver drops her off and she steps out of the taxi into a large crowd of people, who all seem to be climbing to somewhere. She looks up and sees an enormous ornately carved building at the top of a long flight of steps. "Excuse me." She stops one of the passing climbers. "What is this place?"

"Mahalaxmi Temple."

She blinks and looks again at the building. She hears Dadima's voice echoing in her head. *It brings a little bit of peace to my day.* Asha slowly climbs the steps. The narrow walkway leading to the temple is lined with tiny shops selling bright flowers, boxes of sweets, small Hindu idol figurines, and other souvenirs. During her long ascent, raindrops begin to speckle the ground, coming faster and harder, imploring her to quicken her pace. As she nears the top, a breathtaking view of the Arabian Sea spreads out in front of her. She slips her sandals off outside the temple to join the hundreds piled there already. Inside, the floor feels cool beneath her bare feet. At first it seems silent, compared to the noisy bustle of outside, but once her ears adjust she can hear the low murmur of chanting, and waves crashing on the rocks outside.

The temple features three gold statues of Hindu goddesses, each in its own nook, decorated with jewelry, flowers, and offerings of coconuts and fruit. Yellow, white, and orange floral garlands are draped from the center of the ceiling and wrapped around the pillars. Asha sits down on her knees in the middle of the open space, looking around at others for guidance. Standing in front of the middle goddess, a priest with a shaved head and white loincloth is conducting a ceremony with a couple wearing floral garlands. Several heavyset middle-aged women in saris are singing together in one corner. A young man about her age is sitting next to her with his eyes closed, rocking forward and praying.

About her age. She has a brother. Vijay. A brother she's never known about, and one who certainly doesn't know about her. He could be anywhere in this city. He could be here.

The scent of incense reaches her nostrils. She closes her eyes and takes a deep breath. All these years, she's been longing for her parents, dreaming of the moment she would meet them and finally feel complete. She always thought they would be longing for her too. Her face burns with shame at how foolish she's been. The tears flow again. Her parents haven't been longing for her. They don't miss her. They just discarded her.

And in that moment, the dreams she has carried in her heart and in her white marble box are gone. They vaporize into air like the smoke rising from the incense in front of her. Her questions are answered, the mystery surrounding her roots is gone. There is nothing left for her to find out. She doesn't need to meet her parents, just to be spurned again, rejected to her face.

All around her, the singing and chanting engulf her and crowd out the angry voices in her head. The silver bangle slides easily off her wrist. Asha turns it over and over between her fingers. She squeezes, and the soft metal bends under her touch. It is warped in shape, dull with age, imperfect. This, apparently, is all she will ever have from her mother. She holds it between her palms and closes her eyes. Then she puts her forehead to the floor and weeps.

50

A POWERFUL LOVE

Mumbai, India—2005
KAVITA

ONLY THE SHARP TINGLING IN HER LEFT FOOT FORCES KAVITA
to finally change positions. She's been lost in her own head, repeating *mantras* she remembers from her childhood, conjuring up memories of her mother. It's as if time stands still in this inner sanctum of
the temple, with no windows to the outside and the *pandit*'s rhythmic
chanting carrying her on its waves to the past. The *pandit* is conducting a Laxmi *puja* for a young couple, probably newly married. Kavita
herself usually prefers to pray to Laxmi, goddess of prosperity, but
today she sits in front of the goddess Kali who, with Durga, repre-
sents the sacred spirit of motherhood. She feels safe here, with the
familiar aroma of burning incense and the small tinkling of the bell
in her ears, disconnected from the world outside and its troubles.

Other worshippers come and go: young and old, women and
men, locals and tourists. Some walk around the perimeter once
slowly, as if they are visiting a museum. Others come to make a hasty
offering, a coconut or a bunch of bananas, on their way to a job
interview or a hospital visit. That group of plump, rich women in the
corner come here every morning to sing and demonstrate their piety

out loud. Still others, like Kavita, just sit and sit, sometimes for hours. They are the ones, she now understands, who are mourning. Like her, they mourn a loss so wide and so deep and so all-encompassing that it threatens to wash them away with grief.

She kneels and bends forward to the ground to offer her final prayer, as she always does, for her children. Though today she is mourning as a daughter, her duties as a mother never cease. She prays for Vijay's safety and his redemption. She prays for Usha, wherever she may be, picturing her, as she always does, as a little girl with two braids. In all these years, she has never been able to imagine what her daughter would look like as a grown woman, so this is the image she keeps in her mind, a young child frozen in time. She kisses the joined tips of her index fingers, and then the lone silver bangle on her wrist. Reluctantly, she stands up, shaking the stiffness out of her joints. She doesn't want to leave, but there is a train she must catch. Outside, it is now raining. The steady downpour soaks her as she trods down the familiar steps of Mahalaxmi Temple, and around the corner to Mumbai Central Train Station.

KAVITA STANDS ON THE PLATFORM WHILE THE OTHER TRAIN passengers disperse around her. There is no one waiting here for her. Rupa is supposed to come but must be busy with the preparations. Kavita fills her lungs with the familiar scent of earth and sits down on her bag to wait. The fields scattered on the horizon are greener than she remembers, or has her sight become dulled by the gray monotony of Mumbai? Other things have changed since she was last here, nearly three years ago. The dirt roads have been paved over, and there is a telephone booth outside the station. Several cars are parked nearby, of the varied modern types she's used to seeing in Mumbai. Taken together, it is all a little unsettling. Kavita is used to thinking of home as a static place, unchanging.

"*Bena!*" Kavita hears the familiar voice and stands up to be engulfed in Rupa's arms. Her older sister has also changed with age, Kavita notices, her hair more gray than black now.

"Oh, Kavi, thank God you're here." Rupa hugs her tightly and they rock back and forth in their embrace. "Come," she says, finally pulling away. "*Challo,* everyone is waiting."

KAVITA TRACES THE RIM OF THE STAINLESS STEEL TUMBLER WITH HER finger. How strange it is to be served tea, to be treated as a guest, here in her childhood home. Not much has changed, Kavita notes, reassured. The walls are yellower and the floors show more cracks than before, but otherwise, her parents' house looks the same. *How will Bapu look?*

"Don't expect too much, Kavi. He's not the same as he was, this has all been so hard on him," Rupa says, sipping her tea. "Last night he woke up calling for Ba, and it took me a long time to calm him back to sleep." She sighs, puts down her cup, and begins wrapping the end of her sari around her finger, a nervous gesture Kavita remembers from their childhood. "He can't recognize when his own body needs to go to the toilet, but he notices the first night in fifty years his wife is not sleeping beside him." Rupa shakes her head. "I don't quite understand it, but that is a powerful love."

The nursemaid walks into the drawing room and nods her head at Rupa, to indicate she has finished bathing and dressing their father and he can now be seen. "She has been a blessing, Kavi," Rupa says softly as they stand. "She is so patient with Bapu, even when he's cranky. And Ba loved her . . ." With the mention of their mother, Rupa's voice cracks and Kavita feels her own face crumple. They clutch each other as they used to when they shared a bed as young girls. "We must be strong for Bapu," Rupa says, wiping her sister's tears and then her own with the twisted end of her sari. "Come, *bena.*" She grips Kavita's hand firmly, and they enter the bedroom.

The first thing Kavita notices about her father, sitting on the bed with his legs extended, is his sunken face. His cheeks are drawn in, and his jawbones outline a much narrower profile than she remembers. She rushes to him, falling to her knees beside the bed and touching her head to his feet. She is alarmed to feel the sharp angles of his leg bones through the sheet. And then she feels the familiar touch of his hand on her head.

"My child," he says in a raspy voice.

"Bapu?" Kavita looks up at him hopefully. "Do you know me?" She sits beside him on the bed and clasps his two frail hands lightly in hers.

"Of course, *dhikri,* I know you."

She notices the milky gray of glaucoma that has taken over his eyes, rendering it impossible for him to see all but vague shadows right in front of him.

"Rupa *beti,* where is your Ba gone to now? Please tell her I want to see her." He speaks these words looking directly at Kavita. She pulls back for a moment, taking in both revelations at once. Not only does her father not recognize her, but he still doesn't understand her mother is dead. She is at a loss for what to do next when Rupa sits down on the other side of the bed.

"Bapu, it's Kavita. She's just arrived today, she's come all the way from Mumbai!" Rupa's voice is forcefully upbeat.

"Kavita," her father repeats, now following Rupa's voice and looking at her. "Kavita, how are you, *beti*?" He raises a hand to Rupa's cheek. "Do *you* know where your mother is?"

Rupa answers him gently, as she would speak to a child. "Bapu, we talked about this. Ba is gone. She was ill for a long time, and now she is gone. The cremation ceremony is tomorrow."

Kavita sees a brief look of recognition pass over her father's gaunt face, an aching sadness in these eyes that otherwise can see nothing. He leans back on his thin pillow and closes his eyes. "*Ay, Ram,*" he prays softly. Kavita presses her own eyes closed, and the tears squeeze out and roll down her cheeks. She raises her father's hand to her face and kisses it.

"DON'T FEEL BADLY, KAVI. SOMETIMES HE DOESN'T RECOGNIZE me either, and I'm here every day," Rupa says, rinsing a *thali* and handing it to Kavita.

The statement, though intended innocently, delivers a fresh wound to Kavita, a reminder she has not been here for her family. "*Achha,* I know, it's all right," Kavita answers dutifully, drying the *thali* with a cloth.

"It's been so hard on him, Ba's passing. It's as if what little will to live he had left is now going. I'm worried about how the ceremony will affect him. It is good you're here. You bring us all strength." Rupa wraps her arm around her sister and squeezes her shoulder with a damp hand.

Kavita marvels at her sister's ability to be such an adult about this, concerned with everyone else's needs, taking care of the house, handling preparations for the ceremony. All Kavita feels is the deepest sense of despair at the loss of her parents: the death of her mother, the remoteness of her father. It feels as if the very structure of her family is crumbling underneath her. She looks around and is almost surprised to see the walls of the home still standing. She doesn't know quite who she is in the world without her parents behind her. Even though it's been fifteen years since she left Dahanu, this feeling of being a little girl in her parents' home has not changed. She silently admonishes herself for acting like a child, for behaving so selfishly in light of her sister's strength.

"When are Jasu and Vijay arriving?" Rupa says.

"The morning train." Kavita takes the next *thali* from Rupa. She doesn't mention it will likely only be Jasu who comes.

51

MOTHER INDIA

Mumbai, India—2005
ASHA

ASHA SITS AT HER DESK IN THE *TIMES* OFFICE, SURROUNDED BY her notes. In the midst of the paper are two message slips from Sanjay. She has thought about him many times since she first went to Shanti two weeks ago but cannot bring herself to call. The discovery she made in that building lobby on Vincent Road has left her feeling ashamed and confused. She cannot explain it to herself, much less to someone else. She has not wanted to face Sanjay and relive it all again.

Today, Asha has been trying to transcribe her interview footage, but instead she keeps thinking about what Meena said that day at Dharavi—*Mother India does not love all her children equally.* She walks over to the terminal connecting her to the *Times* database. Into the blank search box, she types "India, birth rates" and gets over a thousand unintelligible results. She modifies her search by adding the phrase "girls and boys" and gets a dozen articles. She clicks into the first article, from the United Nations in 1991, and reads how birth rates for girls in India have declined steadily. The corresponding line graph shows both the precipitous decline for girls and the increasing gap between girls and boys. The next article criticizes the spread of lightweight ultrasound machines throughout the country. The advent of the smaller, affordable machines, it seems, made it easier for unscrupulous people to travel around rural India and charge expectant mothers to identify the sex of their unborn children. Although the Indian government outlawed ultrasound for gender identification purposes a decade ago, the practice is still rampant and often leads to sex-selective abortion, a phrase Asha has never heard before.

The third article mentions the infanticide of baby girls, along with bride-burning and dowry deaths, as part of a series on the struggle for women's rights in India. Asha glances over this one only briefly before she has to close her eyes and then the article. Her stomach is starting to churn. She wills herself to look at only one more story, and searches for something uplifting. She finds a profile of a Canadian philanthropist who has established a number of orphanages throughout India. Asha stares at the photo of the older Caucasian woman dressed in a sari, surrounded on all sides by smiling Indian children. Beneath the picture is a quote that overseas adoption of children from their orphanages is not encouraged.

Asha hoists herself out of the chair and back to her desk, where the screen holds a frozen image of Yashoda, the little shorn-headed girl from the slum. Little Yashoda, so full of energy and promise amid the misery of Dharavi. Yashoda, with her sweet smile, oblivious to her lice infestation and the fact that she will never attend school. *Is that what my life would have been like in India?* Over the past several months, she has envied Meena with her great journalism career, and Priya with her salon and shopping lifestyle. But now it is evident to Asha that this would not have been her life. She would have been like Yashoda or her sister Bina—just one of India's statistics, another little girl that nobody values. What kind of future will those girls have? Will they spend their whole lives, childhood to motherhood, in Dharavi like the bruised woman she interviewed? Or will they be the fortunate ones—will they get out of the slums, only to end up like those two women in the tenement on Shivaji Road, saddled with husbands, children, and domestic duties?

All her life, Asha has dreamed about what she missed by not knowing her birth parents—unconditional love, deep understanding, a natural connection. *Is that really what I missed? Or was it just a life without opportunity?* Arun Deshpande's words come rushing back to her. *The fortunate ones are adopted.* She thinks of her childhood in California, her bedroom twice the size of those Dharavi homes, her Harper School uniform and Ivy League education. All those years spent wondering about her parents. Maybe they did her a favor.

Usha. Her mother loved her enough to give her a name.

She stares at her screen, at the thin string hanging around Yashoda's neck, remembering how enthralled the little girl was with Asha's rings. Meena explained later these girls grow up seeing jewelry but never owning any. Her mother loved her enough to give her a silver bangle.

She was a brave woman. She must have been quite dedicated to get you here. Her mother loved her enough to travel all the way from some village to take her to the orphanage. She loved her enough to give her away.

She loved her enough.

She loved her.

Asha wipes away the tears from her cheeks and forces herself to watch the rest of the interview with Bina, trying to find a ray of hope. Seeing herself now on the screen, she realizes how insensitive she was, with her questions about the short hair and school. Parag was only trying to spare those girls some embarrassment, not hamper her interview. The sorrow of Yashoda's life is trumped by the tragedy of the crippled girl who appears next. Asha looks away again when she sees her, just as she did the day of the interview. Then, slowly, she turns back to the screen and leans forward to watch it closely. She doesn't remember seeing the girl's face before. The girl is smiling, and so is her mother. The woman actually looks happy as she sets out on her two-kilometer walk to school with her legless daughter on her back. *How can that be?*

The woman in the next interview, the bruised one in the dull green sari, does not smile at all, except briefly when Asha gives her the fifty-rupee note. *Damnit. Why didn't I give her more?* Perhaps it would have saved her from prostituting herself for a night or two to feed her three kids and alcoholic husband. On the screen, her eyes look hollow. Asha consults her notes and remembers that this woman is her age. She can't imagine having to sell her body, or any of the other things these women do to take care of their families. Asha jots down a few notes, then scrolls back and watches it again, focusing on the women as they talk, explaining what they do every day for their families. The next thought descends upon her like a parachute covering the ground. The real story of life in Dharavi is these mothers. They are the face of hope for these children, born into poverty and desolation. Asha extracts a still image of the crippled girl's smiling mother and copies it to a new screen. On top of the photo she types out a caption: "The Face of Hope: Surviving Urban Slums."

She starts typing, telling the stories of these women's courage. Her fingers fly across the keyboard, racing to keep up with the ideas flowing through her. She glances quickly at the clock on the screen and realizes it's nearly seven o'clock. She will be expected home soon. The familiar rush of adrenaline floods her body, just as it did on a nightly basis at the *Herald,* and she knows she has to keep going, all night if necessary. Still typing, Asha picks up the phone and cradles it on her shoulder. Devesh answers.

"Hi. Asha here. Please tell Memsahib I won't be home tonight. I'm working at office. Be home tomorrow." She speaks slowly, pausing between each word so he understands. She works assiduously through the night until her whole story takes shape. Only then does she lay her head down on her desk to rest.

WHEN MEENA ARRIVES IN THE MORNING, ASHA IS WAITING IN her office. "*Arre,* look what the cat dragged in. You look terrible. Have you been here all night?"

"Yes, actually, but that's not important. Listen, I want to go back to Dharavi, I need to do some more interviews."

"What, you want to talk to some men this time?" Meena takes her sunglasses off and drops her handbag onto her desk.

"No, women. Mothers, actually."

Meena raises one eyebrow. "Sounds interesting." She sits down. "I'm listening."

"Well, I was going to focus on the children, you know. I watched the interviews over and over, and I realized it feels so depressing because the kids are born into those circumstances, they don't choose them and they have no power over them. It's sad, but it's not much of a story. But if you switch the perspective, and tell the children's story through their mothers, it changes everything. You see courage. Resilience. The strength of human spirit."

"I like it," Meena acknowledges, spinning in her chair. "It's a nice angle. But listen, Asha, I'm swamped. I can't come with you."

"What about Parag?"

Meena shrugs. "You'll have to ask him."

ON THE WAY TO DHARAVI, ASHA DESCRIBES TO PARAG THE TYPE of interview subjects she's looking for. She's not sure if he agreed to come out of some sense of professional duty or male chivalry. "Hey listen, I'm glad you're coming with me," she says to him as they leave the taxi. He nods his head in that low-key Indian way. "No, really. I don't know my way around here so well, as you've probably noticed. I really need your help." She detects a slight smile and decides to drop the subject.

Dharavi is full of women, mothers caring for their children. There are plenty of willing participants, but Asha walks down the lane until she finds the first woman she wants to interview. She is sitting quietly, scrubbing clothes in a bucket outside her hut while three children mill around her. Asha does *namaste* to the woman and waits until Parag gets permission for her to turn on her camera. She whispers a couple questions to Parag, and lets him handle most of the interchange while she stands back, capturing the interview on film. After answering several questions, the woman invites them into the hut. Both Asha and Parag must duck their heads to clear the entrance. Inside, Asha sees two thin bedrolls laid out on the floor and, on the wall between them, framed photographs of an elderly woman and man. She's learned such pictures honor deceased family members or gurus, usually with fresh flowers, but these two are adorned with wilted garlands buzzing with flies. In the corner is a small shrine of statues and incense sticks. After filming the interior of the hut, Asha turns off the camera. She asks Parag to thank the woman for her time. He translates and turns back to Asha.

"She wants to know, will you take some *chai*?"

Asha smiles at this woman who has nothing, and yet offers her tea. On an earlier visit, this gesture would have made her feel uncomfortable and guilty. "Yes, thank you. Tea would be lovely." They sit outside while the woman makes tea, and Asha teaches her kids pat-a-cake.

The other interviews they conduct are similar, much easier than last time. They have lingering conversations with the women about their lives, their children, and their hopes for the future. They are invited in to see other homes, and offered more tea and snacks. Asha asks Parag to write down the names of all the mothers they speak to.

By the time they're hungry for lunch, she can see the story coming together in her mind. "We make a pretty good team," she says, offering her raised palm to Parag for a high five. He tentatively returns the gesture, and smiles.

"Hey, do you like *pau-bhaji*?" she says. "I know a great place near here."

AFTER LUNCH, PARAG HAS TO GO TO ANOTHER PART OF THE CITY for his next assignment, so he offers to get a taxi for Asha before heading to the train station. On the corner up ahead, she sees a man selling fresh-cut flowers and garlands.

"That's okay," she says to Parag. "I'm going to stay here a bit longer."

He looks at her, raising one eyebrow, and then back over her shoulder at the slum as a warning. She has never been inside Dharavi without an escort.

"Go on, I'll be fine." She gives his shoulder a playful nudge. After he leaves, Asha approaches the flower vendor and asks for five garlands. Then she goes to the ice cream vendor and buys a dozen *kulfi* ice pops. She enters the settlement again, walking along the path until she comes to the first woman they interviewed this morning, now hanging laundry on the line. Asha holds out two garlands, and gestures toward the woman's hut. A slow smile spreads across the woman's face and she ducks between the hanging clothes. She accepts the flowers, places her palms together, and bows her head. Asha smiles and gives her three *kulfi* pops, then turns back to the path to find the next home, hearing the children's happy laughter as she walks away.

She distributes the rest of the flowers and *kulfi* to the other women in much the same way—no words, no translation, no cameras. After she is done, she hails a taxi and climbs into the backseat. With the chance to finally rest, Asha feels a deep ache in her knees, the residue of staying up all night. Her hair feels particularly greasy, more than the usual degree she's become accustomed to in India. It will be such a pleasure to shampoo it properly once she's back home. When she was little, her mother would patiently brush it out in the morning while Asha watched cartoons. It was one of her favorite times of day, when she would look up from Bugs Bunny to see her unruly hair tamed into two neat ponytails for school.

So many memories like this have been coming to Asha lately. The elaborate birthday parties her mother gave her every year, spending the whole morning to make her cake and frosting from scratch. The annual Easter egg hunt she held for all the neighborhood kids in their yard, always hiding a special stash of eggs for Asha in the same corner of her sandbox. And this camera, particularly the camera. Neither of her parents much liked her interest in journalism at first, but her mom eventually came around to the idea. Just as she did when Asha went to college so far away from home, and chose English as her major instead of premed. Despite making many choices that have upset her mother, some even intended to, Asha has never once doubted the steadfastness of her mother's love. She feels a pang of remorse for how angry she was with her mom before she left, and the short meaningless conversations they've had since then.

It is late afternoon by the time Asha gets back to the office, and although the previous night's sleep deprivation is beginning to hit her, she can't stop yet. She goes through the new interviews, and starts writing. She keeps working until she has the skeleton of her story in place. She reviews it all the way through and sits back in her chair. It needs more material and a lot of editing, but there's a story there, one only she could tell. Asha closes her eyes, and a slow smile spreads across her face. She is exhausted, and there is only one person she wants to talk to. She picks up the phone and dials her parents' number. It rings four times before the machine picks up. "Mom?" Asha says. "Hi, it's me. Anyone there? Dad?" She waits a few more moments, then redials. She tries her mother's mobile phone. No answer. *Strange. Where could she be at five P.M. on a weekday?* Asha hangs up, leans back in her swivel chair, and stretches her arms high above her head as a deep yawn escapes from her mouth. She can feel the fatigue deep in her bones. She'll call tomorrow, after getting some sleep.

52

AS GOOD AS I REMEMBER

Menlo Park, California—2005
KRISHNAN

KRISHNAN PACES WITH PHONE IN HAND, BEGINS TO DIAL, THEN
hangs up. He sits down at the kitchen table. *This is ridiculous. Why am
I so nervous?* He spent most of the return flight from his conference
in Boston thinking of what he wanted to say to Somer, and now he
can't even bring himself to make the call. His suitcase sits unopened
in the front foyer, and a pile of mail demands attention on the kitchen
counter. All he's done since arriving from the airport is listen to the
messages, disappointed to hear none from Somer.

He takes a deep breath and dials again. She picks up after the
second ring.

"Hi, it's me," he says. "I just wanted to let you know I'm back in
town."

"Oh, good. So I'll see you Sunday?" Somer says. Outside of their
weekly joint calls to their daughter, Krishnan has called Asha a few
times on his own, trying to be supportive of her search for her birth
parents. The last time he called, Asha had just gone to the orphanage,
but she was reticent to talk and responded vaguely to his questions.

He found himself feeling nervous about this for the first time, worrying that Asha's discoveries might somehow impact their relationship. For once, he empathized with Somer, he understood how this could unsettle her. Next weekend will be one of their last phone calls, since Asha is due to come home in a couple of weeks. Krishnan has no idea what she will return with, and how their family will be affected by it. He is anxious to reconcile with Somer before then. The slow simmer of longing and remorse he has felt during their separation has increased to a full boil with Asha's imminent return. Now, at the age of fifty-five, he is once again awkwardly courting his wife.

"Yes. Hey, listen. I just picked up the photos from my trip to India and I thought you'd like to see them." He takes another deep breath. "Maybe I can stop by sometime . . . tomorrow evening . . . if you're free? We could get dinner?" In the pause that follows, Krishnan closes his eyes tightly and tries to come up with something better.

"Kris, I have to go into the city for an appointment tomorrow after work," Somer says, then pauses before continuing. "I had an abnormal mammogram last week. It's probably nothing, but I made an appointment for a biopsy just to be safe."

"Oh." Krishnan takes this in. "Well, why don't I drive you up there? We can get dinner afterward."

After another long pause, she speaks. "Okay. My appointment's at four-thirty."

"I'll pick you up at three-thirty." He hangs up the phone and shuffles through the pile of assorted items on the kitchen counter until he finds the camera. He picks up the phone again and dials the number he's memorized for the local pharmacy.

"Hello? How quickly can I get photo prints from a memory card?"

Somer gives Krishnan a smile as she enters the car. They greet each other with a peck, and he notices how good she looks. Her face is glowing, and her sleeveless blouse shows her noticeably toned arms.

"Cal-Pacific," she says, reaching for her seat belt.

The last time he drove his wife to that hospital was for her last miscarriage. The memory of that period of their lives unsettles him now. Krishnan takes Highway 280 to San Francisco, the slower and more scenic of the two freeways and the one Somer always prefers. He glances over at her, gazing out the window at the tree-lined hills.

"I found a small lump in my armpit," Somer says, answering the question he has been hesitant to ask. "The week before last in the shower. I'm sure it's just a cyst, but given my family history, I wanted to check it out. I had a mammogram last week, and the radiologist saw an abnormal mass."

"Who was the radiologist?" Krishnan asks. "Do you have a copy of the films? I could get Jim to take a look—"

"Thanks, but that's not necessary. I looked at the films myself, I got a second opinion. I want a biopsy just to be on the safe side." Her voice is calm, with no trace of the worry or anxiety that overshadowed her while they were struggling with infertility, their last major medical issue.

"Who's performing the biopsy? Mike does a lot of consults at CPMC, I could ask him who's best."

Somer turns to look at him. "Kris," she says gently but firmly, "I don't need you to solve this for me. I just want you to be there, for support, okay?"

"Okay." He tightens his grip on the steering wheel and feels moisture on his palms. He reaches for the air-conditioning and struggles to stay calm while risk factors run like headlines through his mind. Caucasian, midfifties, no biological children, mother with breast cancer: all factors that increase Somer's risk. The only factor in the other column, ironically, is the one that has already caused so much grief—the fact that she stopped menstruating twenty years earlier than she should have.

"Did I tell you I got an e-mail from Asha last week while you were gone? She went to someplace called the Elephant Cave."

"Elephanta Caves. Yes, I told her not to miss it." Krishnan smiles. "It's on an island in the harbor. They're these ancient caves, with sculptures cut right into the rock. It's a big tourist attraction. I never took you there?"

"Don't think so. Apparently there are monkeys all over the place, and they jump down on the people visiting—the tourists and everything—they jump down on their shoulders looking for food. Asha sent a photo of her feeding a banana to one. She looked like she was having so much fun. It reminded me of when she was little. Remember how she loved the monkeys at the zoo?"

"Hey, look," she says, "Red's Java House. Can you believe it's still standing there after all these years?" Somer points out the window to the small white shack where they went for burgers on the weekends when they lived in San Francisco.

He forces a smile. "Yeah, hard to believe. What's it been—twenty years or so?"

"Twenty- . . . seven since we first moved up here. Gosh. Older than Asha. Did we ever bring her here?"

"Hmm. Don't think so. We could afford a little better by the time we had her." They both laugh. The greasy food at Red's was nothing special, but they could both eat for under five dollars, the most important element on their residents' salaries. It feels good to laugh, and Krishnan feels some of the tension leave his shoulders.

AT THE HOSPITAL, WHILE SOMER COMPLETES PAPERWORK AT THE reception desk, Krishnan notices the muscular definition of her legs visible below her knee-length skirt. He feels a sudden urge to walk across the room, lift her hair, and kiss the back of her neck. Instead, he crosses his legs and picks up a magazine. After a few minutes, she sits down next to him and peers over his shoulder.

"*Good Housekeeping*? I didn't know you were looking for Weeknight Chicken Meals," she says, noting the article at which he's been staring.

He puts down the magazine. "I'm a bit distracted, I guess."

"Show me the pictures," she says.

"Pictures?"

"From your trip to India."

"Oh. I think I left them in the car."

"Dr. Thakkar?" a nurse calls into the waiting room.

Krishnan looks up with a jolt until Somer lays her hand gently on his. "Not this time, Dr. Thakkar." She smiles, pats his hand, and follows the nurse.

While he waits, Krishnan permits his mind to wander to the worst places. Mastectomy, radiation, chemotherapy. Survival rates for breast cancer are relatively good, but Krishnan has been around illness enough to know there is usually a cruel injustice about the way it strikes. Cranky patients defy the odds, while the kind ones, the ones who bake him cookies or bring him tomatoes from their garden, always seem to die early. Mortality rates utilize the law of averages without consideration for who is most deserving. *This can't happen. Not to her. Not now.*

The last several months have been difficult. Home, where he spends as little time as possible, is full of reminders of their life together. He never thought he would miss the mediocre meals Somer had simmering in the kitchen when he got home, or the way her clothes were casually strewn on their bed at the end of the day. And the mornings. The mornings, when he woke at dawn to perform surgery, as he showered and dressed, her body was conspicuously absent from the bed. There was no one to kiss as he left for the coldness of the operating room, nothing to look forward to coming back to. His home and his work had come to take on the same sterile feel without her presence.

He stands up and paces, passing in front of the reception desk so many times the woman sitting there stops looking up in anticipation each time. From somewhere inside the purse Somer left here, her cell phone rings. He doesn't like this, the waiting. He thinks of the hundreds of times he has walked into a waiting room to speak to a family, to deliver devastating news. Just yesterday, he told a woman not much older than himself that her husband was brain-dead. He encouraged her to call family members, to say good-bye while he was on the ventilator.

"Good-bye? He's still alive, isn't he?" the woman said to him with absolute conviction.

Krishnan never understood why some of his patients' families clung to them long after brain function was gone and their bodies were empty shells. But now he does. Because it happened like this, in an instant. One moment you were laughing in the car with your wife, and the next, you heard a terrible diagnosis in a hospital waiting room. In an instant. The brain, even with all its amazing neural pathways and capacities, with all the mysteries he had grown to respect, could not handle this kind of news. Those families still saw the person they loved somewhere in there, amid the tubes and machinery keeping them alive. They hung on to the dreams they had, of going to their daughter's wedding, holding their grandchild, growing old together. Now he knows, in the same way, it would not be so easy to let Somer go, even if it was what she wanted.

She reappears in the waiting room and sits down next to him. "Everything go okay?" he asks her. She nods. "Your phone rang," he says.

"Oh. Probably my yoga teacher. I never miss class on Tuesday." Krishnan nods, worried about the strength of his voice. "Hey, thanks," she says, pulling her purse onto her lap, "for coming with me today. I'm really glad you're here."

"Of course. Where else would I be?" He squeezes her knee and leaves his hand there.

"When will you get the results?"

"They're putting a rush on it. Hopefully in a day or two."

Krishnan is surprised by the sudden burst of emotion he feels, the lump rising in his throat. "Come on, let's get out of this place," he says, wrapping his arm around her shoulders and holding her body close to his. "I'm taking you out for dinner, anywhere you'd like to go in this wonderful city. You name the place."

It is a rare spring day in San Francisco, sunny and clear, such that they can see the Bay Bridge perfectly from their picnic table in front of Red's. Somer's hair, usually tied back, is blowing around her face in the gentle breeze.

"It's not quite as good as I remember," she says, holding the foil-wrapped burger in front of her face. She smiles in a way that makes her look ten years younger.

"I think our tastes have changed a little in the last few decades," Kris says.

"Not to mention our metabolism. I bet these fries end up directly on my hips tomorrow morning." She laughs lightly.

"You know you look great, honey," he says.

"You mean, assuming I don't have cancer?"

"No, I mean you really look great. Really toned, fit. You're doing yoga?"

"Yes, and now I've got my mom doing it too. After her last surgery she was having a lot of difficulty raising her arm and lifting things, she was getting frustrated. You know how she likes to do things for herself," Somer says. "So I took her to a few classes with me here, and got her some videos she could use at home. It helped the scar tissue heal, her range of motion improved, and her energy level is much higher."

"That's great."

"I was amazed at the difference it made, and so was her oncologist. I wrote an article for *Stanford Women's Health* magazine on the benefits of yoga for breast cancer survivors. The Cancer Center asked me to give workshops for patients. I think I'm going to have Mom come up and do them with me. She can demonstrate the yoga poses while I go through my slides."

"She's lucky to have you looking out for her," Krishnan says. "We all are." He smiles at Somer, the strong, intelligent, confident woman whom he fell in love with, showing a side he hasn't seen in a long time. *Has she changed that much in the last few months, or did I just become blind to her over the years?* And yet, it's not only Somer who seems changed. The whole nature of their interaction feels different. Whether it's the time apart, the distance of Asha, or the scare of the biopsy, it feels as if a bright light is now shining on them, exposing everything they have suppressed for years. And just as it is on his operating table, while those truths might be unpleasant, seeing them clearly is the first step toward healing.

Somer smiles and plays with the pendant of her necklace, reminding him of their days of overt flirtation. And with that, they leave behind all the unspoken discussion of disease, death, and fear and instead, for the first time since they separated, talk in detail about what they've been doing while living apart. Somer tells him about her biking trip to Italy and the personnel changes at the clinic. He tells her about his upcoming tennis club tournament and the broken water heater in the house. Conspicuously absent from their discussion is the topic of their daughter. Krishnan's photos remain untouched in his car. They sit outside until the roaming seagulls have finished off the rest of their dinner, until the air turns chilly and twinkling lights illuminate the outline of the bridge.

"We should probably go." Somer wraps her arms around herself, shivering.

The drive home passes quickly, and Kris realizes he has driven them to their house, where he's been living alone. They sit inside the car in the driveway, like a couple of high school teenagers. He turns off the ignition. "Listen, do you . . . do you want to spend the night?" he says, feeling strangely sheepish. "I know we still have a lot to—"

She interrupts him by placing two fingers against his lips, and smiles. "Yes."

IN THE MORNING, KRIS OPENS HIS EYES TO SEE SOMER'S SUNNY hair spilled out over the pillow. He sighs and feels the sudden rush of emotion he used to when he was first falling in love. He rolls out of bed, careful not to wake her. Walking down the stairs, he realizes the fridge is still empty from his week away and considers making a quick run to the store for breakfast. While he fills the coffeepot, he notices the red light blinking on the answering machine. The message is from his mother in India. She doesn't say anything except to call back, but even through the crackly telephone lines, Krishnan knows something is not right.

53

A FAMILY MATTER

Mumbai, India—2005
ASHA

ASHA FALLS ASLEEP ON THE TAXI RIDE HOME FROM THE *TIMES* office, so the cabdriver has to wake her up when they arrive. She pays him and enters the building. She's been awake for thirty-six hours now, and most of it is a blur—writing, filming, editing—images of the women from Dharavi flash through her mind. She reminds herself to call her mom in the morning. Asha yawns, knocks on the door to the flat, and waits for Devesh's familiar footsteps. She pulls Sanjay's card out of her pocket. *A promise is a promise.* She'll call him in the morning too, now that she finally has the full story herself. After several moments of waiting and hearing sounds from inside, Asha turns the doorknob to find it unlocked. Inside, she sets down her bag, steps over the assorted *chappals* littering the front hallway, and walks toward the drawing room, where she hears the murmur of low voices. *Who could be visiting at this hour?*

Dadima is on the settee, flanked on each side by women who share common looks of concern. Dadima's head is bowed, but even before she sees her face, Asha knows something is wrong. "This is

Asha, my granddaughter from America," Dadima says as she looks up. "You'll please excuse us for a moment." She stands, shuffles over to Asha, and takes her hand.

"Yes, yes, of course," the ladies say in harmony, bobbing their heads side to side.

Dadima walks silently toward the small room Asha has come to call home over the past year. She sits on the bed and gestures for Asha to sit next to her. "*Dhikri,* your *dadaji*'s time has come. He went peacefully in his sleep early this morning."

Asha's hand covers her mouth. "Dadaji?" She looks around the room, toward the door. "Where . . . ?"

Dadima gently takes her hands. "*Beti,* they've taken his body. He passed early this morning, very peacefully."

This morning, while I was . . . working? Dadima's voice is steady, but her red-rimmed eyes tell Asha the rest of the story. She looks down at the hands lying in her lap, two pairs intertwined: Dadima's bony fingers with green veins visible below the sagging skin, and her own, firm and full of youth. As tears slowly parch the varied brown land-scape of their hands, Dadima grips hers tighter and whispers hoarsely, "I must ask you to do something, Asha. Your father will not be here to fulfill the eldest son's role, so you must take his place. You must light the pyre at your *dadaji*'s cremation ceremony. I have spoken to your uncles and they will be there next to you, but I want you to do the lighting." She pauses before continuing. "It is your duty to your family," she says firmly, to quell any forthcoming protests.

Asha knows quite clearly this is not true. Yes, it is the eldest son's role to preside over his family once the patriarch has passed, but in his absence, other men will also do—uncles, friends, cousins, even neighbors. If there is one thing Asha has learned in India, it is that there is always a long succession of men willing to step into an honored role. She looks into her grandmother's eyes and sees she is resolute. Dadima has swept Asha into the arms of this clan as if she has always been one of them, she has treated her like she is both precious and strong. Your duty to your family. *My family.* People Asha had never met and barely spoken to just one year ago, who have fetched her from the airport in the middle of the night, taken her to tourist sites they had no interest in seeing again, taught her how to wear a *lengha,* fly tissue-paper kites, eat all kinds of new foods. She was not born into this family, she did not grow up with them, but it has made no difference. They have done everything for her.

And now it is her turn. Asha feels the lump rising in her throat and nods her agreement.

THE PIGEONS AWAKEN ASHA AS THE LIGHT OF DAWN SEEPS THROUGH the window. She can hear them pecking and cawing on the balcony, scurrying among the bird feed Dadima scatters there every morning, even today. Asha rises, bathes, and dresses, as her grandmother instructed her to.

In the drawing room, a large framed photo of Dadaji is draped with fresh flowers. Dadima is sitting at the table and gazing out the window, without her regular cup of tea. "Hello, *beti.* Come, let us get dressed. The *pandit* will be here soon." Asha is nervous about entering the back bedroom. Her eyes immediately go to Dadaji's side of the bed. On the bed lie two saris. Dadima picks up the pale yellow one with a thin embroidered border and holds it up to Asha. "Your *dadaji* would have liked to see you wear your first sari. Put on the petticoat and blouse and I will show you how to wrap it."

The other sari remains on the bed, unadorned and pure white, the traditional color worn by Indian widows for the rest of their lives. The absence of color, jewelry, and makeup signals their mourning. Asha marvels again at her grandmother, who can embrace tradition so fully with one hand and shatter it with the other. Before this trip, she would have found this kind of contradiction maddening, hypocritical in her parents or others. But the experiences of the past year have taught her the world is more complicated than she ever thought. She started out seeking one family and ended up discovering another. She came to India with no knowledge of her birth parents but certainty about the rest of her life, and now the opposite is true.

Dadima's sari blouse, tailored to fit a woman whose body has birthed and fed children, is much too big for Asha. When she proposes wearing a fitted T-shirt in its place, Dadima is reluctant but finally relents and even admits it looks good. "I wonder why we don't all do that," Dadima mutters to herself as she pins Asha's sari. When Dadima finishes dressing her, Asha looks at her reflection, and she is stunned. The sari flatters her and is surprisingly comfortable.

Shortly after they are dressed, the relatives begin to arrive. Priya, Bindu, and the other women gather in the drawing room around Dadaji's picture, some singing softly, others in quiet prayer. When the *pandit* arrives, Dadima asks Asha to follow them to the balcony. Asha's stomach rumbles as she passes the kitchen, but Dadima has already told her they aren't permitted to eat until after the ceremony.

Standing outside, the *pandit* bows his head to Dadima. "Where are your sons, Sarla-ji?" he asks.

"They will meet us at the *ghats*," she says, "but Asha will be the one to assist you with the rituals, in her father's place."

A look of confusion passes over his face, then a small labored smile. "Please, Sarla-ji, you don't want to compromise your husband's soul. You should choose a male relative, one of your other sons . . ."

Asha looks at her grandmother, sees her tired eyes. "*Pandit-ji*, with respect, this is a family matter. We have made our decision."

THEY ARRIVE TO FIND HUNDREDS OF PEOPLE ALREADY ASSEMBLED FOR the ceremony. There are dozens of hospital staff dressed in medical coats. She sees Nimish and other cousins, her uncles and more relatives she's met over the summer. Sanjay is standing with his father, his eyes red like hers. She recognizes many neighbors from the building, and even the vegetable merchant who comes to their door every day. Neil and Parag from the newspaper are there. Most of the mourners greet her with head bowed and hands joined in *namaste,* and several of them bend down to touch Dadima's feet in the ultimate sign of respect.

The wooden pyre stands nearly as tall as Asha, with Dadaji's body wrapped in white cloth resting on top of it. Asha stands next to the *pandit* and watches attentively as he begins to sing and chant. He dips his fingers into vessels of holy water, rice grains, and flower petals, sprinkles them over the pyre, and gestures for her to do the same. Before long, the continuous rhythm of the *pandit*'s chanting soothes her, and she becomes less conscious of the people surrounding them.

The *pandit* gestures to Asha's uncles, and they come forward. He speaks quietly, and into their upturned palms he places puffed rice, sticks of incense, a pot of *ghee*. Her uncles walk around the pyre and make their offerings to Dadaji's body. They finish circling the pyre and return to stand by Dadima's side.

Finally, the *pandit* speaks a few words of Gujarati to Asha and points to the flame burning in the oil lamp. Asha looks at Dadima's lined face, into her moist eyes, and then takes a step forward. She picks up the bound branches from the oil lamp. As directed by the *pandit,* she circles the pyre three times, then touches the flame to the end of the pyre. Her hands trembling, she holds it in place until small flames lick up the edge of the wooden branches.

Asha steps back next to Dadima and watches as the flames slowly engulf the wooden pyre and finally, the white sheet–covered figure of her grandfather. Through the flickering flames, she sees the faces of her cousins and uncles. *My family.* Only her father is missing, but she knows her presence here is what he would want. *At some point, the family you create is more important than the one you're born into,* he told her. Asha reaches for Dadima's gnarled hand and holds it firmly in her own as the tears roll down her face.

54

UNCOMMONLY PLACID

Dahanu, India—2005
KAVITA

"DID YOU KNOW THESE WERE HERE?" ASKS KAVITA, HOLDING up a dog-eared issue of *Stardust* magazine from 1987.

"No. What was Ba doing with that? She couldn't even read!"

"I don't know. Maybe she liked the pictures?" Kavita flips through the tattered film magazine. "*Arre!* Look at these outfits, so old-fashioned. Oh, my."

Rupa walks over to Kavita, stands on her tiptoes, and peers into the metal cupboard Kavita has been going through. "*Bhagwan!* There must be a hundred of these in here!" She laughs, pulling out a stack of magazines bound together with string.

"I can't believe she would spend money on magazines, and Bollywood magazines at that. Our frugal mother, who saved every grain of sugar. I wonder why she was keeping all of these?" Kavita says.

"Who knew Ba was such a film fan?" Rupa stacks the magazines next to her mother's saris on the bed.

"Oh, it feels good to laugh. I feel like I've been doing nothing but crying since I got here." Kavita gives her sister a weak smile, feeling guilty again.

"*Hahn*. It was hard this morning, wasn't it? Seeing Bapu there?" Rupa is referring to the cremation ceremony held in the village center. Their father fell to his knees and wept as soon as he saw their mother's body on the pyre. His frail body shook violently with hollow cries. He could not be consoled by any of them. The sight of his raw grief, his utter despair, was more than Kavita could handle. She didn't know which sight was more heartbreaking—the draped figure of her mother's body, or her distraught father at its side. Kavita was thankful to have Jasu beside her, his strong arms bracing her as she wept like a child. Normally women mourned at home instead of attending the cremation, but the sisters could not let Bapu go alone. For some indiscernible period of time that followed, they all stood and watched the fire until the last of the embers died out. The ashes were gathered by the *pandit* with a small shovel and given to them in a clay urn. Their father had not spoken or eaten since they came home. Afterward, in the words and embraces she exchanged with guests, Kavita found herself explaining Vijay's absence as briefly as possible, though she wanted to scream. *No, my son is not here, but his money is—in those marigold garlands, in this food you will eat.*

"Mmm." Kavita nods. "Very hard. I'm glad he's sleeping now. Perhaps it's a blessing his memory is going. Maybe he won't remember it all when he wakes up."

"Unfortunately, it seems to be the only part of his memory that is working, the part that remembers her. It's sweet, really," Rupa says. "Think about it, when they got married, Ba was sixteen and he was eighteen. They spent half a century together. He probably can't even remember life before her."

Kavita nods her agreement. She cannot form the words to answer her sister, because once again, her throat is tight with tears.

The water is uncommonly placid this morning. Delicate ripples on the surface of the water dance coyly with the morning's early rays. Strands of bright sunlight sit in contrast atop the dark water underneath, like gold thread woven into a dark sari. As Kavita digs her toes into the smooth cool clay of the sea bank, she tries to imagine what it would feel like to drift to the depths of this water. To be completely unencumbered, free of the worries and responsibilities of life, free to just float, float . . . float . . . and then disappear.

She knows her mother's soul is no longer in the ashes that fill the clay urn beside her, but she wants to believe some part of her is here today. Her mother would appreciate how peaceful this morning feels. Kavita picks up the urn and wraps her hands around the wide base. "Ba," she says softly, and then smiles, realizing it must be her mother's spirit bringing this calm to the morning. Only years after Kavita became a mother herself did she discover how much of a hand her own mother had in everything—working quietly, purposefully, behind the stage of all of their lives. And, Kavita thinks as she holds the urn in her lap, her mother's impact lives on still. *If the mother falls, the whole family falls.*

"*Bena?*" Rupa appears beside her, with her sari draped respectfully over her head. "He is ready for us now." She inclines her head slightly, indicating the boatman standing alongside his raft floating in the water.

"*Hahn.* Let us go." Kavita stands up slowly so as not to disturb the urn. They walk down toward the waiting boatman, who resembles an amphibious creature himself. His body, bare except for a loincloth wrapped over his hips and thighs, is leathery from the sun. He stands in the water up to his waist, equally comfortable on land and at sea. His limbs are lean but muscular, well suited for running through the water before casting himself atop the raft. Kavita and Rupa sit on either end of the raft facing each other, while the boatman stands in the center between them. He steers with deliberate movements of the long bamboo pole he pushes along the bottom. Kavita imagines other ashes down there, the remains of all the other loved ones scattered in these waters—fathers, mothers, sisters, children. Finally, they are far enough from the shore, and the boatman drives his bamboo pole like a spear into the sand below. The sun is now fully visible on the horizon, its orange glow warming their faces and necks.

They could have asked the *pandit* to come out here, to chant *slokas* as they scatter their mother's ashes. But both sisters wanted to perform this final act honoring their mother alone. Even their father, they agreed, would be best served by his absence today. Two days after the cremation ceremony last month, he went back to asking after his wife's whereabouts. Whether it was his ailing mind playing tricks on him or wisely sparing him the pain of truth, they could not be sure. In any case, they finally decided to tell him their mother had gone to visit her sister in a neighboring village and would return the following day. This aunt had, in actuality, died some years earlier, but this fact did not present a problem for their father. Rather, the explanation served to keep him calm for the duration of the day. The following morning, when he asked again, they simply repeated the lie. Each day, the lie became easier to tell. The days passed, and their father slowly returned to his former routine of simply grumbling about the weakness of his ceiling fan or the tepidness of his morning tea. After a few days, Jasu returned to Mumbai, while Kavita decided to stay awhile longer to perform these last rituals.

Kavita slides the lid from the clay urn and tilts it toward Rupa. Although there is little hierarchy to observe in their family of only daughters, she is showing respect for Rupa's role as the elder. Rupa dips her hand into the narrow mouth of the urn and takes out a small handful of gray ash. As she slowly opens her fingers, some of it instantly disappears off the edges of her palm with the light breeze. She holds her hand out over the water and tilts it sideways until the ash falls to the surface of the water. It floats there for a moment, and then is no longer visible, mixing with the sea and all that it holds.

Kavita reaches into the urn and sprinkles the ash back and forth in the water, a motion she has used many times to spread flour for rolling *rotli*. They watch until it disappears, then Rupa reaches inside once more. They continue like this, each alternating a handful, until the urn is nearly empty. Then, without needing to speak, together they hold the clay urn up over the water and tilt it until the last few ashes are emptied. The silence that follows is broken by Rupa. Hers are small cries at first, and grow louder until her whole body is shaking with them. Kavita wraps one arm around her sister, then another, holding her while she weeps. They watch together until the last remnants of their mother's body have vanished below the surface.

55

THAT'S FAMILY

Mumbai, India—2005
ASHA

"THE *MULLIGATAWNY'S* REALLY GOOD HERE." SANJAY SITS ON
the other side of the booth, his hands carefully folded on the table,
his eyes penetrating hers.

At Dadima's insistence, Asha agreed to have lunch with him
today. He is leaving soon for London, but she's been reluctant to leave
her grandmother's side since the cremation ceremony. So here she
sits, with no makeup, her unwashed hair in a ponytail, in a fine hotel
restaurant with the closest thing she's had to a boyfriend. Asha closes
the laminated menu. "Okay, I'll have that," she says. "Sanjay, what
does *Usha* mean?"

He looks up from his menu. "*Usha?* It means . . . dawn. Why?"

"Dawn," she repeats, looking out the window. "That's the name
they gave me. My birth parents only had me for three days before the
orphanage, but they named me Usha."

He puts down the menu and leans forward. "You found them?"

Asha nods. She hasn't told anybody yet. And once she speaks the
words out loud about the truths she now knows, they will become an

irrefutable part of her. "I found them. I didn't meet them face-to-face, but I found them."

The waiter approaches the table. Sanjay orders for them both and sends him away.

"Their names are Kavita and Jasu Merchant," she continues. "They live in an apartment building in Sion." She pauses. "And they have a son. Vijay. He's a year or two younger than me." She looks for a reaction from Sanjay, who nods her on. "They had a *son* after giving me away. They kept him because he was a boy, and—"

"You don't know that was the reason."

Asha shoots him a look of exasperation. "Come on, I wasn't born yesterday."

"There could be lots of explanations. Maybe they couldn't afford to feed a child at the time. Maybe they were living someplace unsafe. Or maybe they regretted losing you and decided they wanted a child after all. You can't know what's in another person's heart, Asha."

She nods, turning the silver bangle around on her wrist. "She came from some village north of here, a few hours away. She traveled all the way to the city just to . . ." She trails off, feeling a lump grow in her throat.

". . . to take you to that orphanage?" Sanjay finishes for her.

Asha nods. "And she gave me this." She slides the bangle back on her wrist.

"They gave you everything they had to give," Sanjay says. He reaches across the table for her hand. "So how do you feel, now that you know?"

Asha gazes out the window. "I used to write these letters, when I was a little girl," she says. "Letters to my mother, telling her what I was learning in school, who my friends were, the books I liked. I must have been about seven when I wrote the first one. I asked my dad to mail it, and I remember he got a really sad look in his eyes and he said, 'I'm sorry, Asha, I don't know where she is.'" She turns back to face Sanjay. "Then, as I got older, the letters changed. Instead of telling her about my life, I started asking all these questions. Was her hair curly? Did she like crossword puzzles? Why didn't she keep me?" Asha shakes her head. "So many questions.

"And now, I know," she continues. "I know where I came from, and I know I was loved. I know I'm a hell of a lot better off now than I would have been otherwise." She shrugs. "And that's enough for me. Some answers, I'll just have to figure out on my own." She takes a deep breath. "You know, I have her eyes." Asha smiles, hers glistening now. She rests the back of her head on the booth. "I wish there was some way to let them know I'm okay, without . . . intruding on their life."

The waiter arrives and places soup bowls on the table in front of each of them. Asha realizes how hungry she is, having eaten very little the past few days between the all-nighter and her grandfather's cremation. She tastes her soup. They eat for a while, without speaking.

"You know, when I went to the orphanage, I found out my grandmother made a big donation there, after I was adopted," Asha says. "Our family's name is on a plaque outside, and she never told me. Isn't that strange?"

Sanjay shrugs and shakes his head. "No, I don't think so. It makes perfect sense to me. She owed a debt of gratitude." Seeing the blank look on her face, he leans toward her and continues, "For *you*. She was grateful for you."

Asha looks down at her hands. "Really?"

"Absolutely. It's very common here. My grandfather had a well built back in his home village, his way of giving back to all the people who helped him."

Asha takes a deep breath. "It's a little overwhelming to think about all the things people have done for me over the years, most of which I didn't even know about, still don't know about. I'm a product of all that—all those efforts, all these people who loved me, even before they really knew me."

Sanjay smiles. "That's family."

"You know, I think I always held it against my parents that there was no biological connection between us. I used to think something was missing. But now . . . it's remarkable really—they've done so much for me, you know, even without the blood. They did it just . . . just because they wanted to." She wipes her mouth with a napkin and smiles. "So I suppose I owe a debt of gratitude to a lot of people." She takes a deep breath. "And an apology to my mom."

"Speaking of which, you owe *me* a copy of your project, when it's done. I'll give it to my friend at the BBC. And once you're famous, you'll really owe me." He winks. "At least a visit to London."

"We'll see." Asha smiles. "Hey, will you come do something with me tomorrow? I want to go by Shanti to drop something off."

56

CROSSING OCEANS

Mumbai, India—2005
SOMER

SOMER LOOKS OVER AT KRISHNAN IN THE SEAT NEXT TO HER, staring through the window to the empty sky. On the surface, he appears just like the hundreds of other Indian men on this plane, a well-dressed, educated professional on his way home for a visit. But Somer can detect the small indications of something else below the surface: Krishnan's jaw, usually clenched, is slack today. His drooping upper eyelid makes his chestnut eyes seem dull and smaller than usual. And at the corner of his mouth, there is a slight quiver. It is an expression her husband does not wear often, accustomed to projecting confidence in the operating room, intensity on the tennis court, impermeability everywhere else.

She reaches over and places her hand on top of his. His eyes begin to water, and still looking out the window, he grasps her hand, intertwining their fingers. He holds on to her as if it is necessary to his survival, as he did in the darkness last night, when they lay in bed together for the second night in a row after six months apart. All day yesterday, as they went about arranging plane tickets and expediting visas, Krishnan was composed. But last night, after their suitcases stood packed and ready in the front hall, after the taxi had been called for the morning, he wept like a child in her arms for the father he had just lost.

There was no question she would go with him. As soon as he woke her up yesterday morning to give her the news, Somer offered to do so. She didn't want him to have to ask, and he seemed grateful for this. Her place was with her family, and now she knew this in the deepest part of her being.

THEY ARRIVE IN MUMBAI IN THE MIDDLE OF THE NIGHT, TAKE A taxi from the airport, and are shown into the flat by a servant. They sleep a few fitful hours before morning arrives. When they enter the living room together, Somer notices how much older Kris's mother appears, her hair thinner and completely white now. Krishnan falls to touch her feet, something Somer has never seen him do before. He and his mother embrace and exchange a few words of Gujarati. Their conversation at the breakfast table over tea and toast is sparse, muted.

"*Beta,* we have some paperwork to take care of at the bank," Dadima says to Krishnan. He nods and looks at Somer.

"It's fine, you go ahead. I'll wait here for Asha to wake up."

SOMER OPENS THE DOOR TO ASHA'S ROOM AND SEES HER daughter sleeping soundly, her hair splayed out across the pillow, her breathing peaceful and heavy—looking at once older than when she left, and resembling the child she has watched sleep so many times before. Somer closes the door quietly and returns to the living room. She glances at her watch, picks up her mobile phone, and dials.

"Hello, this Dr. Somer Thakkar. Can you please page Dr. Woods for me? I'll hold. Thank you." In the several minutes that pass, she stares at the tablecloth, tracing the floral patterns with her fingernail. Finally, she hears a voice.

"Dr. Woods." His voice betrays the fact that he's been awoken.

"James, it's Somer. I'm sorry to disturb you this late, but—"

He yawns. "That's okay. I've been trying to reach you. It's good news, Somer. Biopsy results came back negative. It's a benign cyst. You're clear."

Somer closes her eyes and breathes her response. "Oh, thank God." She exhales a long breath. "Thank you, James. Go back to sleep. Bye." She puts the phone down and rests her head in her hands.

"Mom?"

Somer turns around to see Asha in a nightshirt, her hair disheveled. "Asha, honey." She stands up, opens her arms, and Asha walks into them.

After they embrace, Asha pulls back to look at her. "Mom? What was that? Who were you talking to just now?"

Somer strokes her daughter's hair and notices it has grown several inches. "Come here, honey, I need to tell you something." She takes Asha's hand, and they sit down together at the table. "I'm fine, I want you to know that first. I had a biopsy a couple days ago on a lump in my breast, and it turned out to be benign. So everything's fine."

The lines etched into Asha's forehead remain. Her eyes are earnest.

"Really, I'm fine," Somer says, touching Asha's knee. "It's so good to see you, honey."

Asha leaps forward and throws her arms around Somer's neck. "Oh, Mom. Are you sure you're okay? Positive?"

"Yes, positive." She grabs Asha's hands and squeezes them. "How are you?"

Asha sits back down in her chair. "I've really missed you, Mom. I'm glad you're here."

"Of course." Somer smiles. "Where else would I be?"

"I know it means a lot to Dadima too," Asha says. "She tries not to show it, but this has been hard on her. I can hear her crying in her room at night."

"It must be devastating," Somer says. "Losing her husband after, what, fifty years?"

"Fifty-six. They were married the year after Independence," Asha says. "She's an amazing woman. I've learned so much from her. Everyone's been great—do you know I have thirty-two cousins here? It's been good, really good."

Somer smiles. "And how about your project?"

Asha's eyes glimmer and she straightens her back. "You want to come to the *Times* with me today? I can show you."

SOMER FOLLOWS ASHA THROUGH THE MAZE OF THE NEWSROOM, impressed with how assured her daughter seems in this environment.

"Meena?" Asha finally stops to knock at someone's door. "I want you to meet my mom."

The petite woman springs out of her chair. "Ah, so this is the famous Dr. Thakkar. Asha speaks very highly of you. It's a privilege."

She extends her hand and Somer shakes it, conscious of how good it feels to be recognized as Asha's mother on sight.

Meena turns to Asha. "Have you shown her yet?"

Asha shakes her head, smiling.

"Bring it in here," Meena says. "I'll turn off the lights."

"We filmed all the interviews I did in the slums," Asha explains, setting up her laptop on Meena's desk. "And I edited some of the highlights together into a short film." The three women huddle together around the screen.

After the lights flicker back on, Somer is unable to speak, still moved by what she just saw. Asha managed to find hope in the most unlikely place. In the midst of the poverty and despair of the slums, she showed the fierceness of a mother's love. And how we're really all the same in that way. At the end of the film, there was a dedication to all the mothers who made the film possible. Asha listed all the women by name. Somer's name was last, on its own screen.

Meena speaks first. "The *Times* is running her story as a special feature next month. Asha will get a byline and photo credits." She puts her arm around Asha. "Your daughter is quite a talent. I look forward to seeing what she does next."

Somer smiles as sparks of pride fire in her chest. *Kris was right. India was good for her.*

"What I'd really like to do next is have lunch. Ready, Mom?"

"THIS PLACE IS GREAT," SOMER WHISPERS ACROSS THE WHITE tablecloth. "It looks new?" The menu of the hotel restaurant appears to have come right out of Florence.

"Yeah, it opened just before I got here," Asha says. "They have a real Italian chef and it's so close to the flat, I can just come here whenever I get tired of Indian food." They order salads and pasta from the waiter and dig into the bread basket.

"So, did Dad tell you the news?" Asha asks.

"I don't think so." Somer feels a reflexive tightening in her stomach, running through the possibilities in her head. "What news?"

"I met a guy. Sanjay," Asha says with a lilt in her voice. "He's smart and funny and so good-looking. And he's got these deep brown eyes, you know?"

"Yes, I think I do," Somer says, shaking her head. "Deadly." They laugh together as they enjoy their meal, catching up on their months apart.

When the tiramisu arrives, Asha apologizes. "Mom," she says,

"I'm sorry I . . . I'm sorry about everything that happened before I left home. I know it wasn't easy for you—"

"Honey," Somer interrupts, reaching across the table, "I'm sorry too. I can see this year has been good for you. I'm so proud of what you've done. You seem to have learned so much, grown up so fast."

Asha nods. "You know," she says softly, "what I've learned is that everything's more complicated than it seems. I'm so glad I came here, got to know my family, learn about where I come from. India is an incredible country. There are parts of it that I love, that really feel like home. But at the same time, there are things here that just make me want to turn away, you know?" She looks to Somer. "Does that sound awful?"

"No, honey." She touches Asha's cheek with the back of her hand. "I think I understand," Somer says, and she means it. This country has given her Krishnan and Asha, the most important people in her life. But when she has fought against the power of its influence, it has also been the root of her greatest turmoil.

57

MORNING PRAYERS

Dahanu, India—2005
KAVITA

EACH OF THE ROUGH STONE STEPS KAVITA CLIMBS BRINGS THE
memories rushing back. Though it has been over twenty years since
she shared this house with Jasu, the soles of her feet remember it as if
no time has passed at all. In all the visits she has made back here to
Dahanu over the past two decades, even to this very house where
Jasu's parents still live, she has never felt this way. Perhaps it is the time
of day, this peaceful hour before the village awakens and the rustlings
of human activity become audible from all directions. Perhaps it is
the season, the last few days of spring when the *chickoo* trees are full
of blossoms, filling the air with their sweet scent. Perhaps it is that
she has come here alone: not to visit her in-laws, not to show Vijay
his childhood home, but by herself. Or perhaps it is her frame of
mind, having just said her final farewell to her mother yesterday at
the seashore.

Kavita left her father's house early this morning before the nursemaid was awake. She bathed quickly and gathered a few things from
the *mandir*—a *diya,* an incense stick, a string of sandalwood beads, the

brass figurine of Krishna playing his flute. Her intention was only to step outside the house to perform her *puja,* preferring the fresh dawn air as the backdrop for her morning prayers. But once she was standing outside with those familiar items weighing in her hands, Kavita felt drawn to keep walking, all the way here to her old house. Her in-laws will be asleep for at least another hour, so she can slip away without anyone seeing her.

Standing on top of the stone landing, Kavita spreads out the worn cloth mat in the same place she used to. She kneels down on it, facing east. One by one, she lays out the items she has brought with her: Krishna at the center, *diya* on the right, incense on the left, beads in front of her. Each movement follows automatically after the last, a series of rituals she has performed so many times it is natural. She strikes a match to light the *diya.* She holds the end of the incense stick into the flame until it catches, then waves it lightly until the dull orange glow appears at its end. When she completes the routine, she sits back on her heels and exhales slowly a long deep breath that she feels she has been holding for many years.

She relaxes the muscles of her body and gazes into the hypnotic glow of the flame until her breath falls into a steady rhythm. The familiar scent of burning *ghee* and incense fills her nostrils. She sees the sun breaking through on the distant horizon, and hears the twittering of birds in the trees above her. She closes her eyes and picks up the beads, feeling the ridges of each one with her fingers, chanting softly. She is filled with something so big it feels like it will break through her lungs. Yet at the same time, she feels hollow. What fills her heart and her mind is an overwhelming sense of emptiness, a deep mourning for all the things she's lost.

Kavita scattered the ashes just yesterday, but it has been nearly a month since she lost her mother. She expected the sorrow, but it has come as a shock just how unmoored she has become with her mother's passing. She left this village years ago, her parents' home years earlier still. She has lived as an adult for a very long time, yet losing her mother has made her feel like a child again. The memories that now echo in Kavita's mind are from so long ago she cannot place them: her mother's cool hand on her feverish head, the scent of jasmine woven into her hair.

Beads between her fingers
A cool hand on her forehead
The scent of the incense and jasmine

Now, she is losing her father too. He is slipping away from her, she can feel it. Some days Kavita feels his spirit close; there are many more when he feels far away. Three days ago, as she fed him rice pudding with a spoon, he called her "Lalita." Tears sprang to her eyes when she heard that name, a name she has not been called in twenty-five years, a name only her father could call her. She cries again now, remembering how it sounded on his lips.

Lalita
Beads between her fingers
A cool hand on her forehead
Incense and jasmine

Was it the right decision to leave here, to leave their families so many years ago? Things might have turned out differently if they hadn't. They did it for Vijay, but in the end, he was lost to them. And how long has it been since she lost Vijay? What has become of that little boy, who played in the dirt with his cousins? Where, along the way, was his innocence lost? What had happened to the child who had been named for Victory?

Victory
Beads between her fingers
Lalita
A cool hand on her forehead
Incense and jasmine

It has been more than twenty years since she lost her two daughters here, the one who was never given a name or a life, and her precious Usha. With thoughts of Usha comes the physical ache in her heart. There has not been a day since Usha's birth that Kavita has not thought of her, mourned her loss, and prayed for the hollow feelings of grief to melt away. But God has not listened. Or else he has not yet forgiven her. Because the heartache has endured.

Usha
Beads between her fingers
Victory
A cool hand on her forehead
Lalita
Incense and jasmine

She has spent twenty years far away from her family. She lost first her daughters, then her son, and now her parents. The only relationship that has prospered, against those many cruel complications, is her marriage to Jasu. Yes, he has made mistakes and poor decisions along the way, but her husband has grown to be a good man. Their journey together has been littered with hardship and sorrow, and yet they learned to bury the regrets and the resentment that could have gathered force during their lives. They have grown together, toward one another, two trees leaning on each other as they age. When their time comes, perhaps she and Jasu will be fortunate to have a love like her parents, enduring beyond all reason and even death.

Kavita thinks about all she still does not know, even now as an adult. She doesn't know where her daughter is. She doesn't know where she went wrong with Vijay. She doesn't know whether Bapu will remember her today or tomorrow. She doesn't know how she will go on without her mother's cool hand on her forehead. The only thing she knows for certain is, for the next few days, she will tend to her father. Then she will pack her suitcase, board the train to Mumbai, and return home to Jasu.

58

PARTING GIFTS

Mumbai, India—2005
ASHA

"MOM LEFT ME IN THE DUST AGAIN." ASHA LEANS DOWN TO unlace her sneakers.

Her father and Dadima are sitting at the table, enjoying a second cup of tea as they do every morning. "And she's only had a week to get used to the lovely pollution of Mumbai," her dad says. "Imagine how she'll outrun you back in the fresh California air." He kneads Asha's shoulders a couple times when she sits down beside him.

"Not bad for an old lady," her mom says, wiping her face and reaching for the pitcher of water in the center of the table.

"Devesh, *limbu pani layavo!*" Dadima calls over her shoulder into the kitchen. Devesh appears with a chilled glass of freshly squeezed lime and sugarcane juice, and places it on the table in front of Asha's mom. Ever since her mother took a liking to this labor-intensive beverage, Dadima has had a glass ready for her after their morning run. "Don't call yourself an old lady! What on earth would that make me?" Dadima laughs.

Her mother takes a sip. "Mmm. Delicious. Thank you, Sarla."

Dadima wobbles her head sideways and excuses herself, leaving the three of them.

"So, you're totally off of coffee, Mom?" Asha says.

Somer nods. "The first couple weeks were rough, but now I find staying hydrated keeps me alert throughout the day, and I don't miss the caffeine at all."

"I can't believe how toned you are." Asha places a hand on her mother's bicep. "Have you been lifting weights?"

"A little. It's mostly yoga though. I found this great studio near . . . uh, near the clinic."

"Yoga, huh? Maybe I should go with you, I could use a little toning after all the fattening up I got from Dad's family. Doesn't she look great, Dad?" Asha turns to him.

"Yes," he says, sharing a private smile with her mother. "Yes, she really does." Her dad encircles her mom with his arms from behind, and kisses her on the head. "And did you know your mom published an article in a medical journal?"

"You did?" Asha says.

"Yeah, how about that? Now you're not the only writer in the family." Her mom smiles.

"ARE YOU SURE YOU WON'T COME, DADIMA? I PROMISE NOT TO tell anyone," Asha says, raising one eyebrow at her and smiling. She puts a stack of folded clothes into a large suitcase on the bed.

"*Nai, nai, beti*. It has not even been two weeks since the cremation. I cannot leave the house except to go to the temple. Besides, what place is there for an old woman like me at the airport? I would just be in the way, like one more trunk for you to look after." She smiles at Asha. "Don't worry. Nimish will take you, and Priya is coming too, no?"

"Yes," Asha says, straining to zip up the overstuffed suitcase.

"They'll be here in a couple hours. But I still wish you would come."

"You'll just have to come back soon then, *beti*. How about next year? Maybe our Priya will finally agree to get married next wedding season."

"I don't know, Dadima. I wouldn't count on it." Asha laughs and sits down on the bed, between the suitcase and her grandmother. In the quiet that follows their laughter, Asha stares at the floor, at her grandmother's ancient, gnarled feet that have walked so many miles with her over the past many months. Dadima tucks a fallen strand of Asha's hair behind her ear, and with this touch, Asha squeezes her eyes closed. She feels her face contort as she begins to cry.

"*Beti.*" Dadima puts one hand on top of Asha's hands and strokes her hair with the other, just repeating this simple gesture while she cries.

"I don't know how to thank you for everything. I can't believe it took me twenty years to get here." She takes a deep breath before continuing. "I thought I had it all figured out before I came here, but I was wrong about so many things. I feel like there's still so much I don't know."

"Ah, *beti*," Dadima says, "that is what growing up is. Life is always changing on us, presenting us with new lessons. Look at me, I'm seventy-six, and I'm just now learning how to wear white." Asha forces a smile. "Which reminds me, I have some things for you." Dadima stands up and walks toward the bedroom door.

"Dadima, no!" Asha says. "I just got my suitcase closed." She falls back on the bed, laughing, and wipes her eyes with the heels of her palms.

"Then you'll just have to take another one," Dadima says as she shuffles out of the room. She returns with a cardboard box and sits next to Asha on the bed. She reaches inside the box, pulls out a thick dust-covered book, and hands it to Asha.

Asha runs her hand over the navy blue cover and the gold letters spelling out *Oxford English Dictionary.* "Wow. This must be fifty years old."

"Older, even," Dadima says. "My father gave this to me for my graduation, about . . . oh, sixty years ago. I told you he was an Anglophile. I found it quite handy when I was giving my tutoring lessons. You will do much greater things in your career, I know. Keep it on your desk as a reminder of the confidence I have in you, just as my father had in me."

Asha nods, tears forming at the corners of her eyes. "I will," she whispers.

"And one more thing." Dadima hands her a blue velvet rectangular box. Asha flips the clasp and opens the hinged lid. She pulls back when she sees what's inside. It is a matching set of jewelry, deep yellow gold encrusted with bright green emeralds: a necklace, drop earrings, and four bangles. She looks up at her grandmother, her mouth slightly parted.

Dadima shrugs. "What use do I have for jewels, at my age? I'm not going to weddings anymore. I wore this at my own wedding."

"Oh Dadima, but don't you want to keep it?" Asha looks at her with disbelief.

Dadima shakes her head. "In our custom, this should go to my daughter. I want you to have it. And so would Dadaji." Asha nods at the dazzling vision of jewels in front of her. "Besides, this looks so lovely on you," Dadima says, holding one of the earrings up to Asha's lobe. "Shows off your eyes." As they embrace, Dadima speaks softly. "Are you going to tell your parents what you learned, *beti,* at the orphanage?"

They disentangle themselves and Asha wipes her face and nods. "After we get home. I don't know how they'll feel about it, especially Mom, but they deserve to know the truth."

Dadima wraps her cool papery hands around Asha's face. "Yes, we all do, *beti.*"

59

RETURN OF HOPE

Mumbai, India—2005
SOMER

SOMER IS PACKING HER SUITCASE WHEN THERE IS A KNOCK AT the door. "Come in," she says over her shoulder, expecting Asha.

Instead, Kris's mother enters the room, carrying a large box. "Hello, *beti,* I have a few things for you."

"Oh, well Krishnan just ran downstairs to say good-bye to one of the neighbors."

"No matter," Sarla says, placing a large bundle wrapped in a thin white cloth on the bed. "These are not for him, they are for you."

Somer moves her suitcase and sits down on the bed, she and her mother-in-law separated by the bundle between them. Sarla begins untying the string around the bundle and unfolding layers of the white cloth to reveal a stack of rich jewel-toned saris.

"I want you to have these. I'll give the others away to charity, but I wanted these—the ones I wore to my various wedding events—to stay in the family." The old woman lays both of her hands, palms down, on top of the pile. "I've kept a few for the other girls, but they have so many of their own. They think mine are old-fashioned, which they are. I know you don't wear Indian clothes, so you can use them for bedspreads or drapes if you want to, I won't mind." Sarla laughs.

Somer unfolds the rich orange-yellow sari on top of the pile and runs her hand over the smooth silk, the ornate gold designs along the edge. It is breathtaking, the color of sunset. "That would be a shame. I'd like to try to wear them, I don't know how but—"

"Asha can show you." Sarla's smile accentuates the deep lines around her mouth.

"Thank you. I know how special these are. I promise to take good care of them," Somer says, feeling the emotion well in her chest. "I appreciate it. And . . . I appreciate you taking such good care of Asha over the past year."

"Well"—Sarla covers Somer's hands with her own—"no one can take the place of a mother, but I tried to look after her for you. She is a very special young woman. I see a lot of you in her. You should feel proud of how you've raised her."

"Thank you," Somer says, tears filling her eyes. The door squeaks open and Krishnan enters. "But I didn't do it alone, as you know." She laughs, cocking her head toward the door. "Your son deserves some credit too."

"Yes, please give me some credit. What have I done this time?" Krishnan says.

"Nothing. Absolutely nothing. Come, sit," Sarla says. "I have some things for you."

Somer lifts the bundle of saris in her arms and walks to the other side of the room while Krishnan sits in her place on the bed. She wonders for a moment if she should leave, to allow them some privacy, but then Sarla speaks to them both.

"I know you have many bodies of water there, where you live in California?" she says. "Perhaps you can find a nice spot, someplace peaceful your papa would like." She hands Kris a small jar filled with gray ash. "And you can sprinkle these."

From across the room, Somer sees Kris's shoulders sink a few degrees as he takes the jar.

"We'll scatter some here in the sea when it's time, but . . ." Sarla juts her chin out and her eyes glisten as she looks at her son. "But he was always so proud of you for being there.

"And, this is also for you. A little old, but it still works." Sarla pulls out of the box a well-worn stethoscope.

Somer immediately recognizes the instrument she saw Kris's father wear every single day on their last visit. He was inseparable from that stethoscope, and it often accompanied him to the dinner table. Krishnan has little need for one now in his own practice, probably hasn't used one in years, but she understands the significance of this gift.

"Are you sure? You don't want to keep it—" he says, turning it over in his hands.

Sarla closes her eyes. "*Hahn, beta,* I'm sure. He made his wishes very clear."

THEY WAIT IN THE AIRPORT LOUNGE, ONE MORE HOUR TO GO before boarding their plane. Krishnan drinks what he deems to be his last cup of true Indian *chai,* and Asha and Somer sip tonic water with lime.

"Mom taught me the sun salutation this morning," Asha says to Kris. "You should have joined us. You're going to be stiff and sore by the time we get home, and we'll be all limber." Kris shakes his head with a smile and turns back to his newspaper.

"You know, I've been thinking about going on a yoga retreat for two weeks next year," Somer says.

"Cool. Where?" Asha says.

"Mysore."

Kris looks up from the paper, he and Asha look at each other, and they both look at Somer. "Mysore . . . India?" Kris asks.

"Yes," she replies. "Mysore, India. They have a big yoga retreat center there. I've been talking to my instructor about it. She thinks I'm almost ready." A slow smile spreads across her face. The first time she came to India, it was for Asha. This time was for Krishnan. Perhaps next time will be for her. "Maybe we can make it a family trip."

"Yeah," Asha says, "that would be great."

"Only you"—Somer reaches over to pat Kris on his belly—"*You* will have to get into better shape if you want to keep up with us." They all laugh.

Asha stretches her arms over her head and yawns. "I am not looking forward to this flight," she says. "Twenty-seven hours? That'll be the longest time we've ever spent this close together." She points to Somer in the chair on her left and Kris on her right.

"Well, not really," Somer says. Kris peers over his bifocals, and Asha looks at her with a furrowed brow. "I believe it was about twenty years ago, we made the same flight?"

Krishnan chuckles. Asha smiles and gives her a playful punch in the shoulder.

SOMER RECLINES IN HER AIRPLANE SEAT, WATCHING THROUGH the window as the glimmering lights of Mumbai recede into the darkness of night. In the seat next to her, Asha is already asleep, her head and pillow resting on Somer's lap, her feet in Krishnan's. They should both try to sleep as well, but she knows Krishnan, like her, is reluctant to disturb Asha. He extends his hand to Somer, and she takes it. They rest their interlocking hands on Asha's sleeping body between them, just as they did the first time they made this journey.

60

SUCH A GOOD THING

Mumbai, India—2009
JASU

HE CLUTCHES THE WORN SLIP OF PAPER IN HIS HAND, TRYING TO compare the letters written there to the red sign hanging on the door in front of him. Looking back and forth from the paper to the door several times, he is careful not to make a mistake. Once he feels certain, he presses the bell, and a shrill ring echoes inside. While he waits, he runs his palm over the brass plaque next to the door, feeling the ridges of the raised letters with his fingers. When the door opens suddenly, he pulls back his hand and gives another slip of paper to the young woman in the doorway. She reads the note, looks up at him, and steps back to let him enter.

With a slight tilt of her head, she indicates he should follow her down the hallway. He makes sure his shirt is tucked in underneath his slight paunch of a belly, and runs his fingers through his graying hair. The young woman walks into an office, hands the slip of paper to someone inside, and then points him to a chair. He enters, sits down, and clasps his fingers.

"I'm Arun Deshpande." The man behind the desk wears thin spectacles. "Mr. Merchant, is it?"

"Yes," Jasu says, clearing his throat. "Jasu Merchant."

"I understand you're looking for someone."

"Yes, we—my wife and I—we don't want to cause any trouble. We just want to know what happened to a little girl who came here twenty-five years ago. Her name was Usha. Merchant. We just want to know if she is . . . well, we want to know what happened to her."

"Why now, Mr. Merchant? After twenty-five years, why now?" Arun says.

Jasu feels his face flush. He looks down at his hands. "My wife," he says softly, "she is not well . . ." He thinks of Kavita lying in bed, hot with fever, whispering the same words over and over in her delirium, "*Usha . . . Shanti . . . Usha.*" At first, he thought she was praying to herself, until the night she clasped his hand and said, "Go find her." After a phone call to Rupa, he learned the truth of what happened twenty-five years ago and understood what she was asking of him. Now, he finds the right words to explain. "I want to bring her some peace, before it's too late."

"Of course. You must understand, our first priority is to protect the children, even when they're adults. But I will tell you what I can." He pulls a file folder out of his desk drawer. "I met this girl a few years ago. She goes by the name Asha now."

"Asha," Jasu says, nodding his head slowly. "So, she still lives nearby then?"

The man shakes his head. "No, she lives in America now. She was adopted by a family there, two doctors."

"America?" Jasu says it the first time loudly, in disbelief, and then again quietly, as he takes it in. "America." A smile spreads slowly across his face. "*Achha.* You said doctor?"

"Her parents are doctors. She is a journalist, at least she was when she came here."

"Journalist?"

"Yes, she writes stories for newspapers," Arun says, holding up yesterday's *Times* from his desk. "In fact, I have one of her stories here in her file. She sent it to me after she went back."

"*Achha,* very good." Jasu nods his head slowly from side to side and reaches for the page of newsprint Arun holds out. Now, more than at any other moment in his life, Jasu wishes he knew how to read.

"You know, she came here a few years ago looking for you," Arun says, removing his glasses to wipe them.

"To look for . . . me?"

"Yes, both of you. She was curious about her biological parents. Very curious. And very persistent." Arun replaces his glasses and squints into them. "Was there something specific you were looking for, Mr. Merchant? Something you wanted?"

Jasu wears a small, sad smile. Something he wanted? He came here for Kavita, of course, but that's not all. Last year, when the police called him to get Vijay out of jail, he yelled at his son, slapped him across the face, threw him against the wall. Vijay smirked and told his father not to worry about him anymore, that next time one of his friends would bail him out. The boy has come to see Kavita only once during the past month when she's been bedridden. Jasu shakes his head a little, looking down at the newspaper article. "No, I want nothing. I just wanted to see how she has fared. There are things in my life I'm not proud of, but . . ." The tears well in his eyes and he clears his throat. "But this girl has done good, no?"

"Mr. Merchant," Arun says, "there's one more thing." He removes an envelope from the file and holds it out to him. "Would you like me to read it for you?"

KAVITA LOOKS PEACEFUL WHEN SHE'S SLEEPING, WHEN THE morphine finally brings her some comfort. Jasu sits in a chair next to the bed and reaches for her frail hand.

With his touch, her eyes flutter open and she licks her dried lips. She sees him and smiles. "*Jani,* you're back," she says softly.

"I went there, *chakli.*" He tries to begin slowly, but the words come tumbling out. "I went to Shanti, the orphanage. The man there knows her, he's *met* her, Kavi. Her name is Asha now. She grew up in America, her parents are doctors, and she writes stories for newspapers—look, this is hers, she wrote *this.*" He waves the article in front of her.

"America." Kavita's voice is barely a whisper. She closes her eyes and a tear drips down the side of her face and into her ear. "So far from home. All this time, she's been so far from us."

"Such a good thing you did, *chakli.*" He strokes her hair, pulled back into a loose bun, and wipes her tears away with his rough fingers. "Just imagine if . . ." He looks down, shakes his head, and clasps her hand between his. He rests his head against their hands and begins to cry. "Such a good thing."

He looks up at her again. "She came looking for us, Kavi. She left this." Jasu hands her the letter. A small smile breaks through on Kavita's face. She peers at the page while he recites from memory.

"*My name is Asha . . .*"

ACKNOWLEDGMENTS

THE SEED OF THIS STORY WAS PLANTED DURING A SUMMER IN college I spent as a volunteer at an orphanage in Hyderabad, India. For that experience and so many others, I thank the Morehead-Cain Foundation of Chapel Hill, North Carolina, and also Child Haven International.

My instructors and fellow students in the SMU Creative Writing Program provided me with the opportunity, the inspiration, and the tools to write.

Fellow writers Cindy Corpier, Lori Reisenbichler, Sarah Wright, and Erin Burdette read the earliest drafts of the manuscript and helped me craft the story I intended to tell, offering both criticism and encouragement when necessary. Every writer should be fortunate to have such a group.

I am grateful to my dear friends Dr. Katherine Kirby Dunleavy, Celia Savitz Strauss, Saswati Paul, and Dr. Sheila Mehta Au, each of whom read key sections and provided critical insights along the way.

Many people contributed invaluably to my research on various places, professions, and experiences: Reena Kapoor, Michele Katyal Limaye, Faith Morningstar, Alice De Normandie, Susan Ataman,

Anjali Shah Desai, Dr. Michael Desaloms, Dr. Irène Cannon, James Slavet, Stephanie Johnes, Jennifer Marsh, Sangeeta and Sandeep Sadhwani, Christine Nathan, Leela de Souza Bransten, Geetanjali Dhillon, and Tushar Lakhani.

During this process, I was fortunate to have my own personal Texas cheerleading squad on the Stanford block, and even from a distance, the Stanford book club was a formidable presence. Many other friends, too numerous to name, were generous with their introductions and unwavering in their support.

My agent, Ayesha Pande of Collins Literary, believed in this project long before there was any good reason to, and generously invested her time, insight, advice, and support. She is a writer's true gift, and I thank Rachel Kahan and Carrie Thornton for leading me to her.

Carrie Feron took on this project with enthusiasm, and I am grateful for her keen instinct and sensitive touch. She and her wonderful team at HarperCollins/William Morrow—Tessa Woodward, Esi Sogah, Tavia Kowalchuk, and Liate Stehlik—expertly shepherded it through to fruition.

The most essential ingredient to this project, as with everything in my life, has been the influence and support of my family across generations and continents, and in particular:

My father, who introduced me to the art of storytelling with his own imagination from the earliest age I can remember.

My mother, who cherished every piece of writing I have ever created in my life as if it were a priceless work of art.

My sister, Preety, who was the first nurturer of creativity and the artistic spirit in me.

Dr. Ram and Connie Gowda, my parents-in-law, who have supported me in countless ways.

My children, for bringing joy and perspective to every day.

And finally Anand, who always has bigger dreams for me than I can possibly have for myself.

FOREIGN TERMS GLOSSARY

Achha—OK, all right
Agni—god of fire
Aloo—potato
Arre—exclamation, roughly meaning "Oh my!"
Asha—female name meaning "hope"
Atman—soul
Ayah—nanny servant

Ba—mother
Bahot—very
Bapu—father
Basti—settlement, slum
Bathau—show me
Beechari—unfortunate woman, girl
Beedi—hand-rolled cigarettes
Ben, bena—term of respect meaning "sister"
Bengan bhartha—eggplant curry
Betelnut—hard nut chewed as a digestive
Beti, beta—term of endearment meaning "dear"
Bhagwan—god
Bhai, bhaiya—term of respect meaning "brother"
Bhangra—lively Indian dance
Bhath—rice
Bhel-puri—snack food, sold at street stalls
Bhinda—okra
Bindi—mark (makeup or sticker) on Indian woman's forehead
Biryani—rice dish

Chaat—snack food
Chai—tea

Chakli—bird

Challo—let's go

Chania-choli—two-piece Indian dress outfit, with a long skirt and short top

Chappals—sandals

Chawl—tenement building with units that consist of one room for living and sleeping, and a kitchen that also serves as a dining room. Latrines are shared with other units.

Chicken makhani—butter chicken

Crore—ten million (rupees)

Dada, Dadaji—paternal grandfather

Dadi, Dadima—paternal grandmother

Daiji—midwife

Dal—lentil soup, staple of Indian diet

Desi—colloquial term for Indian

Dhaba-wallah—tiffin carrier

Dhikri—daughter

Dhoti—traditional Indian men's garment

Diwali—festival of lights

Diya—a flame/light made in a small earthen pot, with a wick made of cotton and dipped in *ghee*

Doh—two

Ek—one

Futta-fut—quickly

Garam—hot

Garam masala—spice mixture

Gawar—insult meaning "village boy"

Ghee—clarified butter, used in Indian cooking

Gulab jamun—Indian sweet

Hahn, hahnji—yes

Hijra—transvestite

Idli—South Indian savory dumpling

Jaldi—quickly

Jalebi—Indian sweet

Jamai—groom's wedding procession

Jani—term of endearment used between spouses
Jhanjhaar—silver anklet
-ji—as a name suffix, respectful term of address

Kabbadi—chasing game
Kachori—savory fried dumpling
Kajal—eyeliner
Kali—goddess of destruction
Kanjeevaram—type of silk
Khadi—buttermilk soup
Khichdi—simple porridge made of rice and lentils
Khobi-bhaji—cabbage dish
Khush—happy
Kulfi—frozen flavored milk dessert
Kurta-pajama—loose-fitting loungewear

Laddoo—Indian sweet
Lagaan—wedding
Lakh—ten thousand (rupees)
Lathi—bamboo stick used as a weapon by Indian police
Layavo—bring to me
Lengha—two-piece Indian dress outfit, with a skirt
Limbu pani—sweetened lime juice

Mandir—Hindu temple
Mantra—chant
Masala dosa—South Indian savory griddle cake
Masi—maternal aunt
Mehndi—henna

Nai—no
Namaste, Namaskar—common Indian gesture of greeting, thanks, prayer, or
      respect, in which the palms of the hands are placed together in front of
      the face
Namkaran—naming ceremony

Paan—leaf-wrapped postmeal digestive
Pakora—battered vegetable fritters
Pandit—Hindu priest
Paneer—pressed cheese
Pau-bhaji—mixed vegetable curry with bread, often sold by street vendors
Pista—pistachio

Puja—prayer ceremony
Pulao—basmati rice with peas and carrots
Puri—delicate deep-fried bread

Raas-Garba—Gujarati group dance
Ringna—eggplant
Rotli—flatbread

Saag paneer—spinach and cheese curry
Sabzi-wallah—vegetable vendor
Salwar khameez—two-piece Indian dress outfit, with pants
Sambar—spicy South Indian *dal,* or lentil soup
Samosa—deep-fried savory turnovers
Sari, saree—traditional garment worn by Indian women, a six-yard rectangle
     of fabric wrapped around the body over a full-length petticoat/skirt
     and short blouse.
Sassu—mother-in-law
Shaak—vegetable dish
Shakti—strength, the sacred feminine force
Shukriya—thank you
Singh-dhana—peanuts
Slokas—Sanskrit religious chants

Tabla—hand drum
Tandoori—made in a tandoor (open clay) oven
Thali—large dining platter made of stainless steel or silver
Tiffin—stainless steel pot carrying food, usually delivered for lunch
Tindora—variety of Indian vegetable

Usha—female name meaning "dawn"

Wallah—vendor

Yaar—slang term for friend

Zari—silver or gold embroidery

A⁺

AUTHOR
INSIGHTS,
EXTRAS &
MORE...

FROM

**SHILPI
SOMAYA
GOWDA**

AND

WM

WILLIAM MORROW

Reading Group Discussion Questions

1. On the way to the orphanage in Bombay, Kavita reflects on "what power there is in naming another living being." She gives her daughter the name Usha at birth, but she is later raised by her adoptive parents as Asha. Kavita's name changed when she was married, and her given name reappears again later in the story. Even Krishnan becomes known as "Kris" in America. What is the significance of these changing names throughout the story?

2. Kavita faces a difficult choice at the beginning of the novel. Did she make the right decision? What would you have done if you were in Kavita's place? What would the repercussions be of making a different choice?

3. Why do you think Somer made the decision to adopt a child from India, and do you believe her reasons were sound? Are there any parallels between how she made this decision, and her previous decision to marry Krishnan? What does this tell us about Somer's character?

4. Both families in the novel leave their home in search of better life—the Merchants leave their village for Bombay, and Krishnan leaves India for America—and this act of migration creates longing for home and feelings of displacement. Did you believe these were good choices at the time? Were the decisions driven more by wanting to

leave home or being attracted to a new place? Would the characters have made different choices if they knew what the consequences would be?

5.   The novel explores the issue of how gender affects one's role in society, both in India and the United States. Despite much of the obvious discrimination women face in India, Sarla Thakkar believes, "you can't always see the power women hold, but it is there. . . ." In what ways is this true? What are the benefits and drawbacks of being a woman in each of these countries? Are there any similarities in the female experience across the two cultures?

6.   An overarching theme of the novel is motherhood, and how that experience can change a woman. Both Somer and Kavita have powerful experiences and emotions around pregnancy, childbirth, and mothering. What are the differences in how they experience motherhood, and are there any similarities? Are there universal aspects to motherhood or is it an individual experience? How do you believe becoming a mother changes you?

7.   Both marriages portrayed in the novel, despite different circumstances and origins, face significant challenges. How did Kavita and Jasu's marriage recover from the dramatic conflict they faced at the beginning? What caused the estrangement between Krishnan and Somer, and how did each spouse contribute to it? Do you believe one marriage is fundamentally stronger than the other? What do you believe the future holds for each couple?

8.   Asha grows up with a deep curiosity about her biological family in India. Is this is a natural curiosity for all adopted children? Could her parents have done anything to lessen the sense of feeling incomplete Asha had as an

adolescent? Can her conflict with Somer be chalked up to that experienced in all mother-teenage daughter relationships, or was it more complicated? What does Asha learn about the true meaning of family, and could she have learned it without going to India?

9. This story turns on a twist of fate that changes the life path of Asha and follows the parallel lives of Asha and her brother in India. Do you believe Asha was better off being taken to the orphanage as a baby than she would have been with her birth parents? Could Vijay have had a different life? What role do you believe gender and socioeconomic class have on our fate? How much of our lives are destined for us, and how much is within our power to change? Reflecting on your own life, what have been the turning points that have been made for you, and those made by you?

10. The importance of relationships across generations echoes through the novel, particularly at the end, with the deaths of Krishnan's father and Kavita's mother. What role do elder relatives play in the story? What hopes and expectations are passed down? What did you think of the relationship that develops between Sarla (Dadima) and Asha? How are these ideas complicated or resolved in the rituals of the cremation ceremonies at the end?

11. What do you believe Kavita and Jasu are feeling and thinking at the end of the novel? Were you surprised at the ending? Did you find it satisfying? How did your view of Jasu's character change from the beginning, and why? What do you imagine happens to these families next?

The Story Behind the Book

Yashoda was three years old when I met her, the summer in college I volunteered at an orphanage in India. She was a beautiful, lithe girl with a shaved head, sparkling brown eyes, and an impish grin. Though I couldn't speak her language, we quickly found ways to communicate and soon became inseparable. She loved to be chased around the courtyard, and delighted in listening to my Sony Walkman while she danced. What Yashoda impressed upon me most, along with the other children at the orphanage, was her joyfulness. Regardless of how they got there, and the fact that many of them had no family at all, those children lived each day with more joy than I was accustomed to seeing in my privileged world.

The orphanage was operated by a nonprofit organization with strict rules against religious conversion and foreign adoption, so it became home to a diverse family of more than a hundred children. They spent their days and nights together: lining up in the courtyard each morning to say their own silent prayers to various gods, sitting cross-legged in rows to eat their meals, sleeping side by side on straw mats. Their lives were simple, but seemed full and happy. I tried not to judge, to believe wholly in what I'd been told: the children were lucky to be there, it was better than being on the street. Still, I could not help think about how limited their opportunities were, about what would happen when they had to leave the orphanage at the age of sixteen. New children arrived all the time, at different ages and for unspoken reasons, sometimes joining relatives already there. Even as we welcomed and cared for these children, I wondered about the circumstances that brought them to our doorstep.

Having grown up in North America and visiting India every few years, I was quite aware of the inequality faced by most women there, even if it didn't materialize as much in my own educated family. One of the most disturbing manifestations is India's gender imbalance. In most of the world, there are 105 females for every 100 males; in India, there are fewer than 93. The accepted reason for this disparity is the practice of female infanticide and abortion. It is ironic that the same advances in medical technology, such as widespread ultrasounds and safer abortions, which have led to women's reproductive freedom in the West, have also led to their demise in the East. According to the United Nations, half a million girls in India are killed this way each year. As a result, fifty million girls and women are missing from India's population. Fifty million.

This year, Yashoda will be twenty-one years old. The lively little girl I have pictured in my mind and in photographs is now all grown up. I've often wondered about her fate, but I know the odds are not in her favor. There's little chance she got a solid education, a good job, a self-sufficient life, if she's even survived all these years.

These ideas percolated in my mind over time, and eventually formed the underlying themes of *Secret Daughter*. How much of our life is destined for us—by our gender, our economic class, or the culture we're born into? How much is within our power to change? By the time I finally sat down to write this story, many years had passed since that summer at the orphanage. Like many people, I now see the world differently through the eyes of a parent.

This story is an alternate history for Yashoda, and the millions of India's other forgotten daughters. Perhaps, despite the odds, Yashoda did get a break. Maybe, one day, on a city street or in a suburban mall, I'll pass by her without even knowing it. I'd like to think so.

Author Q&A

The story is told mainly from the perspectives of the three major characters—Kavita, Somer, and Asha—but also a few secondary characters such as Krishnan, Jasu, and Sarla. Why did you choose to tell the story in this way?

I believe this is a story about family relationships and the way our choices impact others' lives. I thought the best way to illustrate the growing tension within each relationship, between husband and wife, parent and child, was to show it from different perspectives. Each of these characters is flawed and makes choices without understanding all the consequences, but often has good intentions. I think this is how people actually behave, so I was trying to show the humanity of each character without demonizing them.

The story follows two families on opposite sides of the world that face radically different circumstances and environments. And yet, there appear to be some commonalities between the Merchants and the Thakkars. How did you orchestrate the characters' development and was that commonality intentional?

I tried to create each character as an individual with challenges to overcome, which are often accentuated by a spouse or child. I do believe there are some common experiences people face—in becoming a parent, striving for a better life, the push and pull with a child learning to be their own person—even when their outward circumstances are very different. I think one of the greatest roles of art and literature is to draw this out, to help us find ways of seeing commonality between ourselves and someone on the other side of the world.

Your book raises the issue of the infanticide and other forms of discrimination against girls in India. Is the situation as bad today as it was thirty years ago when the events in the book take place?

India is a very large and diverse country, so I hesitate to say things are one way. My aunt likes to say that India lives in several centuries at once, and I think that's true. Although the rates of female infanticide in India have gone down over the past two decades, there are some areas where it is still too common. However, in much of the country, female infanticide has been replaced with sex-selective abortion—choosing to abort after determining a baby's gender through an ultrasound. Sadly, this practice is not limited to rural areas or poor populations, it is also practiced among the educated, urban, and middle-class. There is still a gender imbalance among new births in India, causing a "girl deficit" of 500,000 girls a year. On the other hand, as I tried to illustrate in the book, women in India also play a very important and powerful role in many ways—in the government, in the workplace, and particularly in their families.

What made you want to write about adoption? Do you have any personal experience with it, or how did you learn about it? Are you hoping to promote adoption through this book?

I don't have personal experience with adoption, but I was fortunate to be able to speak with several people who have adopted children from Asia, both recently and in the 1980s, when Asha's adoption takes place. That was important, because the notion of adopting a child from another country was a lot less prevalent thirty years ago than it has become now. There were far fewer intercultural marriages then, and they attracted more attention. You certainly didn't see as many international adoptions, and the families who chose to do it faced a different scrutiny. The conventional wisdom about how to handle those adoptions was also quite different. People thought it was best to assimilate an adopted child to American culture as quickly as possible, so that they would fit in and not feel as different. Today, many families who adopt from overseas make a point of keeping a connection to the child's birth country and culture, which I think is a good thing. It's rather incredible to realize how much things have changed in our society in only a few decades.

I'm not trying to make a statement or promote adoption, I just tried to write a story that was true to the complexity of these relationships. I think these are very personal choices, about whether to have a child or whether to adopt. Each individual or couple has to make the right decision for themselves. Among the adoptive parents I spoke with, there were many paths they took. Some always knew they would adopt one day, others came to that decision quickly after having infertility problems, and still others spent years getting comfortable with the idea. I do believe that raising a child well is one of the best legacies you can leave in the world, no matter how that child comes to you.

There could have been many ways to end this story, and yet the ending you chose is not one that most readers would expect or be prepared for. How did you decide on the ending?

When I first started writing the story, I knew that I wanted it to culminate in something other than Asha and Kavita meeting face-to-face. The more I wrote and the characters came to life, the more strongly I felt about this. The relationship between these two characters is at the heart of the story; it is the vehicle through which each struggles with loss, longing, love, and their own identity. Asha and Kavita are both searching for some understanding of themselves in relation to the other and, perhaps paradoxically, I didn't think the best way for each of them to achieve the personal growth they needed to was to meet each other. I wanted the characters and the reader to feel some satisfaction and peace at the end of the story, without making the events predictable, unrealistic, or too neat. I wrote several different endings before landing on the one that best captured the feeling of bittersweet authenticity I wanted.

How did being the mother of two children affect or change the way you told this story? Do you relate to one of the female characters in particular?

I relate to all of my female characters, and all of the men for that matter, in some way. But I don't think I could have written this story before becoming a mother. The most difficult part of it was putting myself in the shoes of Kavita, Somer, and even Sarla— all of whom lose a child in some way, and have to find ways of coping with that loss. That terrible experience is far away from my own reality, but not so far away in my imagination, where, like all parents, I always seek to keep my children safe.

Stacey Bostrum

SHILPI SOMAYA GOWDA was born in Toronto and raised there by parents who emigrated from Mumbai. She holds an MBA from Stanford University and a BA from the University of North Carolina at Chapel Hill. In 1991, she spent a summer as a volunteer in an Indian orphanage. She has lived in New York, North Carolina, and Texas, and currently makes her home in California with her husband and children.

www.shilpigowda.com

Shilpi Somaya Gowda